Payment
in Full

ALSO BY HENRY DENKER

NOVELS

I'll Be Right Home, Ma
My Son, The Lawyer
Salome: Princess of Galilee
The First Easter
The Director
The Kingmaker
A Place for the Mighty
The Physicians
The Experiment
The Starmaker
The Scofield Diagnosis
The Actress
Error of Judgment
Horowitz and Mrs.
Washington
The Warfield Syndrome
Outrage
The Healers
Kincaid
Robert, My Son
Judge Spencer Dissents
The Choice
The Retreat
A Gift of Life

PLAYS

Time Limit
A Far Country
A Case of Libel
What Did We Do Wrong
Venus at Large
Second Time Around
Horowitz and Mrs.
Washington
The Headhunters
Outrage!

Payment in Full

HENRY DENKER

William Morrow and Company, Inc.
New York

Library of Congress Cataloging-in-Publication Data

Denker, Henry.
     Payment in full / Henry Denker.
        p.   cm.
     ISBN 0-688-10450-9
     I. Title.
     PS3507.E5475P39   1991
     813'.54—dc20   90-45458
                                                                                  CIP

Printed in the United States of America

First Edition

1 2 3 4 5 6 7 8 9 10

BOOK DESIGN BY WILLIAM MCCARTHY

To Edith,
my wife

In appreciation of the valuable
help and warm cooperation of
Pastor T. C. Wilder and his
congregation of the Ajalon Baptist
Church of Palm Springs, California,
the author has used his name and the
name of his church to make them an
enduring part of this novel.

PROLOGUE

1989

The first sign of the trouble appeared when a driver, making an early-morning delivery of warm bagels to a Brooklyn grocery store that had not yet opened for business, spied smoke curling up from the rear of an old wood-frame building that years ago had been converted into a synagogue. He leapt from his truck and ran down the alley, to discover the rear of the building was an inferno. He raced back to the street to find the fire-alarm box.

Within minutes, the sound of sirens roused the neighboring families from their beds to watch as fire trucks swept up to the burning synagogue. Firemen clad in yellow-striped black raincoats catapulted to the ground, dragging hoses, axes, and other equipment with them.

Within the hour the fire battalion chief, the mayor, and the police commissioner had arrived, accompanied by more sirens and the inevitable television trucks and personnel.

Even in civilian clothes, Police Commissioner Sam Armstrong was an imposing presence, tall and of muscular build. Though he was often referred to as a police commissioner who came up from the ranks, Armstrong had received a bachelor's degree from Howard University, a master's in criminal law, and had been graduated from the John Jay College of Criminal Law. But those credentials were more often overlooked than mentioned by the critical media.

Once the battalion chief reported that the fire was finally under control and the initial findings indicated it was of suspicious origin, the mayor and the police commissioner were assailed by a barrage of questions from the television reporters.

"Mr. Mayor, do you think this fire was the result of racial tensions?"

"Commissioner Armstrong, as a black man, do you think

this could be the result of friction between blacks and Jews? Or is this a skinhead crime?"

To put an end to such questions, Sam Armstrong replied, "The fire department will make its investigation. If there is evidence of a crime, I, as police commissioner, working together with the district attorney, will take it from there."

Failing to evoke any newsworthy speculation from the police commissioner, the reporters turned their attention back to the mayor.

"Mr. Mayor, three weeks ago, two blacks attacked some Chasidic Jews coming from this very synagogue. In reprisal, the blacks were beaten by a gang of young Chasidim. Do you think this fire could be an act of revenge, black against Jew?"

"We've already said all we can honestly say at this time," the mayor replied. "Except for one thing: You don't help the situation by irresponsible speculations."

As the mayor turned away to avoid one reporter, another pressed so close to him that his microphone struck the mayor on the face, causing the police commissioner to abandon his reserve and give vent to his feelings.

"Damnit, what do you vultures want? Riots in the streets?" Armstrong demanded.

"We only report the truth as we find it," the television reporter tried to justify.

"You want to report the truth?" Commissioner Armstrong shot back. "Okay! On the six o'clock news, say there was a fire in a synagogue in Brooklyn. And a Jewish mayor and a black police commissioner went there to discover, if they could, whether a crime had been committed. And also to work together to keep peace and quiet in this troubled community. That's it! All we know. And all we intend to say!"

As the commissioner was concluding his last angry words, the battalion chief made his way through the crowd of reporters, followed by a soot-faced fireman, who carried in his arms two long, severely burned objects. The scorched remains had been water-soaked in an effort to rescue them from the flames.

"Mr. Mayor, look what we found," the chief said.

"What are . . ." the mayor started to ask. But being Jewish, hence familiar with the half-burned objects, he realized,

"Torahs? Two burned Torahs? I assume the ark was completely destroyed."

"They weren't in the ark. Whoever did this took them out and threw them on the floor to deliberately set fire to them."

Police Commissioner Samuel Armstrong stared down at the burned fragments of sheepskin parchment on which the holy words of the first five books of the Old Testament had been painstakingly inscribed by hand. Both Torahs were obviously beyond salvaging.

An elderly man, bearded, with the look of a prophet, pushed his way through reporters, police, and curious onlookers.

He touched the burned parchment, then brought his fingers to his lips to kiss them, the age-old ceremony of reverence for the holy words. He shook his head and began to weep.

"Why . . . why . . ." was all he could whisper. "To burn the word of God . . . why?"

Nearest to the bereaved old man, Sam Armstrong attempted to reassure him. "I'm sorry, rabbi. But we'll find out who did this and we'll—" Aware of the limitations placed on him and his department these days by overzealous courts, he concluded weakly, "We'll do everything in our power." A euphemism in which *everything* meant virtually *nothing*.

The rabbi responded, "Everything, Mr. Commissioner? What can you do, catch the criminals, prosecute them? But who will replace these? With all your new inventions, there is no proper way to produce a Torah except by the careful, precise hand of a holy scribe. Word by word, letter by letter. How will we replace these? How?"

The old man started through the crowd, weeping.

Sam Armstrong shook his head sadly as he watched the grieving rabbi mingle with and disappear among his staring, shocked congregants and neighbors.

To Armstrong, the tears in the old man's eyes were a personal and a professional rebuke. Despite everything that had been done in this city during his time in an effort to heal the breaches and conciliate the grievances between various ethnic groups, things had grown not better but worse.

Twenty-four years ago, during his first tour of duty as a

newly sworn in patrolman, he and his partner, Mike Conlin, had been sent to cover another crime in which a synagogue was the target. Two Torahs, along with their silver and gold ornaments, had been stolen and sold to a fence of valuable religious artifacts. Eventually, the perpetrators had been apprehended. That had been a crime solely for profit. But what he had just witnessed this dawn was a vicious act of vandalism, profiting no one and with only one purpose—to destroy.

Hatred, Sam Armstrong was forced to recognize, had replaced avarice as a motive for many of the city's crimes.

Discouraging, most discouraging.

It was late in the evening. Commissioner Sam Armstrong was finally free to leave his office at Police Plaza, across from City Hall in lower Manhattan. He was one tired man.

Starting before dawn, he had attended the scene of the burning synagogue in Brooklyn. Had presided over a heated confrontation with the Police Benevolent Association concerning the case of a white officer accused of shooting too quickly at a teenage black. Had delivered a lunchtime plea to a group of business leaders for contributions to fund a community center for boys in a depressed area of the Bronx. Had tried to mediate a neighborhood conflict in Queens between a group of Orientals and a delegation of Haitians. Had been summoned away from that heated meeting to the scene of a gay protest march, which had tied up all traffic on Brooklyn Bridge during the rush hour. Had been called away from there when his radio crackled with the news that another policeman had been shot by a fleeing suspect. At the hospital he met the mayor and together they paced the corridor anxiously while awaiting news from the surgeons who were trying to save the wounded officer. Finally, assured that the officer was no longer in critical condition, Sam Armstrong was free to return to headquarters to attend to the remaining details of his office.

Now he slid wearily into the rear of his car, settled back, and said to his driver, "Okay, Juan, let's . . . let's . . ." Sam Armstrong suddenly realized that the avalanche of the day's troubles had obscured all memory of his destination.

"Your mother's house, commissioner? It's Wednesday night," his driver reminded.

"Of course," Armstrong agreed. "Some days I forget my own name. Other days I'd like to. This was one of them."

"Yes, sir. We've had a rough day," Juan agreed, for he had witnessed much of it.

The commissioner's car pulled up before a staid old Manhattan apartment house in the East Sixties. As Sam Armstrong got out, he said, "No need to wait, Juan."

"I could get some dinner and hang around," the driver volunteered.

"I'll take a cab home," Armstrong said.

"Give my best to your mother, sir," Juan said.

Elvira Hitchins Armstrong, a tall, woman with graying hair and a strong, distinguished light brown face, stood at her kitchen range browning the pork chops, which she had started as soon as her son's secretary phoned to say he was on his way.

Over her proper, trim businesslike skirt and blouse she wore an apron that obscured the fact that during the day she was dean of students and English professor emeritus at Hunter College. But on Wednesday evenings, whenever she was not away from the city lecturing and her son, Sam, could take time from his demanding schedule, she was a doting mother with the persistent maternal suspicion that once out of her sight, her only son never ate a decent meal.

She was deftly turning the sixth chop in the skillet, careful not to spatter any of the oil, when she heard the front door being unlocked and opened.

"That you, son?" Elvira called.

Sam Armstrong followed the tempting aroma of frying chops into the kitchen. He kissed his mother on the cheek. Seeing them together, one could tell at once that if he inherited his tall, muscular build from his father, he had received his light brown skin and intense black eyes from his mother.

While Sam Armstrong opened the oven door to sneak a look at the golden cornbread baking in the cast-iron skillet,

Elvira laid out the chops on a paper towel to absorb any excess oil, then added milk to the frying pan to make her gravy.

As she stirred, she remarked, "Rough day."

"What happened?" Sam asked with great concern.

"Not me, you," Elvira said. "I've been listening to the radio news."

"I've had worse." He tried to dismiss it, for he did not like to burden his mother with the city's ugly problems during these visits, which, lately, had become too infrequent.

"That early-morning fire over in Brooklyn," Elvira said. "Was it true?"

"Was what true?"

"That whoever did that terrible thing actually took those Torahs out of the ark and tried to burn them?"

"They didn't just try. All that was left were shreds of singed parchment and parts of the wooden rollers."

"How can people do such things?" Elvira protested.

"You should have seen that old rabbi. When he turned to me, weeping, and pleaded, 'How will we replace these . . . how?'"

"It's not easy to replace a Torah. It takes a scribe at least a whole year to write one," Elvira said. "Makes them very costly. I remember when Uncle David wanted to donate one to their synagogue in Aunt Rebecca's memory. It was the highest tribute he could pay her, he revered the Torah so."

She was turning back to finish mixing her gravy when a nostalgic smile brightened her face. Sam noticed.

"Mama?"

"Sam, can't you just picture it? If the Rosens were still alive, first thing Aunt Rebecca would—"

Her son anticipated her, "Aunt Rebecca would form a ladies' committee to raise the money to provide a new Torah."

"And Uncle David would write out a check," Elvira agreed. "Those two, those two . . ." she said, cherishing the memory of them. "But as Aunt Rebecca would have said now, 'Come, sonny. Eat!'"

1 9 3 0

The instant the bedroom door of the little apartment opened, David Rosen quickly ceased pacing to greet the elderly man who emerged.

"Doctor?" David pleaded.

"I'm afraid Rebecca was right," the thin, small man replied as he rubbed his chin, which bristled with a stubble of white beard, indicating that he had hastened to respond to David's early-morning call without taking time to shave or even to comb his unruly gray hair.

"You mean it happened? It really happened again?" David asked. A trace of the Yiddish intonation of his European childhood still escaped him in moments of stress.

Dr. Pomerantz nodded.

"But this is the fourth time," David Rosen protested, an advocate in his wife's cause.

"Yes. I'm afraid she could be one of those."

"One of *what*?" David demanded.

"David, I haven't had any breakfast, so right now a glass of tea wouldn't hurt. Let's go into the kitchen. There we can talk." He did not wish to risk being overheard by the patient, who he knew was weeping by this time.

David Rosen held the dripping perforated silver tea ball over the glass, allowing the last of the strong, dark liquid to drip into the steaming water. His dark eyes, set deep in his lean face, stared across at the old man, who was silently debating: *How much does one tell a young husband? Especially a young man who in the old country had been a Talmudic scholar and is bright enough to be alarmed by all the unspoken consequences of what I am about to tell him.* Better the whole truth than piecemeal, Pomerantz decided as he took the steaming glass from David's hand.

"David, your Rebecca is one of those women who are subject to habitual abortion."

"Abortion?" the young man protested, his face flushed with anger. "Are you suggesting that my Rebecca did something . . . that she . . . she wouldn't! She couldn't! It is against the Torah. Against Halakah!"

"I accuse her of nothing. There is also what we call *spontaneous* abortion," the old doctor tried to explain.

"Spontaneous . . ." David Rosen considered the word. "It just . . . happens?"

"To some women, yes. After it happens three or four times, we label it *habitual* abortion."

"It can't just happen. There must be an explanation, a reason!"

He grew so insistent that Pomerantz gestured he lower his voice for fear Rebecca would overhear.

More softly, but no less intensely, David asked, "Why does it happen? Four times now. Four times! Why?"

"Many reasons—infection, a chronic kidney condition, malformation of the uterus. Or if a woman is what we call hypothyroid, or diabetic . . ."

"Rebecca is none of those," David insisted, the sweat glistening on his angular jaw. "So why?"

"David, we just don't know," the doctor said.

"But it is important that we know, so we can do something about it next time."

Gently as he could, Pomerantz suggested, "David, I wouldn't be so quick to talk to her about next time."

David did not respond but stared into the old man's eyes, demanding an explanation the old doctor would have preferred to arrive at more gradually and compassionately.

"David, in your early years as a student of Talmud, you learned what the rabbis of old said about God's will. We must trust to His wisdom, His mercy. Perhaps it is His plan that for some reason unknown to us, your Rebecca is destined *never* to have children."

"Destined never . . . But we had such plans, such dreams. We promised each other that the education I had to forego would be his."

"And if, by chance, it had been a girl?" the doctor asked. "For her, no education?"

"Education, of course," David replied. "To be a school-teacher. Not a doctor or a lawyer, like a son. But now, bad enough not to have a son to say Kaddish for a man when he dies. But not to have even a daughter, or grandchildren . . . Did you tell her?"

"She should learn the truth, but from someone she loves and who loves her," the doctor said. "And keep me informed."

Rebecca Rosen was a small woman, never quite appearing old enough to justify her thirty-one years. Sixteen years of struggle to survive in a strange land with a strange language had not taken any enduring toll. Except for her four unfortunate attempts to conceive and bear a living child, she considered herself a fortunate young woman. She lived in a free land. She had met and married a fine, intelligent young man with whom she shared roots, since they both came from the same town in Poland. It was ironic that they had not met in that little town, where the Jewish population was so small. They decided it was because he was a *yeshiva bucher* who spent all his days in the synagogue studying Torah and Talmud and the commentaries of Rashi, so he had no time for casual friendships or social occasions. Especially for meeting the daughters of poor or even modestly comfortable families.

Since he was trained for a life of religious study, it was assumed that at the proper time, when he had reached the age of sixteen or seventeen, David Rosen would be betrothed to the daughter of some merchant or manufacturer or goldsmith, who would consider it an honor and a privilege to support this learned son-in-law in religious study for the rest of his life. It was the means by which a businessman earned the approval of God and his fellow men.

For young David Rosen, those plans came to an abrupt end in his fourteenth year. His father, a teamster who owned a single wagon and one old horse, had suffered an unfortunate accident. The horse, being blind in one eye, had strayed off the road, overturning his wagon in a ditch.

Shmuel Rosen died that night, leaving David and his mother with little money and no means of support. However, they did possess one valuable, highly prized asset: an uncle who lived in America! Not only lived there, but—if one were to believe the letters he sent back—he had prospered. A businessman. With his own factory. A boss! Surely he would not turn from his brother's widow and orphan in time of need.

The widow's letter brought the hoped-for reply. Yes, Uncle Shiman would be glad to have David come to America. And he added, "With the news we get over here, there is likely to be a war in Europe soon, so by all means he should come."

As had millions of other immigrants before him, David Rosen, fourteen years old, arrived at Ellis Island to be inspected, thumped, tested for tuberculosis and diseases of the eyes, and finally approved, to be claimed by his relative Uncle Shiman Rosen on March 22, 1910.

Shiman Rosen was a practical man, and quite direct. They were still on the ferry when he said, "David, a man can't trust strangers. They steal you blind. So it's good to have you here. You start in the business tomorrow. In six months you'll know it as well as I do. By the time you're seventeen, eighteen, you'll be the inside man, the factory manager, so I can be completely the outside man. You have to know the language to deal with the storekeepers."

This unexpected rush of plans caused young David to ask in Yiddish, "And about my studies . . ."

"Studies? What studies?" Shiman demanded. "Oh, you mean being a *yeshiva bucher*. Not in this country, boychick. There are no rich religious Jews waiting around to marry off their daughters to someone who can't earn a dollar. Here, shul is someplace you go to pray on Saturday. And what do you pray for? *Parnosseh*. Prosperity. Money. So forget those old-fashioned fairy tales you were brought up on."

That was the first of a number of disappointments for young David Rosen. Being taken to the barber to be shorn of his long, curling sideburns was a shock. Even worse was his introduction to his uncle's factory. It turned out to be a small loft on the Lower East Side that accommodated twenty-four sewing machines at which women and young girls worked at a rapid, harried pace, sewing together pieces of colored fabric, which, when they were done, evolved into cheap ladies' blouses.

He accompanied his uncle up and down the narrow aisle between two rows of clicking machines, their treadles driven by the foot power of anxious operators. Uncle Shiman stood over them, reminding, "Pennies, pennies. It all adds up, girlies. Do your job, and end of the week you can have six dollars. Six whole dollars. If you make your quota."

David did not learn until later that Uncle Shiman had a way of declaring some blouses poorly made and unacceptable, hence a reason for deducting from a girl's wages, so none of them ever went home at the end of the week with a full six dollars.

But Shiman packed the "unacceptable" blouses along with the others to deliver them to the stores. When David questioned the fairness of that, Shiman responded, "Fool! If I didn't do this, there wouldn't be any profit at all. I have a wife and three children to feed. And now, let's not forget, in addition a greenhorn nephew!"

David knew he could not live in his uncle's home or eat his uncle's food if it was earned by the labor of these poor women. So to support himself he found a job in a small hat factory not far from his Uncle Shiman's loft. There he worked twelve hours a day, six days a week, seven days a week during the rush season. It took some years before he indulged in the one luxury he had promised himself, attending night classes five evenings a week at the public school on East Broadway, where, in the company of other foreigners—Poles, Italians, Greeks, and other Jews—he would learn English sufficiently well to become an "outside man," entitled to more respect and income than a mere factory worker.

It was in night school that he met the girl named Rebecca Silverstone. She was small, almost tiny, but with a womanly body even at the age of sixteen. She had an intense and pretty face, framed in a halo of blond hair. David was drawn to her with a feeling that he finally recognized as love, as he had heard it talked about by older men.

He schemed to meet her. Soon he was walking her home from night school to where she lived with her father, mother, and a sister, her older brother having married and moved out to set up a household of his own.

During the day, Rebecca Silverstone worked in a knitting factory in a dim loft on West Broadway. Each week, she brought home her pay of seven dollars to her father, from which he dispensed to her one dollar to spend in any way she chose. This was neither niggardly on his part nor selfish, because in those times families, especially immigrant families, had to sacrifice together to exist.

What appealed to David Rosen as much as Rebecca's beauty was her determination. Other students might be satisfied to learn sufficient English to get by, but Rebecca Silverstone had pledged herself to learn to speak the language and enunciate the words so perfectly that no one would ever again call her a greenhorn.

When, on one of their nightly walks back from school, she expressed that ambition to him for the first time, David joked, in Yiddish, "Yes. Sure. A regular Yankee you'll be."

She had responded in carefully phrased English, "Yes, I will. And so will the man I marry."

That served as a very effective spur to David Rosen to learn to speak English perfectly, a skill he never quite achieved. For under emotional pressure, he was likely to lapse into Yiddish words or the convoluted constructions typical of that language.

Once they had married, David discovered that his lovely young wife was as determined about everything she set out to do as she was about language. Small as she was, she had a will that usually prevailed.

Probably the only victory he scored in the very early days of their marriage was to convince her that since he had gone into business for himself, she must give up working and become a housewife. It would reflect on his manhood, on his standing in the community and in the synagogue, if he could not support his wife. Even if they had to scrimp and save, Mrs. David Rosen would never again work for anyone.

Now, as David stood at the door to their bedroom, he knew that Rebecca would recognize his extreme tension by the way he spoke. So he paused to frame his words in his best English.

To add to his pretense, he had done what he oftentimes did when bringing her a cup of coffee or a glass of tea. He draped a napkin over his arm, pretending to be a waiter. That had always brought a smile to her face and lit up her blue eyes with delight. He knocked, then paused. He finally opened the door, announcing: "Tea for Madame?"

She half turned toward him. Instead of the smile he hoped for, she burst into tears. He raced to her side, took her in his arms, and whispered, "Please, sweetheart, don't cry. Don't cry." He rocked her back and forth. For the moment, she seemed soothed.

"Four times . . . four times now you had a right to expect a son. If not a son, then a daughter. Four times I have disappointed you."

"It isn't your fault," he consoled.

"It's not a matter of fault but fairness. You are entitled to have a son to carry on your name. To say Kaddish for you. Since I cannot give you one, you should think about . . . about another wife."

"What are you talking about? A divorce? A *geht*?" he asked, lapsing into Yiddish. "Absolutely not!"

"Some other woman will be able to give you not only a child but children. Not only *a* son but *sons*."

"Don't speak like that!" he rebuked.

"Why not? In Abraham's time, when Sarah was barren and could not give him a son, she urged him to take a concubine, Hagar, and he did. She bore him a son."

"Yes," David agreed and pointed out, "Ishmael, ancestor of all Arabs."

"Think about it," she urged. "You will come to see the wisdom of what I said."

"I don't want to hear any more about it," he insisted.

"David, I will make an agreement with you."

"Why suddenly do we need agreements?"

"We will try once more. If the same thing happens next time, then out of fairness to you we *must* discuss a divorce."

Painfully aware of Dr. Pomerantz's warning—*I wouldn't be so quick to talk to her about next time*—David tensed. She felt it.

"David? Darling?"

Trying to appear calm and unemotional, he began, "Becca darling, you quoted to me from Genesis about Abraham and Sarah, Hagar and Ishmael. So you also know what happened later. In her old age Sarah did conceive, and bore a son."

"But that took a miracle from God."

"Becca," he said softly. "The age of miracles is over."

It took only a moment for her to realize. "Meaning, for me there is no hope? How do you know?"

"Pomerantz."

"He said that?"

His silence was sufficient confirmation. He could not detect her weeping until he felt the wet warmth of her tears through his shirt.

"Please, Rebecca. You have been everything I ever dreamed of in a wife. Kind. Gentle. Loving. Warm. A partner in love. And in life. A woman with whom I can discuss my good times and my bad. And God knows there have been enough of the bad ones in my business. One day, one day I will be able to give you the riches and the luxury you deserve. But without you, nothing would have meaning."

"But children . . ." she tried to insist.

He pressed his fingers to her lips. "As long as we have each other, we don't need anyone else. We will make the most of what God has given us. After all, how many couples do you know who are as happy as we are?"

That seemed a reassuring answer, for she no longer protested but was content to rest with his strong, comforting arms around her.

The moment of crisis had passed, with less anguish than he had feared.

Until four days later.

2

*I*t *was the* eve of Rosh Hashanah. David and Rebecca made ready to welcome in the New Year. He was dressed in his blue suit, good white shirt, and blue tie, a combination he wore to the funerals, weddings, and bar mitzvahs that courtesy required they attend.

"Becca," David called, thinking she was dallying in the bedroom for one last look in the mirror to be sure she would pass inspection by all the other women, though he knew none of them could equal her beauty; her face, which was heart-shaped, with the hint of a dimple in her chin; her long golden hair, which, when it hung free, caught the light of the sun, which turned it lustrous and shining as it billowed with each swift turn of her head.

His pride in her was always overshadowed by a twinge of guilt. Despite his best efforts, his small, struggling business had not yet enabled him to provide her with the life of ease he had dreamed of when they first married. The little hat factory he had recently established barely supported the very modest Washington Heights apartment they called home. Rebecca had no woman come in once a week to do the cleaning, as did her sister and her sister-in-law.

She always tried to assuage his guilt by laughing about it. "David my darling, what could I find for a cleaning woman to do? This place is so small there's hardly enough to keep me busy."

"That's not the point. It's a matter of . . . of pride! My pride. It is a sign of my failure."

She would embrace him, press her sweet-smelling cheek to his, and whisper, "You are not a failure. You are just starting out. One day you will have the largest hat-blocking business in the city!"

Thus, she could make him believe in himself all over again.

"Becca!" he called a second time. "We'll be late for the services. Becca?" Her silence drew him back toward the bedroom. As he approached, he heard her gasping. "Becca!"

He rushed in to find her sitting in a corner facing away from the light. He took her in his arms, tried to turn her about. She trembled in his arms. He lifted her face. He could see the tears on her cheeks.

"Rebecca? Sweetheart? What is it? What's wrong?"

She shook her head and tried to hide her face from him. He forced her to look up at him.

"Becca?"

"I was putting on my dress . . ." she started to say, then stopped.

"The plum-colored velvet? The one you made especially for the holidays?" David asked. "It's a lovely dress. "What's wrong?"

"When I . . . when I made it, I thought by now I would be five months pregnant, that I would show. So I made allowances, left room. Now . . . it is too big. It hangs on me like an empty sack. An empty sack . . ." she repeated before weeping obscured her words.

"Becca, Becca, you can't keep tormenting yourself. It is not your fault. Even the doctors don't know why it happens. There's no cause for shame."

"It isn't shame," she protested.

"Then what?"

"The other women. Some will have their children with them. Those who don't will brag about the children they left at home—how pretty they are, or how bright. Only I will have no child to brag about."

"They understand," David consoled.

"I don't want them to understand. I don't want them to talk about me behind my back. 'The Rosen woman, very sad about her. Childless. It's a curse. Too bad.' I do not wish to be the subject of their pity."

"My darling, please, you exaggerate. They do not talk about you behind your back."

"I have heard them!" she insisted.

"How could you?" he asked, growing more concerned now.

"In the butcher shop. Yesterday I went in to buy a tender chicken for the holiday. I rejected the ones Olinsky showed me, so he said, 'Okay, go in the back. Pick out from the ones my son is flicking. Maybe there'll be one to suit your fancy-schmancy taste!' So I did. As I was coming out with the bird, I could hear him say to two women there, 'That's Mrs. Rosen. The pretty one.' One of the women asked, 'Isn't she the child-less one?' The other woman said, 'That's the one. Too bad. When I lived in Europe as a child we had a woman like that in our little shtetl. The old women would say, "She's cursed. Cursed."' So, my dear David, they *do* talk. They *do* pity me."

"Becca my darling, powder your nose again. Wipe your eyes. We'll be late for services."

"I am not going," she declared simply.

"You have to go!" he insisted.

"*You* have to go, not *I*." She said it with such finality that he stepped back from her and stared. This was a different Rebecca than he had ever known. He knew, too, that she would not change her mind.

She heard him close the door gently. She sat alone, rocking slowly. In time she rose, slowly removed her slip and her undergarments, undid her brassiere. She stood naked. She stood before the mirror over their dresser. She cupped her hands under her breasts, which were firm and quite ample for a young woman of her diminutive size.

So much to give, she thought. *I need a child at my breasts. A hungry child, suckling at them, drawing life-giving milk from me. Otherwise they are useless. Except for the pleasure David derives from them. God may have performed a miracle for Sarah in her old age. He has made a mockery of me, of my body, my breasts. Those women in the butcher shop were right. Cursed. I am cursed.*

She turned away from the mirror in tears.

David returned from synagogue two hours later to find Rebecca sitting in their dark bedroom, still naked, turned to the wall, as if to hide. He took her in his arms and carried her to their bed. He embraced her, kissed her, sought to arouse her passion, which at other times was quite intense. She remained cold to his wooing. When he kissed her breasts, she thrust him away with great intensity.

For three days her condition not only persisted but worsened. David felt forced to seek out Dr. Pomerantz in his office.

Once David explained, the old man said, "It is not unusual. Some women even suffer from it after giving birth to a perfectly healthy child. We call it postpartum depression. Of course in her case, not having given birth . . ."

The doctor chose not to express his opinion as to the potential danger lurking in Rebecca Rosen's case.

"I will prescribe a tonic for her," he said as he wrote out the prescription. "Have this filled. Make sure she takes a tablespoonful four times a day. No, five times a day. Let me know how it goes."

Five times every day for six days David insisted Rebecca swallow a tablespoon of the cherry-red liquid, which was largely composed of medicinal alcohol. It did nothing to improve her condition. She had not dressed in her usual daytime clothes. She had not cooked a single meal for David, though she had started to several times. She kept to herself in the bedroom. David became accustomed to sleeping out in the tiny living room on the brocade-covered couch.

On the eve of Yom Kippur, ten days after the onset of Rebecca's depression, instead of going to synagogue at the usual time, David went directly to Pomerantz's office. On the point of tears, he explained how much worse Rebecca's condition had grown. Pomerantz listened, nodded, finally said, "David, the situation is serious. More than serious. Some doctors would send you to what we call a psychiatrist or a psychoanalyst. A very long, very costly procedure."

"I don't care about cost!" David protested. "Just help her!"

"It is also a very uncertain procedure," Pomerantz pointed out. "But there may be another way. Give me a day or two."

"It's been ten days now!" David exploded in frustration, then apologized at once. "Sorry, doctor. Very sorry. Do whatever you think best. But, in God's name, do something! Before she destroys herself!"

The next evening, Dr. Pomerantz arrived at the Rosens' modest apartment with the air of a man who had made a grave, perhaps a fateful, decision. He did not ask but commanded Rebecca to dress in her street clothes and accompany him on what he termed a mission of mercy. When she resisted, he insisted. Until she had no choice but to comply.

While she dressed, David asked, "Doctor, what means a mission of mercy?"

"Anche Chesed," was all that Pomerantz said.

"Anche Chesed? That's not our synagogue," David pointed out.

"Not the synagogue," Pomerantz explained. "The orphanage."

"Orphanage?" David questioned.

"Mrs. Feinstein who runs it has her hands full right now; three children with croup, one with possible quinsy, or even a strep throat. And there is always the danger of diphtheria. Someone is needed to maintain discipline among the others. When the lives of Jewish children are at stake, we must all do what we can, Rebecca included."

"She's never been one to shrink from an act of charity. But, doctor, to expose her to taking care of children at a time like this, what are you trying to do, kill her?"

"And what do you think will happen if we let her go on the way she is?" the old doctor demanded. "I say expose her to children like we expose a patient when we inoculate him. Let her build up the ability to cope with the situation. And who knows, David, there may be some child who appeals to her in some special way. It may prove a blessing to her, and to some unfortunate Jewish child who needs a mother. And also a father."

The orphanage of the Anche Chesed synagogue was a drab structure three stories high, of old red brick. It had once been a warehouse for a small company in the spice business. The pungent odor of that trade still hung in the air despite the alterations made to convert it to its present use as a dormitory and dining and recreational center for orphaned children. It had been donated to the synagogue for that purpose by a spice merchant named Isaac Van Dam, an immigrant from Holland.

As Dr. Pomerantz hustled her through the front door of

the institution, Rebecca stopped short, inhaling the unexpected aroma. The old doctor urged impatiently, "Come, my dear, come! They need you."

He led the way to the staircase, past a door that opened slightly once they started up the steps. The woman who peered out stared after them, then shook her head quizzically before retreating behind the door.

The second floor of the institution had been remodeled into two large dormitories. From the voices that erupted from each room, it was apparent to Rebecca that the room on the right was inhabited entirely by girls. The one on the left housed a group of boys, who were not only loud but combative as well, to judge from the pillow that came hurtling out the door.

Pomerantz picked up the pillow and handed it to Rebecca. "Go in there. Set those little savages straight."

As she reached the threshold, all sounds of hostilities ceased. She found fourteen sheepish and wary boys staring at her.

"Whose pillow is this?" Rebecca asked.

One of the smaller boys timidly raised his hand. Rebecca held out the pillow to him. He approached her slowly, as if expecting punishment. Cautiously, he held out his hand. As she passed the pillow to him, he said, "I didn't throw it. They took it away from me. It was them did it."

His eyes blinked as if he were about to shed tears. Rebecca dropped to one knee and took him in her arms.

"Don't be afraid." Her words were addressed to him. Her look was a reproach to the older boys. "No one is going to pick on you anymore, so go to bed."

She released him, watched him trudge back to his cot at the far end of the room, passing between two lines of boys who stood silent and attentive. Peace having been restored, Rebecca turned to Pomerantz. She stared at him, trembling, her eyes beseeching. *I can't do this. Take me home.*

Firmly, the doctor said, "There is the other dormitory to check, my dear."

Rebecca hesitated. The doctor did not relent. She had no choice. She opened the door to find most of the girls in bed. But at the far end of the room, three older girls were gathered around the last cot. They tugged at something while giggling maliciously. Once they became aware of Rebecca, they stopped giggling and turned away from the cot. Rebecca realized that huddled under a blanket, almost totally obscured from view, lay the object of their taunting.

She started down the aisle between the rows of beds. She sat down on the side of the cot. The child pulled back in terror, attempting to hide even deeper within her thin blanket.

Gently, Rebecca pulled the blanket away from the child's frightened black eyes, their whites in sharp contrast to the child's brown face.

A Negro child, here at Anche Chesed? Rebecca thought. She turned to look back at Pomerantz, seeking an explanation. But the doctor himself had been taken by surprise, for he was not expecting this.

There was no time to wait for explanations. The child was trembling in fear. Rebecca took her into her arms. She held her close, rocking slowly back and forth. It took some moments to ease the child's fear, but eventually she relaxed and burrowed between Rebecca's breasts. Rebecca could feel the racing pulse beat in the child's throat begin to slow. She could feel fear slowly drain out of the child's body. Soon her little fingers dared to reach up to touch Rebecca's cheek. But only for a moment, for they came away swiftly, as if burned. They became more venturesome, touching once more, then rubbing the soft skin of Rebecca's cheek, before coming to rest on her own.

Speaking for the first time, the child whispered, "Do it feel different?"

Because Rebecca sensed that the child expected it, she imitated the gesture, touching first her own cheek, then the child's.

"No, my dear, it doesn't feel different."

Her eyes indicating the girls who had bedeviled her, the child said, "They sayin' it do. So they sayin' le's find out. And they rubbin' my face. I don' want nobody to rub my face 'less I let 'em."

At the declaration, Rebecca looked down into the little brown face, the black eyes, and said, "Nobody is going to rub your face again. I won't let them. So you just get under your blanket and go to sleep."

But the child continued to cling to her. Rebecca held her close and began to hum softly to her.

Meantime, Dr. Pomerantz had gone below to the temporary infirmary, which he had set up to care for the ailing children. He found Mrs. Feinstein administering the last of the medications for the night. She half turned to ask, "So?" Meaning, how did it go up there?

"You never told me there was a Negro child," Pomerantz said.

"Until late this afternoon there wasn't," she explained. "You know Mrs. Fleischman . . ."

"Do I know Mrs. Fleischman?" Pomerantz replied. "I curse the day the telephone was invented. She is on the line to me three, four times a week. For free advice, naturally. What does she have to do with a Negro child?"

"You've been to the Fleischmans'. You know they have a Negro woman working there."

"Yes of course. Annie."

"The child is hers."

"But why here?"

"Late this afternoon, Annie was not feeling well. She went to the dispensary at Mount Sinai. She has it."

"Has what?"

"TB," Mrs. Feinstein said mournfully, as if pronouncing a death sentence.

"Tuberculosis? Annie? Oh, that's too bad!"

"They sent her down to Willard Parker Hospital right away. She wouldn't go until Mrs. Fleischman promised her the child would be taken care of."

"So you took her in," Pomerantz concluded.

"Right now the Fleischmans are trying to track down some of Annie's relatives," Mrs. Feinstein said. "This hasn't upset your plan, has it?"

"I don't think so. The main thing is to keep Mrs. Rosen involved with children, any children," the doctor said.

On the floor above, Rebecca Rosen still held the little Negro child in her embrace. Twice the girl fell asleep; twice she woke with a start. Only when she recognized Rebecca's face close to hers did she slip into sleep again. It was almost two hours later before Rebecca was free to lay the child down, cover her tenderly, and leave quietly.

She went across the hall to the boys' room, made sure that all was quiet, then started down.

As she reached the foot of the stairs, the infirmary door opened.

"Mrs. Rosen?"

"Yes, Mrs. Feinstein?"

"How is it going in there?"

"For the moment, all quiet," Rebecca said.

The woman nodded. "The nights are not the big problem. It's the days when I need all the help I can get. So if you can spare the time . . ."

"Time?" Rebecca replied sadly. "Time is all I have."

"Then you'll do it?"

"Yes."

"Good! Very good! Now, a glass of tea maybe? Moscowitz the baker, he always comes by with his leftover rugalach for the children. So if you like day-old rugalach, join me."

Feeling a slight resurgence of her vanished appetite, Rebecca said, "I would have some tea and rugalach. And, personally, I like day-old even better. The cinnamon gets a chance to settle in."

3

Rebecca Rosen returned home so exhausted that David had to restrain himself from asking how things had gone at the orphanage. Instead, he insisted that she have a late supper before she went to bed.

He heated up the chicken soup for her and insisted she come to the table and eat. She began, but after only two spoonfuls, she pushed back her bowl.

"Becca?" he asked, fearful that she still persisted in rejecting all food.

"Her arms," she said. "So tight around me, as if her life depended on it."

"Arms? Whose arms?"

"This little girl, no more than seven or eight. She threw her arms around me and clung. She pressed her head against my breasts, trembling like a frightened bird. I could feel her heart beating."

She could not continue, for she had begun to weep. She rocked back and forth as she had with the child in her arms.

"Rebecca," he declared. "If one evening in that place is going to affect you in this way, then you are not to return."

"But I must. That child . . . all the children—"

"Rebecca!" He grew more stern with her. "As your husband, I forbid you to return!"

"But I promised Mrs. Feinstein."

"You have only one obligation—to your husband. And I say you are not to go back there."

"David, you? Saying that? You didn't learn that in your study of Torah in the yeshiva. These children are orphans."

"I am not a tyrant," he tried to justify himself. "But I refuse to allow you to become so involved with strange children. Enough suffering, enough tears. I forbid you to return there."

She did not respond, only continued to feel that terrified child's arms around her neck, her fingers on her cheek, her face pressed against her breasts, the child's tears wet against her.

The next morning, for the first time in their marriage, Rebecca Rosen deliberately disobeyed her husband and returned to the Anche Chesed orphanage.

The look on the little girl's face, the way she ran to embrace her, her imploring black eyes made Rebecca know that whatever David had said, or what anyone might say, she was vindicated in her rebellion.

Each day for four days Rebecca appeared at the Anche Chesed orphanage. She spent her afternoons with the children, enforcing discipline, telling them stories, teaching the youngest how to read.

Of all the children, the eight-year-old Negro girl, whose name was Elvira Hitchins, looked forward most to Rebecca's arrival. Wherever Rebecca went, the child followed. She stood off at a distance observing her. Whenever Rebecca turned, she discovered the child staring up at her, studying her every move. Rebecca had the feeling that silently the girl spoke along with her, mimicking her words and her speech. At times, she could discern the child's lips moving in consonance with her own. Of one thing Rebecca felt sure: The girl seemed to feel safe only in her presence.

Each day when Rebecca arrived, she would inquire of Mrs. Feinstein, "Any news?"

On the fifth day, the answer was discouraging. "They discovered that Annie Hitchins came from Birmingham, a long time ago. There's no trace of any relatives."

"Any word about Annie herself?"

"They've sent her up to Saranac. It's her only chance."

"She is that bad?"

"Now they want to examine Elvira, to make sure she hasn't caught it. Would you mind taking her down to Willard Parker?"

"No, no, of course I wouldn't mind."

"From the way the health department sounded, this afternoon is not too soon."

While helping the girl dress, Rebecca was disturbed to discover that her clothes were unclean and badly wrinkled. She took Elvira by the hand and marched her out of the orphanage straight to her own home.

There, she stripped Elvira of all her clothes and wrapped her in a blanket. While the girl peered out from between the folds of the blanket, Rebecca proceeded to wash all her clothes in the tub in the kitchen. She wrung them out and then ironed them until the dampness was gone. The aroma of clean, newly pressed cotton filled the kitchen.

Once the child was dressed, Rebecca combed her soft curly hair into a neat arrangement. As she did so, a thought occurred to her. She rooted about in a drawer of her dresser and found a length of red ribbon she had left over from a gift that David had bought her several years ago. She tied it around the child's hair, making a crisp bow. She presented little Elvira to herself in the mirror.

The girl looked proud and pleased. "I wish my mama be seein' me like this. She always say, 'Poor ain't no excuse for dirty.'"

At Willard Parker Hospital, Rebecca was relieved to discover that as far as the doctors could detect, Elvira Hitchins bore no signs of the dread consumption. Rebecca took her little charge back to the orphanage. With a firm grip on the child's hand, Rebecca started up the four steps into the old red brick building. At the top step, the child stopped suddenly and pulled back, bringing Rebecca to a halt.

"Elvira?"

The girl did not respond but stared up into Rebecca's face, her eyes filling with tears.

"Elvira?"

She clung to Rebecca's hand, pressing it close to her face. Rebecca dropped to one knee so they were eye to eye. Without a word, Elvira thrust her arms around Rebecca and clung to her. Cheek to cheek, their eyes averted, Rebecca whispered into the child's ear:

"Elvira, don't you want to go in there?"

"They don' be likin' me in there," the girl said.

"They will. Once they get to know you better." The child did not relent. "Elvira, do you remember any family? Grandma or aunt or uncle or cousin?"

"No," the child admitted.

"Don't you see, Elvira, there's no one else, no place else. And this won't be forever. Only till your mama comes back."

Rebecca held the child back from her to explore her face, to study her eyes. Elvira blinked. Slowly, tears began to trace down her smooth cheeks. Rebecca embraced her, holding her close and, though she had no plan in mind, whispered, "We'll find some way." With that assurance, the child seemed resigned to enter the orphanage.

"What?" David asked, his forkful of potted beef suddenly poised in midair, halfway between his plate and his mouth. "Becca, what did you say?"

Rebecca stared across the kitchen table at her husband. "I was wondering . . . what if . . . that is, only until her mother returns from Saranac . . . What if *we* took the child in?"

"Becca, my darling wife, I know how you feel about children. But this child . . . this child . . . Well, in the first place, she is a Negro."

"But still a child, alone, frightened," Rebecca countered.

"Don't you read the newspapers? There is a madness in this country now. Down South that . . . that Ku Klux Klan is rising up again. And the lynchings! Negroes dragged out of their homes, out of jails, even, then hung in public squares. But worse, the authorities stand by and let them do it!"

"Nobody is going to lynch a little child," Rebecca protested.

"Rebecca! We are not talking only about Negroes. A few months ago Sacco and Vanzetti. Were they black? No. But they were railroaded to the chair. Why? Because they were foreigners. We may think we're Americans, but to *them* we are still foreigners. It is tough enough being an immigrant, tough enough being Jewish, without adding a Negro child to our troubles."

"David, she is still a frightened child," Rebecca insisted.

"Rebecca, it is not only that she is Negro. You told me she is Christian."

"But still a child," Rebecca repeated.

"Besides, where would we put her?" David demanded. "We don't have a big apartment. We are not exactly rich people. Actually, if things don't pick up, I may have to go back to work for Madigan. I would hate to give him the satisfaction. Especially after the way we said goodbye. 'Rosen, it might do you good to go out on your own. To pay rent and wages, phone bills and gas and electric, and with the machinery breaking down so often, then try to wind up the month with enough to live on. It's no fun, my boy. Well, you'll find out. You'll come crawling back begging for your old job.' To have to go back and admit to Madigan he was right—I don't look forward to it."

"David, you never told me . . ." Rebecca rose from her place and went to his side. He looked away from her.

"I was hoping not to have to tell you. I kept thinking, next week will be better, next month will be better. I spend half my time not in the shop but outside looking for business. I have covered every hat store from Wall Street up to Bloomingdale's, way up on Fifty-ninth Street." He grunted in self-deprecation. "I wanted to be an outside man. I find I am not very good at it. Now, with things so bad since the crash on Wall Street . . ." He shook his head grimly.

"If things are that bad," Rebecca said, "I will go back to work."

"No wife of mine will ever go to work!" David declared, pounding the table for emphasis. He left, slamming the door behind him.

She called after him, "David! David! Please . . ." She slipped into his chair, staring at the supper he had abandoned.

He is too sensitive, she thought. *He was not meant for the life of a businessman. He is not used to giving orders to his workmen or begging for business from the men who run those big department stores on which he depends. In his heart he is still a scholar of Torah, and always will be. The thing that torments him now is his sense of moral obligation to a helpless, needy child. I was thoughtless to suggest taking in the child when he has all his other troubles.*

It was past ten o'clock. She gave up waiting for him to return. She went into the bedroom, stripped off her clothes, and slipped into her nightgown, resigned to falling asleep alone. The more determined she was to sleep, the more awake she became. Until it was beyond enduring. She pulled her kimono about her and went out to the kitchen, where she started to boil some water for tea. She was filling the silver tea ball with the dark flakes when she heard the door being unlocked.

She ran to greet him. "David? Darling?"

He was startled and disturbed to discover that she was still awake. He allowed her to kiss him, though he did not return her affection.

"I cannot do it," he declared. "I have walked the streets trying to get my mind off it. But I couldn't. I argued with myself—yes, do it; no, you can't; it's wrong."

Despite her strong resolve not to burden him with arguments, Rebecca asked, "How could it be wrong? Besides, it's only for a short time."

"But it is *not* for a short time. Once you start a practice like this, they expect it all the time."

"Practice? They? Who is they?"

"It may start with one buyer, but words get around the trade," he pointed out.

"Who's talking about buyers and trade?"

He stopped pacing to turn to her. "What do you think I've been talking about? Why do you think I was so upset, so abrupt with you?"

"Why?" she asked.

Realizing she did not understand his dilemma, he explained, "Today, at Macy's, where I have begun to get a little business, I had a chance to talk to the assistant buyer of men's hats. I felt I might get some advice from him. How does a man get his foot in the door at Altman's? Or possibly even Saks? That is the cream of the hat-repair business. If you get Saks, you can also get into Dobbs. And even Knox. The thing is to have a good reference when you go to the other places. Nobody likes to deal with a new repair shop unless they have references."

"David, David, please, what does this have to do with the little girl?"

"I'm getting to that," he said impatiently. "So I am talking to this assistant buyer at Macy's. And while he rubs his thumb and forefinger together, he says to me, 'Rosen, use your head. *Shmeer* a little.' 'You mean offer a buyer a little cut? There's hardly enough to make a profit now!' I said. He smiles and says, 'Rosen, do as I say and there'll be no problem with price. Only one thing, Rosen. Buyers like to pretend there is no such dealing. So deal only with the assistants.' It became clear to me. This was his way of asking me for a bribe. And I . . . I agreed. Now I find I can't do it. I can't."

He shook his head wearily, the sweat glistening on his lean face.

"A businessman could do it. But a *yeshiva bucher*, no. I am doomed to be a failure. Becca, you married the wrong man. You deserve better. A man who can give you all the luxuries. A large apartment, not this small hovel."

"It is not a hovel!" she insisted. "It is a nice, clean, warm, comfortable home. This is all we need."

"You ask me to take in a homeless child for a few weeks—a simple act of charity any Jew should do, but I have to say we can't afford it, we don't have the room."

He shook his head slowly, sadly. "You realize it will not be fair to the child."

"Not fair?" She was puzzled.

"There is not another colored child in this building, on this whole block. Who will she have to play with?" he pointed out.

"I will find children for her to play with," Rebecca said. "And if not, I will play with her myself."

"To my every objection you have an answer," he lamented. "You would have made a very fine *yeshiva bucher* yourself. All right, all right, so take her in for a few weeks."

Rebecca went to him. He tried to turn away from her. She came around to look up into his face.

"Thank you, David, thank you." She stood on tiptoe to kiss him on the cheek, because he did not bend to her as usual or take the initiative.

"Only a few weeks," he warned. "Remember!"

She nodded dutifully.

4

"*Is this everything?*" Rebecca Rosen asked when Mrs. Feinstein handed her Elvira's clothing. She glanced through the pile: five pairs of worn, frequently laundered socks; two pairs of long stockings; several clean undershirts, some mended; four pairs of underpants; two old dresses; one pair of navy-blue bloomers, too large to be Elvira's; and a pair of sneakers from which the white cleaner had flaked off, revealing worn places. Obviously, the shoes Elvira wore were the only ones she possessed.

There was one last possession contained within a neat linen towel. When Rebecca unwrapped it, she found two children's books, the pages worn at the corners, both covers stained. Carefully, she rewrapped them.

After putting Elvira's belongings in a brown paper bag that had been used to deliver stale rolls to the orphanage, Rebecca Rosen took the child's hand and started down the stairs.

Despite the glances and looks of surprise from curious pedestrians and women who interrupted gossiping on the stoops to stare at a young Jewish woman and a Negro child, Rebecca walked with determination, the child's hand in hers.

At the door to Rebecca's building, they met Bertha Youngstein, mother of two and into the eighth month of pregnancy with her third.

"She is back?" Mrs. Youngstein asked. For the moment Rebecca was puzzled. "A week ago, you also had her here."

"Oh. Yes. The day I took her to Willard Parker."

The pregnant woman drew back in fear. "Willard Parker? She is sick? A sick child and you bring her here to infect our children?"

"I took her there to make sure she is *not* sick. The doctor said she is perfectly healthy."

The woman seemed somewhat reassured until Rebecca

said, "I was thinking of asking you, Mrs. Youngstein. She is about the same age as your Molly. It would be nice if they could play together."

"Play together?" the woman echoed. "I . . . I never thought . . . We'll see, we'll see."

"Only for a few weeks. Until her mother comes back."

"We'll see," the pregnant woman said, waddling off toward the corner grocery.

Rebecca had washed all the clothes that came with Elvira. While she was pressing them, the child stood on the other side of the ironing board, stared up at her, her large eyes wide with curiosity but also with a hint of anxiety.

"Yes, Elvira?" Rebecca coaxed as she folded one white blouse. A button was missing and would have to be replaced.

"Do I be staying here?" the child asked.

"For a time," Rebecca said easily.

"And then?"

"Then your mama will come back and you'll live with her again."

Reassured, she pointed at the iron and asked, "Can I be doin' that?" For an instant Rebecca had no answer. The girl misinterpreted her silence. "Not if it's not allowed."

"It's allowed. Come." Rebecca placed Elvira's hand on the handle of the iron. Together they guided it over the worn ironing board cover, whose large brown areas testified to places where Rebecca had let the iron rest too long while it was too hot. The iron slid easily back and forth.

"Would you like to iron something, Elvira?"

"Mama never let me."

"Well, I will," Rebecca said. She seized a dishtowel from the rack over the chipped white porcelain sink. She wet it under the faucet and laid it out on the board. Together they ironed the towel until it was dry and wrinkle-free. When they were done, Elvira looked up and for the first time in all the days Rebecca had known her, she smiled.

Rebecca tried to smile back, but a stab of pain in her belly prevented it. *My child. I would give anything to have my own child smile at me that way*, she realized. She recognized the pain. It was the same as had preceded her four miscarriages.

Determined to put an end to self-pity, Rebecca said, "Come. We are going to find some children to play with."

The child's hand in hers, Rebecca started out of the apartment, up a flight of dark stairs to the door directly above her own. She twisted the knob of the bell in the middle of the door. It rang. Once. Then again. Then a third time. No one came to the door, but from inside Rebecca could hear the voice of Mrs. Youngstein.

"I think I can guess who that is. Don't go near the door!" A child responded in words Rebecca could not quite understand, which called forth another rebuke. "Molly! I said no!"

Embarrassed as well as angry, Rebecca said, "Maybe . . . maybe there's no one home. Come!" She marched the child back to the stairwell.

As they started down, the child asked, "Why she say no to her Molly?"

Rebecca had no ready lie to ease the child's hurt, so she chose not to respond. She could only think, *How does one explain the irony of this life to a child? Mrs. Youngstein, herself a victim of prejudice, could reject an innocent child because of her color. But the child will have time to learn. Unfortunately.*

To put the distasteful episode behind them, Rebecca tried to sound bright and enthusiastic when she said, "Besides, we really don't have time to play. We have to go shopping for supper."

Berkowitz's grocery, right next door to Olinsky's kosher meat market, was of the old-fashioned kind, with a display of fruits and vegetables out front and all dairy products, packaged bread, cereals, and other footstuffs inside.

As Rebecca and Elvira approached, Berkowitz, in his stained white apron, came rushing out to chase two ten-year-old boys who had swiped an apple and run off.

"Bums!" the short, heavyset grocer shouted at them. He took cognizance of Rebecca. "Hello, Mrs. Rosen. And how are you feeling today?" Her recent misfortunes were no secret from anyone in the neighborhood."

"I'm fine," she insisted. "Fine."

"Good. I'm happy to hear," Berkowitz said. He fixed his stare on Elvira, who pressed shyly against Rebecca's thigh. He said nothing, but his curiosity was evident, as well as his disapproval. "So what's going to be today, Mrs. Rosen?"

She read off her list of groceries: a box of dried lima beans to go with the beef flanken she planned to buy at Olinsky's, a pound of butter, half a dozen eggs, two bagels. And for the child, an extra quart of milk and a cereal of some kind.

The other items having been assembled by Berkowitz, Rebecca had to face the choice of cereals.

What is best for a child? she wondered. *My sister, Miriam, always says oatmeal, hot, with butter and milk. But other mothers seem to rely on corn flakes, cold, with milk and bananas.*

She chose the round oatmeal carton with the face of a jolly Quaker on it.

With the big brown grocer's bag in one arm and Elvira's hand in hers, Rebecca started for the door. She stopped only long enough to pick up a box of Oreo cookies.

After all, she argued, *every child loves sweets. One box should do for the time she will be with us.*

Once she had collected two pounds of beef flanken from Olinsky's, they returned home. Rebecca tried to make the child feel at ease, pretending she needed her help in placing each item of food in its proper place on the shelves.

Kitchen chores completed, Rebecca considered making a second attempt at Mrs. Youngstein's door. But rather than risk another painful episode for Elvira, Rebecca remembered those two worn books, part of the girl's few possessions. She decided to read to her.

Ensconced on the couch in the parlor, Rebecca put her arm around Elvira and drew her close. She opened the first book. The binding had been broken long ago. When Rebecca fingered the title page, a corner of it flaked off on her finger. Handling the pages more gingerly, she started to read. The girl seemed comforted, for she burrowed closer, pulling Rebecca's arm tighter around herself.

Pronouncing each word meticulously, to demonstrate the proper inflection and to impart the meaning as well, Rebecca read the first page. Elvira listened. From time to time she nodded.

Carefully, Rebecca turned the page. No longer bound into

the book, it came loose. It slipped from her hand, floating gently away despite her sudden reach to retrieve it. As she leaned forward to pick it up from the floor, the child continued reciting the words from the second side of the page. Rebecca pulled back slightly to look down at Elvira's earnest face as she continued. Then, as she reached the end of the missing page, Elvira pointed to the next page, inviting Rebecca to read on.

"Elvira, do you know this book?"

"Yes, ma'am. My mama be readin' to me—" the child started to reply. Then she stopped quite suddenly. She took a deep breath before she ventured slowly, "My mama, she used . . . to read . . . it . . . to me . . . most times." She enunciated each word, each syllable, with practiced care.

Slowly, it became clear to Rebecca that during those moments when she had caught the child observing her so closely, Elvira had been actually imitating her silently.

"Be that the right way to say?" Elvira asked.

"Oh yes, yes indeed," Rebecca replied.

The child seemed reassured, as if she had passed a crucial test.

"Even when I jus' a chile, I aks myself—why when my mama read to me from the book she sound one way but when she talk to me she speak another way?"

"You asked yourself that when you were just a child?" Rebecca asked, smiling.

"Yes, ma'am," Elvira replied in all seriousness.

"So you decided to learn how to speak like the book speaks?"

"And the way you speakin'." Then she corrected herself. "The way you speaks . . . speak," she finally arrived at. "You teach me?"

"Elvira, I think you are learning quite well on your own. Which is the best way."

Oh, what a child this is, Rebecca realized. *Such a desire for learning. If only David had been here. Wait until I tell him. I wonder. How much more does her shyness conceal?*

Rebecca drew Elvira close once more and resumed reading. She was just about to turn to the next page when a thought provoked her.

"Elvira dear, do you know what's on the next page?"

"Yes, ma'am. My mama teach me."

"Let me hear it," Rebecca invited.

The girl began to recite the lines atop the next page until Rebecca asked, "Can you also recognize the words when you see them?"

"Yes, ma'am."

"Very good. Now let me see what your mama *taught* you." Whereupon Elvira pointed to each word as she pronounced it.

"Why didn't you tell me you could read?"

"You din' ask me," the child responded in all innocence.

"Yes, yes, you're right," Rebecca said, and continued reading aloud. She had not read beyond the third page when she realized Elvira had fallen asleep. Very gently, Rebecca slipped free, lay her down in a more comfortable position, and brought a light blanket to cover her.

As Rebecca studied the sleeping child, she thought, *For the first time she seems at ease, truly at ease.*

Elvira was still asleep when David returned for supper. Rebecca heard him insert his key in the front door. She rushed to open it, her finger pressed to her lips to demand silence.

Startled, he asked, "What's the trouble?"

"She's asleep," Rebecca whispered. "How did it go today?"

"Pretty good," he answered casually.

It was one of his usual evasive responses. *Pretty good* meant not good at all. *Very good* meant at least nothing bad had happened.

"Things'll get better. I know it," she tried to enthuse. She kissed him. He pressed against her body, seeking more encouragement from her than he could give.

"Tomorrow's another day," he said. "Tomorrow I go back to Macy's. I have decided to *shmeer* that assistant buyer. If that's what it takes to do business, I'll do it!"

"If you don't feel right about it . . ." Rebecca said.

"I don't have any choice!" he protested, the strength of his protest testifying to his turmoil.

To ease the moment for him, Rebecca changed the subject. "She is very bright."

"Who?"

"The child, Elvira. She not only knows the book by heart, she can read. And she wants to learn to speak the language as written in books."

"Becca," he asked suddenly. "How long does it take for someone to get cured from consumption?"

"I don't know. Why?"

"I've been thinking. If it takes a long time, maybe she would be better off with her own," he said.

"They are still looking, but so far they haven't discovered any relatives.

"I didn't exactly mean relatives. I meant her own kind."

"Oh, you mean Negroes." Rebecca understood, finally.

"After all, for a colored child to live with white people is not natural."

"Not natural?"

"White people are white people. And colored people are colored people. That's the way God arranged things."

"A child is a child," Rebecca protested.

"But not *our* child," David responded quickly, too quickly. At once, he started to apologize. "I'm sorry, Becca! I didn't mean to say that. I didn't think . . . I don't know what I meant."

"I know," she apologized for him. "It's the business, your worries. I understand, dear, I understand."

But when he went into the bathroom to wash up for supper, she went into the kitchen, and alone, she wept. She heard him open the bathroom door. She quickly dried her eyes and turned to the stove to tend the pot of lima-bean-and-beef soup simmering there. As she turned, she discovered Elvira standing in the doorway staring up at her. To cover her own sadness, Rebecca tried to smile. The girl came toward her. She pressed her head against Rebecca's belly, reached for her hand, and kissed it.

"Please don't cry. My mama, when she cry, I cry too."

"I . . . I wasn't crying. I just had something in my eye," Rebecca said, trying even harder to smile.

"That's what my mama always say," Elvira responded.

David came into the kitchen to discover them so close. For an instant he felt a jolt in the pit of his stomach. If Rebecca had been able to carry that first time, their own child would have been almost eight years old by now.

Later that night, once Elvira had been put to sleep on the living room couch, David and Rebecca were in bed. He embraced her warm body and whispered into her ear. "What I said before, about a child of our own . . . it slipped out. I didn't mean anything."

"I know." She pretended to believe him, but the thought still made her ache.

Even after they had made love and she was physically fulfilled, she still felt that gnawing pain, slight but ever-present.

What is wrong with me? Why can't I be a woman like all other women? A mother like all other mothers?

He was breathing erratically, in troubled sleep. She turned on her side, away from him, and wept silently.

*F*ive days had elapsed. David had mentioned nothing about the business. She assumed, *he hates himself for having stooped to bribery. He does not wish to compound his crime by trying to justify it.*

On the afternoon of the sixth day, one of the older children in the Anche Chesed orphanage brought a note to Rebecca. It read:

Dear Mrs. Rosen:

Can you come to see me at once? I have important news concerning Elvira Hitchins.

Sincerely,
Ida Feinstein

"Saranac?" Rebecca Rosen repeated. "That's a long way from New York."

"Overnight by train," Mrs. Feinstein said.

"Her mother wants to see her?"

"The doctors said her mother will feel better knowing the child is well cared for. The cure consists of rest, good food, fresh air, and sunshine. But also peace of mind."

"Yes, I know. I had an aunt who had it," Rebecca said. "But to send an eight-year-old child on such an overnight trip by herself . . ."

"For the sake of her mother," Mrs. Feinstein said.

"Of course," Rebecca agreed.

Supper had passed without any undue incident. But always sensitive to his wife's feelings, David knew something was troubling her. He waited until the child had been put to bed and they were in the privacy of their room.

"All right, Becca, what is it?"

"What is what?" she tried to deny. His silence had always been the most effective inquisitor, so he waited. Soon, while drawing her nightgown down over her naked body, Rebecca said, "She has to go to visit her mother."

"All the way to Saranac?"

"Overnight on the train."

"That could cost a lot of money," he said.

She loosed her long blond hair, freeing it from the tortoiseshell pins that kept it in place during her day's activities. It fell long and loose over her shoulders. She brushed it, looking into the mirror beyond herself and at David, who lay in bed staring up at the ceiling.

"How much?" he asked.

"I called Grand Central Station this afternoon," she admitted. "From New York to Saranac and back, fourteen dollars. Unless one goes by sleeper. Then it is twenty-three dollars."

"Twenty-three dollars!" he exclaimed. "Do you know how many hats a man has to clean and block to make twenty-three dollars?"

She continued to brush her long blond hair.

"Of course," he said, as if thinking aloud, "a child her age, sitting up all night in a railroad car. It isn't just the loss of sleep. Who knows what could happen? Yes, I suppose she has to have a berth. In a Pullman car there are porters who would look after a child traveling alone, especially a Negro child. After all, all the porters are Negroes."

He had decided. "All right, Becca. We will send her by sleeper. Somehow we'll . . . we'll find the money."

They were both in bed. He lay on his side, his arm around her, cradling her breast. They often fell asleep that way. This night, however, she could not sleep. He sensed her restlessness.

"Becca darling?"

"I . . . I have been thinking, David. Is it right to send the child alone?"

"What are you getting at? As if I didn't know. You think you should go with her. Another twenty-three dollars. Impossible!"

"If we both sleep in the same berth, for me it's only another fourteen dollars."

"*Only* fourteen dollars," he scoffed. "Fourteen plus twenty-three is thirty-seven dollars. I know men who support their families for a whole week on a lot less than thirty-seven dollars!"

She knew better than to argue with him when he was in this mood. So she lay silent, waiting.

"Thirty-seven dollars . . . a fortune. A fortune! Might as well ask for my blood." He was silent once more. Then, "Becca, I know what you were thinking. Now that I did my little business with the assistant buyer at Macy's, things would be better . . . right?"

"Uh-huh," she admitted.

"I was all prepared to slip him an envelope with five dollars in it. I had it in my pocket. I had my hand on it. But if a man has no respect for himself, he doesn't deserve respect from anyone else. No matter what you call it—a *shmeer*, a gift—it is a bribe. I couldn't do it. So business is no better than before."

"I'm sorry," Rebecca said. "If I had known, I wouldn't have asked."

The next morning, after he had unlocked the door to his small shop on the third floor of the old loft building and admitted his two workmen to begin on the few orders that remained, David Rosen decided to go down to his bank, which had a branch on the corner. He reached into his jacket pocket to make sure his bankbook was there. With a curt, "Boys, I'll be back in fifteen minutes," he started out.

The bank teller stared at David Rosen's slip.

"Mr. Rosen, you realize that if you withdraw forty dollars we will have to cancel your checking privileges and convert you to savings."

"You can't do that! I've had an account in this bank for three years!" David protested.

"Sorry, sir, bank rules."

"But I'm a businessman. I pay my bills with checks."

"Mr. Rosen, the rules say every checking account must maintain a balance of at least two hundred and fifty dollars."

"Yes, of course. I understand." He crumpled his withdrawal slip.

He left the bank, tormented. With the fare coming to thirty-seven dollars, and a few extra dollars for emergencies, he needed forty dollars. Where to go? Whom to ask?

The first name that came to mind was Olinsky, the butcher. He was known to carry a customer on the books through hard times. And even to lend someone five or ten dollars in an emergency. But forty? Not likely. Berkowitz, the grocer? He carried customers too, but he never handed out cash. Who? Who else?

There was one other possibility, he realized. Stern Brothers, the big department store up on Forty-second Street and Sixth Avenue. He had delivered his first order to them a week ago and it had been accepted by the buyer of the hat department as perfectly satisfactory. Payment would be due on the tenth of the month. Perhaps they would bend the rules slightly and make payment now instead of seventeen days from now. It was not a matter of dollars but merely of days, David argued to himself. What could be lost by asking for one's own money?

Plenty, he decided. *A man holding himself out to be the responsible owner of a solid business should not have to ask for niggling advances. It could destroy my welcome at Stern Brothers for all time. So Stern Brothers is out. B. Altman? The same.*

Of course there is always Max Gabel, that assistant buyer at Macy's. Any man who will hondel *for a bribe could also bend the rules in other ways. It will mean being indebted to him for future bribes, but if Rebecca has her mind set on accompanying the child to Saranac, what choice do I have? Even the Talmud says, When a human life is involved, rules do not matter. And in a way, a life is involved. Is not the purpose of this trip to give her mother courage and incentive to recover?*

With troubled conscience, David Rosen waited patiently outside the cubicles where Macy's buyers and assistants interviewed salesmen and inspected and judged their new lines of merchandise. His hand dug deep into his pocket, clutching the envelope that contained the five-dollar bill intended as the bribe.

He debated. Was it wise to offer Gabel the five dollars before making his request? Or should he be more forthright and put the matter on a straightforward basis? *Move up my payment date and I am ready to "do business."*

His name was called. He started toward the cubicle where he had always met with Gabel. Even before he reached it, he could see that sitting behind the table was not young Gabel but another man, an older man in his late forties, his pince-nez adding to his look of age and severity.

"Rosen?" the man called.

"Yes," David replied.

"Come in, come in." The man rose to a height of more than six feet. He held out his hand, saying, "Callahan."

As they shook hands, David realized, this is the aloof Mr. Callahan one heard of but never expected to meet, buyer of men's hats not only for Macy's but for Bamberger's in Newark as well.

At Callahan's gestured invitation, David sank into the chair across the small table that separated them. His hand, sweaty from added uncertainty, still clutched the now-damp envelope. Through his mind kept racing the tormenting question: *Does one bribe buyers as well as assistant buyers, and if so, is five dollars enough? Surely if five is enough for Gabel, it cannot be enough for an important man like Callahan. Then how much? And how does one open the subject?*

"Rosen, I hear your work is quite satisfactory."

"Thank you, sir. Mr. Gabel told you," David assumed.

"Not exactly," Callahan said, taking off his pince-nez to polish them. "The reason I am here to see the trade today is that Mr. Gabel is no longer with us."

David's heart stopped for a full two beats. "No longer here?"

"He left quite suddenly," Callahan said. "But before he did, we had quite a long talk, Mr. Gabel and I," Callahan said as he carefully clamped his pince-nez back in their accustomed place, fitting them into the red indentations on each side of his long straight nose. "Quite a talk. He said that you were one."

"One? I was one?" David felt accused suddenly.

"I do not like to discuss this," Callahan said, his distaste obvious on his face, "but I was forced to fire Mr. Gabel yesterday. It seems he was making outrageous demands on resources like yourself. During our talk, I went down the list of all our suppliers and servicers. There were very few who resisted his demands. He mentioned you as one."

David's hand inside his pocket, clutching the damp envelope, went lax.

"I have always opposed bullying suppliers or extorting money from them. Whatever other buyers do, I will not put up with it! I want you to know you do not have to bribe your way into Macy's. Now then, what did you come here to show me today?"

"Today . . ." David began. "Today I came here to show you . . . no, I didn't come here to show you anything. I came here because . . . because . . . because I need help!"

Callahan pulled back from the table, prepared for almost anything but what he was about to hear. Out of David's mouth poured the reason for his presence this morning: about the child, her mother, the need to go to Saranac, the cost, the trouble at the bank.

"I came here to ask Mr. Gabel if he could arrange that I be paid for work already done, which adds up to seventy-four dollars and fifty cents."

"We pay all bills on the tenth of the month," Callahan said.

"And promptly," David agreed.

"We don't make exceptions. Or else in times like these, manufacturers would be using us as bankers. Still . . . your case." Callahan pondered, then finally decided. "No, I'm afraid I can't ask Accounts Payable to advance you any money."

David tried to conceal his deep disappointment. "I understand, Mr. Callahan. And no hard feelings, believe me."

"I'll tell you what I *can* do," Callahan said. "*I* could advance you the money."

"You? You mean . . ."

"It would be a personal transaction. But purely business. Callahan advances money to Rosen. Rosen promises to repay it on the tenth of the month. How about that?"

"Oh, Mr. Callahan, thank you. Thank you more than I can say. And believe me, on the tenth you will have your money. You have my word on it."

"I accept that," Callahan said. He reached into his pocket and took out a wad of bills held together by a gold money clip. He started to peel off bills, asking, "How much did you say?"

"Forty dollars," David ventured.

"We will make it fifty. That's an easier number to remember. And it will give your wife some leeway for contingencies. One never knows."

"Thank you, Mr. Callahan," David said.

As he was handing over the money, Callahan remarked with some wonder, "A little colored girl, you said?"

"Yes."

"Hm!" was all that Callahan said in reply, giving no indication of whether he approved.

David took the money, half turned away, then turned back to ask, "Mr. Callahan, if you have half a minute, I'd like some advice."

"Advice? Sure. Shoot."

"I am thinking of putting in a machine to conform opera hats. Do you think it is a wise investment?"

"Not bad," Callahan said. "Not bad. We would send you some business. But if you want my advice, go into manufacturing."

"Against the giants?" David asked.

"Specialize, Rosen, specialize—derbies in fall and winter; straws in spring and summer. Makes a balanced year-round line. Leave the expensive XXXX beaver felt hats to the big boys in Danbury. But specialize. That's the secret for small men like you."

"Thank you, Mr. Callahan. I'll think about that. And I will see you on the tenth of the month, Promptly."

"I hear it is very cold up in the mountains," Rebecca said over their early morning coffee.

"Cold? The mountains?" David responded, taken aback, for he had been deep in thought about Callahan's suggestion of the day before.

"Saranac. It's high up in the Adirondack Mountains."

"So? You'll wear your winter coat," David said, eager to pursue the possibilities that were racing through his mind.

Aware of the resistance she would evoke, she said, "I wasn't thinking about myself."

For the first time, David looked up from the slice of brown cornbread he was buttering. He stared at her. An explanation was called for.

"Elvira has no coat. Some underwear, one old dress, and a pair of gym bloomers—not hers, because they're too big for her—but no coat."

"So?" David asked, as if challenging her to continue.

"So I was thinking, maybe if I took her down to Klein's on Union Square I could find a warm coat for her for seven or eight dollars. Sometimes they have great bargains. We could save a lot of money."

"From saving money that way, we could go bankrupt." He resumed buttering his bread.

Rebecca did not pursue the matter. She watched him eat and sip his coffee. Then, as had become the habit between them, she anticipated his desire for more hot coffee and poured it even before he had to ask. He was stirring the fresh steaming brew when he said, "You're sure it couldn't be more than eight dollars?"

"According to Klein's ad in the *Daily News*," she said.

"The *Daily News*," David scoffed. "You should read the *Times*. They're never right about anything, but at least it's a higher-class paper."

"Klein's doesn't advertise in the *Times*," she reminded. The comment cut more deeply than she had intended, for she could see in his eyes how hurt he was by the reminder that she geared her reading to their income, to what they could afford to buy. She hastened to apologize. "I'm sorry, David. It was wrong of me to bring up the matter of the coat. Perhaps I can borrow one from one of the neighbors' children."

"Absolutely not!" he rebuked. "We are not rich, but we are not beggars, either."

He figured hastily: With the extra money Callahan had insisted on for "contingencies" and if he stalled paying the gas bill in the shop and the phone bill, he could manage. After all, this could be considered one of those contingencies.

He reached into his pocket and pulled out a small collection of worn bills. He counted out thirty-seven dollars.

"Here. The fare." He counted out another eight dollars. "And for the coat." Then he added five more dollars. "For contingencies."

He had left himself five one-dollar bills. Before she could remark on it, he said, "I have some payments coming by the end of the week." He was lying, or at least exaggerating. She knew it. But said nothing.

When he returned home that evening, Rebecca and Elvira were waiting for him so they could all have supper together. He came in, said his good evenings, and went to wash up. While he did, Rebecca whispered to the child, "Go. Quick. Put on your new coat."

When he came into the kitchen to pour his presupper glass of schnapps, Elvira was waiting for him, dressed in a neat navy-blue coat of chinchilla cloth, tailored like a military uniform, double-breasted, with bright, shiny gilt buttons. The pride of ownership on the girl's face, her shining eyes, gave him a surge of satisfaction that he grudgingly had to admit. He glanced above Elvira's beaming face at Rebecca, who stood behind her.

"Five-fifty," Rebecca said. "It was on special sale."

"Good!" David said. "Very good. Now, let's eat."

6

*T*wo *mornings later*, Rebecca Rosen worked hurriedly in the kitchen preparing sandwiches for the journey. At the same time, she was reading the printed instructions from the sanatorium. Train to take, time of departure from Grand Central, arrival time next morning in Saranac, transportation from station to sanatorium.

She continued slicing rye bread and challah, left over from the Sabbath, already a little dry. She made the sandwiches in two separate groups—one of sliced chicken, the other of sliced egg. For the chicken she used the white-bread challah, first covering the slices with a layer of chicken fat, then adding salt. Those sandwiches would be for the day's lunch. For the egg sandwiches, she covered slices of rye bread with a thick layer of butter to keep them moist until suppertime. Since she was forbidden to mix the meat of the chicken with the butter of the egg sandwiches, Rebecca wrapped each group separately, so they would not commingle even by chance.

She prepared supper for David and left the pot on the stove so he had only to light the gas flame when he returned in the evening. She also wrote a note.

Darling David,

We will only be gone two nights, the longest separation of our married lives. It will seem forever. All my love.

The train had left Grand Central Station more than an hour before. With Elvira on her lap, Rebecca sat on the dark green velvet seat of the Pullman car. They stared out the window at the Hudson River on their left as the train raced by countryside that was dappled with the red and gold of late autumn. As they drew closer to Albany, the bright colors of late fall gave way to the drab sight of that industrial city as the train slowed and clanged its way into the station. The conductor came through the car calling out, "Allllbany! This station is Allllbany!" When the doors were opened, a rush of cold air invaded the car, bringing with it the acrid smell of burning coal.

Elvira shuddered. Rebecca slipped the new coat around her shoulders. The child drew it close, rubbing her cheek fondly against the soft curled chinchilla fabric. Whatever momentary difficulty the coat had created between her and David, Rebecca felt it was worth it to see the look on Elvira's face now.

New passengers came aboard. More than one paused when coming upon the white woman with a little Negro child. Then, reminding themselves that staring was rude, they searched for their assigned seats. Some looked back until Rebecca caught them at it. Then they continued on.

The train had pulled out of Albany, bumping its way noisily over various switches. Soon it picked up speed and was on its way once more.

"Hungry, my dear?" Rebecca asked.

"Yes, ma'am," Elvira replied.

"Elvira, can you call me something else besides ma'am?"

"What?" the child asked.

It was a better question than any answer Rebecca had ready.

"Perhaps you could try Mrs. Rosen," Rebecca suggested.

"All right, Mrs. Rosen," little Elvira attempted.

"Hungry, my dear?"

"Yes, Mrs. Rosen."

"Then we shall eat."

She proceeded to open the brown paper bag containing the chicken sandwiches. It was apparent that Elvira was more than hungry. She was ravenous. But she had been too polite or too afraid to give any hint. She held the large challah sandwich in her small hands, so that it almost obscured her face.

Unaccustomed to the confines of a Pullman berth and the rocking, swaying motion of a train that raced along at seventy miles an hour, both Rebecca and Elvira slept fitfully, jolted awake from time to time by the steam whistle that screamed in the night. Rebecca woke often to make sure the child, who had become a bundle of warmth pressed into her belly, was asleep and comfortable. Twice, the girl reached out to pull Rebecca's arm tighter around herself. Rebecca drew her even closer. They slept that way for the rest of the night.

The next morning, the train pulled into the Saranac station in slow jerking movements, creating a grinding noise that echoed in the frosty mountain air. In anticipation, bundled up in her navy-blue coat, Elvira stood with her face pressed against the window of the car door. The genial conductor had to coax, "Little girl, 'less you stand back, I can't open that door so you can go see your mama."

As Rebecca reached for the child's hand to draw her back, she could not help wondering how the conductor knew. He read her glance. "We get lots of little ones come to see Mama or Papa. Hope this time it's *good* news." Then, in a louder voice, he called to the passengers waiting to disembark. "Button up, folks. We get 'em real cold like this up here this time of year. Even worse comes real winter."

As Rebecca knelt down to make sure that Elvira's coat was buttoned to the very top, a Negro porter, his white jacket showing under his overcoat, brought Rebecca's small old suitcase to her. He handed her the paper bag of sandwiches.

At the same time, he whispered, "Ma'am, you never been here before, have you?"

Curious as to the reason for his question, Rebecca said, "No. Why?"

"There's taxis and carriages at the end of the station. Supposed to take folks to any sanatorium they want to go. If it's the child's mother, you'll likely be going to the Roosevelt Sanatorium."

"That's the name they gave me," Rebecca said.

"Sometimes there's trouble getting a ride, since that's the place for colored patients."

"They'd refuse a little girl?" Rebecca asked.

"Might. So best thing, *you* hire the taxi first, *then* let 'em see the child."

"Thank you," Rebecca said as she dug into her pocketbook.

"No thank you, ma'am," the porter said, refusing the tip even before it was offered.

After a slow drive over a winding rutted road, between banks of high white snow that sparkled in the sun, the old taxi pulled up at a large two-story log building bordered on all sides by a wide-open deck. While Rebecca counted out the coins for their fare, little Elvira stood staring at the huge building. Rebecca took her hand. They started up the wooden steps, which had been cleared of snow and ice only an hour earlier.

Inside the door everything was white—the walls, the clothes of the nurses and doctors, the medicine carts, even the information desk. The place was alive with the early-morning bustle of a hospital—dominated by doctors and nurses asking for or receiving reports on the condition of patients since last night's rounds.

Elvira, who had been eager up till now, became shy and afraid. Rebecca took her hand. They approached the desk.

"Mrs. Hitchins, please?" Rebecca asked of the plump middle-aged nurse in charge of information.

"Hitchins?" the woman said, looking down the list on the desk. When she did not find it at once, she repeated, "Hitchins? Are you sure?"

Rebecca felt little Elvira's hand tighten on her own. For the same thought that had occurred to Rebecca had obviously occurred to the child.

If her mama is no longer on the list . . .

But the woman said, "Hitchins. Oh yes. Ward two sixty-four. Second floor, end of the hall. Take those stairs and turn right."

The woman's moment of doubt had left a deeper scar on Elvira than Rebecca suspected, for she lagged when they climbed the stairs. At the landing, when Rebecca turned to the right, the child hesitated. Rebecca held out her hand. Elvira took it. They set off down the long hall, their heels sounding sharply on the polished pine-colored wood floor.

They passed ward after ward. A swift glance revealed rows of white beds, all occupied. The staccato of wracking coughs explained why. Anticipating what Elvira might find and how it would affect her, Rebecca tightened her grip on the girl's hand and picked up their pace.

They were at the end of the corridor. On their left, on the last open door, was printed neatly in plain black type: WARD 264.

They stood in the open doorway, looking down the aisle between the two rows of beds. All the patients were Negroes—some old, some young, some even in their teens. There were three gaps, where beds had been and were no longer.

Rebecca led Elvira into the room. Some patients lifted their heads from their pillows to identify the visitors, concentrating on the child, then assessing the anomaly of a colored child with a white guardian.

Rebecca whispered, "Elvira?" meaning, *Which one is your mama?*

The girl searched from bed to bed, from face to face, at first puzzled, then distressed, then terrified at not finding her mother.

"My mama? Where's my mama?" She began to cry then, demanded loudly, "My mama! I want my mama!"

Rebecca dropped to one knee to embrace the child and comfort her, holding her tear-stained face against her own. Looking across Elvira's shoulder at the other patients, she asked, "Mrs. Hitchins? They said she was in this ward."

"She was," one of the women volunteered, while pointing to the empty space across from her bed.

Rebecca felt herself in need of solace as well as courage. She concealed her fear from the child as best she could. She rose, took Elvira by the hand, and ventured, "Where . . . where is Mrs. Hitchins now?"

"Took her down for X rays," several women volunteered at once.

"Let's go find her," Elvira insisted.

"Oh, you can't do that, child!" an elderly gray-haired woman warned. Addressing Rebecca, she said, "Just go down the hall and wait. There's a visitors' room there. They'll come get you."

They had been waiting for more than half an hour. During that time Elvira was restless, climbing up on one of the lounge chairs, then down, never finding a place that seemed comfortable. She talked, giving vent to her feelings and fears.

"Could be it could be good."

"What, dear?" Rebecca asked.

"X rays. Maybe they tryin' to see if'n . . ." she blurted out excitedly, then corrected herself, and began once more: "Maybe they are trying to see if . . ." She hesitated to evaluate that, then continued, "To see if she's all right to come home."

"Maybe," Rebecca agreed quickly, to calm the child's anxieties as well as her own.

"If she be very sick . . ." She paused, then corrected, "If she is very sick, they wouldn't need X rays to know. When we go to the doctor that first time, he just listen to Mama's back and right away he say . . . said, 'Mrs. Hitchins, you got to go to the hospital.' He didn't need no X rays. So X rays could be good. Couldn't they? Couldn't they?" she pleaded.

"Yes, they could," Rebecca agreed with as much conviction as she could muster.

A white-clad nurse appeared in the doorway. "Are you the people asking about Mrs. Hitchins?"

Even before Rebecca could respond, Elvira raced across the room, demanding, "Where is she? Where is my mama?" Tears streamed down her face as she pleaded, "Where is she?"

"Come with me, child," the nurse said.

Elvira burst into ward 264, calling out with great expectation, "Mama! Mama!" She looked about, saw the still-empty place where her mother's bed should be, then whispered, "Mama . . ."

"Out on the porch," the elderly woman said, pointing the way.

The child raced to the door at the far end of the ward. She had difficulty pulling open the tall, heavy glass-and-wood door, but she managed it finally. One look, and she cried out in relief, "Mama!" She raced across the open wooden porch to the bed where her mother lay, swathed in a heavy flannel hospital gown, thick white blankets, and a white mask that contrasted with the rest of her thin brown face.

"My baby, my baby," Anna Hitchins cried, struggling through her blankets to embrace Elvira and lift her into her arms. When Elvira attempted to kiss her, Anna Hitchins turned her head to avoid her. "Not there, baby. Not there." Elvira was content to feel her mother's arms around her. She pressed against the blankets, which were as close to her mother as she could come.

Rebecca stood at the door, glancing through the glass at this reunion. She felt extremely happy for the child and considerably relieved for herself as well. Once she realized that she also felt a pang of jealousy. She turned away to find the nurse at her side.

"Dr. Flanders would like to see you, ma'am."

Rebecca found the doctor in his office studying the chest X rays of a patient. He was a younger man than his beard testified. He was dressed in a white lab coat, a habit he had acquired from the German doctors under whom he had studied after graduating from medical college in Michigan. When he heard the door open behind him, he called out, "Mrs. Rosen?"

"Yes, doctor."

Still turned away from her, he asked, "Are you a social-services worker?"

"No."

"Then what *is* your connection with the Hitchinses?"

As briefly as possible, Rebecca told him how the child had come into her life.

"It was very decent," Flanders commented. "Very humane of you and your husband to do that."

"A child alone—it would have been inhumane to refuse."

"And now?" Flanders said, turning to face Rebecca for the first time. He stared at her for a long moment.

"Something wrong?" she asked, self-conscious.

"The nurse said you were white. From your name, I assumed you were Jewish. I expected a woman with a darker complexion, darker hair. She did not say you were blond. Also . . . so . . . so beautiful."

Rebecca felt herself blush. In the society in which she lived, one did not pay such compliments to another man's wife. Flanders noticed and apologized.

"I'm sorry. I did not mean to be so . . . so personal," he said. "I asked you to come by for a professional consultation."

"So I assumed," Rebecca responded, still blushing and self-conscious. "I have several questions myself. How soon will her mother be released so they can be together again?" Rebecca asked.

"Mrs. Rosen," Flanders began. "This place, with its snow-capped mountains, its clean mountain air, is very deceptive. When you ride through our picturesque town and see those rosy-cheeked, clean, well-dressed people, it gives one the feeling of being in an Alpine skiing village at holiday time. But those rosy-cheeked people are not holidayers only unfortunates fighting for their lives."

Flanders tugged at his short beard before admitting, "And the sad truth is there is little we can do for them. Fresh air? Yes. Sunshine? That, too. Good food? Of course. And medical intervention. Does it help? Not much."

"What are you trying to tell me, doctor?"

"This is a treacherous disease, most times beyond our control. It has a way of galloping through the entire body, inflicting damage beyond the lungs, until it becomes uncontrollable."

"So this is a . . . a farewell visit . . . a final visit?" Rebecca said, more to absorb the fact than to give words to it.

"We don't make it a practice to anticipate the event. But in this case—the mother of a child with no other family—we thought someone should be making plans."

"Yes, yes, of course, plans," Rebecca said, still stunned by the sudden news.

The interview at an end, she knew she should go but found herself unable to rise. She sat pondering the consequences of what Flanders had said.

"Mrs. Rosen," he said gently.

"Yes. Of course. I was just leaving."

Anna Hitchins lay in her bed out on the deck, breathing the cold, sharp, dry Adirondack air. Wrapped in heavy white blankets, with a mask to cover her nose, she breathed deeply, thinking, *The cold air gonna cure me, the cold air gonna cure me, the colder the better*. In the crook of her arm lay little Elvira, her face pressed against the wool blanket that intervened between her and her mother's bosom.

The child was content to lie there, more content than she had been for many days. Her mother realized that and kept up a steady flow of promises in answer to her young daughter's questions.

"Tell me, Mama, how it gonna be," Elvira asked.

"It be like before, baby, better than before," her mother said. "We'll have more time together. I won't be working for the Fleischmans anymore. Not for a while, for a long while."

"We'll be together all the time?" Elvira asked, begging for reassurance.

"All the time." She felt a fit of coughing coming on. She turned away from her daughter to lift her mask and clear the bloody residue from her mouth. She recovered, breathing deeply several times before continuing: "All the time, baby. Of course, until then . . . you like Mrs. Rosen?"

"Oh yes, Mama. Mister, sometimes he be . . . like very angry. But the rest of the time he be nice, too."

"I'm glad. She seem like a fine woman."

"She bought me this coat," Elvira said proudly.

"And a lovely coat it be."

Elvira put her arms around her mother. But the woman spoke gently. "Not too close, baby, not too close." It was painful to say, but necessary.

"Mama, be we goin' to Central Park again, too?" the child asked.

"The park? Of course."

"A picnic? Fried chicken?" Elvira anticipated.

"My best," her mother promised.

"Much as I want?"

"Much as you want, darling."

"'N' ice cream? Eskimo pies?" the child asked.

"Eskimo pies? I am going to fill your little belly with Eskimo pies. Hundreds of them."

Elvira smiled. "You jokin', Mama? Hundreds of Eskimo pies? Two or three, maybe."

"Then you be havin' two or three," her mother promised.

"*When*, Mama, *when* you be comin' home?" Elvira asked.

"When . . . whenever the doctors say, baby. Whenever they say—" She was interrupted by another fit of coughing. She reached out to stroke Elvira's cheek.

"So pretty, my baby. 'N light-skinned. Such nice hair. From your papa's side. Such a handsome man. 'Most white. People was use to say, 'If he wanted, he could pass.' But not him. Not him. Proud."

The woman hesitated, debating whether to continue. *She not yet old enough to hear it, but if I don' tell her now, I never going to be able to.*

"They don' like no proud black man down there where we was livin'. That day, I beg him not to talk back. He's takin' me to the doctor since I'm so close to birthin' you. And they standin' out there, front of the general store. One of 'em call out, 'Hey you! White nigger! Whyn't you marry that bitch 'fore she whelps your little bastard?' Which was a lie, since we been married two years by that time. I could feel the anger in him. 'N I say, 'Homer, don't you say a word back! They's Klan.' But 'fore I get all the words out, your papa is turning on 'em and . . . 'N' the las' words he ever say to me, 'Take care my chile.'"

"He call me his chile?" Elvira asked.

"Oh yes, yes. And he make such plans for you . . . such plans. When we bury him, I promise at his grave, 'Homer,' I say. 'Your chile is going to have a different way—a better way.'"

Tears began to trace down her thin brown cheeks.

"Your papa had bigger dreams than I could do for. You got to do 'em. Y'hear? 'N you hold yourself proud, like he did. 'N be what he wanted you to be from even before you was born."

She patted Elvira on the cheek, her thin, bony fingers enjoying the feel of the child's smooth skin.

"Chile," she said. "You go through this life, don't you pile up no burden of debt. People do you good, you do good back to them, so you can feel free. Don't you leave this world owin' nothin' to nobody."

She reached out and drew her daughter close, to kiss her. But fearful of infecting the child, she turned away and was overcome by a fit of coughing, which ended with her spitting up some blood into a piece of gauze.

All this Rebecca observed from the other side of the tall glass door. She felt on the verge of tears but replaced them with a smile as she stepped out onto the deck to fetch the child for lunch.

"Elvira, time now," Rebecca said. "Time for lunch."

"Mama?" the child asked, seeking permission.

"Of course, baby, you go with Mrs. Rosen."

The child tried to kiss her mother on the cheek.

"Not too close, baby, not too close."

As Elvira turned from her mother to join Rebecca, Anna Hitchins's eyes pleaded, *Stay a moment, Mrs. Rosen, I beg you.*

Rebecca allowed Elvira to enter the ward. She approached the bed. Mrs. Hitchins indicated: Bend closer to me. Rebecca leaned over so they were face to face. Behind the white mask Rebecca discovered a pair of watery eyes, black as coal and filled with the suffering of her illness and her life.

"She be a good child," the woman began.

"I know."

"She deserves better'n I could give her. Promise me one thing—the family she finally go to, they be good, God-fearing folk. And a clean, decent home."

She broke into a fit of coughing. Rebecca felt helpless to aid her in any way. When her coughing subsided, Rebecca said, "We will do our best to see that she is placed with a good family."

"Don't just give her away," the woman pleaded. "I mean, ask after her from time to time. Make sure she be all right . . . well treated. Make sure."

"I will."

"One thing. Don't never let them put her into no orphanage. I couldn't rest where I'm goin' thinkin' she be in some friendless place. That child be fragile in herself. She couldn't stand up to it. It must be some family. Promise me!" the woman insisted, peering at Rebecca over the white mask that covered her face.

"I promise. She will not go to an orphanage," Rebecca assured her.

At noon the next day Rebecca Rosen, her hand wrapped around Elvira's hand, boarded the train for Albany and New York City.

As the train made its way through snowy mountain country, fresh flakes began to fall, brushing against the windows. Rebecca had her arm about the girl as they both stared out at the new flurries that swept by.

Suddenly, Elvira said, "Luna Park. I din' get to ask about Luna Park." She cast an upward glance at Rebecca. "She be takin' me . . . she'll take me to Luna Park, won't she?" the child corrected herself.

Rebecca could not resist becoming an unwilling co-conspirator. "Of course, Luna Park. Mr. Rosen and I used to go there when we were courting."

"What's courting, Mrs. Rosen?"

"Courting is when a young man comes to call on a young woman with the idea of asking her to marry him."

"You think any young man ever come courtin' on me?" the child asked.

"When you grow up, you will be so beautiful there'll be many young men who will come courting you," Rebecca promised.

Rebecca thought, *This child keeps asking questions calculated to evoke promises. What am I to do? But, more, what are we to do when the doctor's prognosis finally comes true?*

"We go to Luna Park once," Elvira said. "Mama working this job for some rich people. And they be goin'—" She stopped to correct herself. "And they were going away for the summer. Since Mama didn't have no job all summer, they give her—gave her—a little present. Not a real present, but extra money. And Mama says . . . said, 'I don't know when we be having extra money again.'" The child interrupted herself to explain, "That's what my mama said, so I can't correct that." Then she continued: "'I don't know when we be havin' extra money again, so let's have a good time.' She took me to Luna Park. We went on all the rides. Not *all* the rides. On one ride there was this man with two kids and he say—said, he said, 'My kids don't ride in no car with no niggers.' So Mama just take my hand and she walk me away. She say . . . said to me, 'Not all white folks be like that.' Next time she takes me to Luna Park we will go on that ride. I know if I aks her . . . I know if I . . . ask her, we will, we will!"

The ride along the Hudson River from Albany to New York was uneventful, save for Elvira reliving and cherishing the promises her mother had made.

"And Mama say we be having a picnic in Central Park. Fried chicken and all. My mama makes the best fried chicken in the whole world. And Eskimo pies." Then she appeared sheepish as she smiled and said, "My mama don't make the Eskimo pies. She buys 'em. White ice cream all covered with chocolate."

"I know," Rebecca said. "And they are delicious."

Elvira pulled Rebecca's arm tighter around her. Suddenly, she asked, "Will you come?"

Taken by surprise, Rebecca asked, "Come? Where?"

"When Mama and me have our picnic. Will you come?"

"Well . . . well, yes, if you invite me."

"I invite you," the child said. "And so will my mama."

"Then I will come," Rebecca said, unable to avoid making another futile promise of her own.

Reassured, the child turned to stare out the window at the late-fall scene that rushed past the train window.

7

N*ine days later*, early in the morning, the ringing phone intruded on the Rosen household. David was already at the door, leaving for business, so Rebecca answered. He lingered to learn if the call was for him. When he heard his wife respond with a hushed, pained, "Oh, no, no!" he came back to her side.

"Becca? What? What is it?"

She gestured him to silence until she had completed the call. "Yes. Yes I understand, doctor. You will hear from me."

She hung up the phone.

"Dr. Flanders. In Saranac. Elvira's mama died at four o'clock this morning. He wants instructions as to what to do with her remains."

"Remains?" David commented. "Is that what we all become?"

"We'll have to do something. Something," Rebecca said thoughtfully. "But first . . . first I will have to tell her."

"You may need me. I'll stay."

"No, you go, take care of the business. I'll let her sleep. When she wakes . . ."

David kissed her tenderly. "God, how do you tell a child something like that?"

It was past nine o'clock in the morning. Rebecca had been cleaning and cooking in the kitchen, very quietly so as not to disturb Elvira, who was asleep on the couch in the living room. Rebecca was just skimming the fat off the boiling chicken soup when she heard Elvira stir. She had already determined she would not tell her until after she had had her breakfast.

Breakfast over, Rebecca took the child into the living room and sat her on her lap. With her arms around her, she said,

"Elvira my dear, this morning I had a telephone call from up in Saranac."

"Mama's coming home!" the child exulted. "When? Will we go to that station to meet her?"

"Elvira my dear . . . listen to me," Rebecca pleaded. "Your mama is not coming home . . . not the way you would like." The child stared up at her. Rebecca forced herself to continue: "The doctor told me that early this morning your mama died."

"Died . . ." The child spoke the word as if it were foreign to her and had no meaning. "Died," she repeated. She was silent until she asked, "Do that mean we not be havin' any picnic?" Puzzled, stunned, she made no effort to correct herself.

"I'm afraid that's what it means. But also, your mama won't be coming back anymore."

"Not coming back anymore . . . ever?" Elvira shook her head. Refusing to accept that, she did not weep. She looked up to stare at Rebecca, her black eyes accusing. *Why are you telling me lies?* She slipped from Rebecca's embrace to stand at the window. Then she turned suddenly and raced to the bathroom. Rebecca followed in time to hear the child vomiting up her breakfast. Rebecca went in, took the girl in her arms, wiped her damp face dry with her apron, held her, and rocked her.

"Elvira my dear, you mustn't be afraid. You are not alone in the world. Mr. Rosen and I will see that you find another family."

"My mama . . . I want my mama!" the child protested, then broke free and raced into the living room to put on her street clothes. Half-dressed, shoes untied, blouse unbuttoned, she started toward the door. There, Rebecca caught her, held her despite her fierce struggle, and pleaded, "No, Elvira, no. It won't do any good. It won't."

"My mama . . . I want my mama . . . I want my mama . . ." she continued to protest until gradually her struggles ceased and she finally began to weep. Hot tears traced down her face. Rebecca held her tightly.

"Cry. Cry, Elvira darling. That's the best way. Just cry."

She held the child in her arms until her young, thin body went soft and limp as anger turned to grief.

With the plain wood coffin that brought Anna Hitchins's body back to New York came a worn suitcase, barely held together by a piece of clothesline with frayed ends. Inside it were all the worldly possessions of the woman.

Rebecca and David sorted through them.

"Nothing worth keeping," he said.

"The child should make that choice," Rebecca said.

That afternoon, before she dressed Elvira for the funeral, she laid out her mother's clothes for the girl to examine and choose. Angry at being abandoned, Elvira rejected them all. "I don't want to be keepin' anything of hers! Anything!" She began to cry. After a time she sniffed back her tears and resumed looking through her mother's last possessions. Of them all, she selected only the red-and-white kerchief.

"My mama wear this when she be workin' . . . when she used to work around the house." She demonstrated by wrapping the kerchief around her own head. "Other people's houses."

Something in Rebecca rebelled. *That's like Aunt Jemima on the box of pancake flour. I won't allow it!* Until she realized: *She is not my child, I have no right to say what she will or will not wear, do or will not do. Besides, who knows what this prejudiced world will let her do?*

Helped by Dr. Pomerantz, Mrs. Feinstein of the Anche Chesed orphanage, and the Fleischmans, the family for which Hitchins had last worked, enough money was raised to provide a simple funeral.

From his medical practice, Dr. Pomerantz knew the pastor of a Baptist church in upper Harlem, the Reverend Elton Bruton, who consented to preside. The service, conducted in a funeral chapel in Harlem, was attended by Elvira, Rebecca and David Rosen, and Dr. Pomerantz. The body was laid out in front of the altar. Before the service, Rebecca took Elvira by the hand and led her to the open casket. There, the child stood on tiptoe to look down at the peaceful face of her mother.

"Mama," she said softly, as if speaking louder would have

disturbed her. "Mama . . ." She turned to Rebecca. "She never leave me without a kiss goodbye."

Rebecca lifted the girl so she could kiss her mother.

Elvira reached out to pat her mother's cold cheek. "You go to heaven now, Mama, hear?" the child instructed.

Once the tiny company of mourners took their places, the Reverend Bruton delivered a eulogy. He spoke glowingly of a woman he had never known or even met, endowing her with all the qualities that every child would love to remember about her mother. Throughout, Elvira continued to nod her head.

The service concluded, Reverend Bruton paused only long enough to say to Rebecca, "Mrs. Rosen, I will do everything in my power to find a suitable home for the child. Though, in these times, that won't be easy. People . . . colored people . . . have trouble enough feeding their own. When white folks have a depression, black folks have a disaster. But there must be a family somewhere . . . somewhere," he promised.

It was obvious to Rebecca that despite his intentions, he knew his promise was vague, given in desperation.

In the days that followed, during which Elvira suffered hours of depression and weeping, Rebecca tried to keep her mind occupied. She attempted to entice her back to reading. When the child would not join in, Rebecca read to her. Elvira lost interest. Even when Rebecca read to her from the two treasured books that were her only inheritance, she did not respond as she had earlier.

On the eighth day after Anna Hitchins's soul had been consigned to God, there was a call from Reverend Bruton. He had located a family in Harlem who would consider taking in a child of eight—provided there was the usual city assistance paid to foster families.

"Reverend, did you say it was to be a foster family?"

"Yes, Mrs. Rosen."

"If it's for the money, no, I'm sorry. I can't permit it."

"Mrs. Rosen, I must point out that your feelings are of no consequence in this. In fact, you have no standing in this situation at all."

"I can't permit this child to be passed around among foster homes," Rebecca insisted.

That evening, after Elvira had been put to bed, Rebecca reported to David her confrontation with the minister.

"But, Becca, he was right. We took the girl in, in an emergency. But aside from that, what are we? Not relatives, surely. Not foster parents. Not possible adopting parents. That minister is right. A colored child belongs in a colored family. And soon. Before . . ."

He decided it was not wise to continue. But Rebecca insisted.

"Before *what?*"

"Nothing," he said abruptly. "I said all I have to say about this matter."

"Before *what?*" she insisted.

He took both her hands in his. He looked down into her soft blue eyes. "Before you become *too* attached to her."

"What does that mean, 'too attached'?"

"She is a nice child. Very smart. You, being the woman you are, may find yourself unable to give her up when the time comes."

"Meaning I, being a woman who has not been able to have a child of her own, would look upon her as a substitute?"

"I didn't say that," he protested. "You are simply too softhearted. Since her mother's death, you have shared every moment of grief with that child. This house has become a house of mourning—for both of you."

"David, my darling, are you saying that I have been neglecting you for the sake of the child?"

"No," he denied emphatically. "I never said that, never thought that."

"There must be something more than you've told me." When he did not respond, she urged, "David? Darling? Are we to begin having secrets from one another?"

He did not respond but left the kitchen to slip quietly into their bedroom and undress for the night.

They lay in bed, unable to sleep, unable to make love.

He was silent for a time. Then, "What I was thinking . . . I am afraid."

"Afraid? Of what?"

"If you become attached to the child, when the time comes to give her up—and we *must*—it will be like . . ."

She continued on her own, "It will be like after my fourth time. . . ."

"Yes," he admitted, relieved that she had said it. "I can't tell you how afraid I was. If Dr. Pomerantz hadn't suggested that you help out at the orphanage, I don't know what would have happened to you. And now, if you become too attached to this child . . ."

"Well, you don't have to worry," Rebecca assured him. "I know we must give her up. And we will. But for adoption."

Reverend Bruton listened to Rebecca's decisions gravely and without interruption. When she finished, he said, "Of course, first thing is to have the child examined."

"Examined? Why? What for?" Rebecca asked defensively.

"Considering her mother's illness and death, I would have to assure any family who might consider adopting her permanently that she is in good health," the minister explained.

"Yes. Of course," Rebecca said, less tense now. "And then?"

"And then we must place her in an orphanage, an orphanage for Negro children."

"I promised her mother no orphanage!" Rebecca protested.

"I must make her available to be seen by potential adopting families."

"Why can't she stay with us until then?"

"Mrs. Rosen, I trust I do not have to point out to you that this situation is quite . . . shall I say unusual. The girl belongs with her own. Her own people. Her own religion."

"But to take her from a home just to place her in an orphanage . . ." Rebecca considered grimly. "And then what happens if no home is found for her?"

"She would remain in that orphanage until the age of fifteen or sixteen, when she will be put out to work to support herself."

"At fifteen?" Rebecca asked.

"You've seen them—colored women standing at subway stations on cold mornings, waiting to be picked out by some white woman for a day of housework. It is little better than the slave auctions of old."

"She is a bright child, very sensitive. To condemn her to such a life would be criminal. I can't let that happen!" Rebecca protested.

"Mrs. Rosen, I understand your feelings. But we have so few choices unless we want the Department of Welfare to step in, and the domestic-relations court, which I dread most of all; to throw any child, especially a colored child, into the hands of petty bureaucrats. She would be swallowed up, out of your hands and mine forever."

"Then what can we do?" Rebecca asked.

"Have faith." Then he added, "And at the same time, enter into a little conspiracy. While I search for some family to take her on a permanent basis, you take care of her. But we must keep her out of the hands of the court."

"Are we now involved in conspiracies?" David asked.

"Better that than turn her over to some place where she will be just another Negro child."

"Actually, Becca, I've been asking about this too," David confessed. "Business, all kinds, even one as small as mine— we have our refuse collected by private garbage people. One of our men is a Negro, a big, strong young man. So yesterday I started up a conversation with him. He's married. So I thought . . . but it turns out his wife is already pregnant and he can't consider another mouth to feed."

"A child is more than a mouth. She is a human being who has many hungers besides food. Especially this child. Especially—" Her words stopped suddenly.

David detected a stifled sob. In the darkness, he reached for her, drew her close. He felt the tension go out of her body, felt her softness.

Gently, chiding her in good humor, he said, "If I were a more sensitive man, I would be jealous, Becca. All you talk about, think about, is her. Since she arrived, no questions about me, about the business."

"The business?" Rebecca asked in alarm. "Has something gone wrong?"

"For a change, something has gone right," he boasted.

"What? Tell me!"

"The idea that Mr. Callahan gave me—"

"Derbies?"

"Right, derbies. I have made arrangements for the equipment that is needed. A small deposit, which I was able to borrow from the bank. And monthly payments."

"David, what do you know about manufacturing derbies?" Rebecca asked.

"That's what started it. Callahan. I was making a delivery last week. He told me that the foreman from Gillideau—they make the best derbies—was dissatisfied. He was looking to leave, Callahan said, 'Get hold of him, make a deal, he's the best there is.' So I did. Then Callahan, what a fine man, he says, 'Davey,' . . . he calls me Davey now . . . 'Davey, I am going to start you out right: an order for ten dozen derbies. Black. Sizes six and seven-eighths to seven and five-eighths.' We are on our way, Becca, on our way!"

He shared his enthusiasm with her by kissing her passionately and exuberantly. She felt the warmth of desire stirring in her and then in him. They made love.

In the silence that followed, she said softly into his ear, "You see, David, how God has rewarded us for doing a small act of kindness and charity toward a needy child?"

"Becca, isn't it possible that this would have happened if there had been no child?"

"David, you *are* jealous."

"Not jealous," he protested. "But I would like some recognition for what I have done. And for Callahan. He's been very good to us."

"He sounds like a very nice man," Rebecca said.

"He is, he is. One day I asked him, 'Why?' He gave me a very strange answer. He said, 'Davey, we Irish and you Jews have a lot in common. We both suffer from prejudice. So we have to stick together.'"

"Strange," Rebecca said. "Reverend Bruton . . . he said that Jews and Negroes should understand each other because they, too, suffer from prejudice."

The Reverend Bruton called often to inquire about Elvira. But only three times did he have a new family to suggest.

Each time, Rebecca dutifully boarded the subway to go downtown to Harlem to interview the family, inspect the living conditions, and inquire about their attitude toward a child of eight coming into the household.

Each time she came away deciding, *This is no place for Elvira.*

The evening of her third visit, David was washing up before supper when he asked, "Well?"

That single syllable had come to have a special meaning in the Rosen home: *Did you go, what did you find; what kind of people; what kind of home?*

"I didn't like the way the children looked," Rebecca said.

"How are children supposed to look? Weren't they clean? Weren't they decently dressed? Weren't they fed?"

"Their eyes," Rebecca said.

"Their eyes?" David asked. "Colored children, at least the ones I've ever seen, all have black eyes, brown eyes. What's wrong with that?" He was becoming impatient with her when Elvira appeared in the doorway, drawn by his argumentative tone. At once his attitude changed. "Good evening, Elvira. You look very pretty tonight. What a nice hair bow. Such a lovely color."

Shyly, she fingered the green bow Rebecca had taught her to tie earlier in the day.

Conversation during supper was mainly confined to David's opinions about the news he had heard on the radio. Business conditions in the country were growing worse despite everything President Hoover said or did.

"But you wish to know what troubles me most?" he demanded, brandishing his fork for emphasis. *"The New York Times."*

"Darling," Rebecca reminded quietly. "Hardly a day goes by that something in the *Times* doesn't trouble you most."

"Rebecca, don't make fun! This morning in the *Times* the word *depression*?"

"What about it?" Rebecca asked, truly puzzled.

"Today for the first time *The New York Times* spelled depression not with a small *d* but with a capital *D.*" He enunciated the word with rolling emphasis and added length: "Depression! With a capital *D!*"

"Which means?"

"Which means, my darling wife, that it is no longer a severe business problem. It is now an institution. *The Depression.* Like The Woolworth Building. The White House. The Supreme Court. The Depression has become permanent, a way of life," he pontificated.

Throughout, Elvira sat between them, her eyes wide, her head turning first one way then the other, depending on who was speaking. While she could not grasp the full import of David's words, her child's instinct told her that bad times for the world were especially threatening to children like herself. She ceased eating until Rebecca reminded, "Elvira sweetheart, eat your soup." When that failed, she resorted to the one argument that always succeeded. "Your mama would have wanted you to eat."

Elvira resumed eating but remained sensitive to anything David might say. One glance from Rebecca caused David to change the subject. He talked enthusiastically about the shop, about a new order he had received that morning from the men's hat department at Stern Brothers. Evidently, word was getting around the trade that Rosen makes a good derby. As the tone of the conversation took on a brighter note, the child seemed reassured, for she ate with more appetite.

But once Elvira was asleep, David resumed questioning, "What about their eyes?"

Taken aback, Rebecca asked, "Eyes? Whose eyes?"

"Those children you saw today."

"Oh, those eyes," Rebecca said, then added only, "Fear."

"Maybe they were afraid because a stranger, a white woman, came prying into their home."

"They can't be afraid of me," Rebecca insisted.

"How can you be sure?"

"Because I know children."

"A few months with this one child and already you know children?" he rebuked.

Tears rushed to her eyes. "A woman does not need to have children of her own. She only needs to have been a child herself."

That ended the discussion until they were in bed and both found sleep impossible.

"Rebecca," he whispered. "Suppose someone were to come here to inspect *us*? What would they say? The place is too small to accommodate a child. The husband is so concerned about his business he has no time for a child. The wife is overprotective. And besides all that, this family is white and the child is a Negro."

"I never said I intend to keep her!" Rebecca replied.

"No. But if there is no other family fit to take her, what is left? An orphanage? Her mother said no to that. You are leaving us no choice."

"What do you want me to do?" she asked, resigned.

"Inspect those families with a little more . . . understanding. Bear in mind that there is no such thing as a perfect family. Keep an open mind. Promise me!"

"All right, David. I promise."

In the ensuing week, the Reverend Bruton could supply only two more possible families who might be considered potential adoptive parents.

Rebecca visited them, firmly determined to adhere to her promise to David.

The children in both households were freshly bathed, the hair of the little girls neatly plaited, their dresses so freshly pressed that Rebecca could almost smell the starch and the aroma of ironing.

Each time, she found little to criticize. She had only her own instinct to fall back on. Something within her said, *No, not for Elvira. She is a special child, with special needs. Or is David right? Will I never find a home good enough? Is it her mother's plea? Do deathbed promises, which many times are no more than extortion or bribery, have any validity? Should they?*

That evening when David returned, she told him quite forthrightly, "Today was no better. I did not find a family I would entrust her to."

Within several days the Reverend Bruton called again. "Mrs. Rosen, I think I have finally found the right family for Elvira. They come highly recommended. They are anxious to take in a child. If Elvira meets their expectations, they will adopt her."

"Elvira will meet their expectations," Rebecca said staunchly.

Bruton made no comment but thought, *She is as proud of that child as if she were her own.*

As Elvira stepped out of the tub, her slender body glistening, Rebecca enveloped her in a large white towel. She dried her vigorously. She combed the girl's hair and wove it neatly into two braids that she joined in a halo atop her head.

"Red," the child said, naming the color of the bow she wanted.

All the while, Rebecca continued speaking softly, "I've been told all about them, Elvira dear. You will like them."

"Mrs. Jackson, she be like my mama?" Elvira asked.

"Elvira, your mama was a very special person. But Mrs. Jackson is a fine woman. You will like her. And Mr. Jackson, too."

The girl having been completely dressed, Rebecca stood off from her to inspect her. "Turn around, Elvira." She made a slow complete turn, her eyes fixed on Rebecca as long as she was able. They kept asking, *Am I all right, am I pretty enough, will they like me?*

"You look lovely. So pretty," Rebecca enthused.

"I wish my mama could see me now, so dressed up," the girl said. "You think she knows? About me and going to new folks?"

"Yes, dear. I think where she is she keeps watch over you all the time," Rebecca said. "And she is proud of you. Very proud."

The child held herself more erect.

"Remember what I said, Elvira. Don't be shy. If they ask you questions, answer them. And don't be afraid. The Jacksons are eager to love you. Give them the chance."

"Yes, ma'am," Elvira responded.

"Put on your coat, dear," Rebecca said. She watched as the girl slipped on her navy-blue coat with the shiny buttons.

Elvira having been made ready, Rebecca took her hand. As they passed the living room on the way to the front door, she stopped, looked in, and whispered, "Goodbye, house."

The words stabbed at Rebecca. Determined, she tightened her grip on the child and started for the front door.

On the subway ride down to Harlem, Elvira sat very still and silent. Whether it was the noise of the train or fear of the impending parting, she appeared grim, her eyes wide, staring, fixed.

With the slip of paper in one hand and Elvira's hand in the other, Rebecca walked along West 119th Street. It was a street of drab tenements that in other days had been considered quite fine apartment buildings, tenanted by middle-class people, white people.

Times being so bad, there were many idle Negro men and women on the street and on the stoops who stared at them. Rebecca overheard more than one comment from which she gleaned that they considered her a teacher bringing a recalcitrant child back from school for some infraction. Or else she was a white city employee returning another runaway colored child.

Elvira herself saw little, heard little, being totally in the grip of fear of what lay ahead. Her hand was damp and sweaty in Rebecca's.

Rebecca matched the number on the slip with the number in faded gold lettering above the double doors of the building. She guided Elvira from the entryway into the darker hallway. They found the steps and started up.

They reached the top of the third flight of stairs and were on the fourth landing. They found apartment 4B.

Rebecca knelt down, examined Elvira's face, tidied her hair, straightened her coat, then prepared to knock. Before she could, the door opened.

A tall man, his black face contrasting with his gray hair, his brown eyes warm and welcoming, asked, "Mrs. Rosen?"

"Mr. Jackson?"

"Yes, come in. Come in."

They started into the apartment, which appeared dark until they emerged from the narrow hallway into the rest of the place, which consisted of a kitchen on their right, a bedroom beyond that, and at the end a parlor, which had two windows and was bright with winter sunlight.

One quick glance and Rebecca knew that this apartment was clean, tidy, and well cared for. The furniture, though old and well worn, was neatly arranged. The carpet showed small areas of long wear so bare in spots that the hemp-colored fiber of the backing showed through.

One thing was instantly obvious and disturbing to Rebecca: the absence of the woman of the house.

Jared Jackson had anticipated her. "Mrs. Jackson is out shopping for a minute. She be back. She be back." Now he turned his attention to Elvira. He smiled. "So this is her, little Elvira . . ." He dropped into the easy chair and beckoned. "Come here, child."

Elvira did not move until Rebecca gently nudged her forward, at the same time apologizing, "She's a little shy."

"And why not?" Jackson replied. "I remember being 'bout her age. And I be going to see my granddaddy for the first time. He lived in Mississippi. He be a farmer. Old as he was, he was a powerful big man. Except by that time he no longer gets around so fast. Rheumatiz, he called it. I think it was his age. Age and a hard life. He was sitting on the porch of his house in his old rocker, and he says to me, 'Come here, boy.' Just like this little one, I hangs back. Then my daddy say, 'Go on, Jared. That's your grandpa.' I went to him. He says, 'Jared, I want you to look around this place. I want you to look at your old granddaddy. And I wants you to promise yourself, "I ain't never going to be a broken-down old nigger like my granddaddy." You go back up North and never come South again. 'Cept maybe for my funeral.'"

Jackson shook his head sadly. "Hardly best way for a boy to meet his granddaddy. Saddest part be I found out things wasn't much better up here."

He appeared to be self-conscious about his reminiscences because he abruptly turned to Elvira. "Well now, child, you have to forgive an old man for recallin' things from the long past. Comes with age, I guess. But about you . . . I see for myself how pretty you be. And the Reverend Bruton tell us how bright you be. Are you?"

Elvira drew back, pressing against Rebecca for protection.

"She is bright, extremely bright," Rebecca said. "But as I said, she is also shy."

"It become a child to be shy. I consider modesty a virtue, a Christian virtue."

He was interrupted by the sound of the front door opening. Jackson called out, "Mary! She here!"

"Just let me put my shoppin' down."

In moments Mary Jackson came bustling into the room. One look and she exclaimed, "My Lord, what a pretty child! Come, dear, I be having some milk and cookies for you in the kitchen." She took Elvira by the hand. The child went reluctantly, looking back at Rebecca, who gestured: *Go, Elvira, go with Mrs. Jackson.*

"Mrs. Rosen, I can't tell you what this child means to us," Jackson said, "It's a chance, a chance to make up. Our own Agnes, she died of the consumption. Later Cillie, she went the same way."

"Cillie?" Rebecca asked.

"Cillie, our granddaughter. So we know what this child has been through. We feel like we be doing for her what we woulda done for Cillie if she lived."

"I see," Rebecca said. She hesitated, debating the most gentle way to suggest it. "Mr. Jackson, have you considered that you and Mrs. Jackson might be a little . . . a little too advanced to be taking on such a responsibility?"

"Too advanced?" Jackson considered. "You mean too old?"

"Well . . . yes, sir," Rebecca said.

"Why, I'm spry and chipper now as ever I was. The only reason I'm not workin', company rule of some kind."

Elvira and Mrs. Jackson returned. The child had a white film of milk on her brown upper lip. Mrs. Jackson was smiling. But Elvira seemed as tense and ill at ease as before.

"My, this little one, she have an appetite no bigger'n a bird." She patted Elvira on the head.

Mr. Jackson brought out some toys and a doll, a white doll, which he placed in Elvira's arms. "This was Cillie's. My, how she loved it. Called her Cinderella. Ain't that a nice name for a doll? Cinderella? From the story. About the girl with the stepsisters . . ."

For the first time, Elvira spoke. "Yes, sir, I know. Mrs. Rosen and me we be readin' it together." Then she remembered and corrected herself. "Mrs. Rosen *and I* . . . she always says it that way, Elvira and I. So it's Mrs. Rosen and I."

"Well, now, that be a bright child!" Mrs. Jackson said, brushing back strands of her gray hair that had come loose.

Elvira tried to play with the doll, but Rebecca noticed that her interest soon flagged.

"Well, Elvira dear, I think this has been long enough for a first visit, don't you?"

"Yes, ma'am," the child said.

"You've found something to criticize about every family," David accused. "Too poor. Too many other children. Too untidy to suit you. Now it is too old. These Jacksons had a child of their own, then a grandchild. They have a great deal of love left over to give. What do a few years more or less have to do with it?"

"What happens three years from now, five years from now? What about when Elvira is in high school and the Jacksons are too old to take part in school activities? If they are even alive at the time."

"What leads you to believe that any of us will be alive in five years? A man crosses the street and gets hit by a trolley car, it doesn't matter how young he is. Or there is another flu epidemic like during the war. I remember as a child, relatives, neighbors dying like flies. And it didn't matter old or young."

Rebecca remained adamant.

"Becca, you admit these are two nice people—religious. Bruton told us that. You said yourself the woman runs a clean household. They are both eager to have the child."

"To replace their own granddaughter," Rebecca argued.

"Is it a crime if they also get joy and satisfaction out of it, is that wrong?"

Rebecca faced him defiantly. "Say it. You've hinted at it, now say it. If you don't, I will. I am no different from the Jacksons. They want to replace a dead granddaughter with Elvira. And I want to replace the child I never had, the four children I never . . ."

She could not continue, for she had begun to weep. He tried to embrace her. She shrugged him off, turning away.

Their voices grew so loud that Elvira awoke and listened.

Me. They're talking about me, she realized. She slipped from the couch. On bare feet, she approached their door very cautiously. She stood there trembling from fear as well as cold. She listened as Rebecca wept and David pleaded to be forgiven for words he had never spoken.

Unaware, puzzled by the references that passed between husband and wife, which had given rise to Rebecca's tears and David's apologies, Elvira knew that all this related to her. And in a terrifying way.

She heard Rebecca recover from her tears to say, "All right, if you feel that way, tomorrow I will take her there and leave her."

She heard David try to ease the conflict for his wife when he said, "Tell them it's only a trial stay, that if the child is not happy with them, you will take her back."

Elvira lingered at the door but heard no more beyond Rebecca's weeping. In her child's mind she knew one thing: *She is going to give me away. She is going to give me away tomorrow. I don't want to leave her . . . I don't . . .*

On cold feet she went back to her couch. She could not sleep the rest of the night. She drew the blanket tight around herself, huddled up, and tried to keep from trembling.

8

Rebecca and Elvira stood at the bottom step of the stairway. In Rebecca's left hand was Anna Hitchins's small, battered suitcase tied with clothesline, in her right, the cold but sweaty hand of the child. Rebecca looked up toward the faint glow from the skylight, then glanced down to find Elvira staring up at her, her dark eyes pleading.

"Come, dear," Rebecca said firmly, as much to steel herself as to encourage the child. They started up.

At the Jacksons' door, Rebecca rang the bell. They could hear the stir of excited voices from within, the approach of footsteps, and then the door was opened. Mrs. Jackson's face lit up with a smile of delight. She looked down at Elvira. "My, my, child, you are even prettier than before. Come in, come in."

Mr. Jackson was right behind her, reaching to take the suitcase from Rebecca's hand. Mrs. Jackson preceded them down the hallway to the front room, which faced out on the street. There, waiting for them, was a pot of tea and a plate of homemade sugar cookies. Mrs. Jackson had set out her best doilies, several frayed with age.

"Sit, please, both of you. I go fetch a glass of milk for little Elvira." She was off to the kitchen.

Elvira sat alongside Rebecca on the couch. She was stiff and straight, her hands tightly clasped in her lap. Mrs. Jackson returned and handed Elvira a glass of milk. Mr. Jackson held out the plate of cookies. Elvira stared at them but did not take one.

"Come on, child," Mr. Jackson urged, smiling. "Ain't nobody in this world makes better sugar cookies than my Mary."

To avoid embarrassment for the child or the Jacksons, Rebecca said, "Elvira, they look delicious. Try one."

The child finally took one, nibbled at the edges, and washed it down with a gulp of milk. Jackson held out the plate to Rebecca. She hesitated, wondering, *Are they baked with lard and not kosher? On the other hand, I cannot insult these two nice people. Besides, for the child's sake I want everything to go smoothly. I had better take one, and trust that they were made with butter. In any event, for the child's sake, I'm sure God will forgive me if I'm wrong.*

She selected one, bit into it, discovered it was tasty, crisp and sweet.

"Well?" Mrs. Jackson asked. "Any instructions?"

"She has no special foods. Only, she doesn't eat nearly enough. She's a good sleeper, though sometimes she will have a restless night. As for school, she hasn't been to school, since we didn't know where she was going to live," Rebecca explained. "But she's a good learner. Bright. Very quick."

Uncomfortable in the face of such praise, Elvira stared down at the worn carpet.

"She is also somewhat shy," Rebecca said, "which I find a very nice trait in little girls." Elvira raised her downcast eyes just enough to cast a glance at Rebecca. It was a silent exchange of love and admiration between them.

There was more talk, all of it stilted and uncomfortable. The Jacksons asked questions. Rebecca answered. Elvira remained silent.

Finally, Rebecca realized the moment of separation had arrived. "Well, I will leave you three to become acquainted."

Elvira stiffened. Her hands began to tremble. She tried to conceal it, but the wavelets of milk in her glass betrayed her.

"Elvira dear, don't you want to be showin' Mrs. Rosen to the door?" Mrs. Jackson suggested.

"Yes, ma'am," Elvira said obediently. They started down the dark hallway to the front door. She clutched Rebecca's hand so tightly it was a desperate plea: *Don't leave me with strangers. Please?*

At the door, Rebecca knelt down and embraced Elvira, whose arms went around her neck and clung to her.

"Elvira, these are very nice people. And they like you. Soon, if you give them the chance, they will love you."

"Don't leave me," Elvira whispered.

"These are the kind of people I promised your mama I would find for you," Rebecca said. "She would be very pleased, I know it."

"Don't leave me," Elvira pleaded.

The girl tightened her embrace, pressing against Rebecca, who tried gently but firmly to free herself. Still, the child clung to her.

"Is it because of Mr. Rosen?" the child asked.

"Of course not, my dear. This is the best thing. For your sake. To be among your own people."

"Will you come see me?" Elvira asked.

"If you want me to," Rebecca promised, though she knew that a clean break was probably more desirable.

"I want you to," Elvira said. "I want you to. A lot."

After another fierce and frightened hug from the child, Rebecca was able to free herself.

"Now, go, else Mrs. Jackson will think you don't like her." Rebecca watched as Elvira started slowly down the dark hallway toward the light of the front room.

Rebecca started out of the flat. By the time she reached the front door of the tenement, she realized she was running. *Like a criminal, escaping the scene of the crime*, she thought. She deliberately slowed to a normal walking pace. She tried to justify herself. *Elvira belongs here, with her own. The Jacksons seem like good people. Certainly, they are eager to have her. They have no other children now. She will be the center of their attention and their affection. As for Elvira, she is young and pliable. She will adjust. Give her a decent home, affection, and attention, and she will grow to love them. Once they send her to school and get that bright mind of hers involved, she will be fine. Better than fine!*

Rebecca Rosen was restless that night. She could not sleep. Fearful that she was disturbing David, she slipped out of bed and padded out to the living room. He needed his sleep, especially these days, with virtually two jobs to do—hat renovation and the new derby business.

She would sleep on the couch the rest of the night. She lay down and covered herself with the same blanket Elvira had used. She was even more restless than before. She sat up, pulled the blanket around her, and started rocking. She could not free herself of the feeling of the child's arms clinging around her neck. She determined that in the morning she would go back to the Jacksons and explain that the whole thing was a mistake. She would take Elvira back.

And if I did? Consider the impossibility of the situation. How does a white religious Jew bring up a Negro child who is a Christian? And where do I send such a child to school? To a school of white children? Jewish children? There is no other available in this neighborhood.

Despite how strongly she felt about Elvira, Rebecca could see the impossibility of the situation.

She resolved. *Now that I am free, I will help Mrs. Feinstein at Anche Chesed. There are plenty of orphans there who need looking after.*

She was able to fall asleep after that.

She woke in response to muffled sounds from the kitchen. She sat up, listening carefully. From the clumsy rattling of dishes, she realized David was making breakfast for himself. She hurried into the kitchen.

"Sorry, Becca, I tried to be quiet," he apologized.

She took over, taking the coffee pot from his hands, emptying it, and starting to make the coffee properly.

"You had a bad night. I thought you needed your sleep."

Without warning, she started to weep silently.

He took her in his arms. "Becca, no. It was simply something not meant to be So, don't cry. Please?"

He wiped her tears away with his fingers. He kissed her. She nodded, determined to control her weeping. She did. Until he left for work. She started to weep once more. Finally, she decided, *If I remain here, alone, I will never learn to control it. I must go to the orphanage. Perhaps there will be some other child who needs a home, like Elvira did. A Jewish child. A child David would accept more readily. No, that isn't fair to him. He did like Elvira, more than he could let on. But I must go, I must.*

She dressed hurriedly, before doubts or tears could change her mind. She raced down the stairs to the front door, where she almost collided with a policeman who was trying to discern the names of the tenants from the mailboxes in the dark entryway.

"Lady, would you happen to know a family named Rosen?" the policeman asked.

"Rosen? Why? Something happened to my husband!" she exclaimed.

"Your husband?" the man asked. "You Mrs. Rosen?"

"Yes, yes, now tell me! David! What happened, where is he?"

"Hasn't to do with your husband, ma'am. Do you know a little nigger girl named Elvira?"

"I know a *Negro* girl named Elvira," Rebecca corrected. "What about her?"

"Is she here with you?"

"No. If you're from the courts or the welfare, she is perfectly safe with some nice people named Jackson down in Harlem," Rebecca said.

"She isn't there, that's for sure," the policeman said.

"How do you know?"

"Because it was people named Jackson who called in to report her missing."

"Missing? Elvira missing? I've got to find her," Rebecca insisted. Her tears started once more.

"Get a hold of yourself, ma'am," the policeman said, seizing her by the arms. "You can't just run out and go searching. Running around the city like a madwoman ain't going to help. In most cases like this, what happens is the kid gets hungry and starts begging for food. Someone realizes it's a lost kid or a runaway and they turn them in to us."

"Where is your station house?" Rebecca demanded.

"Down in Harlem. Why?"

"I have to go there."

"You'll just be in the way," he pointed out.

"I don't care. I want to be there!" she insisted. "Take me!"

As they entered the Twenty-sixth Precinct station house, Rebecca spied the Jacksons, both seated on a hard wooden bench, he with his arm around her, she in tears. She had been crying for some time, for the salt of her tears had stained her face.

At the sight of Rebecca, both Jacksons exclaimed at once, "Oh, Mrs. Rosen . . ." The three of them embraced.

"What we say, what we do to make her run away?" Jackson asked. "I swear to God and Jesus, we try to make her feel at home. If anything happens to her, if anything happens . . ." By now Jackson himself was weeping.

Rebecca went to the desk to inquire of the sergeant, "Is there any word? What can we do? What are you doing?"

"Lady, all we can do is what we done. We sent out an all-points to the whole city. We don't think she coulda got far enough to be out of our jurisdiction. Now we just wait and see."

"How long?"

"If we don't hear in six hours, I would start to worry. Until then, these runaways usually turn up."

"But she's only eight years old."

"Give us six hours," the sergeant pleaded.

Rebecca returned to the bench and sat down alongside Mrs. Jackson. She reached for the woman's hand and pressed it. It was cold. As cold as her own.

Each time the phone on the sergeant's desk rang, Rebecca and the Jacksons half rose from their bench, only to sink back once they realized the call had nothing to do with Elvira. Rebecca kept her eyes on the wall clock behind the sergeant's desk. She listened intently to his every conversation. Two hours had gone by.

After the third hour and many calls, the sergeant received one that put a grim expression on his face. He listened, then only said, "Give me a description. Yeah. Got it. Got it. Got it. Okay." He hung up the phone, but his hand still clung to the instrument. Then he decided. He approached Rebecca.

"Tell me, near you can, how tall was the girl?"

Rebecca froze. *He is using the past tense. He did say* was. She rose to her feet and indicated with her thumb just below her breast, "She came up to here on me."

The sergeant estimated. "About forty-six maybe forty-eight inches." The fact appeared to concern him. "Would you say she was a light Negro or dark?"

Rebecca turned to the Jacksons.

"Not high yaller, not real black. Kind of light brown," Jackson said, looking to his weeping wife, who nodded.

"Did she have any distinguishing marks?" the sergeant asked.

"She has a vaccination mark on her left arm," Rebecca said. "About here," she added, indicating on her own arm.

"Thank God! the sergeant said, obviously relieved. "They . . . they found a little girl, about the size you said. She was light in color, but she had no marks. Not even a vaccination."

"But at least they found her," Rebecca said.

"Dead, ma'am. Dead." The sergeant turned back to his desk.

By the clock on the wall, four hours and fifty-seven minutes had gone by. Twice the sergeant had urged them all to leave, promising he would call them as soon as there was any word. They insisted on remaining.

Policemen came in from patrol and reported. None had seen any child who appeared lost. They had asked on their beats but elicited no clues or leads.

Phone calls kept coming in, none having to do with a lost child. Several calls came from desperate women pleading for help and protection from violent husbands and lovers. The sergeant's response was always the same, "Lady, I don't like to say this, but we don't run a protection service for wives. Sorry!"

The clock hands showed 4:41. It was growing dark outside. More than the six critical hours had elapsed. Rebecca was painfully aware of it. As was the sergeant. The Jacksons had not been privy to that conversation, so to them time had merely passed, but it was not accompanied by the chilling knowledge of what a lapse of six hours could mean.

The sergeant subtly beckoned Rebecca to the desk. "I think," he began, "that it would be a good idea to convince those folks to go home."

"They're as concerned as I am," Rebecca said.

"It might be better for them, and for us, if they weren't here," he replied.

"You expect the worst, don't you?"

"Lady, I am in a business where the worst happens. Every day. So do what you can to convince them. Please?"

"I'll try, but I can't promise."

She turned from the desk, trying to summon up words that, if not sincere, would at least be convincing enough to accomplish the purpose.

"Mr. Jackson, Mrs. Jackson, the sergeant says that if there is no word by now, chances are that there won't be until morning. So he thinks we had better go home."

Jackson did not respond. His wife shook her head stolidly and gave no sign of moving. Jackson glanced at Rebecca, his dark, watery eyes saying, *There's your answer, Mrs. Rosen.* He took his wife's hand. They sat side by side, silent, waiting.

The sergeant had gone off duty. He had been replaced by another officer, a younger man, who had been briefed on the case. He too suggested that they leave, promising to let them know when there was word. When they refused, he sent out for sandwiches and coffee to make their vigil less onerous.

At a quarter to nine, on a night when routine calls were running at an increased rate, there was one call that brought the new desk man to an alert posture, which made Rebecca suspect that, finally, happy or tragic, there was word. The sergeant hung up the phone, contemplated his next move, and decided to do nothing for the moment. Rebecca rose from the bench. Trying to appear casual, she approached the high desk.

"You just received a call," she said.

"Yeah," the sergeant said, busying himself with making an entry in the log.

"About the child," she insisted.

He hesitated, then admitted, "Yes, about the child. Or a child. We won't know for a while."

"She fits the description, doesn't she?"

"Could," he evaded.

"Tell me. Tell me everything!" Rebecca insisted.

Because he suspected she was on the verge of hysterics, he lowered his voice. "Keep this to yourself until later. The report I just received concerns a girl, light brown, about eight years old. She was found in a subway station in Brooklyn. The way she was discovered, she was screaming because a man was dragging her into the ladies' room."

"Oh God, no!" Rebecca started to protest. But his gesture forced her to stifle her outcry.

"We don't know the details. But a squad car is bringing her in right now."

"If she's been hurt, if that man, whoever he is, has done anything . . . I will kill him!" Rebecca vowed.

"Lady, I feel that way myself. Ten times every day."

Within half an hour, a squad car pulled up before the police precinct. A patrolman stepped out, carrying a child in his arms. As he reached the door, the child could see through the glass panels. She struggled to free herself. The officer set her down. She pushed through the door and raced across the waiting room to throw herself into Rebecca's arms.

"Mrs. Rosen, Mrs. Rosen . . ." She began to cry.

Rebecca embraced her and lifted her face to kiss her. Elvira was disheveled, her face smudged with dirt, her dress wrinkled and torn.

"My baby, my poor baby . . ."

The Jacksons surrounded them, looking down, weeping with relief.

"Thank the Lord, thank the Lord Jesus," Mrs. Jackson kept repeating.

"Why, child?" Jackson asked as he bent down to look into Elvira's eyes. "Why you run away? We do you any harm? Do we not treat you nice? Why?"

The child was unable to respond to the kindly man's questions.

"Elvira?" Rebecca prodded gently.

"I . . . I . . . got lost on the subway," she said.

"Child, how in the world you even get on the subway?" he asked.

"I sneaked."

"And where was you going? Someplace? Or just running away from us?" Jackson asked.

"When Mrs. Rosen took me down we come by subway. So if the subway take me down, sure it can take me back up," Elvira said.

"You were running away from us to go back to her?" Jackson asked. Elvira did not respond. She didn't have to. Jackson knew all he had wanted to know. He turned to his wife.

"Come, Mary, the child is safe. There ain't no need for us any longer." He helped his wife to her feet. She kissed the child before she took his arm. Jackson lingered just long enough to say, "Mrs. Rosen, the little one evidently needs you. But how you manage—a white woman, with a colored child—I don't know. I don't even know if the law allows such a thing. But you take good care of her, good care."

Because of the lateness of the hour and the exhausting events of the day, the sergeant had Rebecca and Elvira delivered home by squad car. As the car pulled up before their building, Rebecca spied David out front, surrounded by a crowd of neighbors. She realized, *I should have called, I should have left a note, to keep him from worrying.* She leaped from the car and ran to him. "I'm sorry, I'm sorry, but she's all right. She's fine. Fine!"

"And you?" he asked.

"I never want to live through a day like this again," she said.

Elvira submitted herself to a hot bath. She did not protest when Rebecca soaped her hair and then poured pans of warm water over it to rinse out the suds. After Rebecca drew the clean, sweet-smelling nightgown over her head and straightened it along her thin body, Elvira threw her arms around her and kissed her. She pressed her face against Rebecca's neck and whispered in a barely audible voice, "I was so scared I never see you again."

David had waited patiently for his own supper until Elvira had eaten and gone to sleep on the living room couch. Rebecca sat across the table from him, staring down at her soup but not eating. She was considering the least contentious way to open a discussion that was now unavoidable.

"Foolish thing for a child to go on the subway alone," David said. "Trying to find a place when she didn't even know the address."

"David, we are going to have to do something about her."

"Take her back to that Reverend Bruton. What else can we do?"

"There is something else," she ventured.

Before she could continue he interrupted. "Oh no! Not that!"

"Why not? She was running away to come back here. To us."

"To you, maybe, not to me. The child does not like me."

"But she does," Rebecca insisted.

"Even if she does, we are not able to bring up such a child."

"David, husband, that child loves us, needs us. I love her. I do not think a child needs much more than that."

"Women! Take a perfectly sensible woman out of her kitchen and right away she loses her mind." With exquisite emphasis, he proceeded to point out, "In the first place, my dear wife, a child cannot sleep all her life on a couch in the living room. She needs a bed. In the second place, I will not even mention the expense of another mouth to feed, another body to clothe, doctors' bills, dentists' bills, and God knows what else. Even if she were white and Jewish, we couldn't afford it." He laid out the words with great emphasis and precision: "We . . . can . . . not . . . afford . . . it."

Thinking he had disposed of the question, he felt free to resume eating.

"David," Rebecca began, catching him with a full spoon in midair between bowl and mouth.

"Yes?" he asked suspiciously.

"Last week, before the Jacksons, I did some asking."

"Asking?" he repeated gingerly. Even more suspicious now, he put down his spoon.

"From some superintendents in the neighborhood. It turns out, conditions being bad as they are, apartments are going begging."

"They are giving them away? Rent-free?" he replied, sarcastic now. "Where do we go to get one?"

"Not exactly rent-free," Rebecca replied. "But they are giving concessions. A free month at the start of the year, a free month at the end, so that you get twelve months' occupancy for only ten months' rent."

"And who pays for the ten months? J. P. Morgan? Or President Hoover?" he demanded.

"I figured it out. We are now paying thirty-one dollars a

month for a three-room. That comes to four hundred thirty-
two dollars a year. Down the block we could get a four-
room—two bedrooms, if we make the dining room into another bedroom—for forty-seven dollars a month. With two
months' concession, that comes to four hundred and seventy
dollars a year. Altogether, a difference of only thirty-eight dollars for the whole year. Surely we can afford thirty-eight dollars more."

"And what about moving expenses? Even moving down
the block costs money."

"Forty dollars," Rebecca said. He glared at her. "As long
as I was asking about a new apartment, I thought I would ask
about moving as well. Two men, one truck, for half a day,
forty dollars. If they can do it without a truck, thirty-five dollars."

"I never knew you had such a mind for details," David
said to evade a commitment. "And there's the deposit with
the electric company. And the telephone."

"They just transfer them, so no new deposits are necessary."

"Apartments, moving expenses, deposits. If there is anything else, tell me now. I don't want to find out later."

"I spoke to Dr. Pomerantz. He spoke to the rabbi. The
rabbi said that the highest virtue of a good Jew is to give aid
and shelter to an orphan."

"A Negro orphan? A Christian orphan? Did Pomerantz tell
him *that*?"

"No."

"Aha!" David exclaimed victoriously, as if he had scored
an important point in a talmudic debate.

"But *I* did," Rebecca said. "And the rabbi said the Torah
does not specify color, it says only to care for the widow and
the orphan. Therefore, it would be a mitzvah to take in such a
child."

"You went to talk to the rabbi without me?" His standing
as a student of Torah having been impugned, he appeared
deeply hurt. "Rebecca, this is no decision to arrive at lightly.
We are dealing with the life of another human being, a child
of eight. She has fifty, sixty years of life left. What we do now
will affect her all those years."

"What we do . . . and what we *don't* do," Rebecca corrected softly.

"What do we really know about this child? For instance, her mother died of consumption. How do we know if this child is healthy?"

"Pomerantz confirms what the other doctors said. Her X rays are clean."

"I know now what is meant by the expression leaving no stone unturned. You, my dear Rebecca, are surely a stone turner of the first order. So, granted the child is healthy, what do we really know about her? Not much. Who knows what is lurking there that could come up later. You know, these *shvartzers*. Cute they are, as children. But once they grow up, God knows."

"David," Rebecca said, now relying less on softness and subtlety. "I don't know about the future. I only know that now she is a shy, bright child who is frightened and alone. She needs a home. Not an orphan's home, but a real home."

Having lost his appetite, David turned away from the table.

"Well," he procrastinated, "we'll see. We'll see. I have to think about it."

Two evenings later, David was late returning from his little factory. Elvira had already had her supper and was out on the couch with Rebecca, reading one of the two books her mother had left her.

Rebecca tucked her in before she went to serve David his supper. While she was at the stove, he tried to appear casual as he said, "Tomorrow, go see apartment 3C in 229 down the block." She turned to him. "If you like it, tell the super. I already set the price with him. And this is a five-room, not four."

"Oh, David!" She went to him and kissed him on the cheek.

Always self-conscious at being caught performing some act of charity, he tried to joke. "If I knew you were going to kiss me, I would have shaved."

"Oh, David, I have such plans . . ." Rebecca said.

"Please! No plans! Not before I have my supper!" he commanded. "If a man can't enjoy his supper after a long day's work . . ."

She set the plate before him, slices of potted breast of beef, in rich brown gravy, with a mound of steaming kasha brimming over the side.

My David, she thought. *He may be a hat man, but no one will ever change the* yeshiva bucher *in him. By ancient law, charity should be done not for public acclaim or self-aggrandizement. And the more he grumbles, the easier he is to convince. I think grumbling is his only defense before he surrenders.*

She slept much better that night.

9

*R*ebecca Rosen *turned* the key in the lock but had difficulty opening the front door, fresh but dried paint having added a new layer between door and jamb. But she pushed until it gave way. Though the painter had left all the windows open since the day before, the apartment, too, smelled of fresh paint.

"Now?" Elvira asked.

"Now!" Rebecca said. "You go first."

The girl entered the empty apartment, which, with its bare floors, created an echo when she said, "It's so big." She made a wide circle in the dining room.

"Yes, yes, it is big," Rebecca said, at the same time thinking, *It'll take more furniture than we have, even after we buy the bed and dresser and chair for her. What will David say to that? However, one problem at a time.*

They explored each room together. In her mind, Rebecca began arranging furniture in the most advantageous and economical way. Dining room, living room, large bedroom, finally they came to the smaller bedroom.

"And this, darling, is your room!" she announced.

Elvira stood at the door, looked in. "Big. It's so big." She ventured into the empty room as if into a fairy-tale land. She wheeled around, spinning so fast that Rebecca had to catch her as she became dizzy.

"Window. I have a window."

"All rooms have windows," Rebecca said.

"Not my mama's," Elvira said. She proceeded to describe the room where she and her mother had lived during the last job, with the Fleischmans. Obviously, it was a maid's room that had been cut out of a larger room and was the half without the window. It was the last place Elvira Hitchins would remember having lived with her mother.

*　*　*

"A chair is a chair," David argued. "A dresser is a dresser and a bed is a bed. What difference does it make if it's new or used?"

"New is new," Rebecca insisted very softly as she leaned over the stove to stir the pea soup that was dancing in small bubbles.

"Stubborn, stubborn, stubborn." He shook his head. "Believe me, in the old country a wife had respect for her husband's decisions."

"David," she reminded. "In the old country *you* would be a yeshiva bucher, not a successful businessman."

"Successful!" he deprecated. "Rockefeller I'm not. Believe me, if at the end of the week there is a little left over after I pay the bills, I'm lucky."

"Then you must be very lucky."

"Which means, my darling wife?" he challenged.

"I happened to get a look at your checkbook last week," Rebecca said. "Six hundred and forty-seven dollars."

"A condition of temporary prosperity," he pleaded. "There are bills to pay—the security rent on this place, the moving expenses. . ."

"All paid for," she announced.

"What do you mean all paid for?"

She put aside her ladle. "David, your mother never had a *knippel*?"

"A *knippel*?" he repeated. "You mean you too?"

"The mother of a Jewish bride may not tell her how to behave with her new husband, but she is always sure to warn her, build up a *knippel*. Save a little from the grocery money. Walk instead of taking the bus. Every nickel helps. At the butcher, a few soup bones can sometimes take the place of a pound of flanken. Little by little, build up your *knippel*, but make sure your husband never knows. That way there'll be money for a rainy day."

"So behind my back this has been going on." David pretended to be hurt and betrayed. "If a man can't trust his own wife . . ."

"Forgive me?" she asked.

He pretended to consider such a grave step and finally asked, "You paid the security *and* the moving bill?"

She nodded. He kissed her. He whispered in her ear, "There is nothing you will not do for that child, is there?" She did not respond but pressed her cheek against his. "Rebecca," he whispered. "How much? The moving, the security?"

"Altogether? Fifty-nine dollars."

"All right," he finally conceded. "New furniture."

The two men who delivered the new furniture for Elvira's room were experienced hands at their trade, for they groaned with every exertion required to ease the dresser through the doorways so as not to scratch the paint.

"Watch out, watch out!" the older one warned the younger. "Else you'll damage this beautiful dresser."

Rebecca watched, thinking. *He's hinting for a tip. Let him hint. He'll earn it before they leave.*

Dresser, chair, small white desk, and bed frame had been carried in. Rebecca looked around as the two men waited to be paid, the older man mopping his brow as if it were wet with sweat from his exertions.

"I think," Rebecca said, "the dresser would be better here. And the desk there. Let's see how it looks."

They moved the dresser, then the desk. She asked to have them moved again. And yet once more. Until the older man protested, "Lady, please, make up your mind already. We got other jobs to do."

"You mean you're leaving without setting up the bed frame and the bedspring?"

Accompanied by groans and other sounds of effort, they put the bed together, brought in the bedspring, and placed it in its proper place.

"Now the mattress," Rebecca said.

"The mattress too?" the old man protested.

Once the mattress was installed, Rebecca called out, "Elvira! Darling! Come see!"

The child came racing into the room. She looked around, her eyes wide with excitement. "Mine? It's all for me?"

"Missus," the boss demanded angrily. "You put us to all that trouble for a little . . ."

"Don't you dare say that word!" Rebecca forbade in a hoarse whisper. She counted out their payment, adding, "Here's a dollar for your trouble."

The old man took the dollar, crumpled it, and tossed it on the bare wood floor. "Thank you," he said in bitter sarcasm.

Rebecca felt tears of anger well up in her eyes. How much had Elvira understood of what had occurred? Evidently, not too much, since she was bouncing up and down on her new mattress.

"Do you like it, darling?"

"It be . . . it *is* the bestest bed in the whole world!" she responded, still bouncing.

"Now, we'd better make it up. Pad, sheets, pillows, blankets. Come!"

Elvira was helping tuck in one side of the bottom sheet when she said softly, "My mama . . ." Then she slipped out of the room. She returned carrying one of her undershirts, neatly folded. She proceeded to open it as she would unwrap a precious package. Rebecca realized that it contained a faded, worn photograph.

"Elvira?"

The child appeared reluctant, almost frightened, to show it. Rebecca took it, handling it like a fragile artifact. She discovered the faces of a young Negro couple, the man very light complexioned and handsome, the woman no more than seventeen at the time the photograph was taken. She was light brown, with high cheekbones, concave cheeks, and a strong chin. Rebecca recognized the resemblance between the young woman in this photograph and the sick, wasting woman she had seen in the sanatorium in Saranac.

"Your mama and papa," Rebecca said softly. The child nodded. "You've been hiding it all this time."

"I like . . . I kinda would want . . . to put them here." She went to the dresser to try to lean the picture against the mirror. She turned to Rebecca, her sad young eyes asking, *Would you mind very much?*

"It won't stand up that way," Rebecca said. "We'll have to get a frame for it."

"Frame? Then it's all right?" the child asked.

"Tomorrow we'll go shopping for a frame."

In relief and gratitude, Elvira rushed into her arms. While they embraced, Rebecca suddenly felt the child stiffen as a new problem presented itself. Elvira looked up at her gravely.

"She is my mama. What do I call you?"

"What would you like to call me?"

"My mama, she sometimes talk about her Aunt Lettie. How she so nice. Aunt Lettie this, 'n Aunt Lettie that. Could I call you Aunt Lettie?"

"Maybe Aunt Rebecca would be better."

The child pondered it before attempting, "Aunt Rebecca, Aunt Rebecca . . ." She nodded, then smiled, reassured. "Aunt Rebecca," she repeated, more firmly now.

"Tomorrow, Elvira, you and Aunt Rebecca will buy a picture frame."

That evening, when David came home to their new apartment for the first time, he brought with him a shiny golden tin mezuzah. A small, flat, hollow object, only thick enough to contain a few passages of Holy Scripture, it was to be affixed to the doorport of their home, to announce to the world that this was indeed a Jewish household.

Whatever mythology accompanied the custom, no Jewish family, religious or otherwise, dared to ignore it. With a mezuzah at the front door, and a *pushke* in the kitchen, a household was complete. The white *pushke* was a small tin cannister, bearing blue printing in Hebrew and in English, that announced the contents were being accumulated for the support of Jews who had returned to the Holy Land. Some Jewish housewives slipped their donations in through the little slot regularly each week: a nickel, a dime, sometimes only a few pennies. Others only did so when there was a momentary abundance of money and then would insert as much as a quarter or even two. When the *pushke* was full, someone from the charity came to collect it and install an empty *pushke* in its place.

Once David had said the proper prayers to accompany nailing the mezuzah to the doorport and had mounted the *pushke* on the wall of the freshly painted kitchen, he felt he had sanctified their new apartment. He was ready to take his usual drink of *bronfen* before sitting down to the table for supper.

With great anticipation, he inhaled the aromas that filled the kitchen. He remarked cheerily to Elvira, "Vegetable soup and blintzes! I could smell my Rebecca's blintzes all the way from the subway station. Tell me, little one, you know what are blintzes?"

"Yes, Uncle David," Elvira replied.

At this unexpected term of address, David Rosen glanced toward his wife, his surprised look, his arched eyebrows conspiring to ask, *How did I suddenly get to be an uncle?*

Rebecca responded with a look of her own: *Don't make an issue now, I'll tell you later.*

"So, Elvira, tell me, how come you know what are blintzes?"

"My mama, when she work for the Fleischmans, she be . . . she used to . . . make them. Flour'n eggs'n milk for the pancakes. Then mix up cheese, lot of cheese, with sour cream'n salt'n sugar for the fillin'."

"You watched her do all that?"

"She was teachin' me readin' while she be cookin'—was cooking."

"You mean you never went to school?"

"No, Uncle David," Elvira replied. "With my mama's teachin', no need for me to go to school."

Once Elvira was asleep in her new bed in her new room, David asked, "Becca my darling wife, how did I suddenly become an uncle?"

"If I'm an aunt, you're an uncle."

"You're an aunt?" he asked.

"We are not her mother and father, and she can't keep calling us Mr. and Mrs. Rosen. So we decided, Elvira and I, that Aunt Rebecca would be nice. That's how you became an uncle."

"You and Elvira decided," he remarked, without further comment. "One thing, Becca. A child her age who has never been to school, that cannot be allowed to continue."

Public School 173 was so designated because it dominated the corner of 173rd Street and Fort Washington Avenue. Three stories tall, of red brick and clean white sandstone, with a tall wrought-iron fence surrounding it, it was the newest school

in upper Manhattan. With trees in front and a small park
across the street, it presented a most inviting atmosphere.

In the outer room of the office of Principal Marcus Goodman, Rebecca Rosen waited nervously. Beside her, Elvira was
perched on the edge of the straight-backed hardwood chair.
She wore a simple plaid cotton dress that Rebecca had made
for her. Her hair was neatly plaited and tied with a bright
bow. To encourage her, Rebecca forced a smile, though she
herself was in need of confidence.

"Lady! Out there! Come in, come in!" Principal Goodman
commanded.

They entered his office, Rebecca first, Elvira shyly lagging
a step behind so that Rebecca had to urge her in.

"Well, now?" the man demanded as he turned to peer at
them through his steel-framed glasses. His look turned to one
of surprise and disapproval. "Well, quickly, what can I do for
you?"

"I would like to register Elvira in school," Rebecca said.

"Madam, in this school we register children at the registration office. That may not make sense to *you*, but that's the
way *we* do things around here. That office is down the hall in
room one-o-four!"

"We've already been there, Mr. Goodman. The woman
sent us to see you."

"Me? She sent you to see me?" he demanded.

"Yes, sir. They asked for her record. Her . . . I didn't quite
get the word."

"Transcript," the principal corrected intolerantly. "Transcript."

"Yes, sir, her transcript," Rebecca said. "You see, due to
certain circumstances, she has never been to school before."

"A child in New York City, eight years old, who has never
been to school?"

"Her mother was a domestic servant. She worked and
lived with a family who did not mind the child living in with
them. Her mother kept her at home and taught her by herself.
So she has no official school record."

"What about her father? Didn't he care enough to see that
she had schooling?"

"She . . ." Rebecca felt most uncomfortable in the child's
presence. "It seems . . ."

The principal presumed, "And naturally, she has no father that she is aware of. Right? Of course, right. After all, she's . . . she's what she is."

"You happen to be wrong, sir," Rebecca started to protest.

Goodman denied her the chance. "Look, Mrs. . . ."

"Rosen. Rebecca Rosen."

"Mrs. Rosen, I have no choice. According to the rules, if the child has no school record we have to start her in first grade."

"But she is eight years old and can read and write," Rebecca protested.

"We will start her in first grade and see how she develops."

"Sir, I can assure you—"

"The rules, Mrs. Rosen," he interrupted. "The rules. Go back to the registration office. Have them register her. And bring her back tomorrow, ready to start."

"Yes, sir," Rebecca finally agreed.

On the way home from P.S. 173, Rebecca and Elvira stopped at the small stationery store on upper Broadway. There, Rebecca invited Elvira to select a pencil box. The man brought out several of imitation leather that folded over and snapped shut and also two of fragrant wood, the covers of which slid open to reveal their contents.

He announced the prices: "The leather ones are a dollar sixty-nine. These," he said, indicating the wooden-box type, "are on special, ninety-seven cents. Complete. Pencils and all."

Elvira stared longingly at the leatherette cases but said, "I like a wooden one."

"And a bag?" the man suggested. "Every child needs a schoolbag." Before Rebecca could protest, he brought out several bags, some in solid colors, some in black-and-white plaid, trimmed in red oilcloth piping. "All one price," he announced. "One forty-nine. Bargains like these don't show up every day, missus, take my word."

Rebecca was performing her private arithmetic. *Ninety-seven cents for the pencil box; sixty-four cents for a dozen eggs; at least a dollar ten for chicken; twenty-seven cents for a large piece of cornbread; twelve cents for soup greens, another fifty cents for vege-*

tables and fruit; maybe more if there are some good fresh melons this week; milk, fourteen cents; a pound of coffee, forty-six cents; butter; cream cheese; fresh bagels—all in all, there goes the five dollars David left on the bureau before he went to work early this morning. And now, now, a schoolbag, which is a dollar forty-nine. Back to your knippel, *Rebecca, back to your* knippel. *Which is now gradually fading away.*

She picked up the plaid schoolbag and slid the strap over Elvira's shoulder so that the bag rested against her side. She placed the wooden pencil box in it and strapped the bag closed.

"Fits just like it was made for her," the man said.

As Rebecca waited for change of her five-dollar bill, Elvira started out proudly, the bag over her shoulder. The man held out his closed hand with Rebecca's change. Before he released it, he said softly, "Look, you don't mind my asking. What is a nice Jewish woman like you doing with a child like that?"

Something within Rebecca rebelled—perhaps it had been her encounter with the principal—for she heard herself saying, "My husband. He's a Negro, too."

"Oh my God!" the man whispered, as if blasphemy had been committed in his presence.

10

"*Look, Uncle David*, look," Elvira said the next morning as she twirled around before him, displaying her new schoolbag. "And inside . . ." The child swung the bag around to unstrap it to show her shiny wooden pencil box.

With a reproving look to Rebecca, since he could estimate the cost, he said, "Lovely, dear, very nice."

"All right now, Elvira, time to go. You know the way. And if you don't, just follow the other children."

"Becca, have you lost your senses? You send a child off to school on her first day without . . . quickly, quickly, the honey. A book, some child's book. Quickly. I don't have all day!"

"Elvira, your book!" Rebecca ordered as she went to the cabinet over the stove to find the jar of honey. The child returned with one of the books her mother had left her. David opened the jar of honey. He dipped his little finger in and deposited a single drop of honey on one of the pages.

"Taste, Elvira, taste," he said.

Confused, the girl hesitated, then glanced up at Rebecca. Rebecca nodded. Elvira raised the page to her lips and licked the drop of honey.

"Sweet?" David asked. The child nodded. "Just remember, learning is sweet. The sweetest thing in this world. I remember from my studies of the Torah. It is written in Proverbs, 'My child, eat honey, for it is good. And the drippings of the honeycomb are delicious to your mouth. But know that wisdom is more delicious to your soul. For in wisdom lies your future and your hope.' You may not understand that now, child, but one day you will. Now, go! And have a good day. A good day!"

He patted her on the head. Elvira waited for Rebecca to kiss her, and then she was off. Once they heard the front door close, Rebecca turned to discover him deep in thought. *Memories*, she *realized. He is reliving his memories of when he was a student at yeshiva, looking forward to a whole lifetime of study of Torah.*

"David," she said softly. "What are you thinking?"

"Thinking? Who was thinking?" he attempted to evade. Then he admitted, "I was thinking. The Torah speaks of the honeycomb, not the moneycomb."

"There is no disgrace in being a businessman if one is honest and hardworking and making it possible for others to earn a living too. Life is not lived in synagogue studying."

"I wasn't even thinking about that!" he attempted to deny, but too strongly.

"Then what were you thinking?"

"Thinking . . . I was just thinking, the drop of honey, the sweet taste, it works for Jewish children. But what about gentiles? Does it work for them too?"

He had avoided the subject of his discontent. He was ready to go downtown to his shop. He had much planning to do. Callahan had been right about the derby business. But now with spring coming on, he must consider summer headwear. Sennit straws, perhaps.

David was gone. Rebecca was alone. Alone for the first time since Elvira had entered their lives. She missed her. She missed washing her hair, making it up into pigtails, missed tying the bows. She missed Elvira's questions. Missed having her at her side when she cleaned house, when she shopped, when she cooked, explaining every step in the process to her.

It was afternoon, well past three o'clock. Elvira should be home by now. Rebecca found herself looking at the kitchen clock so often the hands seemed not to move at all. Twice she had poured Elvira a glass of milk and laid out two freshly baked cookies for her. Twice she had put the glass back into the icebox for fear it would sour.

Finally, she could abide it no longer. She grabbed her coat from the rack at the door and rushed out.

Where is she? What could have happened to her? Something terrible, most likely. The things you read in the papers these days.

She reached the bottom of the stairs and was on her way toward the street when she was halted by the sound of a child crying. She turned to look but saw no one. She went around behind the staircase. There she found her. Sitting on the floor, crying.

"Elvira? Darling?" The child turned away from her to hide in the darkness. Rebecca bent to her and tried to make her look up. The child resisted, then she suddenly reached for Rebecca, pressing against her.

"I'm not going back," Elvira declared. "I'm not!"

"It was only your first day. You can't tell from just a first day."

The girl buried her head in Rebecca's belly and continued to weep. Rebecca tried to console her by gently caressing her head. Only then did she notice the schoolbag still slung over her shoulder. It was torn, one seam ripped open.

"Elvira darling, what happened?"

"They did it!"

"Why? Why would they do something like this?" She sought the child's eyes. "Elvira, did you do anything?" She shook her head. Even in the darkness, Rebecca could read the child's eyes and knew she was telling the truth.

"Elvira dear, tell me, did they *say* anything to you?"

The child nodded, then said softly, "Nigger. They called me nigger."

Rebecca embraced her once more, held her close and whispered into her small, delicately shaped ear. "Tomorrow we will go to school together."

When David arrived home, his first question after he had kissed Rebecca and patted Elvira was, "Well, little one, tell me. How was it, your first day at school?" He misread her reticence for the usual difficulty a child might have adjusting to a new situation. He attempted to dispel that by chuckling. "You think you had a hard first day? Let me tell you, the first day I went to *cheder*, that's school in Yiddish, I was only five years old. No bigger than a minute. I wore one cousin's pants, cut down of course, and a jacket from another cousin who had outgrown it before he left for America. My mother wanted to walk me to the synagogue school. But my father said no. 'Let him learn how to go by himself.' Five years old."

He laughed, hoping Elvira would join him and lose the sad look that had distressed him so. Instead, she began to cry. David glanced toward Rebecca, his puzzled look asking, *What happened? What did I say? Why is she crying?*

"Elvira, get your schoolbag," Rebecca said.

Once David had examined it, his face grew stern, then angry. "Elvira, my dear, you have to learn to take care of your things. A dollar forty-nine is real money. A family can eat for a whole day on a dollar forty-nine."

"David, it wasn't her."

"She must have done something. Children do not do this kind of thing without some provocation."

"But they do," Rebecca said pointedly. "They carry out their parents' prejudices."

"They called her . . . names?"

"*The* name," Rebecca said.

"Rebecca, there is only one thing to do."

The next morning, while Rebecca and Elvira remained outside the door, David Rosen entered the principal's office, brushing by his assistant, a chunky, plain-faced woman who stood aghast at such disrespectful conduct.

"Mr. Goodman?" David demanded.

"Who are you? And what can I do for you?" the principal asked. David slammed the damaged schoolbag down on Goodman's desk. Resentful of such conduct, but in response to David's angry glare, Goodman picked up the bag and examined it. "It appears to be torn. Well, children do that kind of thing. Careless."

"This was done by students in your school."

"There must have been a fight," Goodman said. "Kids get into all kinds of mischief over the most trivial things."

"This was no trivial thing," David insisted. "It was done intentionally."

"I know, I know," Goodman replied impatiently. "Your child's version of the story is he did nothing, but the other kids just ganged up on him. You can't believe everything children tell you. You should know that, if you're any kind of father."

"My child does not lie!" David turned toward the door. "Elvira, come in here."

Rebecca urged Elvira forward. Shyly, slowly, staring down at the floor, Elvira entered the principal's office. David reached out and lifted her face by the chin.

"So this is your child?" Goodman commented. "I knew there'd be nothing but trouble once we admitted her. How do you happen to have such a child, may I ask?"

"You may not!" David replied. "Now, Elvira, tell this man!"

Elvira repeated the events of yesterday afternoon. Concluding with, ". . . the big kids, they chase me and tell me I am dumb being in with just first graders, so they call me a dumb nigger. And they catch up with me. They knocked me down 'n tear my bag. And they said, 'Don't you never come back to this school again.'"

She was in tears. David drew her close in support.

"Now, Mr. Principal, tell me this child is lying. Or that she made this up," David defied.

Goodman's face began to exhibit both impatience and embarrassment. "Mr. Rosen, must I say it in front of the child?"

"Say what?" David demanded angrily.

"The children here are not used to having such a child in their school."

"Well, she lives in this school district, so they will *have* to get used to it!" David said. "And as long as I am here, we might as well clear up something else. I do not like our little girl being put in first grade."

"She has no school record, no credentials," Goodman explained.

"Credentials? Is that what you want? Credentials?"

David looked about the office, spied some books in a cabinet, examined the titles, discovered a reader, pulled it out, opened it, turned to Elvira, and said, "Elvira darling, page one. Read!"

Elvira took the book in her trembling hands and began to read, slowly at first, enunciating each word, then proceeded more easily, with more confidence. When she was done, David said, "Page two! Read!" Elvira read the second page. "Page three! Read!" When she had completed reading page three, David turned to the principal.

"There! Those are her credentials! She belongs in a class with children her own age!"

"Mr. Rosen, I grant you the child can read. But we have rules in this school," Goodman protested.

"Rules?" David considered. "Rules." Then he asked suddenly, "Goodman, one Jew to another, what is the holiest day in the year?"

"What has that to do—" Goodman started to dispute, then granted, "Yom Kippur, of course," with considerable irritation. "What has that to do with this child, who is obviously not Jewish—"

Undeterred, David persisted. "And what is the solemn duty of every good Jew on Yom Kippur?"

"To go to synagogue and to fast."

"Exactly! A Jew goes to synagogue and he fasts. Even if he doesn't go to synagogue, he must fast. That is the rule. More than the rule: It is custom, tradition, a holy obligation. Yet the rabbis of old have debated this and they have come to the conclusion that if a person is sick or a woman has an infant to nurse, God provides that they are exempt. The rules are suspended. Now, my dear Goodman, are you telling me that God in His wisdom can suspend the rules of Yom Kippur, the holiest day in the year, but Goodman in his infinite wisdom can't suspend a trivial board of education rule for a child who is so well qualified? God says yes. But Goodman says no! I would like to hear what your rabbi would say about such chutzpah! Rules!"

"Well, I . . . I grant you there is something to be said . . ." Goodman mumbled.

"There is only one thing to be said. Goodman, do yourself a favor. Put this child in the grade where she belongs and this whole matter will remain a secret. Forgotten. Like it never happened!"

"Well," Goodman finally conceded, "I will have one of our third-grade teachers test her. And if she meets the standards, we will . . . we will waive the rules in her case."

"Goodman, you are a wise and compassionate man. As Jew to Jew, I salute you. But if I can make a suggestion, wouldn't do any harm you should teach your pupils to have a little respect and consideration for others. Not nice for Jewish children to be intolerant. Not with our history. Not nice at all."

Rebecca trailed alongside David as he hurried toward the subway station to get downtown as quickly as possible.

"David darling, I can't tell you how impressed I was. The way you spoke up to that principal."

"What's to be impressed? All those years of studying Torah and Talmud finally came in handy," he replied diffidently. "What a child learns he never forgets. The main thing, the little one will no longer feel ashamed."

They were at the subway stairs. He kissed her and started down swiftly. She watched him go, thinking, *Her own father could not have been more zealous on her behalf. But more, David called her "our little girl."*

11

"*P* *assover?" Elvira repeated* as she submitted her head to Rebecca's careful combing.

"It's a holiday we celebrate because years ago, thousands of years ago, Jews were slaves in Egypt and—"

The child interrupted. "Like my mama said we was—were—slaves once?"

"Yes, Elvira. But God sent Moses to Pharaoh, king of the Egyptians, to tell him, 'Let my people go.' And after God punished the Egyptians with many plagues, Pharaoh finally did let the Jews go free. So every year at this time, we celebrate our freedom with Passover. That's what we will be doing tonight at my father's house. So I want you to look your prettiest and wear the new dress I made for you."

"How do you do that?"

"Do what, dear?"

"Celebrate freedom," the child said.

"We recite the *Haggadah*."

"What's that?"

"The Haggadah is a storybook, the story of how we were set free," Rebecca explained. "The children at the table always ask the same four questions about why we do certain things differently on Passover than on other nights. Then the grown-ups answer them by reading Haggadah out loud."

"Is it a nice story?"

Rebecca embraced the child. "Darling, any story that ends with people being set free is a nice story, a very nice story."

While they were close, arms around each other, Elvira asked, "What questions?" Rebecca drew back to look into the child's inquisitive eyes. "Those same four questions . . ."

For a moment, a provocative thought, an almost impudent thought, flickered in Rebecca's mind. She banished it at once. For her father had already made known that as it related to

Elvira, he did not share his daughter's concept of charity or good works.

Suddenly, that impish impulse not only returned but took complete possession of Rebecca's mind. She was surprised to hear herself say, "Why not?"

In response to the puzzled look on Elvira's face, Rebecca said, "Darling, say after me, very slowly, *mah nishtanah.*"

"*Mah?*" the child asked, seeking an explanation.

"Just say it, Elvira. *Mah nishtanah.* Once we've gone through the rest, I'll explain."

The entire family had gathered in Meier and Gussie Silverstone's flat in the tenement on Fifth Street on the Lower East Side of Manhattan. Though he could have afforded a slightly better apartment farther uptown, Meier Silverstone, an elderly Orthodox Jew, could not tear himself away from the synagogue where he had worshiped since he had arrived in this new country, or from the dwindling congregation where he still had his old friends.

On this first night of Passover, Rebecca, David, and Elvira came down from Washington Heights. Rebecca's older brother, Simon, his wife, Chana, and their two sons came down from the Bronx. Her sister, Miriam, and her husband, Abe, brought their daughter and their son from Borough Park in Brooklyn.

Each of the younger Silverstones would have preferred to hold the Passover Seder in his or her own home, but as they agreed each year, "Papa enjoys presiding, and after all, how many years does he have left?"

When Rebecca, David, and Elvira arrived, they found everything in readiness. The two extra leaves had been inserted into the dining room table, so it extended to its utmost.

In the center of the table was the holiday plate with green bitter herbs, grated white horseradish, the roasted shinbone of the paschal lamb, and the haroseth, the mixture of chopped apple, nuts, cinnamon, and wine that symbolized the mortar Jewish slaves had been forced to use in building the Pyramids. Before Meier Silverstone's place at the head of the table was the large plate with three squares of matzo wrapped in a

fresh white linen towel. At his right hand was a bowl of saltwater to be used later for dipping the bitter herbs.

Every straight-backed chair in the house had been commandeered to accommodate the thirteen celebrants.

At Meier Silverstone's place was the armchair, with a pillow draped over one arm, to pay symbolic service to that part
of the four questions where the child intoned, "On all other
nights we eat sitting up or reclining. Why on this night do we
recline while eating?" Behind that question lay the concept
that once the Jews had been set free, each Jew was king in his
own house and hence reclined while eating, in the way of
kings in that ancient time.

Everyone in place, Meier Silverstone began the ceremony
of the seder. He pronounced the proper preliminary prayer of
thanks to the Lord for allowing this entire company to survive
to celebrate the holiday again this year. He blessed the matzo
and the wine, inviting the celebrants to drink the first required sip. Soon came time for the four questions, which
would invite the telling of the Passover story. By tradition,
those questions were asked by the youngest family member
capable of either reading or memorizing them. To avoid any
familial slights, in the Silverstone family the questions were
assigned among the children of Simon's and Miriam's families.

Since Simon's older son, Jacob, had already been bar
mitzvahed and thus was a man, he was no longer considered
eligible to ask one of the questions. His younger brother, Marvin, had that honor. Under the watchful and judgmental eye
of his bearded grandfather, the lad began in the singsong
manner in which he had been taught:

*Mah nishtanah halailah hazeh mikohl halaylos? Shebchol halaylos
awnu ochlin chametz oo'matzah. Halailah hazeh culo matzah?*

"Why is this night different from all other nights? On all
other nights, we eat leavened or unleavened bread. But on
this night we eat only unleavened bread."

Whereupon Miriam's daughter, Sarah, continued with the
second question: *Shebchol halaylos awnu ochlin she'or yerakos.
Halailah hazeh culo maror.* "On other nights we eat all kinds of
herbs. But on this night we eat only the bitter herbs."

Miriam's son, Irving, youngest of all, was appointed to ask

the third and fourth questions. Valiantly, and not before a timid glance in his grandfather's direction, little Irving began: *"Shebchol halaylos ain awnu matbillin afiloo pa'am echas. Halailah hazeh shtai payamim.* "On all other nights, we do not dip into the dish even once. But on this night, we dip twice."

Having gotten by the third question without any mistakes, Irving was ready, with great relief, to ask the fourth and final one. Until Rebecca said softly but quite firmly, "Elvira, your turn."

Everyone at table, especially David, was startled. They turned to focus their attention on eight-year-old Elvira. Behind his gray beard, Meier Silverstone's face reddened in surprise and anger. Elvira was silent until Rebecca reached under the table to take her hand and urge softly, "Go on, darling."

After a moment of hesitation, the child began. Haltingly but determinedly, she enunciated in correct Hebrew. *"Shebchol halaylos awnu ochlin bayn yesubin u'bayn m'subin. Halailah hazeh culanu m'subin."*

Rebecca dared to glance toward the head of the table at her father.

Meier Silverstone glared at her, then turned his gaze on the child. "Tell me, little one," he said in English. "Do you have any idea what you just said?"

Elvira looked toward Rebecca, then back at the old man. "Yes, sir. On all other nights, we eat sitting up or reclining. On this night, we all eat reclining."

Her rehearsed and correct answer seemed to satisfy the old man. But he was surely not prepared for what followed.

"Which is why you have the pillow on your chair. So you can eat like a king in your own house."

Meier Silverstone cast a look of rebuke at his younger daughter before he began to answer the questions of the children by intoning the story of the Exodus of the Jews from Egypt thousands of years ago.

In accord with Silverstone tradition, each of the adults read a portion of the story until the story of the Exodus had been completely told.

The ceremony was followed by a meal at which everyone overindulged in chicken soup with Mama's matzo balls, her gefilte fish, roasted chicken, potted beef, vegetables, and *tsimmes*, a rich dish of steamed carrots and sweet potatoes.

The evening was over. It was growing late. Each visiting family had a long subway ride home. As Rebecca, David, and Elvira were starting for the door, Meier Silverstone called in a tone that Rebecca knew from past experience was prelude to a rebuke, "Daughter!" It was accompanied by a gesture of his head that ordered: Follow me! She preceded him into the bedroom. He closed the door.

"I didn't want to upset the seder," he said in Yiddish, "but that was a . . ." he groped for the word. "It was unusual. Also unexpected. *And* unwise."

"Papa, she is a very sensitive child. For the other children to ask, two of them younger than she, and she to remain silent—she would be made to feel ashamed. I know her, Papa. She is a bright child."

"She must be if she could memorize the four questions *you* taught her," he accused. "*And* the explanations," he added.

"I didn't want her to feel out of place, less than the rest."

"*Why?*" the old man asked. "*Why* did you teach her?"

"I told you—"

He interrupted her. "I know what you told me. But, daughter, you were wrong."

"Papa, you, of all people, saying it is wrong to teach a child?"

"Daughter, daughter, if you were sitting in my place it would have been clear to you. Chana's Marvin asked, Miriam's Sarah and her Irving asked. You were the only woman at the table without a child of her own who could ask."

Much as she tried to control it, Rebecca felt hot tears starting down her cheeks.

"If you are saying I used the child for my own purposes . . ." she started to protest, but could not continue.

The old man held out his arms to embrace her. "Child, I do not say this to cause you more pain than you've already had. There is another reason, even more important—the welfare of the child. She is not a Jewish child. Her soul belongs to God, but in her own religion, the religion of her mother, her own people."

"I wasn't attempting to convert her."

"You owe the child more than that, daughter," the old man said. "More than that," he repeated.

12

*R*ebecca *Rosen climbed* the stairs of the 135th Street station of the new Eighth Avenue subway. Reaching the street level, she looked around cautiously. This was a shabby neighborhood even compared with her own modest street. The houses here were older than those up on Washington Heights. Here, the people were Negro. She sensed they were staring at her. She felt out of place, alone. And a little afraid. Nevertheless, she glanced at the slip of paper she held and started walking north.

The number she sought had been given to her by the Negro woman who cleaned two days a week for Mrs. Dwyer, her new next-door neighbor. She kept checking the address against the aged, fading, once-gilt numbers on transom windows. Not all the numbers had survived the wear of time.

Finally, she found the building she sought. Wedged between 2319 and 2323 was a building with no address but only a small bulletin board, which announced: AJALON BAPTIST CHURCH.

She tried the door and found it open. It was dark inside. There were no sounds of activity. She called out timidly, "Hello? Anybody here?" There was no reply. She discovered the double doors that led to the sanctuary. She peered through the glass insert. The area was dark, so dark that she could barely make out the pews and the altar. Behind the altar loomed several rows of benches.

She had never been inside any church. She opened one of the doors and she ventured in. Instinctively, her eyes went to where the ark of the scrolls would be in a synagogue, with the eternal light above it. Here there was no ark, no light.

Instead, behind the upper rows of benches was a large cross. Tall as a man, golden in color, it dominated the wall. Rebecca stared up at it. She had never seen a cross so large, had never been so close to one. In a terrifying flood, it brought back to her all fear and resentment of a lifetime, the days of her early childhood, when the Jews in her little town in Poland lived in dread of pogroms on Christian holidays. Suddenly, she knew she could not go through with her plan. She turned from the cross and raced back to the double doors to escape. She flung open one door and burst out, only to collide with a tall, lean, gray-haired Negro in dusty overalls. Shock compounding her fears, she cried out, "Please! I didn't do anything. Don't touch me!"

"Ma'am," the man said. "Calm down, please. Just take possession of yourself." He started to reach out to give her physical reassurance, but faced with her tense condition, he decided that any contact, despite its intent, was too risky for a Negro man to make.

In face of his calm, reassuring tone, his soft eyes, and his obvious concern, Rebecca felt less threatened. Finally, she managed, "I was told that I would find the minister here, Reverend Wilder."

"Yes, of course, Pastor Wilder. Well, if you just wait there in the office . . ." He pointed to a door at the end of the short corridor.

She started toward the door, then stopped, looked back, still not completely reassured.

"Go on, ma'am, it's open. Just go right in."

She reached for the white porcelain doorknob, turned it, and eased the door open. She found herself in a small room, no more than ten feet by eight. One wall was of plain white bookshelves, filled with books of various sizes and colors, some stacked, some lying on their sides, some leaning in seeming disorder. A small desk dominated the room; behind it was a worn swivel chair that tilted slightly. The desk, too, was cluttered with books, including a well-thumbed Bible with many slips of paper marking off passages for reference. Across from the desk was a single plain wood chair for visitors.

Rebecca slipped into that chair to await the arrival of Pastor Wilder. Though the room was unlighted, there was sufficient light from the window that faced the alleyway so she could make out the wording of the single framed article that hung on the walls and was not a religious picture. It was a diploma from a school of which she had never heard—Morehouse College. The degree was a bachelor of arts in Literature. She knew she was in the office of a man of education. She felt more encouraged. He would understand her problem.

She was taken by surprise when the door opened behind her. She stood up and, turning, began, "Pastor Wilder . . ." She discovered that she was facing the same man she had met before. This time, however, he was dressed in a simple, worn, somewhat shiny black serge suit, white shirt, and black tie. "I'm sorry," Rebecca said. "I thought you might be Pastor Wilder."

He smiled. "I *am* Pastor Wilder."

She hesitated an instant before she was able to shake his extended hand. It was cool; the skin was smooth. It was a strong hand, quite used to physical work.

He was aware of her hesitation. This was the first time in her life that she had shaken the hand of a Negro. She felt out of place and uncomfortable. She was also obviously curious about his change of apparel. About that, he could set her mind at rest.

"Please," he said, indicating that she sit down once more. He went around the desk to sit opposite her. "Earlier I had been down in the basement working on the furnace. While the weather is springlike, is a good time to get ready for next winter, so I tinker a bit."

"You do your own . . . your own work here in the church?"

"Not only here," he said. "I'm the janitor for twenty-three seventeen, twenty-three nineteen, and twenty-three twenty-three as well."

Instinctively, Rebecca gestured toward the diploma. "You mean, a man with a college education is a janitor?"

"My small congregation cannot support a pastor full-time. If you can suggest a better-paying job . . ." He had no need to say more. "Now, then, what can I do for you, Mrs. . . ."

"Rosen. Rebecca Rosen."

"Rosen," he repeated, drawing the inevitable conclusion. "Well, Mrs. Rosen? You came here to see me. Why?"

"I was told you could instruct me on how to bring up a

child in the Christian faith." She tried to assess his reaction to that declaration before she felt compelled to add, "A Negro child. A girl. Eight years old, almost nine."

Wilder did not respond at once. He was trying to assimilate the almost bizarre request the woman had just made. Feeling insecure, anticipating a refusal, Rebecca sat up more staunchly to conceal her qualms.

"A child. Almost nine years old. Negro," Wilder evaluated. "How does she happen to be your responsibility?"

Rebecca explained about Elvira's mother, about the attempt to place her with a Negro couple, and how Elvira insisted on returning to the Rosens. Throughout, Wilder nodded. Rebecca had no inkling as to how he would react.

"My dear Mrs. Rosen, Christianity cannot be learned out of books alone. Especially Negro Christianity. It has to be experienced."

"You mean, there are no books . . ." Rebecca started to ask.

"Oh, there are books," Wilder anticipated, rising to the bookshelves on the wall. "I could pick out half a dozen that would tell you what it's all about. But Negro Christianity is something one can only learn in concert with other Negro people. It is something one feels, something one is part of, with body as well as mind, with fervor as well as intellect. There is really no way to explain it without demonstrating it. That can only be done here, in the church."

"You won't help me?"

"I want to help," Wilder assured. "And we will do *our* part. The question is, will *you*?"

"What can I do?"

"Bring her here every Sunday morning for Sunday school. Have her remain for the church service."

"If that's what it takes," Rebecca said, "yes!"

"Then it is possible. You see, the church plays a special part in the lives of Negro people. In the days of slavery, we were forbidden to congregate or discuss anything except in church. So to us, the church means not only religion; it is the center of our social life, and our politics as well. *And*, if you are a Negro, as the girl is, a refuge when the world has dealt badly with you. As it will," he warned sadly. "As it will."

Rebecca nodded sadly. She had never heard the burden of the Negro past put so plainly and clearly.

"This may be difficult for a white person to appreciate—" Wilder continued.

"Less difficult than you think," Rebecca said. "I can still remember from my own childhood when a rumor would sweep through our quarter of the town that some drunken peasants were headed our way. My mother, like all Jewish mothers, would snatch me up under one arm and my sister under her other and start for the synagogue, calling to my brother, 'Warn your father.' Soon all the Jews in the town were gathered in the synagogue for closeness and protection in time of our greatest danger. It was our refuge in time of trouble, too. So I know, I know."

"Mrs. Rosen, we may have more in common than first appeared. I am quite hopeful that we will be able to help you."

He reached to a stack of pamphlets on the corner of his desk. He picked up two of them.

"These are for our younger children. If you read these to the girl, it will be a place to begin."

"Elvira reads quite well on her own," Rebecca replied firmly.

"Good, good," Wilder replied, thinking, *Spoken like a proud mother. The bond between them must be strong, very strong.* "Sunday morning, at nine-thirty, have her here and I will see she is placed in a class with her peers."

"Thank you, Reverend." Feeling indebted, she said, "There must be a fee for these booklets."

"No, Mrs. Rosen. But when you bring her on Sunday, see that she has a few pennies to put in the collection plate, so she can acquire the habit of giving—and feel part of the congregation. To a child of almost nine, belonging is very important."

Rebecca sat in the jerking, speeding subway car, the religious booklets clutched in her hands. Curious as she was about their contents, she dared not open them to reveal to the other passengers that she, Meier Silverstone's daughter, was reading forbidden materials. Despite how strongly her father felt about Elvira's right to her own religion, Rebecca refused to contemplate what he would say now. It was one thing to share the feelings and deprivations of another minority, but to venture into this source of so much travail and misery for Jews through many centuries was quite another.

The subway ride seemed endless. At the 175th Street station, she fled the car and raced up the stairs toward daylight. Then she collected herself and started quickly along Broadway to arrive home before Elvira returned from school.

She grew even more self-conscious as she approached her house. As she passed the familiar faces of her neighborhood, white faces in this area populated mainly by Jews, she realized that she clutched Pastor Wilder's booklets close to her breast to conceal them.

Each time a neighbor called, "Hello, Mrs. Rosen!" she blanched. When one woman asked, "And how is the little one?" she felt unable to do more than smile and hurry on, as if her own apartment were a refuge she must reach to be safe from exposure.

Home at last, she dared to examine the first of the two booklets. The cover was a pastoral scene of biblical times: the hills of Judea and, in the distant background, the artist's conception of ancient Jerusalem. Her first response was a surge of protest. What right had they to lay claim to her land and her holy city?

The more painful challenge lay ahead. Would she dare to open the booklet? She hesitated, her fingers playing with the edge of the cover. She turned the page. What she had feared most now confronted her. There *he* was. With his arms outstretched. In a white robe. His beard, his flowing hair, his intense eyes.

All her life he had been held up to her as a symbol of the torment of Jews in pogroms and inquisitions. Yet here he was, looking so loving and benign.

She had dwelled too long on the image. She forced herself to begin reading. She wanted to be ready when Elvira returned from school, so she could have the books out of sight by the time David returned for supper.

> *Instructions to the Teacher:*
> Lesson Number sixteen, for Sunday
> morning, April 2: Jesus enters
> Jerusalem to celebrate the Passover.

Passover! She rebelled. *What do they know of Passover? Were they slaves in Egypt? Did God work miracles through Moses to set them free? It is our holiday, not theirs.*

I must stop thinking "they" and "us," "theirs" and "ours," she realized. *Else Elvira will become one of "them" and I will be one of "us."*

> Jesus enters Jerusalem to celebrate
> the Passover.
>
> *Lesson:* Mark 11: 7, 8, 9, 10.
> Golden Text—Blessed is He who
> cometh in the name of the Lord.
>
> *Scripture Lesson Text:*
>
> And they brought the colt to
> Jesus, and cast their garments
> in the way; and others cut down
> branches off the trees, and
> strewed them in the way.
> And they that went before, cried,
> saying Hosanna! Blessed is he
> that cometh in the name of the Lord!

Rebecca read on. *The Notes On The Lesson* told the story in colloquial English and gave the history of the event and a summary.

> *The Object in View:* To teach that
> the death of Jesus was a holy event
> ordained by God and known to Jesus.

Why is it, she demanded silently, *that in their books they teach that Jesus' death was ordained by God, but they accuse us of crucifying him? I must ask David. He has studied a great deal. He must know about this. But then if I start to ask, he will want to know why and I will have to tell him.*

She realized, *I will have to tell him in any event. I have never had secrets from him. And surely I cannot have them now.*

And I must stop superimposing my feelings on what I read in these booklets. Else I will not be fit to teach Elvira.

She read on, discovering much that she had never known before. She read about the Last Supper and Jesus' foretelling his fate. She continued through the seizure of Jesus, his betrayal by Peter, his appearance before Pontius Pilate, his dispatch to the temple for trial.

She was relieved when the doorbell rang. It must be Elvira, back from school. It continued to ring insistently. She went to let the child in. Elvira raced into her arms, brandishing a paper in one hand.

"Look, Aunt Rebecca, look!"

Rebecca examined it eagerly. It was an arithmetic test. In a column along the right-hand side there were red check marks at each answer. Ten red check marks. At the top, also in red crayon: *100%. Excellent, Elvira!*

"This is wonderful, darling! Uncle David will be very happy."

"Will he be proud of me? Real proud?" the child asked.

"He's always proud of you, dear," Rebecca assured.

"Then will he be prouder now?"

Rebecca smiled. "Yes. He will be prouder now." She kissed the child once more. "Now, for some milk and cake."

The child raced toward the kitchen. As Rebecca watched her, she thought, *With this new teaching, will she change toward us? Will we change toward her?*

David had come home, washed up, had his one drink of whiskey, and sat down at the table. He pronounced the blessing over the bread and was ready for one of Rebecca's special dishes, the aroma of which already promised much. As was his custom now, he looked at Elvira. "And how was it in school today?"

She did not respond, but there was a mischievous twinkle in her dark eyes that caused David to call in singsong to Rebecca, who was at the stove, "Something is going on here tonight. Rebecca!"

"I'm sorry, David, I have no idea," she said as she approached the table, carrying a steaming tureen of fragrant veal stew. But she exchanged a conspiratorial glance with the child. "What in the world could it be, Elvira?"

Elvira pulled the paper out of her lap and waved it. David

took it from her. One glance was enough to cause him to break into a great beaming smile.

"One hundred percent!" he exclaimed. "One hundred percent! We have to celebrate. Some way, something. I know! Sunday morning we all go down to Central Park, to the zoo. Have you ever been to the zoo before, Elvira?"

"No."

"Then first the zoo. Later we will go to the Automat. You know about the Automat, Elvira? It's a restaurant where you put in nickels and get all kinds of wonderful things—chocolate-covered doughnuts, hot chocolate, egg sandwiches, macaroni and cheese. You can pick whatever you want!"

Thereafter, supper was a joint exercise in enjoying Rebecca's stew and planning the outing for Sunday.

They were in bed. After having made love and just before falling asleep. David had his arm around Rebecca, her head resting against his chest.

"That child, that child," he said. "She is full of surprises."

Rebecca did not respond directly but said softly, as if venturing into forbidden territory. "David . . . today . . . today I went downtown."

"Downtown? What for? If there was anything you needed, I could have picked it up for you on the way home."

"I went to the Ajalon Baptist Church."

"Oh!" he said with the resigned air of a man who had been expecting troublesome news that finally arrived. "And?"

"It won't be as easy as I thought," she announced.

"They won't help?" he assumed.

"No. The man, the pastor, was very nice. Very understanding. He wants to help. But I must bring Elvira there every Sunday morning. For Sunday school. And then for church."

"So you mean we can't go to Central Park?"

"He . . . he also gave me some books. To teach her about . . . about . . . you know."

"About *him*?" David asked.

"Yes."

David was silent for a time. "I expected it would come up," he said finally.

"What do I do?" she asked, for she would not proceed without his knowledge and agreement.

"As your own father said, even if she asked to be converted, she is not of a proper age to give consent. So do what you have to. And if any of the neighbors ask where you go every Sunday morning, don't be bashful. Tell them. To see that a child is instructed in her own religion is no reason for shame."

"Thank you, David," she said softly. "It would have been difficult enough, without feeling that you were against it."

"I just hope they won't teach her to hate . . . to hate Jews," he said.

"Not that old pastor."

"Good, good," David said.

He was about to fall off to sleep when she asked, "You said nothing about the business today. Is something wrong?"

"Wrong? An order for four dozen derbies, in two different-shaped crowns, from Stern Brothers. Is that something wrong?" he responded proudly. "What's more, the buyer liked my samples so much he asked, 'Rosen, with Al Smith having made such a thing of the brown derby during his campaign for president, do you think you could come up with a few dozen in brown if I asked?'"

"Oh, that's wonderful, darling, wonderful!"

"So Gilleaudeau no longer has a corner on the derby market in New York! There is now David Rosen to consider."

He has accepted the idea of Sunday school, she thought, *of Elvira going to church, even of my taking her. Now, if only I can conquer my own qualms about being able to see it through.*

The next afternoon when Elvira returned from school, Rebecca insisted she have her milk and a large piece of fresh, fragrant cinnamon-nut cake she had baked. While the child was enjoying her snack, Rebecca said, "Today, instead of going out to play, we are going to do some reading together."

"Reading?" The child looked up, still chewing, puzzled.

"Reading," Rebecca repeated. "About religion. And God. And . . ." Feeling she was betraying generations of her ancestors, she found it difficult to pronounce the name. But finally found the will to do it. "And about . . . Jesus."

"Jesus, yes. My mama used to tell me about him."

"Then we'll read about him together," Rebecca said.

Later, with Elvira sitting alongside her on the living room couch, Rebecca opened the book and began to read: "'So Jesus went up to Jerusalem. He went there to celebrate the Passover.'"

"Who asked the four questions?" Elvira asked.

"It . . . it doesn't say in here."

"Oh," the child replied, but she was obviously disappointed at not knowing.

Rebecca continued to read the brief lesson.

13

*R*ebecca *stood at* the door to the small basement classroom watching the children file in. Boys, ages eight to ten, some dressed in knickers, some in long pants, all in white shirts, ties mostly askew despite their mothers' efforts. Then followed the girls, in short, crisply starched dresses, hair neatly combed and sectioned into squares, each square topped by a short pigtail tied in ribbons of red, blue, or yellow. As they filed by, they could not resist stealing furtive looks at Rebecca.

In public school, the children were accustomed to the fact that most of their teachers were white. But to be suddenly confronted by a white woman here in their own church was startling. They were doubly curious that this white woman held a young Negro girl by the hand.

Once the others were all inside, Rebecca knelt down to whisper, "Now, Elvira, you go in. Be a part of the class. Remember all the stories we read together."

Rebecca patted her on the head, then set her free. As she watched her disappear into the classroom, she thought, *She looked as neat as any of them, and as clean too. But her hair. I've got to learn how to do hair like their mothers do. Those neat squares. Those cute little pigtails.*

The young teacher closed the door, leaving Rebecca aware that she had an hour to pass on her own, in a strange place. Where to go? What to do? She decided to spend the time quietly up in the sanctuary. She climbed the stairs, then pushed open the door to discover the sanctuary was not empty. A group of adults filled the first three rows. Between them and the altar stood a tall woman, attired in a flowered dress, wearing a large picture hat that set off her handsome brown face. She was lecturing on precisely the same events that Rebecca and Elvira had studied. This was, Rebecca realized, a Sunday school class for adults.

Silently, Rebecca slipped into the last pew, resigned to listen. But the teacher had already noticed her. "Sister, wouldn't you like to come down front and join us?"

"No, I . . ." Rebecca tried to reply. "I . . . thank you, but I would like to be out of the way if you don't mind."

The lesson continued.

In the small basement classroom, Elvira Hitchins sat in her assigned seat in the first row with all the other girls. Her hands were clasped tightly before her, reflecting the anxiety she experienced in an unfamiliar place, among new children, while listening to a teacher who was a stranger to her.

But as the lesson progressed and she heard a repetition of what she and Aunt Rebecca had read aloud together, she began to feel more reassured. When she glanced from one side to the other and was met by the curious yet friendly smiles of the other girls, the tightness in her hands gradually began to give way. Soon they lay loose and relaxed in her lap as she became absorbed by the storybook manner in which her young teacher retold the story of Jesus entering Jerusalem at Passover time.

Once finished, the teacher proceeded to review the lesson by means of questions and answers.

"Now, boys and girls, why did Jesus go to Jerusalem?"

Several boys and girls raised their hands, some almost jumping out of their seats in their eagerness to answer. But one boy, without permission, blurted out, "To celebrate the Passover!"

"Correct, Alvin. But next time, wait until I call on you. Now, who knows what Passover is?"

No hands went up until Elvira timidly raised hers.

"Yes, Elvira, you know what Passover is?"

"Yes, ma'am."

"Then tell us," the teacher coaxed.

Elvira began shyly, "Well, it is a time when Jewish people celebrate their freedom from the Egyptians."

"Correct!" her teacher said, unprepared for what would follow.

"And all Jewish children ask four questions which go like this: *mah nishtanah halailah hazeh* . . ."

Elvira proceeded to recite the four questions in Hebrew,

followed by their English translation. She continued relating all the ceremonial detail her perceptive young mind had retained from that night at Meier Silverstone's house.

When she had finished, her astonished teacher said, "Elvira, that was very interesting. A little more than my question called for, but very interesting. And it also seems to have brought us to the end of our class time. So let's all go upstairs for the regular church service."

Rebecca watched the children file out of the classroom straight to the stairs that led up to the sanctuary. As Elvira emerged, her eager eyes searched for Rebecca. They lit up to reassure Rebecca that she had survived this first test. She continued up the stairs with the rest of her class.

Rebecca followed. At the doors of the sanctuary, she hesitated. From behind, she heard the calm, cheerful voice of Pastor Wilder. "You're welcome to come in." Undecided, she hesitated. "I promise not to baptize you," he said, smiling.

"Could I just sit in the back, where no one will notice?"

"You are our guest, Mrs. Rosen. You may sit anywhere you like."

He stood aside to permit her entrance. She could not offend this kindly man who, in his long black clerical robe, appeared far different from the old janitor she had first encountered. She chose the end seat of the pew against the back wall. She scanned the pews in front. Hers was the only white face in the entire church.

Is this how it feels for them all the time? she wondered. *To be the only one in the white households where they clean, or on the bus or the subway when they leave here and go uptown to work. Being a Jew in these times is difficult enough. We can avoid being singled out so readily. They can't.*

Rebecca remained perched stiffly on the edge of a pew worn smooth over many years. The door alongside her opened. A dozen men and women, all very neatly dressed, all wearing spotless white gloves, filed in, the deacons and deaconesses of the church. They went down the aisle, taking their places before the altar, facing the congregation. As they did, Rebecca was startled when the organ suddenly came to life. Now, behind her strong voices were raised in song. She turned to discover a line of men and women, robed in white silk gowns with blood-red stripes extending across their shoulders like epaulets and down the length of their sleeves. With great vigor they sang a hymn, clapping their hands in rhythmic unison. They made their way down the aisle, but slowly, taking a step, then pausing. Step, pause, step, pause, step, pause; they went in cadence to their singing. In they marched, in single file, until they reached the altar. They climbed to the two rows of benches. There they stood, the men in the front row, the women behind, still singing, still clapping their hands in accented rhythm. The congregants joined in one by one until the entire church rocked with the sound of voices and the clapping of hands.

It was impossible not to be moved by the sheer religious fervor that filled the small, bare church. The words of their song became louder and clearer: "Praise the Lord and sing! Let our voices ring!"

The singing concluded and the service continued. To Rebecca's surprise, unlike a rabbi or a cantor, Pastor Wilder did not take command. He quietly made notes as he sat below the chorus and behind the altar. A younger man, a deacon, dressed in a white suit and wearing white gloves, stepped to the pulpit to make announcements. There would be a cake sale next Sunday afternoon and a brotherhood service with a church up on Amsterdam Avenue. He had also succeeded in getting a permit to use one of the baseball diamonds up in Van Courtlandt Park, so there would be a church outing three weeks from today. As a special inducement, a star of the Negro League, Satchel Paige, had agreed to umpire the game. In response to that news, one of the congregants called out, "Tell 'em, man, tell 'em!"

Rebecca thought this most disrespectful in the midst of a religious service, even if the topic was not particularly religious in nature. *This surely would not happen in a synagogue,* she rebuked silently.

After the announcements, the choir members rose to their feet and commenced singing once more. With a single subtle cue from Pastor Wilder the whole congregation, young and old, rose and joined in. The choir swayed from side to side in unison, clapping their hands on each accented word. Soon the

entire congregation was welded into a single singing, swaying, clapping group.

It was so inviting, enticing, intoxicating, Rebecca felt
tempted to join in the rhythm and the swaying, until she
noted that when engaged in religious ceremony, Negroes
swayed from side to side. Jews, on the other hand, rocked
forward and back.

Why? she wondered. *What is the significance? I must ask
David. He should know from his studies.*

She was engaged in thinking of such things when an elderly woman, also dressed in white and wearing white
gloves, stepped to the pulpit and read one of the Psalms. This
passage was from the Old Testament and familiar to Rebecca.
The woman read the first line, and the congregation responded with the next line. So it went: the woman reading,
the congregation responding. From time to time a voice in the
congregation would call out: "Amen! Hallelujah!" Once a man
in the front pew called out: "Tell it, sister, tell it loud and
strong!"

Rebecca thought, *Surely that nice soft-spoken pastor will not
put up with such interruptions for very long.*

She was greatly relieved when the choir rose to sing once
more.

Once they finished, one of the deacons, an elderly man,
stepped to the pulpit to announce: "We are now ready to receive your offerings."

The choir rose, humming softly, then descended from
their benches above the pulpit and marched down to drop
their contributions into a basket that rested on the altar. Continuing to hum in rhythm, they returned to their places,
whereupon the congregation rose and, one pew at a time,
filed down the aisle to deposit their offerings.

Rebecca watched as Elvira's little group rose and took their
place in the line. She strained to see Elvira approach the basket and drop her pennies in. At the same time, the child
turned to look in Rebecca's direction, seeking her approval.

Once the last worshiper had returned to his place, the
choir burst into a hymn that rocked the small church with its
explosive opening notes.

> Where would I be?
> Without the Lord at my side
> Where would I be?

This evoked an even stronger response from the entire congregation. When they had finished, Pastor Wilder came to the pulpit, smiling. "Now brothers, sisters, that is what I call making a joyful noise unto the Lord."

Wilder raised his eyes toward heaven and intoned, "Our Father . . ."

The congregation responded by singing the opening phrase of the Lord's Prayer, "Our Father . . ."

"Which art in heaven," Wilder continued.

"Which art in heaven," the congregation sang in response.

Thus they continued, the pastor pronouncing the Lord's Prayer phrase by phrase, the congregation repeating it in song. Until the final phrase, when congregation and pastor sang together in a rousing crescendo: "For Thine is the kingdom and the power and the glory forever. Amen."

Pastor Wilder continued: "And the Lord said, six days shalt thou labor, as I did when I created the heavens and the earth, but on the seventh day shall you rest. So remember the Sabbath and keep it holy."

From the congregation a voice called out "Amen!"

"I say to you He meant more than physical labor. For during those six days we also labor at being angered and hostile to those around us. So I say to you, on this seventh day let us make it holy with love and forgiveness. Stand up, brothers, sisters. Turn to one side and the other, turn back, turn front, to all those around you. Shake his hand, her hand, embrace 'em, kiss 'em. Let us have a moment of fellowship for all. Come, now! On your feet. Let this little church overflow with love and fellowship!"

Rebecca watched as they greeted one another, men shaking hands, embracing. Women embracing and kissing. The children watched, then imitated their elders.

Suddenly, the woman sitting directly in front of Rebecca turned to her and greeted, "Sister! Good to have you here! Welcome!" Rebecca felt herself being embraced and brought tight to the woman's large bosom. Rebecca felt withdrawn at first, until the warmth of the woman caused her to relax and surrender to the embrace. Now, on each side of her were others who shook her hand and welcomed her.

The period of fellowship over, Rebecca sank back into her seat, looked about shyly, wondering, *What was I so afraid of? Why did I hold back? Because I came in here carrying with me my own little bundle of prejudices. God, I hope I did not offend them.*

Pastor Wilder was in the pulpit once more. This time he laid before him his pages of notes. He reached into his robes and pulled out a big silver watch, which he placed on the lectern. Rebecca had seen Rabbi Kahn do exactly the same. She knew the sermon was about to be delivered.

"Brothers, sisters," Wilder began, then looked down into the pews before him, where the Sunday school classes were seated. "And you little ones—you don't have to be big to be a brother or a sister. What we are going to talk 'bout today is for you, too. So listen good, real good."

He raised his eyes to address the entire congregation. "Now, last week we dwelled on how Jesus made His triumphant entrance into Jerusalem, how He was seated on that donkey and the disciples they took the reins 'n they said, 'Let's go!' They started up that long, long hill to Jerusalem. And the people, they knew, they felt it, felt it in their bones. Just like you do. They knew they was in the presence of the Christ. That Jesus was their Lord!"

"Praise God, brother!" a man called from a corner of the small church.

"And what did that crowd do? Why, they took the shirts offa their backs. They laid them on the ground before Him. They wasn't standing around discussin', 'Am I giving too much? Am I dirtying my one good shirt?' Out of their love for Jesus they gave the shirts offa their backs! And they ran alongside Jesus crying out, and what did they cry out?"

Many voices called back: "Hosanna! Hosanna! in the highest!"

"Right! And one thing more, Blessed is he that cometh in the name of the Lord!"

"Tell it, brother, tell it!" the old man in a side pew called out.

Wilder thundered: "Now, you and me, if'n we got such

greetin' we'd be sayin' to ourselves, 'Man, I am somethin'.' But there was a sad look in Jesus' eyes. If you and me was standin' on the corner watchin' we'da said, 'That is one sorrowful man.' And why? Why, friends?"

"'Cause He knowed, He knowed," a voice called out.

"Right, brother! He knowed what was waitin' for Him. He knowed then like we know now what is waitin' for *us*. Prejudice. And bigotry. But for Him, more. Much more. Now His friends, His disciples, His followers, they didn't know. Not till late that night, when He brought them together for the feast. The Passover feast."

Rebecca felt herself go stiff. She feared that this man, who had appeared soft-spoken and cultured in his modest little office but who had now become a man afire, would open old wounds between Christians and Jews.

"Now, why do you suppose that Jesus picked that particular time, that particular way to gather His closest followers and lay the truth on them?"

"Why, pastor, why?" a woman down front called out.

"I think Jesus say to Himself, 'This is hard news I got to tell them. And if I come straight out with it, it is gonna shock 'em. So I got to put them at ease. But at the same time, I got to teach 'em some lessons and get 'em ready for the future. Now, how best do I do that?' And He said, 'I know! I will say, "Let us celebrate the Passover together." Then, when they are all together, I will do like I always done. I will show them with signs and examples.' So Jesus had 'em all in to celebrate the Passover. And after they had done the Passover part of things, when the supper is over, He does a strange thing. He gets up from the table. He starts to take off His clothing. Till there He is, standing naked before them. Naked like He came into this world. Like you, brother, and you, sister. We all come naked into this world. A human being can't be poorer than that. Then He wraps a towel around His middle, like it says in John thirteen. And while they were all watching, He pours water into a basin and then, then He begins to wash the disciples' feet.

"Now, they are sittin' there watchin' as He goes from one to the other washing their feet, then takin' off the towel to wipe 'em dry. And they are looking from one to the other.

Just picture 'em. Matthew, the publican, lookin' to John and John lookin' to Andrew, the fisherman. Their eyes is askin', What's He doin', man? He is the Christ and He is washin' our feet. How come? Why?

"Now, He comes to Simon Peter and tries to do the same, but the big fisherman pulls back his feet. He says, 'Lord, you mean you going to wash my feet?' And he is hiding his big clodhoppers from Jesus. But Jesus says, 'Simon, you don't un- derstand now why I have to do this. But one day, one day . . .' And just picture it, brothers, picture Jesus' eyes when He is thinkin' of what He knows is waitin' for Him. 'One day, Peter, you will know.'"

"Amen!" several voices cried out.

"But Peter said, 'Lord, you ain't goin' to wash my feet. No, sir!' And Jesus looks up from the floor where he was kneeling and he says, 'Peter, if I don't do this, you'll be no part of me.' And that big man, why, he melts like a baby and says, with tears in his eyes. 'In that case, Lord, not just mah feet, but mah hands.' And get this, 'And also mah heart.'"

"Tell it, man, tell it!" a woman cried out.

Now Wilder raised his voice even more strongly as it took on inflections that sounded more like singing than speaking.

"Now, Jesus declares to them, 'Brothers, the reason I be doin' this is that I want you to learn humility. Whoever would be greatest of all should be least of all.' Now, that is not the same as being told, 'Nigger, know your place.' Humility is not somethin' that is forced on you, like we have to endure if we are cleanin' women."

"Say it, brother, say it!" came the voice of a pained and indignant woman from some part of the sanctuary. Others joined in with, "Amen, sister! Amen!"

"Or if we are ridin' the trains like Pullman porters or dinin' car waiters and we got to fetch and tote for white folks. And they thinkin' or else sayin' that colored man was born to serve my needs and desires. 'N we got to smile 'n nod 'n bow 'n scrape. That, brothers, that, sisters, is not humility. That is degradation. That is not somethin' we choose but somethin' that is forced upon us."

"Tell it, pastor, tell it all!" an elderly white-haired man cried out. Rebecca knew from the sound of his voice, from the depth of his feeling, that he had spent a lifetime in such menial service.

Wilder nodded in the man's direction, then, raising his arms as if to encompass the world, called out, "Now, ask yourself, why did Jesus choose the Passover for this lesson? Sure, you be sayin' Passover was a time for religious Jews to go to Jerusalem. True. But why Passover *and* humility? He is reachin' out to you, sister, to you, brother! He's sayin' put aside your false humility, your polite speakin', and your empty smiles. He is sayin' remember the Passover. Remember what it means. Freedom! Freedom, sisters! Freedom, brothers! He was sayin', you want to be in a position to show true humility? Then first get free, like Moses said, 'Let my people go!'"

Now Amens erupted from all sides of the modest little church. "Hallelujah!" And one man cried out, "Say the word, Lord, say the word!"

"The word is freedom! Freedom from the slavery of poor jobs, at poor wages. What is the difference 'tween a naked colored woman at a slave auction up for bidding and a colored woman in an old coat, too thin to keep out the winter winds, standin' at the subway station waitin' for some white woman to come bid a measly dollar for her whole day's work?"

"No difference, Lord!" a woman cried out.

All the guilt that Rebecca had ever felt in witnessing such transactions was suddenly doubled and redoubled. She was thinking, *Not Elvira; that will never happen to Elvira.* But the next instant she thought, *If an educated man like Pastor Wilder is forced to be a janitor, what hope is there for any colored person?*

In his fervor, Wilder swept on, his voice rising and filling the small church. "The day be comin', brothers, sisters, when we will be able to speak the truth not only within these four walls but out in the open. For the whole world to hear. When we will be demandin' of the world . . ."

He seemed to falter, groping for the correct words, which did not come to him, until one woman just in front of Rebecca cried out, "Help him, Lord, help him find the words!"

Thus encouraged, Wilder took fresh breath and continued: "When we will be demandin' of this world, let *my* people go!

Loud and clear, proud and strong, for the whole world to hear: Let my people go!"

A torrent of Hallelujahs burst upon him from all corners of the church, accompanied by "Praise the Lord!" and "Oh, yes, Lord, yes!"

"And when that day come," Wilder continued, his voice rising even higher, "when we be free and equal, we not goin' to be forgettin' the lesson of the Passover supper, when our Lord Jesus humble Himself. When we be free and strong, don't any of us forget humility."

"No, Lord, no!" an old man shouted in a tremulous voice.

"Therefore," Wilder resumed, "let us join together and say . . ."

He stretched out his arms and swept them upward to the heavens to invite the entire congregation to join him as he sang out, "He who would be greatest of all, let him be least of all!" which was followed by Amens and Hallelujahs from the entire congregation.

Including Rebecca Rosen, who had been moved by the emotion of the old pastor. At once she felt self-conscious, embarrassed, and grew silent, hoping no one had detected her outburst.

Wilder appeared spent, his face glistening with sweat as he lowered his arms. He stepped down from the pulpit to take his place before the altar. As the choir sang, "Is Your All on the Altar," Wilder stretched out his arms wide in invitation to discipleship. Several men and women came forward to clasp hands with him and with each other.

Elvira watched, feeling a desire to join and be part of them. Her shyness prevented her, until the young boy alongside her started forward. After only a moment of hesitation, she rose to follow, glancing back at Rebecca, who encouraged her with a smile and a nod. Elvira reached the group and joined hands with the boy on her left and the woman on her right, completing the circle. Thus joined, Elvira swayed with the others while the choir continued to sing and clap their hands to accent the beat of the music. Her momentary shyness overcome, Elvira raised her voice to sing in concert with the choir, while across the circle from her Pastor Wilder encouraged her with a broad, warm smile.

The service was at an end. The congregation rose, formed a line, and came forward to greet the pastor. Wilder shook each hand, kissed each woman and each child on the cheek. Once they had filed out, Wilder took his Bible and notes in hand and started toward the door, where the departing worshipers were bidding Rebecca farewell and inviting her to return.

Wilder reached her side. "If you have a moment, Mrs. Rosen . . ." She followed the old minister down the steps into his office.

"Well now, Mrs. Rosen, that wasn't so difficult, was it?" he asked, smiling. "Especially the way little Elvira caught the spirit. So you can relax." Rebecca thought she had concealed her nervousness. "A minister gets to read people by their littlest signs. Posture. Hands." He pointed. She became aware of how stiffly clenched her hands were. "Eyes."

"My eyes?" Rebecca asked.

"Surprise there. And questions. Many, many questions. First you're thinking, Why so much singing? Why not the speaking of many prayers as written in the prayer books? Like in your synagogues. Or in white churches. Why all that swaying and clapping of hands? And this strange minister, why does he speak one language in the privacy of his office but another language when he is up there in the pulpit?"

Blushing at having her thoughts exposed, Rebecca nodded.

"No need to be embarrassed, Mrs. Rosen. That diploma on the wall behind me attests to the fact that I am an educated man. I can speak the language as well as any white man. Better than many. Why then, when I get up in the pulpit, do I speak as I did? Because every Negro preacher has *two* languages—white English to win that college degree, and our own English to preach to our own. Our English is to us like Yiddish is to you: our common language. What sound like mistakes to you are native to us."

He rose from his squeaking swivel chair to pace. "That diploma—I was thirty-two before I was able to achieve that. Had to work at some mean jobs before I could save enough to go to college. But when I was done, I had what no other man in my family had ever had, a college education. Oh, I had no illusions. I was still a Negro, still barred from most jobs. But I had to believe that a better day was coming, if not for me then for my little ones. Doesn't seem that way now. But I've got to go on hoping.

"Meantime, I preach to my people. Now, you don't see up on that wall any diploma from any divinity school. Because most of us have learned our preaching from other preachers. I learned how to translate the Bible's words into words my people understand, so they fall on the Negro ear with a familiar ring."

He paused in his pacing to smile down at Rebecca. "After all, Mrs. Rosen, you don't think that God spoke in King James English, do you? So why not our kind of English? You have to remember that we are not yet seventy years free from slavery. And from being forbidden by law to learn to read and write.

"I mean to say, Mrs. Rosen, there is good historic reason for everything you witnessed in my little church. Singing, swaying, clapping was the only way for us to join together when we were slaves. The speaking was left to the preacher. And he spoke to them as I did this morning. Negroes need to become part of the sermon, not by listening to a parable as it is written in the Bible. Those parables are dehydrated, boiled down. 'A certain man went down from Jerusalem to Jericho and fell among thieves.' From *The Good Samaritan*. We Negroes want to know that man. We want to know his family, why he was going to Jericho. We want that story to come alive. That's where Negro preaching comes in. We have to rewrite the parable so it becomes an exciting story. With a plot. With villains. Heroes. Conflict. Suspense. So real and so exciting that my people begin to live it, become part of it and, yes, join in."

He was chuckling as he said, "Surprised you, didn't it? The way my people chime in. Agree with their pastor. Urge him on. Call on God to help him. None of that in those refined white churches. No, ma'am. That would be inelegant, rude. Mrs. Rosen, that's the best kind of worship, ecstasy coming from within, not being force-fed from without. My people *feel* their religion. After centuries of living in a hostile white world where we had to be close-mouthed and poker-faced to survive, we need a place where we can open up. If a Negro is master no place else, he is master in his own church."

His eyes, which had been soft, were piercing now. His face again glistened with sweat.

"Mrs. Rosen, all I wanted to say was this: It is one thing to see that little Elvira comes to Sunday school and to church. But what you have undertaken is going to demand more. There is a word for what I want to say: *soul*. To us, soul is a festive, feeling-oriented approach not only to religion. Soul is an approach to life itself and to every phase of it. That child will have to find her soul to find her place in the Negro world. That is your challenge, Mrs. Rosen. And a few Sundays or a thousand won't change it. It will take more. Think about it. And if I can help, call on me."

He took her hand and covered it with his other hand. She stared up at him and nodded.

14

*R**ebecca was fumbling* in her purse for the keys to
the apartment when the door opened suddenly. David was
there to welcome them home. In his left hand, his forefinger
inserted to keep his place, he held a worn, old volume on
Torah interpretation that he browsed in from time to time out
of nostalgia for the early days, when his life had consisted of
religious study.

By the probing look in his eyes, Rebecca could tell that he
was most anxious about what had happened in church.

"Well?" he asked. "So? Tell me already."

"Look what I got, Uncle David," Elvira said, holding
out the new Sunday school instruction booklet she had received.

Rebecca had planned to introduce that subject more gingerly, with a proper prelude. David glanced at the illustration
on the booklet and, to Rebecca's great relief, said only, "Very
nice, my dear, very nice." But Rebecca noticed that he did not
return it to the child.

"Hungry?" Rebecca asked with forced enthusiasm. "Some
lunch, darling?"

"Oh yes!" Elvira said. "Can we be havin' . . . can we *have*
bagels, Aunt Rebecca? I love bagels."

"Of course. Bagels. Lox. Cream cheese. And don't forget
your milk."

Once the child was having lunch at the kitchen table, in
their bedroom behind the closed door, David asked, "So? Before I bust, tell me, what happened? What do goyim do in
church?"

"They sing a lot," Rebecca said.

"What's the matter? Jews don't sing?" he asked defensively.

"Yes, but it's different."

"What do you mean, different? Singing is singing," he insisted. "The words, yes, the words are different. We sing in Hebrew, they sing in English. Or is it Latin?"

"Catholics sing in Latin," Rebecca pointed out.

"All right, so Negroes sing in English. What else?"

"When they sing, they clap hands. And they sway."

"In the middle of praying they clap hands? What is it, a vaudeville show?" he demanded impatiently. "I never heard of such a thing!"

"I know it seems strange to you. It did to me when I first saw it. Until I realized those people are more a part of their religion, their prayers, than any people I've ever seen."

"Rebecca! Are you saying those people believe more, pray better than Jews?"

"No. Only, what they feel, they express. Each on his own or her own. When they feel it and as they feel it," Rebecca tried to explain.

"Don't they read prayers out of a book together?"

"A few. Mostly they say it by singing. Then the minister delivers a sermon."

"Aha! Finally, thank God! Something that makes sense! So what was the sermon about?"

"Passover."

"Passover!" David exploded. "What do they know about Passover?" he demanded, insisting on his proprietary rights in what he considered his own personal holiday.

"You heard about the Last Supper?"

"I know, I know. I saw a painting once."

"Well, the Last Supper," Rebecca ventured gingerly. "That was a Passover seder."

"*Who said?*" David demanded indignantly.

"That's the way it's written in their Bible."

"If you're going to believe what's in *their* Bible . . ." he tried to dispose, but then asked, "All right, so what did this minister say in his sermon about Passover?"

"He said Passover was a celebration of freedom, that Negroes in this country still don't have real freedom. But when they do, they should have the same humility as . . ."

Rebecca paused, realizing that she had led the conversation right to the one name she had wanted to avoid.

"The same as?" he coaxed anxiously.

"It seems that . . . that at the seder, Jesus washed the feet of all his disciples—to show them that even the greatest of them was no better than the least of them." She debated continuing and finally did. "I thought that was . . . was quite . . . quite nice."

"Nice, shmice. What did that minister *really* say?"

"I just told you."

A dubious look in his eyes, he asked, "You mean to tell me he said nothing against Jews?"

"David, if you knew the man, you'd know he wouldn't ever say anything like that. In fact, those people are more like us than I realized."

"I'm relieved. Very relieved. I would not want Elvira to change her feelings about us . . . because of something she heard there."

"I'm sure she won't."

"Good, good," he said. Then, more brightly. "We're standing here talking and I'm starving! Let's have some lunch!"

She had served David his bagels, lox, and cream cheese with a steaming glass of coffee. As had become a custom, she filled another glass with milk, adding just a few drops of coffee to turn the color from pure white to very light tan. This was Elvira's and made her feel quite grown-up.

As David ate, he asked, "So, Elvira, you liked it there in that church?"

"Oh, yes. Such a nice teacher. And Pastor Wilder, I like him."

"Rebecca tells me they sing a lot," David said.

"Yes," Elvira replied.

"Show me," he coaxed.

Proud to demonstrate, Elvira was quick to put down her glass and rise to her feet. She took a place in the center of the kitchen. She began to sway from side to side, clap her hands, and sing:

What a friend we have in Jesus
All our sins and griefs to bear
What a pri-vi-lege to car-ry
Ev-erything to God in prayer.
O, what peace we of-ten for-feit
O, what need-less pain we bear
All because we do not car-ry
Ev-erything to God in prayer.

From the very mention of the name Jesus, David listened with forced but fragile patience. Rebecca hoped he would not give vent to his anger. Elvira finished. She turned to David for approval.

"You have a very sweet voice, my dear. Very sweet," he said.

Later, in the privacy of their bedroom, he observed to Rebecca, "She does have a lovely voice. And as songs go, not bad. As a matter of fact, very nice. But did it have to mention . . . him? You know—Jesus?"

In a timid voice that concealed her determination to see this through, Rebecca suggested, "David, I'm afraid you'll have to get used to that. Unless—" But she did not continue.

"What means unless?" he asked. "You women have a way of torturing us. I just happen to mention . . . I barely mention I would like that song better without mentioning *him*. The next thing, like some kind of *shtuch*, some little jab in my side, you say unless. Then you let it hang like a sword over my head. So, my dear devoted wife, what follows *unless*? Hm?"

Softly, gingerly, Rebecca replied, "Unless you think it is a serious mistake, Elvira being here."

"Did I say such a thing?" he demanded at once. "Or even think such a thing?"

"Then I'm afraid you'll have to get used to that," she reiterated.

"You see! That's exactly what I mean. No matter what I say, things always wind up your way. Okay, okay! So I'll get used to it. But I am never going to that church! Never!"

"David, my dear devoted husband, who invited you?"

"What's the matter? I'm not good enough? Or you think I would stand up and make trouble? If I want to go, I'll go. But I don't need permission from you or anybody else!"

It was Friday afternoon. Rebecca had chopped into a fine mixture fillets of whitefish and carp. She added some matzo meal for consistency, then spiced the mix with salt and pepper. She was now ready to form the pinkish concoction into individual portions. Around each she would wrap some of the skin she had saved from the fish, to hold each portion together while it cooked in a savory broth of carrots and other vegetables she had added for flavoring.

She was interrupted by the sound of the front door opening. She called out, "Darling?"

"Yes, Aunt Rebecca!" Elvira called back as she came racing into the kitchen. "Look! Look what I got!" She flaunted a paper she took out of her bookbag.

Rebecca wiped her damp hands quickly on her apron, took the sheet from Elvira's outstretched hand. "My, my, another one hundred in arithmetic! Wonderful, darling, wonderful! Now, come have your milk and cookies. To keep up your strength."

"I got pretty good strength," Elvira said. "My gym teacher said I do."

"Of course. From the milk and cookies. I baked some fresh ones today. The kind you love. The flat ones with sugar and cinammon on top."

Elvira sat down at table while Rebecca poured her milk and placed three cookies beside the glass. Rebecca returned to her fish, asking, "So what else happened in school today?"

"Aunt Rebecca, Mayor Walker. Is he Jewish?"

"No, darling, he's not."

"Then why does he have the same first name as your father?" the child asked.

Rebecca smiled. "No, darling, mayor is a title. Mr. Walker is the mayor of this whole city. Like Hoover is the president. And that title is spelled m-a-y-o-r. But my father's name is spelled M-e-i-e-r. They only sound the same."

"I see. Mayor and Meier." But she was still puzzled. She came to the stove to watch Rebecca forming her fish portions and placing them in the large aluminum pot.

"What are you doing?"

"Making gefilte fish. You know, like we have every Friday night."

"Is that what it looks like?" Elvira asked, staring at the pink gelatinous portions wrapped in fish skin.

"Before it's cooked. You see, I take the fish—two different kinds. I chop them in that wooden bowl with that chopper soaking in the sink. Then I add some matzo meal, salt, and pepper, until it is thick enough to hold together like this. Then I do what I'm doing now. Would you like to help?"

"Oh yes!" Elvira said.

"Take a handful. Like this."

Slowly, Rebecca reached her right hand into the mixture. The child imitated her. Rebecca used her left hand to pat the amorphous mass into a semblance of a portion. Elvira tried but did not quite succeed. But Rebecca encouraged her: "Very nice, darling, very good."

"Not so good as yours," Elvira said truthfully.

"It takes practice, years of practice. I learned from my mother. She learned from her mother."

"Will you teach me?" Elvira asked.

"Of course, darling. Next Friday I will not start the fish until you come home from school."

"Oh good!" Elvira beamed. "Next Friday."

The child picked up her bookbag on her way to her room. Rebecca tended the other pots on the stove. In the largest one, a chicken was boiling in water, making a fragrant broth from the parsley, carrots, celery, and other tangy vegetables. The soup was almost done. She added the matzo balls she had prepared earlier. She turned back to tend her gefilte fish. As she did, she recalled the words she had spoken to Elvira:

It takes practice, years of practice. I learned from my mother. She learned from her mother.

It became distressingly clear to Rebecca Rosen. This is *not* what little Elvira Hitchins would have learned from her mother, who before that would have learned from *her* mother.

Pastor Wilder's message came back to her with sudden and striking impact: Soul is an approach to life itself, and to every phase of it.

Negroes do not eat gefilte fish. Or matzo balls. Or bagels and lox. If one day Elvira is to take her proper place as a Negro woman in her own world, no amount of instruction in kosher cooking would help.

For the rest of that day and evening, Rebecca was tormented.

15

"*You don't have* to walk me to school," Elvira said on Monday morning as Rebecca was slipping into her coat.

"I thought since I have to go out we could go together. Wouldn't you like that?"

"Oh yes!" The child was delighted. Her black eyes lit up.

At the schoolyard gate, Rebecca kissed her and started off on her own mission. She walked quickly north on Fort Washington Avenue toward the Eighth Avenue subway station. While still a block away, she strained to see. The usual collection of cleaning women was waiting. Two white women were also there, bargaining for a day's housework with the Negro women, who competed for the paltry opportunity.

As Rebecca approached, she could overhear the disheartening transactions in process.

"Yeah, ma'am, I do floors, windows, laundry, anything you aks," one older woman said. "'N I got 'sperience. More'n some of these younguns."

The white woman approached her, decided the woman was too old to be energetic enough for the work. She bypassed her to negotiate with a younger woman. The old woman grabbed her by the arm. "I be tellin' you, I kin do it, lady! I'm not old. I jes look old! And I is strong! Real strong!"

The white woman broke loose. "You touch me again and I will call the police!"

The old woman fell back, withdrawing her hands as quickly as if she had been burned. "Sorry, ma'am. I din' mean no harm. Nothin'."

Rebecca waited until the other women had completed their bargaining and departed with their day helpers. The Negro women who were left looked around, staring up and down the block to see if any other buyers were approaching. None

were. They began to drift away. Some started down the subway stairs, others walked. Another five-cent fare to complete
a futile trip was a waste of precious pennies. The old woman
started slowly toward the stairs, reaching for the handrail to
steady herself.

Rebecca called, "Lady! You!" The old woman turned with
a curious but gingerly look on her wrinkled face. More than
her age, it betrayed the difficult life she had led.

"Missus, you callin' me?"

"Yes. Can I talk to you?" Rebecca asked.

"Don' cost nothin' to talk," the old woman said, but it was
apparent that she was growing suspicious and tense.

As Rebecca drew close, several of the younger women
gathered to form a protective guard around the old woman.

"I don't mean any harm. I just want to know, do you
cook?" Rebecca asked.

"Cook?" the old woman repeated skeptically. "Lady, one
look 'n I know you Jewish. I don' cook for no Jewish folks.
Tried that once. You heard that spiritual 'Nobody Knows the
Trouble Ah Seen'? Well, nobody has seen trouble till they
cooks for a Jewish lady. Can't mix milk with this. Can't mix
meat with that. Got to keep this dish from that dish, this pan
from that pan. They got some crazy law—"

"You mean keeping kosher."

"Yeah! Tha's it! Tha's the word." The old woman seized on
it. "They got to have difrint sets o' dishes for difrint things."

"One for meat meals and one for dairy," Rebecca explained.

"'N God forbid you make a mistake. Darn fool woman
blame me. Says now she be throwin' out the pan I used. Unclean. So I said, 'Don' take no fit, lady. I will scour it good,
real good.' Wasn't good enough for her. So, no thank you,
lady. No cookin' in no Jewish house. Not for me!"

Patiently, Rebecca tried to explain, "I don't want you to
cook kosher food. You may not have to cook at all." Her
strange statement evoked even more suspicion from the
young women, as well as the old woman herself.

"First you aksin' kin I cook. Then you say I don' have to
cook. What you got in mind, lady?" the old woman demanded.

"For reasons, certain reasons, I have to learn to cook what Negroes eat," Rebecca explained.

The old woman stared at Rebecca, looking into her eyes deeply. She took Rebecca by the arm and drew her away from the other women. She lowered her voice to ask, "Lady, you tryin' to tell me somethin'? Like you are thinkin' of marryin' a colored man? Ain't there 'nough trouble in this sad world without you stirrin' up more?"

"I am married to a nice Jewish man. But I have a problem. And I think you can help. I'm willing to pay you for a day's work. It's that important."

"I kin help you?" the woman asked skeptically.

"Yes. Come with me. I'll explain. And I will pay you, I promise. In fact, if it will help convince you, I'll pay you in advance. Right now."

The old woman obviously believed her, for she said, "No need, no need. Le's go."

Once home, Rebecca started to explain her need to learn about Negro food and how it was prepared.

"I want you to know how important it is that I learn to do it right, Mrs . . ." Rebecca halted, unable to continue.

The woman realized and informed, "Custis, Martha Mary, being named for the two sisters of Lazarus."

"You can see, Mrs. Custis, how important it is,"

"You bringin' up this Negro child?" the old woman asked.

"Her name is Elvira. Just turned nine. I want to be able to teach her how to cook like a Negro woman. Someday she will have to."

"Yeah, yeah, I kin 'preciate that," the old woman said, great sadness in her voice. "Lord help us, how this is goin' to turn out."

To ease the woman's deep concern, Rebecca explained, "I've started her in Sunday school and church."

"Tha's good, tha's helpful," Mrs. Custis said. "Now, le's get to the cookin' business."

"First, what kind of foods do Negroes like to eat?"

"Eat or *like* to eat? They's two different things. We eats what we kin afford. But if there be a choice, we like chicken, ribs, greens, cornbread. 'Course pork chops is big eatin' with colored folks."

Rebecca hesitated for a moment, trying to decide how to broach the subject. "Jewish people don't eat pork chops. Or pork. Or ham."

"That kosher thing again?"

"Yes."

"Cornmeal. How 'bout that?"

"That's kosher," Rebecca said. "In fact, I have some here now. We use it to make *mamaligah*."

"Don' even bother to tell me what that means. We goin' to have 'nough trouble as it is," the woman said quickly. "But if'n you got cornmeal, whyn't we start with that? Make us some cornbread. Good with mos' anythin'. Even a glass of milk after school."

"Very good." Rebecca was pleased.

"Le's see. Got cornmeal. We needs some white flour, sugar, salt, baking powder, milk 'n eggs."

Rebecca hastened to produce each ingredient.

"Also, Ah'm goin' to need a nice big mixin' bowl, a ladle, 'n a pan. 'Less you got a cast-iron skillet. They's best."

With all the equipment and ingredients before her on the kitchen table, Martha Custis rolled up her sleeves, washed her hands at the sink, and was ready to commence. Rebecca watched her closely, writing down precise notes as the woman began by mixing cornmeal, flour, baking powder, and milk, stirring it into a batter. Then she cracked and added two eggs and mixed the batter once again.

After she stirred the mixture with great energy, she raised a ladleful to let it drip slowly back into the bowl. The yellow mixture met with her expert approval, for she said, half to herself, "Now, how I forget that? Never forget in my own kitchen. Lady, we needs to heat up that skillet."

Rebecca moved swiftly to turn on the gas flame in the oven.

"Lady, lady," the old woman interrupted. "First we got to grease it. Got some lard?"

"Lard?" Rebecca repeated in such dismay that the old woman shook her head.

"I knew it'd come to this. Jewish people don' use lard."

Rebecca had joined her on the last three words, ". . . *don't use lard.*"

"Well, we got to grease this skillet with something," the old colored woman said. "Crisco? What about that?"

"Crisco might be . . ." Then Rebecca remembered, "*Nyafat!*"

"What kind of fat?" the puzzled woman asked.

"*Nyafat*. It's made especially for Passover. To use instead of butter or chicken fat. Because it's *pareveh*."

"It's *what*? Or maybe I'm better off not askin'."

"*Pareveh* . . . well, that means it can be eaten with both meat and dairy products."

The woman's eyes opened wider. "First you say you can't mix meat and milk, now you tell me this parvey thing is okay with meat and milk."

"You see, the rules are—"

"Lady, please don' 'splain. Because the more you 'splain, the more confusin' it gets. If that stuff you mention is any kind of fat at all, it'll do."

Once she had rubbed a light layer of *Nyafat* on the bottom and sides of the skillet she poured in the mixture, then placed the skillet in the oven.

"'N now we jes' wait for nature to do its work. Since we got the time, we better get on to your other troubles."

"Troubles," Rebecca commented with great concern.

"'Tween what we colored folks eat and what you Jews ain't allowed to eat, a person kin starve to death. 'Course now, chicken, you can't have nothin' against chicken. I remember Mrs. Shapiro, she's that lady I tol' you I walk out on, I 'member she was serving chicken soup all the time. Can't make chicken soup less'n you use chicken."

"Oh, chicken is fine. As long as it's kosher."

"Lady, you messin' me around? You mean there's some chickens ain't kosher?" the woman asked, shaking her head in confusion. "How you tell the one from the other? By color? Like white folks do with us?"

"Oh no," Rebecca protested.

"Then how you tell?"

"Well, first the chicken has to be completely healthy."

"Ah 'gree with that," Mrs. Custis said.

"Then it has to be slaughtered by a *shochet*." The frown of doubt on the colored woman's face made Rebecca explain, "A *shochet* is a man authorized by the rabbis to slaughter animals without pain. Then when we get the chicken home we open it up, get rid of the insides, spread the chicken on the drainboard, sprinkle a lot of coarse salt on it, and let it drain."

"Salt?" the woman questioned. "Coarse salt? Could kinda ruin the taste."

"Oh no," Rebecca explained. "We wash all the salt off before we use it."

"Then why do you put it on in the first place?"

"Helps drain out the blood," Rebecca explained. "Jews aren't allowed to eat meat or chicken which contains any blood."

"And after all that, you still got 'nough chicken to do with?"

"Oh yes," Rebecca insisted.

"Well," the skeptical woman conceded grudgingly, "we could try. But Ah got mah doubts."

"What were you going to do with chicken?" Rebecca asked.

"Ain't nothin' in this world tasty as good home-fried chicken. *Mah* home-fried chicken! 'Course mine's done in lard. But that *Nyafat* stuff might do if'n folks don' know better."

"Can you show me?" Rebecca asked. "It wouldn't take long. The butcher's just down on the corner."

"Well . . ." the woman considered, then conceded, "Figure we could try. 'Course I don't have my spices 'n all."

"I have lots of spices," Rebecca said.

"We give it a try," Martha Custis finally consented.

Rebecca grabbed her jacket off the hall rack and was on her way down the stairs when she stopped suddenly. *What am I doing, leaving a total stranger in my home alone? The woman could rob me blind and be gone before I ever get back. And especially a colored woman. Relatives, friends, neighbors warn me all the time: You can't trust them. When they come to clean, you have to watch them every minute.*

She was tempted to invent some pretext and turn back when it struck her. *What am I thinking? Pastor Wilder is colored. Could that man ever be dishonest? And those people in his church. Dishonest? Definitely not. So why am I trembling with doubt about leaving that harmless old woman alone in my home?*

* * *

Rebecca returned with a freshly killed chicken. To save time she had had Olinsky, the butcher, clean it inside and out so all she had to do was place it on the drainboard, tilt the board over the sink, and sprinkle a few handfuls of salt over it. Once the mix of salt, blood, and water began to drain slowly into the sink, she took Mrs. Custis into the living room, where they could both relax.

"Coffee?" Rebecca asked.

"Can't do no harm," the woman replied.

Over coffee the women exchanged bits of information. Rebecca told how she came to have Elvira in their home. Mrs. Custis related how she was born the same year that her mother was set free. "Wasn't much use to bein' free, my mama used to tell me. Hard times. Very hard times. That's why I come up North. To find a new day and a new way. But things no better up here. I keep tellin' my little ones, the gran'children, that is, how things are goin' to get better for them. But I can tell you, Mrs. Rosen, in my heart I don' hardly believe it. When I look at this picture of your little Elvira, I think, this chile'll grow up with all sorts of strange ideas. Till she runs into that world out there. They gonna tell her what she is. And what she ain't."

Improvising with Rebecca's collection of spices, Mrs. Custis mixed them in with the flour. She dipped the cut-up parts of the freshly koshered chicken into egg batter, then into flour, and placed them in the deep cast-iron frying pan that bubbled with *Nyafat*. She needed no timer or clock to tell her when to turn the pieces. While she watched and turned, she continued to talk.

"Greens, ma'am. Colored folks need their greens. Collard greens or mustard or turnip greens. You kin get 'em at any store in Harlem or maybe over on Amsterdam. First you pick 'em."

"Pick 'em?" Rebecca asked.

"Break off part of the long stems. Then wash 'em. Chop up the big leafs. Meantime, you is boilin' up the water. While that is goin' on, you drop in a nice piece of pork to flavor it—" She stopped abruptly. "Ah know, Ah know. No pork. Well, a bit of somethin' for flavor'd do. Once that is cookin' up pretty lively, you drop in the greens. Add some salt. Your own

taste'll tell you how much. Then, when it's done, add a little
pepper. 'N at the end, just a touch of la . . . no, better make
that butter," the old woman corrected hastily.

"Butter if the greens are served with dairy. And chicken
fat if with meat," Rebecca agreed.

"Exactly," Mrs. Custis agreed. "'Course colored people is
big on fried pork chops smothered in gravy. But I seen veal
chops used 'stead of pork. 'Less you Jewish folks has anything against veal."

"No. I can get kosher veal at my butcher's," Rebecca said.

"Well then, all you do, you spice them chops up good
with pepper, salt, garlic, or seasoning salt, dip 'em in flour,
then right into a hot, oiled skillet. Mind, you got to turn 'em
often, like this chicken. Till they done."

"You know, we do the same thing," Rebecca said.

"You do?"

"We use veal chops, of course. But we dip them in matzo
meal instead of flour and we use chicken fat instead of lard.
But it comes out very much the same," Rebecca explained.

"'Course the gravy is the important part. Once you take
those nice brown chops out, you add some flour to what's lef'
in that skillet. Stir it up real good till it makes a thick paste.
Then you adds hot water, maybe another dash of pepper, and
it's ready. You pour that over the mashed potatoes or the
chops."

"We pour the chicken fat over the potatoes," Rebecca said.

"Ah don' know about chicken fat, but you set my dish of
chops and gravy before a man, with some greens and cornbread, that man is goin' to b'lieve he is in heaven. You Jewish
folks b'lieve in heaven, don' you?"

Thinking it unwise to open that subject, since some religious Jews believed in heaven and some did not, Rebecca
simply nodded.

"Guess we take a look at that cornbread now."

Toothpick in one hand, potholder in the other, Martha
Custis opened the oven door. She stuck the toothpick into the
cornbread, which was becoming a rich golden color, brown at
the edges. She pulled out the toothpick and examined it like a
doctor reading a thermometer.

"'Tain't dry yet." She shoved the pan back into the oven.

As she turned to Rebecca, her look of indecision made Rebecca uneasy.

"Something wrong, Mrs. Custis?"

"They is . . . they is one kind of eatin'. Well, I don' know." The woman debated.

"Why?"

"We got this dish called chitlins."

"Chitlins," Rebecca repeated in an effort to learn.

"They comes from . . . lemme see how to say this. In the old days, *my* mama's time, field niggers got to eat what vegetables they raised on their own. But for meat 'n other things they got what the white folks in the big house didn' eat or didn' want. Like parts of pigs, insides. You know?"

"Insides?" Rebecca asked, puzzled.

"Real insides."

"Oh, you mean the . . . the stomach, the intestines?"

"You said the word, I didn'," Mrs. Custis pointed out. "But that is it. Now, you be sayin' to yourself, How in the world kin folks even think of eatin' things like that? Well, I tell you how. You clean those pigs' intestines real, real good. Open each piece. Scrape off the fat. Then cut them up into pieces 'bout so long." She held her thumb and forefinger as wide apart as she could. "You soak 'em in saltwater overnight. Then you cook 'em with cut-up onion, chopped celery, lil season' salt, maybe a cup or so of chicken broth. You keep that simmerin' on the stove for a few hours and you got somethin' close to heaven. Oh, forgot. Peppers. Dried red peppers'll do wonders for the taste. 'Course later, if you like, you kin fry 'em. Dip 'em in egg, roll 'em in crumbs, and fry 'em. Now, you wouldn't 'spect in a million years that somethin' looks so grimy startin' out could wind up being so delicious, would you?"

"Why not?" Rebecca replied. "We do the same thing."

"You forgettin'. Them things come out of pigs."

"We do the same with cows' intestines—clean them, cook them. Only we fill them with stuffing and spices, then bake them and eat them. We call it *kishka*."

"Well, I'll be . . . Jewish chitlins," Martha Custis remarked in surprise. "Mrs. Rosen, you think maybe sometime way back, I mean back in Bible times, we was the same, one people?"

"Could be," Rebecca said.

"Time to test that cornbread again."

This time the toothpick came out dry. Martha Custis removed the pan from the oven to allow it to cool. She turned back to her frying chicken. Satisfied with the rich brown color, she forked the pieces out of the hot oil onto a clean white kitchen towel to permit the excess oil to drain off.

The golden pieces looked so tempting, smelled so delicious, that Rebecca could not resist. "May I?"

"They wasn't made for show."

Rebecca tasted a leg. The coating itself was delicious. The meat was so tender it came off the bone begging to be eaten. "Mrs. Custis, this is the best-tasting chicken I've ever had."

"'Course you ain't had gravy with it, nor grits."

"You'll have to show me. One day a week, say, every Tuesday, you come up and teach me so I can teach Elvira. Bring what you need and I'll repay you. As long as—"

Mrs. Custis interrupted. "Ah know. Long as it's not lard or that other stuff that ain't kosher."

Rebecca smiled. "Yes, as long as you understand."

"Ah din' say I understand, I only said I know what to bring."

After Martha Custis left, Rebecca returned to the kitchen. She picked up the delicious fried chicken leg she had left half eaten and proceeded to finish it. She cut herself a sample of the cooling cornbread. It was fragrant, soft, crumbly, and very pleasing.

So this is colored food. Negro food, she thought. Why Negro food? Anybody with a taste for delicious food would love it.

16

*E*ach *Tuesday, Martha* Mary Custis arrived to instruct Rebecca Rosen in the art of Negro cooking. Soon Rebecca's file of recipes was expanded to include fried okra, fried catfish, the fillets of which had to be soaked in milk before breading and frying, dictating that the entire meal be of the dairy variety. She learned the mysteries of hoppin' John, made with black-eyed peas, rice, onions, black pepper, and water. In place of the pieces of bacon that Martha's recipe called for, they substituted corned beef. The result was less than Martha expected, but to spare Rebecca's feelings, she said, "It'll do. For them as don' know better."

Each week Rebecca passed on to Elvira her newly gained knowledge.

One Tuesday afternoon, when Martha Custis stayed later than usual to perfect Rebecca's technique with hoppin' John, she was still there when Elvira returned from school. It was the first opportunity the old woman had to see the girl. Once Elvira was absorbed with her after-school milk and cookies, Martha took Rebecca aside into the living room.

"My, my, what a pretty child. All the time you be talkin' 'bout her, even when I see her picture, I kep' thinkin' she black. Leastways, dark brown. But she is light. And such good hair, hardly kinky at all, 'n soft." She drew Rebecca as close as propriety would permit. "Comes the time, you make real sure she marries lighter."

"Lighter?" Rebecca asked, puzzled.

"The lighter the better," Martha Custis said. "Wish my daughter'd listened and done the same. Makes a big difference, Mrs. Rosen, big difference."

Rebecca Rosen had been indoctrinated into yet another of the mysteries of the Negro world in which Elvira would one day have to live.

*   *   *

After weeks of instruction passed on from Martha Custis to Rebecca Rosen to Elvira, the child was ready to attempt a meal on her own. They selected a night when, without apprising David, Elvira would prepare supper for the family.

Elvira and Rebecca waited impatiently for his return. While he was having his usual drink, he asked, "Well, Rebecca, what's for supper tonight?"

They both responded at once: "Fried chicken and cornbread."

"Fried chicken and cornbread? Cornbread is fine with a thick layer of butter, a nice fresh radish, or a slice of onion. But cornbread with chicken? This I got to see."

As they had arranged between them, Elvira brought the plate of cornbread to the table while Rebecca presented the platter heaped with fried chicken, freshly heated but still moist and glowing. David observed the ceremony with great curiosity, which continued to grow. When both offerings had been placed before him to serve, he asked, "So where's the cornbread?" When Elvira proudly pointed to it, David said, "Darling, this is not cornbread. Cornbread is a nice big piece of thick brown bread, a crust like shoe leather, with poppy seeds on top and inside, too. This, this looks like some kind of cake. Smells like it, too."

"No, Uncle David, it's delicious. I had some with my milk," Elvira said.

He turned to Rebecca. "Becca dear, tell her. Tell what is cornbread."

"This, David, is *really* cornbread."

"Impossible!" he insisted.

"No, darling. It's made from yellow cornmeal, eggs, and flavoring."

"See, already you're wrong. From yellow meal you don't make bread, you make *mamaligah*. However, to prove I am not stubborn, I will taste it." Which he did, the flaky bread crumbling as he brought it to his mouth. "Bad, it isn't. But cornbread? Absolutely not!" However, he did help himself to another piece.

He enjoyed the chicken enormously, remarking, "This chicken we could stand again sometime. Very good. But now,

I got something I have to do. So if you ladies will excuse me."
With that, he rose from the table and started for the front
door.

"David?" Rebecca called out, puzzled by his sudden departure.

"I'll be back," was all he said.

David Rosen entered Moscowitz's bakery, which was just
two doors north of the corner of Broadway and 176th Street.
Moscowitz was waiting on one last customer, who was selecting from among the remains of the coffee cakes he had baked
early that morning. Once the woman left, Moscowitz addressed David: "Well, Rosen, what can I do for you?"

"I would like to see a nice piece of cornbread," David said.

"I got left only one piece, little more than a pound."

David interrupted. "Don't tell me! Just bring out a piece of
cornbread!"

Moscowitz shrugged, went back to the bread case, and returned with the remainder of what that morning had been a
round five-pound loaf of brown, thickly crusted bread, fragrant with the tangy aroma of rye and poppy seeds.

Adopting the same imperious tone as David had employed, Moscowitz said, "Here! Cornbread!"

"Exactly!" David said. "*This* is cornbread."

"It's what you asked for," Moscowitz began to argue.
"No?"

"Yes!" David agreed, also argumentative.

"So do you want it or don't you?" Moscowitz demanded.
"Because I'm getting ready to close up."

"First tell me something," David said. "How do you make
cornbread?"

"Why? You thinking of going into the bakery business?
Take my word for it, Rosen, you wouldn't like it. Up at four in
the morning to start baking. Rolls, bread, cakes, cupcakes,
cheesecakes, all kinds pastries. So they can be ready for seven
o'clock when I open up. Then they come in, the *all rightniks*.
Especially that Mrs. Blumenthal. One day she doesn't like
this; and the next day she doesn't like that. Believe me,
Rosen, it's no fun. Stay in the hat business!"

After having patiently endured Moscowitz's plaint, David asked once more, "So tell me, how do you make cornbread?"

"But why—" Moscowitz tried to ask.

"Just tell me!" David was beginning to shout in frustration.

"All right, all right." Moscowitz tried to mollify him. "First, rye flour. Then white flour. A little salt. And water, of course. You mix it all together and knead it."

"That's all?" David asked.

"Of course. What else?" Moscowitz asked, puzzled.

"Cornmeal, cornmeal!" David insisted belligerently.

"Rosen, please, don't get excited. There is no cornmeal in cornbread."

"Then how can you call it cornbread?" David demanded.

"It's been cornbread since before I was born and it will be cornbread after I'm gone."

"I can't believe it. Cornbread without cornmeal," David realized.

"Look, Rosen, you want this piece bread or not?" Moscowitz demanded.

Embarrassed, David said, "You don't think I come into a bakery and then don't buy bread, do you?"

When he returned to the apartment, Rebecca was going over Elvira's arithmetic homework at the kitchen table. He entered and put down the bag containing the piece of cornbread.

"Here," he said, a defeated and humbled man. "A Jewish miracle. Cornbread without corn. After all, why not? If we could make matzo while fleeing from Egypt, why couldn't we make cornbread without corn?"

After Elvira had gone to sleep and David was having a late-night glass of coffee with Rebecca, he asked sheepishly, "Becca darling, you got any of that other cornbread left?"

"Half a pan."

"Cut me a little piece. Not too little, you understand? With some butter, a little jelly, couldn't be bad."

From that night onward, Elvira's cornbread made from cornmeal became a staple in the Rosen household, as much so as bagels and that other, tougher, cornbread made from rye flour.

Rebecca set aside one night every week for Elvira to prepare one of the dishes she had learned under instructions from Martha Mary Custis: fried chicken, okra, collard greens, cornbread, fried catfish, veal chops and gravy, chicken and dumplings.

To which dish David always remarked, "Why call them dumplings when they are so much like matzo balls?"

Eventually, there was hardly a meal that was purely of one cuisine or the other. Most meals were a blend of both. All of which David enjoyed, though he often took the opportunity to remark, "Very good, Elvira, delicious. In fact, with a little chicken fat, you couldn't tell it from my mother's."

Whereupon he would launch into a detailed description of how his mother used to remove the fat from the chicken, simmer it in a pan with an onion until the fat was reduced to a thick liquid that, when it congealed, became a rich and tasty spread for bread or matzo or for use in cooking.

To tease him, Elvira would ask mischievously, "Uncle David, is that like drippin's?"

"Darling, believe me, between 'drippin's' and chicken fat there is absolutely, positively no comparison."

After which he would dig in and proceed to enjoy Elvira's culinary contribution to the evening supper.

Meantime, Rebecca Rosen had the satisfaction of knowing that when the time came for Elvira to be a wife and a mother, she would be prepared for her role.

Elvira stood in the doorway of the Rosens' new bedroom watching with wide-eyed curiosity as David tied his new tie into a neat, firm knot with the correct crease in the middle. When he noticed her dark eyes studying him, he smiled, anticipating her question.

"I learned how to do this from a window trimmer at Macy's. Every time I pass through Men's Shirts to get to Men's Hats, I notice how the ties on the display dummies are always neater and straighter than they are on real men. So I asked one day. And he was nice enough to show me how it's done. He said, 'Tie a dollar tie this way and it will look like a five-dollar one.' And, my dear, as you can see, he's right.

Now, does that answer the question that put those little wrinkles in your nice smooth forehead?"

"No," the child said simply.

"No?" David demanded, hurt that his explanation had failed to satisfy her. "What did you expect, that I would write you a book on how to tie a tie?" The hurt look on Elvira's young face made him reach out. "I'm sorry, my dear. Come here."

She hung back until he coaxed, "Please?"

She drew close. He lifted her face with a gentle finger under her chin. "When you get that look of curiosity in your bright eyes, you deserve a better explanation. What is troubling you tonight?"

"Holidays," the child said. "So many holidays."

"Why we are getting dressed to go to synagogue again so soon?" David asked. The child nodded. "You know, little one, when I was your age I never thought about that. I just took it for granted. After Rosh Hashanah, beginning the New Year, in ten days comes Yom Kippur, the day of atonement for all our sins during the past year. Then four days later comes a whole week of Succoth, when we celebrated harvest time in the olden days. And the very next day is Shemini Atzerteth, which now even most rabbis don't know what it's for.

"You know, sometimes I think there are two possibilities why Jews have so many holidays. Either because we are such an ancient people that we've had more time to collect holidays, or else we've had so much suffering in our history that we invent holidays to have something to celebrate."

He felt that he'd given Elvira a more than adequate explanation, until the child reminded him, "You didn't say anything about tonight."

"Tonight, ah, tonight," David Rosen said. "To me, it is the most important holiday of the whole year, next to Yom Kippur. Simchath Torah. A *simcha* means a celebration. And *Torah* is the Torah. So it means a celebration because God has given the Jewish people the Torah. Understand?"

Instead of acquiescing, Elvira asked, "Torah, what is that?"

"The Torah is . . . well, it's the first five books of the Bible. What Christians call the Old Testament. And it is written by hand, word by word, letter by letter, on parchment scrolls."

"On scrolls?" Elvira asked, her forehead wrinkling once more.

"Of course, on scrolls. How else?" David asked, beginning to demonstrate by mimicking the rolling and unrolling of the traditional scrolls on which Jews had written the Bible for thousands of years. But when Elvira still did not seem satisfied, he stopped. "There is only one way to satisfy such an inquiring mind." He called out, "Rebecca!"

Accustomed to that cry for help, she came running from the kitchen.

"Yes, David?"

"Why not?" he asked.

"Why not what?" she asked.

"Why not get the little one dressed nicely and take her with us."

"If she would like to go, why not?"

"Exactly what *I* said," David pointed out. "So now, my dear child, you will actually see a Torah. And not have to depend on my poor description."

While Rebecca combed Elvira's hair and tied it neatly in ribbons, David explained, "In the Torah, Jews find not only their early history—the Creation, Adam and Eve, Noah and the flood, Abraham, Isaac, and Jacob, the story of Joseph and the slavery in Egypt and the Exodus to freedom, like you saw at Passover, and Moses and finding the Promised Land—but even more important, they find how to live a good life. How to follow truth, mercy, righteousness. A man could live a good, pious life by what's written in the Torah. Without it there would be no Jewish people."

He paused before revealing, "When I was younger—about your age, my dear, maybe a little older—I thought I would spend my life studying the Torah and the Talmud and the Commentaries, and possibly even add a bit of wisdom to what has come down to us through the ages. But it was not meant to be, not meant to be."

Elvira looked up into his eyes and thought she saw tears there. But she told herself, *Little girls cry, sometimes even little boys. But not grown-up men.*

On this night of celebration, the rabbi departed from the Orthodox practice and permitted whole families to sit together instead of confining women to the balcony.

The ceremony began with the gathering of all children to the center of the synagogue before the platform on which stood the ark. When Elvira hesitated, Rebecca urged her forward so that she stood under the outspread prayer shawl that served as a canopy over the children while the rabbi pronounced the same prayer the patriarch Jacob had intoned over his own grandsons.

Once the children had returned to their places, the rabbi drew back the deep maroon velvet curtain on which were inscribed in gold thread the Ten Commandments. He carefully pushed aside the wooden doors to reveal the contents of the ark: two large scrolls, decorated in silver and gold, adorned in velvet coverings. He drew out one of them and presented it to the two men who waited alongside him. They proceeded to undress it, first removing the crown of intricately carved silver, to reveal the finials of silver and gold that decorated the rollers of the scroll.

All this Elvira watched with her eyes fixed in wonder on the elaborate ceremony.

While one man held the scroll, the other man removed the breastplate that hung by its silver chain around the two rollers. Then he lifted off the purple velvet mantle with its gold decoration to reveal the Torah itself, the folded-up parchment, which was now held together by a wrapper of red silk. Then the man laid the scroll on the velvet covered table on which it would rest while it was being read.

"See, my dear," David whispered, indicating the naked scroll. "That is the Torah—each word, each letter, written by hand, by a holy scribe, as it has been done for thousands of years."

Meantime, an elderly man who required assistance to ascend the two steps to the platform, approached the Torah, and touched fringes of his prayer shawl to the place on the parchment at which he would commence to read. Having kissed the fringes, he read in Hebrew the final portion of the last of the five books of Moses, which were the epitaph of Moses himself after he had led the Israelites to, but not into, the Promised Land.

As soon as the old man had finished, the scroll was rewound to its beginning, and a younger man was summoned to read the opening words: *Barashess boroh Elohim* . . . "In the beginning God created the heavens and the earth . . ."

David drew Elvira close to whisper, "You see, my dear, this we do every year. We read a portion of the Torah during every week, until we finish on this day. Then at once, we start over again from the beginning. For thousands of years we have done this. And God willing, we will do it for thousands more."

The child nodded, but he could see in her eyes that his explanation was too complex for such a young mind to fully comprehend.

Then the Torah was dressed as it had been undressed and there began the part of the ceremony that was accompanied by joyous singing on the part of the congregation while each man in the synagogue had the honor of carrying one or the other of the Torahs in his arms while he walked the length of one aisle, across behind the last bench, and down the other aisle. Meantime, all those within reach stretched out their hands to touch the holy scrolls and then kiss their fingertips.

Of all this Elvira would remember most the look on David Rosen's face when it came his turn to carry the beloved Torah in his arms. After he had circled the synagogue and returned to the platform, he seemed reluctant to surrender it to the man next in turn.

So it went until every man, age thirteen or older, had performed this cherished duty.

On the way home, as Elvira walked between David and Rebecca, he asked, "Well, my dear, now do you know what a Torah is?"

"Yes, Uncle David," Elvira said. "But why—"

"And they say only Jews answer every question with a question," David remarked to his wife. "Yes, Elvira?"

"If the Torah is so important, why don't they let the women carry it too?"

17

*R*ebecca and Elvira were returning from a visit to the Museum of Natural History, one of the treats she had promised the child for her good report card. She had just inserted her key in the lock when she heard the phone ringing. Something about its persistence made her hurry. She flung open the door to rush to the phone on the end table beside the living room couch.

"Hello?"

"Rebecca?" she heard her brother, Simon, ask.

She knew from the way he had spoken her name that there was trouble. Her only question was: *How serious?*

"Papa."

"What about Papa?" she asked, feeling a chill.

"A heart attack. At first the doctor said it wasn't serious. But an hour ago . . ." He broke off in mid-sentence. She heard him sob.

"I'll come right down to be with Mama!" Rebecca said.

She hung up, her mind a jumble of frantic thoughts.

Shall I call David at once, or not? Take Elvira with me or not? What about her if I don't take her? What about David's supper? What if he comes home to find no one here?

She was trembling with grief and uncertainty. Finally, she paused long enough to think more rationally.

David? No. I won't call him. Not yet. Elvira. There must be a way. Yes, I must arrange about Elvira.

She raced to the apartment next door and rang the bell. There was no immediate response. She proceeded to ring frantically. At last she heard the voice of her neighbor, Mrs. Veronica Dwyer. Though in the months since the Rosens had moved in they and the Dwyers had not been very close, whenever they met in the hallway or down at the front door, they were always polite and cordial.

"Michael, answer the door, will you?" Rebecca heard Mrs. Dwyer call out.

In a moment the door was opened by Michael Dwyer, a man in his early sixties, already retired on a city pension from his job as clerk in the county court. In addition to his pension, he had acquired one other characteristic from his previous civic employment. He was never to be found without a cigar in his mouth. During his years in the county court, he had been the recipient of a cigar from every attorney for whom he had ever filed a paper or to whom he had revealed a file. Now, retired, he still smoked cigars. He had a cigar in his mouth and the *Daily News* in his hand as he opened the door for Rebecca.

"Well now, and where's the fire . . ." Dwyer started to ask, a bit resentful. Until he saw the tears in Rebecca's eyes. "Oh, Mrs. Rosen. What's wrong? Veronica? Come quick. There's trouble. Mrs. Rosen, is it the child? Veronica!"

Veronica Dwyer came out of the kitchen, where she had been preparing supper, took one look, and exclaimed, "Mrs. Rosen, my dear child . . . you're crying. What happened? What's wrong?" She drew a handkerchief out of her apron pocket and wiped Rebecca's tears.

"My father . . . so I have to go be with my mother."

"Of course, my dear, you need someone to look after the little one." Mrs. Dwyer understood at once. "Well, send her in. I'll be glad to have her. Has she had her afternoon milk yet? And would you like for her to have supper with me and the mister?"

Greatly relieved, Rebecca said, "Thank you, Mrs. Dwyer, thank you very much."

On the evening of the next day, after Meier Silverstone had been laid to rest for eternity in a cemetery in Queens, David Rosen brought Rebecca back home. It had been decided that since Rebecca had the responsibility of caring for a child, she should not observe the week of mourning at her mother's. She would carry out the traditional ritual of shivah in her own home.

David was most considerate and respectful of her feelings. He fetched her slippers so she could shed her shoes in accord with custom. He was overly cautious as he tried to make the slit in the hem of her dress so that it did not destroy the dress for future use.

"David, it is only a gesture, a symbol—from biblical times, when people would tear their garments to indicate grief. Just cut it, and never mind the dress!"

"Sorry, sweetheart, I was only trying to—"

"I know what you were trying to do," Rebecca responded angrily, until she burst into tears again and sobbed. "I'm sorry, David . . . sorry . . . sorry . . ."

Shod in slippers, face washed, with no touches of powder or other makeup, attired in the simple dress with the razor slit in the hem, Rebecca was seated on the low crude box David had managed to secure from the fruit market. She was prepared to mourn for her father, whom she had not only loved but respected. During the next seven days, friends and relatives would come to call to express their condolences and exchange memories of old Meier Silverstone. Twice a day, early in the morning and late in the afternoon, ten Jews who would be gathered by the rabbi at their synagogue were to assemble in her home to take part in the morning and evening prayers so that Rebecca might intone the prayer of Kaddish, which one said for the newly departed.

All this had been arranged for her and still Rebecca felt something was missing.

"Elvira," Rebecca said through her tears. "Go next door, David, get her."

In moments she heard the front door open and then heard Elvira's troubled voice, "Aunt Rebecca?" She heard Elvira's footsteps move down the long hallway until she appeared in the archway to the living room. She came running across the floor to fling herself into Rebecca's arms, to press against her. Soon Rebecca felt warm tears on her neck. She gently urged Elvira back from her to see the tears trickling down her face.

"No, darling. No need for you to cry," Rebecca said, wiping back her own tears with the palms of her hands.

In the archway, Mrs. Dwyer waited uncertainly, unused to the mourning customs of another religion. "Now, if there's anythin' I can do. I mean, if you need the house tidied or shoppin' or anythin', don't you stand on ceremony. Mr. Dwyer and I'll be glad to help."

"Thank you, Mrs. Dwyer. Thanks for taking care of Elvira. I hope she wasn't any trouble."

"Trouble? Why, good Lord, that child is a pleasure. She was tellin' me about Jesus and all. Anytime you've need of it, we'll be glad to have her.

The child slipped out of Rebecca's arms to go off to her own room. She reappeared dressed in the dress Rebecca had bought her for her mother's funeral. In place of her shoes she wore her bedroom slippers. She came to Rebecca's side, slipped down onto the box alongside her, and took her hand. She was ready to join Rebecca in mourning.

"You don't have to, darling."

Elvira insisted on holding Rebecca's hand, patting it gently as she recalled Rebecca had done for her in the time of her own bereavement.

In the evening, friends and those relatives who lived uptown came to pay their condolence calls at Rebecca's house rather than make the long subway trip down to her mother's house. They brought delicious cakes, cookies, and candy, a symbolic way of sweetening the time of mourning.

Rebecca's Aunt Mollie, a large and domineering widow, took charge as she usually did at family functions. She accepted each gift of sweets, ransacked Rebecca's kitchen cabinets, appropriating plates, dishes, and bowls in which to lay out the delicacies.

The visitors exchanged memories of old Meier Silverstone, mostly amusing memories, hoping to elicit a smile, possibly even a laugh, from Rebecca. Except for an occasional forced smile, Rebecca was somber and dry-eyed, inhibited by the presence of others from giving way to the tears she felt need to shed.

She sympathized with their fruitless efforts to cheer her. But she became more conscious of the fact that many of them, not excluding Aunt Mollie, had come as much out of curiosity about Elvira as to pay their respects. She could tell what they were thinking by the first look they bestowed upon the child who sat beside her:

So this is the colored child she took in. Aren't there enough Jewish orphans who could use a good home?

As the evening wore on, David could sense the resentment building in her.

"Come, Elvira," he said. "We'll make some coffee. Come!"

The child left Rebecca's side to join David in the kitchen. When the coffee in the large percolator finished bubbling, he poured cup after cup.

"Go on, sweetheart, start taking the cups out, one at a time. But very carefully."

Holding the saucer in both her hands, walking with extreme caution so that the coffee did not slop over, Elvira served the first cup to Aunt Mollie. The woman accepted the saucer from her hands and smiled indulgently. "Very nice. Your mother would have been very proud of you."

David, standing in the doorway to the kitchen, was barely able to stifle the resentment he detected in Rebecca's eyes. With a pleading glance, he beseeched her not to give vent to her anger.

The visitors had left. Aunt Mollie, as usual, was the last to leave, and then not until she had made sure that all the cups and saucers were soaking in the kitchen sink. At the door, she said to David, "Such a nice child. And the way she served. Then later bringing the empty cups and saucers back into the kitchen. Frankly, if she was ten years older, I'd give her some day work myself."

Rebecca had overheard her, but she made no comment until after Elvira had gone to bed.

"David, that child is not going to grow up to be a day worker in someone else's house. Or a maid. She's too good for that. Much too good," Rebecca insisted.

"Becca sweetheart, I have in my shop a man named Lucas Simpson who has been to college for two years. He speaks better English than most people we know. Can I send him to Macy's or Altman's or Stern's as a salesman? No. Because he's a Negro. So what does he do? He blocks felt hats and sews in sweatbands. When there's a rush order, he delivers the finished hats to the stores. Is it fair, is it right? A college-educated deliveryman? Of course not. But that's the way of the world."

"Not for Elvira," Rebecca insisted. "I may not be able to change the *whole* world, but I can change *that* child's world!"

"It could be a mistake," David warned.

"How can it be a mistake?" she demanded.

"It could be a mistake to give her unreasonable ambitions and expectations. Else she'll find herself, like so many young Jewish doctors and lawyers, all educated and with no place to go. You'll break her heart one day."

"That child is not going to grow up feeling she has to be like her mother," Rebecca said with a finality that made David know her mind could not be changed.

18

*D*avid Rosen walked quickly past the towering Empire State Building at Fifth Avenue and Thirty-fourth Street. He looked up, as he always did when he passed this way on his route from B. Altman on Fifth to Macy's and Gimbel's on Herald Square. His envy of men with the daring to raise such a costly structure in a time of national adversity grew with each day. It gave him confidence as well.

Thus encouraged and determined, he directed his thoughts to the immediate problems of his business. Today, December 11, was not exactly a banner day for the hat business. People were thinking of Christmas. And for Christmas women bought their men shirts, ties, pajamas, sweaters, mufflers, gloves, shaving lotion, and a crazy new fad—a razor that worked on electricity. But no hats.

Because of that, it was doubly necessary to keep his own name and his product before the buyers and assistant buyers. What better way than with an appropriate gift at Christmastime? There was Callahan at Macy's, Joe Lacks at Stern Brothers, Vincent Riordan at Altman's. What would impress men like them yet not be too costly? Cash would be in poor taste. Gloves? You have to know the size. The same with shirts. Ties? You didn't need to know the size. But then they would be getting too many of them. Something . . .

His thoughts were interrupted by a sight far down 34th Street. People were gathering at the corner in that haphazard but urgent way that signaled some serious accident. Out of sheer curiosity and a sense of foreboding, David found himself running. As he drew closer, he realized the crowd was gathered at the doors to the bank on the corner. People were hammering on the metal gatework. Loud, angry voices demanded admittance.

Breathless, and in a sweat, David arrived at the corner to

realize that this was a branch of the Bank of the United States, a bank he passed half a dozen times every business day. Yet here it was Wednesday, a business day, only two weeks before Christmas and the bank was closed. A big bank, with sixty branches in the city, closed! Closed! Failed! Insolvent!

David felt relief, then a pang of guilt as he found himself thinking, *Thank God, not my bank.* Even before he could savor that shred of comfort, he was asking himself, *How do I know not my bank?* He resumed running. Down Seventh Avenue, 33rd Street, 32nd Street, 31st, block after block, faster and faster, sweating so profusely that despite the cold day, he felt his shirt sticking to his neck and back. He reached 23rd Street and Seventh Avenue. There on the corner was his own bank, the Public National. As he turned the corner, he discovered a crowd there as well. He felt a sudden sharp pain in the pit of his stomach. His bank too! He drew close to hear the uniformed guard calling out, "People! There ain't nothing to worry about. This bank is open! Get in line and you'll be taken care of. Just get in line! Everybody! Wait your turn and you'll be admitted!"

Sweaty, fighting to catch his breath, David Rosen took his place in line. When he finally reached the teller's window, the man inquired briskly, "Yes, sir?"

"Wallets," David replied. "Every man needs a new wallet . . ." The strange look on the teller's face made David realize his immediate situation. "I would like to withdraw twenty dollars."

It was late evening. Elvira had done her homework, taken her bath, kissed them both good night, and gone off to bed. Rebecca followed to hear her prayers and tuck her in. David had not reconciled to hearing the child say her prayers. He remained in the living room, making his list of business gifts. In the background, the Atwater Kent droned on about the most urgent news of the day—the failure of the Bank of the United States. There was talk of fraud; there were threats of criminal prosecution.

Rebecca returned. "David, I have to talk to you. About Christmas."

Without even looking up, he replied, "No problem. I have it all figured out."

"You have?" she replied, feeling somewhat encouraged.

"I decided this afternoon. Not only the perfect gift, but I can make a deal. Lieberman, on the fifth floor in my loft. He's in leather goods. I need exactly fourteen wallets. For fourteen of an item he should give me at least thirty percent off. Actually, I'm helping clear his overstock. Maybe fifty percent off. So if you want to worry about Christmas, worry about those poor people with their money in the Bank of the United States. People who saved all year in Christmas clubs and now can't get a penny out in time to buy presents."

"Yes. It is too bad," Rebecca agreed, debating with herself whether to raise her own question.

"How does it sound to a gentile to hear that a family named Marcus and another family named Singer are responsible? Marcus and Singer. Might as well be Cohen and Levy," David lamented.

Rebecca decided this was not the best moment to broach the subject. So she resumed repairing a rip in Elvira's bloomers, caused in her extreme effort to mount a gym horse, which had proved too high for her. Meantime, the radio droned on with more news about the great bank failure, augmented by speculations that hundreds if not thousands of other banks might be engulfed in the same disastrous situation.

"And all the while Hoover sits there in the White House doing nothing," David commented bitterly as he wrote out his list of Christmas-gift recipients.

Rebecca continued stitching Elvira's blue serge bloomers. When she had finished, she took them into the kitchen and set up the ironing board to press the seam so it would barely be noticeable. Not soon thereafter David entered and turned on the flame under the coffee pot. A bit self-conscious, he asked, "Happens there's some of that cornbread left over from supper?"

"The bread box. In wax paper. Keeps it fresh," Rebecca said, continuing to run the hot iron back and forth over the fresh seam.

He added some milk to his glass of coffee and seated himself at the kitchen table. Since he now seemed relaxed, Rebecca decided to risk it.

"David," she began, staring down at the bloomers so as to avoid looking at him. "I was thinking. Sunday in church, Elvira learned all about Christmas."

"Where else is she going to learn about Christmas? In shul?" Suddenly David exclaimed, "Aha! I can see already something is going on in that pretty head of yours. Okay! It's been a pretty good year. And since today we were lucky, my bank is still open, go ahead, buy her a Christmas present. I understand children like to get a lot of presents on Christmas. So buy her not *a* present but *presents, plural*. There! Happy now?" he beamed in self-righteous appreciation of his own open-minded, tolerant attitude.

"There's one other thing," Rebecca broached gingerly. "We will need someplace to put the presents."

"You're right!" David agreed at once. "Kids should be surprised so they can believe that Santa Claus brought them when they were asleep. Mrs. Dwyer! She wouldn't mind keeping the presents until we need them. She always says yes when it has to do with the little one. You know, she's such a nice woman, sometimes I forget she's Catholic. She'll be glad to do it."

"I know. I've already asked her," Rebecca admitted.

"So what's the problem?" David asked, until he began to suspect his wife was taking too roundabout an approach. "Rebecca?" he persisted in the rising inflection he employed at such times.

"When I said we need someplace to put the presents, I meant someplace to put them on Christmas morning," she said, then held her breath.

"Someplace to put them," he began to consider when suddenly it dawned on him. He exploded with a loud, "No!" He slammed his glass down on the kitchen table so hard that some coffee splashed over the flowered oilcloth. "I don't want to hear it! Not in my house!" he shouted, while Rebecca scurried to wipe up the coffee before it could run off the edge of the tablecloth onto the floor. David commenced pacing back and forth, continuing his tirade with a nonexistent third person, a tactic he used when he did not wish to confront his wife.

"You understand what she was saying? She wasn't even *saying*. She was *hinting*. When my Rebecca hints, wise men run and hide. Well, I am not hiding. I am saying right here, right now, there will be a Christmas tree in this house over my dead body! End of discussion!"

Meantime, Rebecca had poured him a fresh glass of coffee. As he turned, he caught her at it. "You're appealing to my softer side? At a time like this I *have* no softer side!" he proclaimed. "But you could add a little milk. Or do I have to do everything myself?" She poured just enough milk from the bottle to produce the exact shade of coffee he loved.

"There's more cornbread," she suggested softly.

"Cornbread," he seized on the word. "That's the way it starts. The minute I said we could have cornbread in this house, it began! Oh for the old days, when cornbread was cornbread, with an aroma that could tempt the dead back to life. But once you start with *this* kind of cornbread, yellow, soft, sweet, what comes next? Christmas trees! What else?"

He sat down once more, ate in silence, drank in silence, until he exploded: "How would it look? A menorah on one side of the room and a Christmas tree on the other? People would think we are *meshugge*." He turned again to his invisible colleague. "You ever heard of such a thing? A Christmas tree in a Jewish household? Only a woman could get such a crazy idea!"

"It's not a matter of believing," Rebecca pointed out. "After all, we don't believe in Christmas, but you are still going to give presents to those buyers."

"That's business," David protested.

"It wouldn't be something we did because *we* believed in it. It would be because *other* people believed in it. Like Mr. Callahan, the buyer at Macy's."

"Callahan is a devout Catholic. Naturally he believes in Christmas. So as a gesture of respect, I give him a gift."

"Elvira is a Baptist," Rebecca said. "She also believes in Christmas. Isn't she also entitled to a gesture of respect?"

"Don't be a Talmudic scholar on my time, thank you!" he declared. "It's not the same. With Callahan it's a matter of business. With the little one it's . . . it's just not the same."

"Are you telling me that business is more important than a child's feelings? David, you?"

"You're twisting my words. I am simply saying there will

be no Christmas tree in this house. Period. Exclamation point!" He rose brusquely. "I am going to bed!" He stalked out of the room.

Most of the night he tossed and turned. Rebecca lay beside him unable to sleep. She had expected his initial refusal, but not that it would be so vehement. She would ask Mrs. Dwyer to allow Elvira to find her gifts under their tree. It would be better than no Christmas at all. Thus resigned, she finally fell into an uneasy sleep.

When she awoke, dawn was just barely visible around the edges of the window blind. Instinctively, she reached behind her. David's side of the bed was empty. She rose hurriedly and started out to the living room, where she found him sitting in the darkness, rocking back and forth in deep thought.

"I remember when I was just a child back in the old country. I studied with Reb Shiman ben Shlomo, who himself had studied under the Vilna gaon, than whom there was no more religious Jew in all of Poland. He used to say—Reb Shiman, not the gaon—he used to say a man of goodwill can always find a way to make peace instead of war. What has been going on in this household in the last eight hours has been a war. And over what? My wife has this foolish, ill-conceived, sadly mistaken notion that there should be a Christmas tree in this house. If therefore she is so wrong and misguided, it behooves me, as a wise man of goodwill, to seek to effect some compromise to bring an end to this war."

Aware of his staunch pride, which often masqueraded as humility, she knew it was incumbent on her to say, "In times like this I'm happy for your early training as a *yeshiva bucher*. They say the wisdom a child learns in his early years shapes the man he becomes. As you proved that day with Principal Goodman. What kind of compromise, David?"

"There absolutely cannot be a Chanukah menorah and a Christmas tree in the same room!" he declared.

"Agreed."

"So, therefore, the menorah will be in the kitchen on top of the icebox. And the Christmas tree will be in the living room. But there is no need to have one of those tall ones like on the cover of the *Saturday Evening Post*. Somewhere there must be small trees. *Kleinichkeh* trees, about so high." He held his hand up to the level of the windowsill.

"Whatever you say, darling," Rebecca was quick to promise, now that she felt the battle almost won.

"Wait! Not so fast!" he interposed with dictatorial firmness. "You are never, you hear me, never to tell anyone in my family about this."

"Agreed. Anything else?" she asked.

"I am not going to put on a silly Santa Claus suit. Let Mr. Dwyer do that if he wants to, not me! Understood?" he demanded. "And if he does, tell him not to have that damn cigar in his mouth. He'll set fire to the beard!"

"Yes, David. I'll make sure to tell him."

"Now I got to take a shower and get dressed," he said, greatly relieved that the conflict had been resolved. "I have to get those wallets and some wrappings. Which reminds me, Rebecca, when I was in Macy's the other day I saw a doll there that I think the little one would like. Shall I get it for her?"

"A doll is always a nice gift for a little girl. Especially at Christmastime," Rebecca said, and kissed him.

Accompanied by Mrs. Dwyer, Rebecca Rosen participated in her first attempt at purchasing a Christmas tree. She was looking for one tall enough to delight the child yet small enough not to irritate her sensitive husband. At the neighborhood fruit market she found several trees that seemed to accomplish both purposes. But Mrs. Dwyer would reach out, rub the needles between her fingers, then with a single shake of her head indicate her disapproval. Only after they passed the tree would she whisper to Rebecca, "Too dry. Won't last the week."

Finally, they selected a tree that passed their criteria. Holding it by its crest, Rebecca followed Mrs. Dwyer to the neighborhood stationery and toy store, where she purchased a string of electric lights and some colored balls, red, green, and silver.

Back home, Rebecca placed the tree on its stand and stood it first in the corner to the right of the living room windows and then to the left. She decided the right side was the least obvious.

Now, for the first time in Rebecca Rosen's life, under Mrs. Dwyer's directions, she trimmed a Christmas tree. She wound the cord of the lights around and through the branches of the small tree. She hung a decorative ball here and there, as Mrs. Dwyer indicated, until there was a pleasing distribution of shiny red, silver, and green.

"Does it look all right?" Rebecca invited the older woman's approval.

"Fine, just fine, my dear." But then Mrs. Dwyer burst forth in a horrified, "Oh my God!"

"Mrs. Dwyer, what is it?" Rebecca asked. "Did I do something wrong? If I did, I'm sorry. Very sorry."

"Not you, child! Me. I forgot," she explained. "The star. The Star of Bethlehem. Every Christmas tree needs a star at the top."

"A star . . . a star?" Rebecca said, thinking, then, "I have one! I'll get it." She raced off to the bedroom, searched the upper shelf in the clothes closet for the shoe box in which she preserved all manner of odd keepsakes. She sorted carefully through a collection of old wedding invitations, bar mitzvah invitations, birth announcements, and notes she had received concerning memorable family occasions. At the bottom of the box, wrapped in tissue paper, was a gold metallic star she had received as a reward for sending in her *pushke* money for the pioneers in Palestine. She unwrapped it carefully. It was still whole and in good condition.

She presented the star to Mrs. Dwyer, who approved. Rebecca held it against the top branch of the small tree. When Mrs. Dwyer nodded, Rebecca used some yarn to secure it. Both women stood back to admire their handiwork. Rebecca felt a sense of accomplishment until Mrs. Dwyer said softly, "Oh, my dear . . ."

"What's wrong now?" Rebecca asked.

"Six points," Mrs. Dwyer explained with regret.

Baffled, Rebecca repeated, "Six points?"

"I don't know how to say this, child, but the Star of Bethlehem has only *five* points. That's the way it was, that star in the sky the night our Lord was born."

"But the Star of David always has six points."

"I know, I know," the woman said, greatly distressed at being confronted with such a serious discrepancy.

"Do you think it matters so much, five points or six?" Rebecca asked.

"Since I was a child I don't remember a Christmas tree with a six-pointed star," Mrs. Dwyer said with great concern. "Now, wait, just you wait. I think I may have one." She was gone. She returned some minutes later carrying an old, slightly tarnished silver star, explaining, "From the times we had the big tree at our house and the children were all there." She presented it to Rebecca.

It was just slightly bent, but carefully Rebecca managed to straighten it. She held it up against her own six-pointed star. Aside from size, there was little difference. But bowing to custom, precedent, and the religious convictions of Mrs. Dwyer, she began to loosen the yarn that held the Star of David in place. Mrs. Dwyer watched with approval until Rebecca suddenly stopped, saying softly, "I wonder . . ."

"Yes, my dear?" Mrs. Dwyer said.

"Going to church with Elvira every Sunday, hearing the Christmas story taught, I learned about when he was born. Jesus was a Jewish child, of the family of David."

"Yes," Mrs. Dwyer agreed gingerly, not knowing what to expect.

"Since he was of the house of David, why not both stars?"

Mrs. Dwyer's eyes widened with great concern. "Both stars?"

"One star for what he was born and one star for what he became. Kind of brings the two together."

Mrs. Dwyer took a moment to absorb the idea before she agreed. "What a nice thought, Mrs. Rosen. I must tell the mister."

Rebecca fixed both stars in place, the smaller one centered in front of the larger one. Mrs. Dwyer took in the total scene, then commented, "Very nice, my dear, very nice. Maybe add a little snow around the tree, but otherwise very nice. Unique, one might say. I'm sure Elvira will love it."

"Thank you, Mrs. Dwyer, for taking the time."

"A pleasure, my dear, anything for the little one."

Mrs. Dwyer had gone back to her own apartment. Rebecca stood in the living room, admiring the little tree with its lights, colors, and two stars, and thinking, *Five-pointed stars, six-pointed stars. On such little details hang the differences between peoples.*

When Elvira returned from school, she was delighted with her tree. She spent much time unplugging and plugging it to make the lights go off and on. Rebecca enjoyed the child's fascination with her first very own tree. Still, Rebecca was apprehensive. David had given his approval, true, but when confronted by the reality of this symbol of Christmas in his own home, how would he react?

Elvira had gone to her room to do her homework. Rebecca bustled about her kitchen, preparing a supper of chicken fricassee and noodles, all the while keenly aware of the clock on the wall ticking away. In another hour, maybe a little more, David would be back. Usually, he would come in and drop the *Times* on the armchair near the living room arch on his way into the bathroom to wash up. Then he would have his one drink of whiskey, settle down in his chair to read his newspaper, and listen to the radio news until he was called to supper.

But on this night Rebecca wondered: What would David do when he reached the arch and faced the reality of a Christmas tree, lit up and decorated? Rebecca continued working at the stove, in dread of the sound of the door being unlocked and opened. Finally, she heard it. She braced herself for his entrance.

"David?"

"President Hoover it's not," he replied.

He's had a bad day, or he's expecting one, she thought. She braced herself as she came out of the kitchen to see him reach the archway. He took only one look, then, without a word, dropped his newspaper and continued into the bathroom to wash up. He came out, poured himself his usual measure of whiskey, and drank it down in a single gulp. He went back into the living room, sat down, opened his *Times* with more than his usual angry rattle, then proceeded to lose himself in it. Though Rebecca could not read his face, his silence was warning enough. She hoped he would say nothing that would destroy the child's enjoyment.

Supper was silent in the main. Even Elvira became sensitive to the heavy mood, for she chattered only a bit before falling silent herself.

When supper was over, Elvira offered to help Rebecca clear the table, but she suggested the child go finish her homework. Elvira was gone only a short time, during which David sat in his chair, finishing his *Times* and only occasionally glaring at the tree in the corner. Rebecca continued to do the dishes, all the while thinking, *Don't say anything in front of the child, please.*

Soon Elvira returned, holding in her hand a single sheet of paper. She stood in the archway, hesitated, then said softly, "I wrote a poem." Slowly, David lowered his newspaper to stare. Rebecca came out of the kitchen, wiping her soapy hands on her apron.

"A poem, Elvira?" Rebecca asked. "Homework?"

"No," Elvira said. "Just 'cause I wanted to."

With a gingerly look to David, Rebecca said, "Well, darling, let's hear it."

The child set herself, cleared her throat, and swallowed several times before she was able to summon up the courage.

"Poem. By Elvira Hitchins," she began. Rebecca smiled to encourage her. She continued:

My Tree

I came home to see
A Christmas tree just for me.
With lights and colored balls
An' two nice stars and all.
So I said, I wish my mama was here
To see how much they care.

She broke off to explain, "They, that's you, Aunt Rebecca and Uncle David."

David cleared his throat but said nothing. Elvira assumed that to be an expression of criticism. She defended, "I know *here* and *care* don't exactly rhyme. I really wanted to say *love*, but *here* and *love* don't rhyme even worse. So I said *care*. Is that all right?"

Rebecca held out her arms. "It's a very nice poem, darling,

very nice." The child raced into her arms and they kissed. The child freed herself and went across the room to where David sat. She waited only an instant before he dropped his newspaper and took her in his arms.

"You know, Elvira, in Hebrew poems, the words don't rhyme."

"Poems that don't rhyme!" the child asked, astonished.

"In Hebrew poetry the ideas rhyme," David explained. He could see from the frown on her face that the concept was too intangible to grasp. "Let me see . . . how shall I . . . ah, I know. There is a psalm I studied as a child. It went like this," He was about to recite in Hebrew, but then realized, and translated, "A song of David, King David. It went like this: 'The Eternal God is my light and my salvation, whom shall I fear?' Second line: 'The Eternal God is the fortress of my life, of whom shall I be afraid?' See, same thought, said twice in different words. The thought rhymes, not the words."

It was evident from Elvira's expression that she required more. So he explained: "For instance, where you say, 'I wish my mama was here to see how much they care,' in Hebrew it would go like this: 'I wish my mama was here to see how much they care. Because it would make her happy to see how much I'm loved.' See, same idea said in two different ways. The ideas rhyme. So your poem is a very nice poem. And I was very proud of you as I listened to it."

"You think from now on I should write Hebrew poems?" Elvira asked.

David smiled. "I don't know how your Miss Hillgrove would feel about that. But for me Hebrew-type poems are good enough." He patted her on the cheek. "Now, it's after your bedtime."

The child ran off to her room, Rebecca following her to hear her prayers and tuck her in. When Rebecca returned, she found David wrapping the small cardboard boxes of wallets in bright paper but doing it very badly. She took the work out of his hands and started all over again. David had many virtues and talents; manual dexterity was not one of them.

They were both silent until she had wrapped the last box and he had written out the last card. As she was slipping the card under the ribbon, he said, "That poem was a nice thing for her to write. And she always thinks about her mother, which is also nice. She is a very thoughtful child."

"She's older than her years," Rebecca said. "I guess because she's lived through more."

"She really loves that tree, doesn't she?"

"You should have seen her face when she came home."

"I'll bet she was surprised, right?" David said.

"Surprised? Her eyes lit up like the lights on the tree."

"And why not? After all, it's no ordinary Christmas tree," David said in a way that made Rebecca turn to stare at him. "You know, Rebecca, going from store to store as I do, I see lots of Christmas trees. But somehow I have never seen a tree with *two* stars."

"Just an idea I had," she explained casually.

"A Star of David on a Christmas tree. Who else but my Becca would think of such a thing."

"Do you mind very much?" she asked.

"Mind? I'm relieved you didn't sprinkle salt on it to make it kosher." Then he smiled and said, "Come, Becca, come, time to go to bed."

On the following Tuesday when Elvira returned from school, she found Rebecca polishing an eight-branched candelabra of a kind the child had never seen before.

"What is that, Aunt Rebecca?"

"A menorah. This is the only thing David's mother left him when she died."

"Why are you polishing it now?"

"Because tonight is the first night of Chanukah."

"Chanukah?"

"It's a holiday Jews celebrate because more than two thousand years ago, the Syrians invaded our land. And they tried to force us to give up worshiping God and worship idols instead. But some Jews refused. And they fought the Syrians. And finally drove them out. Then the Jews took back their great Temple in Jerusalem. They cleaned it of the filth the Syrians had brought in. And they relighted the eternal light, which always used to burn there. But that light could only be fed by purified holy oil. And there was only enough oil for one day and one night. But, somehow, that little bit of oil kept on burning, for eight days and eight nights."

"Like a miracle?" Elvira asked.

"Like a miracle," Rebecca agreed. "So ever since, on Chanukah, we celebrate by lighting one candle on the first night, then two on the second night, then three and so on, for all eight nights. And we give gifts to one another."

"Like on Christmas," Elvira said.

"I wouldn't say that when Uncle David lights the candle tonight," Rebecca cautioned.

David Rosen stood at the kitchen table, prayer book in hand. He placed a single candle in the first of the empty arms of the menorah. Then he lit another candle, and while he held it, he recited the prayers. Then he used it to light the first candle and recited another prayer. He deposited the lighting candle in the center of the candelabra and recited yet another prayer. He closed his prayer book. He dug into his pocket and produced a small package wrapped in silver foil. He handed it to Rebecca. Then he reached in and brought out another package. He handed it to Elvira, who had watched the entire procedure wide-eyed.

"Here, Elvira, your first Chanukah gift," David said.

"To celebrate freedom from the Syrians," Elvira said.

David smiled and shook his head. "This child, she knows everything."

And Rebecca could see that her husband was greatly pleased.

Pastor Wilder sat back in his creaky swivel chair and gave his attention to Lydia Caraway, the young woman who taught Elvira's Sunday school class. Plump, kindly, twenty-two years old, she worked as a temporary cleaning woman at Harlem Hospital despite having been graduated from high school with better than average grades. But when she applied to nursing school, she had been turned down. She found an outlet for her intellectual inclinations by teaching Sunday school, for which she prepared conscientiously each week.

Standing before her pastor now, she was shy and reticent.

Wilder coaxed gently, "Speak freely, sister. What made you ask to see me?" When she did not respond, he ventured, "You're not satisfied with your Sunday school class. You'd

like an older class. Or has something come up to interfere
with your teaching and you wish to be relieved?"

"Oh no, Pastor Wilder," Lydia protested. "I love the work,
the children. What I wanted to discuss . . . it may be none of
my business, but when she told the class about it, I thought I
should say something. After all, a Christmas tree with two
stars . . ."

Confused, Wilder replied, "A Christmas tree with two
stars? Who told you?"

"Elvira Hitchins," Lydia informed. "Seems she has a
Christmas tree of her own."

"I think that's very nice, don't you?"

"Yes, but two stars. One five-pointed and one six-pointed
star," Lydia pointed out gingerly, for she felt she might be
trespassing on a religious question.

Pretending this was a grave matter, Wilder stroked his
chin thoughtfully. "What do you suppose we should do about
that, sister?"

"Well, there is this nice couple in the congregation, Elisha
and Lettie Brockway, whose union has not been blessed by
the Lord with any young. I think maybe they might be willing
to take little Elvira and save her."

"Save her?" Wilder repeated. "How? By having a Christmas tree with only one star?"

"I don't know, pastor. That child is bright. She comes
every Sunday with her lessons all learned. And she is always
raising her hand to answer my questions. But somehow . . .
somehow . . ."

"Somehow it just don't feel right," Wilder articulated for
her.

"Exactly!" Lydia was relieved that it was out. "And maybe
there's others who feel the same."

"I'm glad you called the matter to my attention, sister."

"Do you want me to say something to the Brockways?"
Lydia asked.

"Not quite yet," Pastor Wilder continued thoughtfully.
"Not quite yet."

Pastor Wilder sat alone in his small office contemplating
the problem Lydia had presented. He had expected the ques-

tion might come up when Rebecca Rosen and Elvira first appeared at the church. But coming after Elvira and the Rosens had developed such a close and warm relationship, it presented a far more troubling challenge.

He must do something about it as soon as possible. Since he did not wish to alarm either the child or the Rosens sooner than might prove necessary, he decided that on the following Sunday he would casually suggest to Rebecca that she drop by and visit him some afternoon without Elvira. And to do so soon.

Rebecca Rosen found Pastor Wilder at work in his overalls, trying to hang the new blackboard in the larger of the two classrooms in the basement of the Ajalon Baptist Church.

"Pastor, I hope I'm not interrupting," Rebecca apologized.

"I was hoping someone would. Because this is a job for four hands, not just two."

"How can I help?" Rebecca volunteered.

"I'll hold up the blackboard while you help me decide where it would fit best. When we do, you just make a mark on the wall with that pencil at all four corners."

"All right," Rebecca said, standing back to appraise the proper height and placement of the blackboard.

The pastor spoke while he raised the blackboard in place, lowered it, raised it once more, shifted it slightly to the right, then to the left.

"Rebecca, this is a difficult subject to broach, but better we do it than the authorities."

"Authorities?" Rebecca Rosen repeated with great concern.

Wilder was quick to sympathize. "Among the things we colored people share with Jews is our fear of uniforms, courts, and government agencies. Which is precisely why I say better we than they." He turned his attention back to the job at hand. "Am I holding this high enough?"

"A little higher, I think," Rebecca said, somewhat breathless at the alarming thoughts that now assailed her. "You're hinting at a problem, a serious problem."

Raising the blackboard somewhat, Wilder asked. "Have

you and Mr. Rosen given any thought to the . . . the relationship between you and little Elvira?"

"We get along very well," Rebecca protested. "Do you have reason to doubt it?"

"Not at all," Wilder reassured quickly. "But what I meant—well, for example in her school records, what are you and David to her?"

"When we were filling out some forms we came to the question *Whom to notify: parents, next of kin.* David said, 'Her parents we are not. Not even next of kin. And after all, even though she calls us uncle and aunt we are not, not really. Since there is no space on the form for exactly what we are, guardians is the best word, he said."

"I agree," Wilder replied. Then he lowered the blackboard to the floor, turned to Rebecca. "My dear Rebecca, one day Elvira will be starting high school. There will be more forms to fill out. And later, such things as insurance, possibly even job applications and, who knows, possibly even college. In a hundred different ways the question will keep coming up."

"So we will keep writing in *guardians*," Rebecca said.

"There should be a more formal recognition. I would not want, nor would you, to have someone intervene and say, "This child does not belong with this white Jewish couple.""

"Why would anyone do such a thing?" Rebecca challenged.

"There are people," Wilder said, "who with all righteous intentions become self-appointed meddlers in the lives of others. So I suggest you speak to a lawyer and find out the legal thing to do."

Rebecca shook her head slowly. "I keep thinking of the old saying, 'Leave well enough alone.' Once you start with lawyers, courts, and city departments, God alone knows what could happen."

"But to live with uncertainty, as if hiding some guilty secret—I say, confront the problem before it confronts you," Wilder advised.

"Aunt Rebecca, did I do something wrong?" Elvira asked as Rebecca combed her hair and tied it neatly with red ribbons.

"No, darling, you didn't do anything wrong."

"Then why do I have to see a judge? That's only for when someone commits a crime."

Rebecca embraced her and, while holding her tight, said, "Elvira darling, you did nothing wrong. All the judge wants to do is look at you and, maybe, ask you some questions."

"Is it a test?" Elvira asked.

"Not really," Rebecca replied.

"But if there are going to be questions . . ." Elvira said.

"I guess you could say that in a way it *is* a test. A very important test."

"Then shouldn't I study for it?" the child asked.

"Mr. Mandell said," Rebecca began to explain.

"Mr. Mandell? Who is he?"

"The lawyer Uncle David retained."

"There's going to be a lawyer too?" Elvira asked.

"Yes, darling. You see, we will go to a place called the domestic relations court. There we will see a judge. She will talk to us."

"A lady judge?" Elvira asked.

"And Mr. Mandell says she is very tough. That's why he said for me not to tell you any answers to any questions. Because she would know if I did. Anyhow, she will ask us all questions. You, Pastor Wilder, Uncle David, myself. We will answer them. And then . . ."

Rebecca could not bring herself to discuss the possibilities for fear of upsetting Elvira even more. So she contented herself with, "And then, then we will see."

The child's hand felt sweaty in hers as Rebecca and Elvira entered the chambers of Judge Patricia Brosnan. The room had evidently been prepared for their arrival since five chairs were arranged in fanlike formation facing the judge's desk.

"Judge Brosnan will be coming off the bench in a few minutes," the judge's secretary announced. "So make yourselves comfortable."

Rebecca, David, and Pastor Wilder were each involved in anticipating the judge's questions and trying to prepare answers that would satisfy her to evoke the hoped-for decision.

Only Elvira prepared no answers, for she had no intimation of what questions she might be asked.

In minutes, the door was flung open. A short, plump woman, made to appear even more so by her black judicial robe, burst into the room. Thinking she was addressing her secretary, she called out, "If that loudmouth lawyer had opened his mouth one more time, I'd have held him in contempt—" She stopped short once she realized she had visitors. She stared at them a moment.

"Your Honor," David's lawyer, Bernard Mandell, intervened to remind her. "We're here on the Hitchins matter."

Judge Brosnan proceeded briskly to her desk and selected one file from a tall stack. Meantime, she surveyed the five faces before her: two white men and one white woman; one Negro man and one Negro child. She opened the file, refreshed her memory about the contents, then said softly, "Ah, yes." She put aside the file. "Now, then . . ."

Taking that as his cue, attorney Mandell began: "Your Honor, as I explained in my petition, this case deals with a most unusual circumstance—"

Judge Brosnan interrupted. "Counselor, your petition stated the matter well enough. And I have no time for long explanations since I have to be back on the bench in half an hour."

"Half an hour?" Rebecca demanded. "You are going to decide a child's lifetime in half an hour?"

"Mrs. Rosen, please," Mandell tried to silence her, embarrassed that he had lost control of his client.

"It's quite all right, counselor," the judge intervened. "These hearings are always an emotional ordeal." She turned her attention to Rebecca. "Mrs. Rosen, I happen to agree with you. We never have sufficient time in this court to give every case the attention we would like. But we do the best we can. Mainly, we try to protect the child. In the interest of everyone involved, let us keep this brief. I have read Mr. Mandells' petition, read the statements of Mr. Rosen and yourself and the letter from Pastor Wilder." She turned to him, "I assume you are Pastor Wilder?"

"Yes, Your Honor, I am," Wilder replied.

"That was a most touching letter, sir. Now, since I have

not heard from the one person involved, I would ask all of you except—" she consulted the file for the child's name, "—all of you except Elvira to leave the room."

"But we came to—" Mandell started to protest.

"Counselor, before I retire I would like just one lawyer to believe that this judge, granted, a woman judge, knows what she's doing. Please wait outside!"

Once the adults had cleared the room, Judge Brosnan beckoned Elvira to come stand beside her.

"That's a very pretty dress, Elvira."

"Aunt Rebecca made it for me," Elvira said proudly.

The judge reached out, ostensibly to straighten the white crocheted collar on Elvira's best dress. Actually, she was testing to see if Elvira would flinch. She did not.

Good, the judge thought. *She gives no evidence of having been punished physically. And the way she clung to Mrs. Rosen's hand, very significant. However . . .*

"Tell me, Elvira, do you understand what's going on here today?"

"Yes, ma'am," Elvira responded too quickly, then admitted, "No, ma'am, not exactly."

"They didn't tell you? Didn't instruct you what to say?"

"No, ma'am," Elvira said. But she sensed the judge was hinting at matters more grave than her young mind had imagined. "Is there something wrong, ma'am? Did I do something?"

"No, child," Judge Brosnan reassured. "I assume they didn't tell you because they didn't want to upset you."

"No, ma'am," Elvira corrected.

"Oh?"

"Aunt Rebecca said if she told me what to answer, you would know it. Because Mr. Mandell said you are a very tough judge."

"Called me tough, did he?" the judge remarked. "Elvira, you are here because I had to decide whether to let you remain with the Rosens or give you to some Negro family."

Her security suddenly threatened, Elvira asked, "Judge, are you allowed to do that?"

"Allowed to do *what*?" the judge demanded, unaccustomed to having a child of nine question her authority.

"Allowed to just, just give me to some family," Elvira said. Though the judge's eyes were fixed on her, Elvira felt compelled to speak up no matter the consequences.

"Once I heard Uncle David say, it is written that whoever saves just one life is the same as if he saved the whole world. Because in the eyes of God every human being is precious."

"And so?" the judge asked, puzzled by the relevance of Elvira's argument.

"Well, if that's true, can you just *give* a human being away? Even if she is just nine years old and colored?" Elvira dared to ask.

"I will not just be giving you away," Judge Brosnan bristled. "I will have a thorough investigation made of any colored family willing to take you. I will make sure they are good, respectable people who can give you a nice, clean home. Make sure you are well fed, well cared for. Understand?"

"No, ma'am," Elvira said.

Judge Brosnan was beginning to resent the child's resistance. "What don't you understand?"

"I already live in a nice, clean home. And I am well fed. I even learned how to cook Negro food. Aunt Rebecca and me, we cook together. She helps me fry chops and chicken and cook greens and bake cornbread and things. I help her make the gefilte fish on Fridays. And Uncle David, he loves it all. They are both good people. Like you just said, respectable. So, you see, judge, I'm being well cared for now."

"There's something to be said for that," Brosnan granted.

"So you can go back on that bench and never worry about me ever again."

"Oh, can I?" Brosnan asked, concealing her amusement at the forthright manner in which the child argued her own case. "Elvira, there is another very important question. Wouldn't you feel better being with your own people?"

"But I am with my own people," Elvira protested. "Sunday school, church, activities, Pastor Wilder. I'm with my own people then." Now, the full import of Judge Brosnan's question became clear to her. "Ma'am, you mean I have to choose? Between Aunt Rebecca and Uncle David and a colored family?"

The judge nodded. "That's what I have to decide."

Elvira considered the judge's statement for a long moment, then asked, "Judge, can't you just decide to let me stay where I am? With Aunt Rebecca and Uncle David? Please?"

Before she responded to Elvira's question, Judge Brosnan weighed the conventional disposition of such cases: Always place a child with its own group, by either religion or race. Yet this child stood before her secure in her desire and able to speak for herself. That argued extremely well for the people in whose care she now lived. She stared into Elvira's black eyes, which reflected her earnest plea.

"Elvira . . . it's going to be all right, all right."

"You mean I can stay? I can stay?" Elvira asked eagerly.

"Yes, my dear, you can stay," Judge Brosnan granted.

Once the others had been returned to her chambers, Judge Brosnan said, "Mrs. Rosen, Mr. Rosen, off the record and within the confines of this room, my personal advice is, never attempt to move for adoption. The bureaucracy in this city will not permit it. You love the child. She loves you and is happy with you. That's good enough for me. Mr. Mandell, submit your request in the form of an order appointing the Rosens guardians of the child, and I will sign it."

She started out briskly on her way back to her courtroom, pausing at the door only long enough to say, "Quite a child you have there, quite a child."

1 9 3 6

"What do you mean, an entrance examination?" David demanded, as if his own qualifications had been impugned. "A child with her school record should be accepted in *any* high school!"

"David, there are two high schools for which a girl has to be especially qualified—Wadleigh and Hunter, special schools for special girls."

"Special?" he scoffed. "You know what I think? *Special* is a word to keep a bright young girl like Elvira *out* of school. The way it asks on all those forms, race: white or Negro? With Jews they tell by names. With Negroes, they tell by that little box on the form, race!"

"If she doesn't take the exam, she *surely* won't be admitted," Rebecca pointed out.

"Okay! All right! *Take* her down. *Let* her take the exam. Just don't make her any big promises or predictions."

"I have to give her confidence," Rebecca said.

"Confidence, yes! Big promises, no!" David ruled, allowing Rebecca to sort out the difference. "Now, I better go say good night to her so she can get to sleep early."

"David!" He turned to her. "I have to talk to you about something else, too."

"So, Becca, talk!"

"You keep calling her a bright young girl. A pretty young girl."

"Am I exaggerating? Bright she is and pretty too! Anyone can see that!"

"Bright, yes. Pretty also. But she is no longer a girl."

"What are you trying to tell me?"

"You don't notice such things, but lately she began to develop little hints of breasts. Soon, very soon, she will probably begin to have her periods."

"That child? Periods is for a woman."

"David, she is almost fourteen. She *is* a woman. So she must be treated differently from now on."

"That's life. A child grows up. A boy becomes a man. A girl becomes a woman." There was regret in his voice and in his eyes. "I shall be more careful, more respectful of her new state. Am I still allowed to go in and kiss her good night?"

"Of course," Rebecca said.

David knocked on the door, calling softly, "Darling, you asleep?"

"No, Uncle David," Elvira called back.

He slipped into the dark room and sat down on the side of her bed. "So, tomorrow is the big day. Well, with your record, your marks in school, you have nothing to worry about."

"I've never taken a test like this before," Elvira said, revealing her fears.

"So what? That's the excitement of living, to dare to do things you never dared before. Aunt Rebecca and I were born four thousand miles away, in another country, with another language. But we came over here, something we never did before, learned to speak English, which we never did before, and as a result we have a much better life than we had before. That's what we call progress. Tomorrow you are about to take another step in your progress."

In the faint light from the hallway, he studied her eyes. They appeared more moist and glassy than usual. He reached out to touch her cheek. It felt warm, a little too warm.

"Darling, do you feel all right?"

"Yes, Uncle David, I'm fine, fine, really!"

"Good. Now get a good night's sleep so tomorrow you'll be ready." He kissed her on the cheek.

"I don't like the look in her eyes," he told Rebecca.

"She's nervous," Rebecca explained.

"It's more than nervous," he urged. "Go see for yourself."

Rebecca leaned over Elvira and pressed her lips to her forehead. Warm, Rebecca realized.

"Darling, how do you feel?"

"Fine, fine," Elvira protested too readily.

"Your throat? It doesn't hurt?"

"No."

"No headaches?"

"No, I'm fine. Honest."

"Maybe I should take your temperature," Rebecca suggested.

"No, I'm fine," Elvira protested. "Just sleepy, that's all."

"Well, go to sleep, and in the morning we'll see."

"See what, Aunt Rebecca?" Elvira asked, tense now.

"If you're not feeling well, maybe it would be better not to take the test."

"But I have to!"

"We'll see, darling, we'll see."

Rebecca closed the door quietly. Elvira lay in her bed and pulled the blanket tight around her, for she felt again the chill that she had concealed from Rebecca.

She could not fall asleep but lay awake, thinking, *I have to take that test. I have to! I must go to Wadleigh! My mama used to say, 'Child, you are special. And don't let anything or anybody make you believe otherwise.' Unless I pass that test, how will I ever know? So I have to take it, to pass. Getting sick can wait. There'll be time after—after I pass.*

She was seized by another chill. She burrowed more deeply into her mattress, seeking its warmth.

Tomorrow, she thought, *tomorrow I can't let Aunt Rebecca see that I'm sick. Else she won't let me go.*

The burning in her throat woke her before it was light out. She slipped from her bed and silently padded into the bathroom. She climbed up on the washstand so she could stare into the large mirror on the medicine cabinet. She opened her mouth as wide as she could to look deep into her throat. She could only see her tongue and the forepart of her palate. She climbed down, filled the bathroom glass with cold water, and sipped it slowly, feeling it flow over the burning spot deep in her throat. Her bare feet on the cold tiles made her shiver. She went back to bed to try to fall asleep again.

Just before they left the house, Rebecca again suggested taking her temperature, but Elvira insisted. "No, Aunt Rebecca, I'm fine. I feel good, very good! Just a little nervous, that's all."

Finally, Rebecca relented, "As long as you feel all right."

"I do, I do!"

As Rebecca was slipping into her coat, David said softly, "The test can't take long. If there is something wrong with her, you'll be back soon. A few hours can't make that much difference."

Wadleigh High School for Girls, on 115th Street, was a hangover from the days when medieval architecture was considered the only style suitable for academic institutions. Rebecca and Elvira approached the building from the Eighth Avenue subway station at 110th Street.

Rebecca wanted to blurt out, *Darling, just go in there and do your best. They have to judge you by your answers, not by your color. But if I raise the question it will only add to her nervousness.* Finally, she admitted, *David's right. Her race will be a factor. Why have I permitted her to blunder into this situation?*

They were at the entrance to Wadleigh. Rebecca knelt down to impart some last words of advice.

"Sweetheart, don't try to answer everything at once. One question at a time. Think. Then write. And if you don't know an answer, don't waste time. Go on to the next question."

"Yes, Aunt Rebecca, I remember."

Just before Rebecca let Elvira go, she kissed her—partly to encourage, but even more to test her suspicion that the child was really ill. This time her cheek was no longer too warm. It was hot. Rebecca was tempted to seize her by the hand and start for home. But she knew how fervently Elvira had set her mind on proving herself.

"Darling, are you sure you're all right?"

"Yes, Aunt Rebecca, I'm sure," Elvira insisted.

Like the other mothers around them, Rebecca watched Elvira enter the imposing building. With two hours to wait, Rebecca looked about for some place to pass the time. She spied a luncheonette and coffee shop across from the school. It seemed a clean place, and it was empty at midmorning.

Elvira entered the examination hall, a room large enough to accommodate several hundred desk-chairs for all the applicants eager to earn the cherished right to attend Wadleigh High.

Elvira looked around. She had never before been in competition with so many girls. Her anxieties, unsettling as they had been, were suddenly magnified. Nevertheless, she approached the teacher who sat behind the desk on a raised platform waiting to receive the document that attested the candidate's academic record entitled her to take the entrance examination. Elvira handed up her paper. The teacher, a stout woman with graying hair and rimless glasses, studied Elvira's qualifications, then glanced down at her.

"Very nice," she said, unable to conceal her surprise. "Take the last seat in the right-hand section."

Elvira stared around the large room, at more than two hundred other eager and aspiring candidates. There was not a single Negro among them. She remembered Rebecca's instructions for moments like this: *Proud. Be proud.* She drew herself up and started toward the last chair, passing many girls who stared at her and some who edged back from the aisle just a little until she had gone by. She took her place in the last seat and clasped her hands in her lap to keep them from trembling while she waited the arrival of the proctor, who had begun to hand out the test papers.

Elvira forced herself to swallow hard, to see if she could soothe that burning spot deep in her throat. She summoned all the saliva her dry mouth could offer, then let it trickle down slowly, hoping it might possess some remedial powers. She was almost relieved to receive her test papers and booklets so she could ignore her throat and concentrate on the challenge she really feared.

She opened the test paper, cautioning herself not to rush, and scanned the questions. She recognized some at once. This gave her the confidence to unscrew the top of the fountain pen Uncle David had loaned her for this occasion. She began to write her answer to question one.

After what seemed the longest two hours of Rebecca's life, the doors of Wadleigh opened. Girls began to emerge. One of the women in the luncheonette recognized her daughter, calling, "She's out! My Natalie! The first one out! Brilliant! That child is a genius!" So saying, she raced out to cross the street and greet her daughter.

Other women followed, crossing the street to greet their

daughters. Gradually, more applicants emerged, until most of them had appeared. Rebecca waited anxiously, straining to see inside the doors each time they opened. The number of remaining applicants had dwindled down to very few. Still no sight of Elvira. Rebecca grew more tense. Her hands were icy cold. Strongly tempted to go in and find Elvira, she restrained herself. She did not wish to jeopardize the child's chances by causing a scene. Torn thus, she struggled to control herself until she could no longer resist. She started for the doors.

To her great relief, before she reached them, one door opened. Elvira appeared. Rebecca raced to her, embraced her, clutched her so tightly that the child asked, "Something wrong, Aunt Rebecca?"

"The others kept coming out and I didn't see you. I was worried."

"Oh. There was a composition. I wrote so much I had to refill my fountain pen. It took them some time to find ink."

"And I was so worried," Rebecca said, relieved. "Well, let's go home, darling."

"Yes, let's," Elvira said, then admitted for the first time, "My throat feels kind of funny. And my head hurts—a little."

They had just arrived at their front door when Elvira said suddenly, "Aunt Rebecca, open up, quick!" As soon as Rebecca unlocked the door, Elvira raced to the bathroom. She leaned over the toilet bowl and gave up the remains of her breakfast. Rebecca followed and held her while her young body heaved and strained. When it was over, Rebecca wiped her damp face dry, then soaked the towel in cold water and bathed her forehead, which was hot to the touch.

After she put the child to bed, she called Dr. Pomerantz.

Dr. Pomerantz withdrew the thermometer, studied the silver line in the thin glass tube. It extended far beyond the red mark that denoted normal. But he said only, "Sweetheart, a little aspirin, a little grapefruit juice, and you'll be good as new." He covered her up, pressing the blanket close around her, for her knew she was suffering a chill.

Elvira stared up into his eyes in such an inquisitive fashion that he forced a smile as he said, "Tell you what, just to make sure that you do everything I said, I will come back tonight to check up on you, young lady."

He turned away, giving a silent signal to Rebecca, who stood in the doorway awaiting his diagnosis.

"A hundred and four and a half. Vomiting. Headaches. When did this all start?" the doctor asked.

"I suspected it last night. But she kept insisting she felt all right. And she did want to take that test."

"She shouldn't have gone out today. Give her a child's aspirin tablet every two hours and a glass of cold juice every hour. More if she can stomach it. We'll try to drive that fever down. But that vomiting . . ."

"And if her fever doesn't go down?" Rebecca pressed him.

"We will have to watch for signs of strep throat. Or diphtheria."

"Diphtheria?" Rebecca echoed in a hush.

"It's not that serious in these times. Now there's a vaccine which is quite effective." Then he was forced to concede, "Most times."

"What if—" Rebecca started to ask.

To avoid a question he would rather not answer, Pomerantz chided her: "What if . . . what if . . . We will just wait and see. Don't worry. I'll be back around six."

Intended to reassure Rebecca, it served only to alarm her. Two visits within six hours by a busy physician indicated the gravity of Elvira's condition.

Dr. Pomerantz plodded down the stairs from the Rosen apartment, thinking, *My attempt to downplay the danger of diphtheria was not a hundred percent successful. Not with a young woman as perceptive as Rebecca Rosen. But at least I avoided getting into the more serious dangers that might lie ahead. For diphtheria, there is at least a vaccine. But not for meningitis. And the signs are there. A highly febrile patient. Vomiting. Headaches. Must watch for signs of stiff neck and back. And there's her mother's history of fatal tuberculosis. Sometimes it leads to meningitis. And with her lungs in their present condition, a mere stethoscopic examination proves nothing. Should have the child X rayed again. If she were less febrile, I would. But I don't dare move her now, except to a hospital. A dangerous picture, with grave possibilities. But we'll see, we'll see.*

Pomerantz had returned, examined Elvira once more, found her temperature had risen slightly, to just under 105.

By now she was lethargic, in a state of drowsiness that alarmed the doctor more than he would admit to Rebecca and David, who waited just outside Elvira's door while the examination proceeded.

When Pomerantz emerged, they followed him to the living room, where he proceeded to report, "Her fever, instead of lessening, has gone up. She is drowsy, but not dangerously so. However—"

"What means dangerous drowsiness?" David interrupted to ask.

Pomerantz hesitated only a moment before he decided, *Why not the whole truth, to prepare them?*

"It's too early to tell yet, but she presents certain signs of meningitis."

"Oh my God!" Rebecca exclaimed.

Pomerantz persisted. "If it is, then drowsiness generally leads to stupor. And . . . and eventually to coma."

"There must be something we can do!" Rebecca blurted out.

"All we can do is try to control her fever, bring it down. I want her to have alcohol rubs every half hour. Double the aspirin dose. Try to get more fluids into her—fruit juice, milk, even water. We can't let her become dehydrated. If she gets any worse, we'll either have to take her to the hospital or get a nurse in, because she will need intravenous feeding to keep her from becoming dehydrated."

At that moment, they were alerted by a cry from the bedroom.

"Mama . . . Mama . . ." Elvira called out in her delirium. Rebecca raced back to tend her. David started to accompany her until Pomerantz put a hand on his arm.

"Yes, doctor?"

Pomerantz drew him closer so he could whisper, "David, prepare yourself. The situation is worse than I've indicated. Coma is one thing—but dehydration can also lead to vascular collapse, which leads to shock. And shock . . . Well, what can I say?"

"There must be something we can do!" David insisted.

"David, between *should* be and *must* be is a world of difference. There should be something we can do about polio, to save so many thousands of children from paralysis and death. But is there? No. There is a limit, a very severe limit, to what we doctors know and can do. Yet to patients we are gods. I only hope—"

He stopped, considered the consequences of what he felt compelled to say, and decided to say it. "I only hope we won't soon be treating more than one patient."

"You mean, if anything happens to Elvira, the effect on Rebecca?" David asked.

"We know what happened before," Pomerantz said. "Maybe it wasn't such a good idea to get her involved with a child. Well, I will be back in the morning, early. Meantime, do what I said."

David saw the doctor out, then went back to Elvira's room, where he found Rebecca sitting on the side of the bed holding the child in her arms, rocking her back and forth. The child rested her feverish head on Rebecca's shoulder and cried softly, "Mama . . . Mama . . ."

Rebecca looked to David, her eyes pleading, *If only there was something I could do for her.*

With the doctor's warning still echoing in his mind, David said, "Becca! We have work to do. Aspirin! Double dose this time! An alcohol rub to cool her body. Then juice! Lots of juice!"

Rebecca leaned over Elvira's naked body, gently rubbing the alcohol-soaked cloth along her legs, her arms, over the chest, and then her back. The girl, asleep or in a stupor, did not resist the treatment or even seem to be aware of it. David stood by watching, seeking some hint of improvement. There was none. Meantime, the bedsheets had received more of the alcohol than her young body had, so Rebecca said, "I should change her sheets. You hold her, David, while I make up her bed again."

He picked up Elvira, held her in his arms, and stared down into her face. She opened her eyes for only an instant, then cried softly, "Mama . . . I want my mama . . ."

"Shh, quiet sweetheart, Aunt Rebecca is here, Uncle David is here."

Elvira grew more restless, until David said, "You'd better take her. I'll do the bed."

Once the girl passed into Rebecca's arms, she seemed more content. She no longer called for her mother but pressed her feverish face against Rebecca's bosom.

With Rebecca's shopping instructions ringing in his head, "Alcohol! Milk! More oranges and grapefruit! And don't forget the aspirins! Child-strength!" David rushed out to shop before the stores closed for the night.

When he returned, laden with an oversupply of the five items, he helped Rebecca force fluid into their patient. David held her up while Rebecca carefully urged small sips of milk into her mouth. When it ran down her chin, Rebecca wiped away the excess and continued. It became a process of a sip at a time and a wipe, a sip and a wipe. Patiently, Rebecca persisted until the glass was empty.

"You think she had enough?" David asked.

"We'll give her more in a while. Now, her aspirin. And then another rub."

David laid Elvira down, covered her, and felt her brow. Still hot. Still unnaturally dry. Ever aware of the doctor's warning about *two* patients, David said, "Becca, it's late, past midnight. You go get some sleep. I'll watch her."

Exhausted, Rebecca acquiesced with only a brief reminder, "Don't forget—alcohol, then aspirin, then another feeding. Can you manage alone?"

"I can manage. I can manage," he insisted. "Just get some sleep."

She kissed the child and went off to their own bedroom. David sat alongside Elvira's bed, watching, wondering, *What signs are there that indicate a child is improving? Or growing worse? Is she just sleeping, worn out by her fever? Or is she slipping into a stupor, as Pomerantz warned she might?*

He tried to recall how much time had elapsed since her last alcohol rub, then argued, *What harm can it do if her rub is a little early? Or even if she receives an extra rub?* So he added alcohol to the basin, dipped in the cloth, and began to pass it tenderly over her brow, her face, her chest, her arms, and her legs. He placed his hand on her belly, trying to determine if she felt any cooler now. At first he thought she did, but then on second touch he realized that it was the evaporation of the alcohol that made it seem so. She was still hot and feverish.

He dozed off in the chair, then woke with a start, looked at his big gold watch and tried to recall: When was the last time he had given her some juice? He decided it didn't matter. She should have some immediately. He went out to the kitchen to squeeze more grapefruit and more oranges. If the juice of one fruit was good, the juice of two together must be better. When he returned, he found Rebecca lying alongside Elvira, embracing her, her lips pressed to the girl's brow.

"No better, no better," Rebecca whispered.

"Becca, you're supposed to be asleep," he rebuked.

"I couldn't. I lay there trying, but I couldn't. Not when I should be in here with her."

"Then help me feed her," he relented.

This time Rebecca held Elvira and David fed her, sip by sip, wipe by wipe.

At dawn they were both still in Elvira's room, persevering in their vigil, trying to detect some sign of change. They were both disappointed.

"She's been quiet for the last few hours," David observed, out of need to find something hopeful to say.

"She hasn't called for her mama."

"Maybe, just maybe, she is past the crisis," David said. "It could be a good sign."

"Maybe," Rebecca agreed. "David, you'd better take your shower. Get ready to go downtown."

"Downtown! Who'd help you feed her? I can take a day off. The business won't disappear," he protested.

"You don't have to stay on my account," Rebecca said.

He stole a glance at her, wondering, *Does she suspect what Pomerantz warned me about? Two patients?*

The doorbell rang, sounding unusually loud at this early hour. David realized, *The Doctor. And so early. He must be even more concerned than he let on.*

Pomerantz bustled in and started straight for his patient, asking of David, who trailed beside him, "Any change? Any improvement? Did you manage to get any fluid into her? Did she swallow her aspirin?" His torrent of questions left no room for David's answers. By that time Pomerantz was in the bedroom, staring down at Elvira. He felt her brow, pressed gently on her belly, lifted her arm and let it drop. He took her temperature, held the thermometer up to the daylight now beginning to stream in through the window.

"Hm," he grunted in his enigmatic way.

"Well, doctor, well?" Rebecca asked anxiously.

"Down. Not by much. One hundred and three point five. But at least down."

David reached out to draw Rebecca closer to him and held her in his embrace while they watched Pomerantz perform basic neurological tests. He studied Elvira's eyes and her reactions to pinpricks on her soles. All the while he made little sounds of significance to himself but baffling to Rebecca and David.

"Well, doctor?" Rebecca pleaded.

"I find no neurological deficits. And with her fever starting down, I think we may have avoided the worst possibilities. Continue the rubs, fluids, and aspirin. Take her temperature every three hours and call me at the office each time."

He started out as briskly as he had entered. From the door, he called back, "And some milk. To keep up her strength."

Through the morning hours they tended Elvira, held her, forced fluid into her mouth, rubbed her down, placed aspirin tablets in her mouth, and held it closed until she swallowed them.

At ten o'clock her temperature had receded to below 103. By noon it was down to 101.9. When they called Pomerantz to report, he sounded under pressure from his office duties, for he only grunted, "Good. Call me at three."

Shortly after six in the evening, Pomerantz came back, hurried to Elvira's side, and took her temperature, which was still 101. But he appeared far less distressed than he had been. He leaned close to her, whispered in her ear, "Elvira sweetheart, can you hear me? Dr. Pomerantz."

Elvira turned in his direction. Her eyes flickered open, then closed once more.

"Elvira?"

She opened her eyes again to discover Rebecca standing behind the doctor.

"Aunt Rebecca," she whispered.

Rebecca pushed by the doctor to embrace Elvira.

"Oh, baby, baby . . . darling . . ." Rebecca crooned softly as she pressed Elvira's damp face to her own.

"Good, good," Pomerantz said, then in his brusque fashion said, "Tonight a little clear chicken broth. Tomorrow some cereal. And call me every time you take her temperature."

Through the rest of the evening and the night, Elvira's temperature fell, rose slightly, then fell again. David and Rebecca sat at her bedside ministering to her. It no longer required two of them to feed her fluids. Her body seemed less flushed and feverish. She slept more serenely. In her waking moments, she appeared relieved to find them there. She smiled and slipped back into restful sleep.

Before dawn, David insisted, "Becca, you must get some sleep."

"Now that Elvira's so much better, I find I don't need any sleep. It's enough to sit and watch her. I guess this is what parents call *naches*. Of course, we're not parents . . ."

"You means aunts and uncles are not entitled to have a little *naches* too?"

"Watching her, I ask myself, how much more could we have done or cared or worried, if she really were our own? The way she looked at us when she woke was worth everything, everything."

The next afternoon, after David left for the business, Elvira and Rebecca were alone for what proved to be a moment of shared triumph. Elvira's temperature was finally down to near normal, 98.8.

"There, you see, darling, perfect. Well, almost perfect! Which, considering two days ago, is very very good."

"Aunt Rebecca, how long was I . . ."—she groped for the proper word—"was I sick asleep?"

"Three days and nights, sweetheart."

"Was . . . was my mama here?"

Rebecca tensed, but tried to conceal it. "Elvira darling, you know what happened to your mama."

"But she was . . . it was like she kept bathing me 'n feeding me. Uncle David was here, and I kept thinking, Mama and Uncle David don't even know each other. How can they both be taking care of me? It was strange, like a strange dream."

"Yes, dear, like a dream, a strange dream," Rebecca said, thinking, *In her delirium is it possible her mama and I became one? That she should feel so deeply about me as about her mama . . . Now I know truly what joy is, what happiness is.*

"Aunt Rebecca, did we hear?"

"Hear? What?"

"Did we get the letter?" Elvira asked.

"Letter?" Rebecca repeated, suddenly brought out of her own thoughts.

"Wadleigh, Wadleigh!" Elvira insisted.

"Oh, darling, it's only been five days. It's too soon to hear anything. They have to mark all those papers, see who passed. That all takes time."

But Rebecca was thinking, *The condition she was in when she took that test, we had better prepare her for a rejection.*

Four days later, nine days after the entrance examination, an envelope arrived in the mail. WADLEIGH HIGH SCHOOL FOR GIRLS, OFFICE OF THE PRINCIPAL appeared in the upper left hand corner. The letter was addressed to MRS. REBECCA ROSEN. She debated opening it. If this were an acceptance, it would have been addressed ELVIRA HITCHINS, CARE OF DAVID ROSEN. It must be a rejection. Resigned, she opened it. It was a brief note:

> Dear Mrs. Rosen:
> Would you please come to see me
> on Monday? I will be in my office
> from two until four.
>
> Sincerely,
> Marie Flaherty, Principal

Rebecca Rosen sat in the subway car, her hand in her coat

pocket clutching the letter. She had not mentioned it to Elvira. When she had shown it to David, he glanced at it and shook his head sadly. "We . . . we must not make it seem like a big disappointment to us. Go. See. Listen. Then we'll decide."

As the train rattled from one station to the next, Rebecca reviewed all the possibilities.

If Elvira had been accepted, the letter would have been addressed to her. On the other hand, if it was a rejection, to whom would it be sent? Maybe they spoke to the parents first to soften the blow to the child. Or did Elvira fail to qualify for Wadleigh, but the principal had another school to suggest? Or was it possible that they were willing to give her another examination, a second chance? Or, finally, does it come back to the most logical assumption of all: If Elvira had been accepted, this letter would have been addressed to her?

She waited patiently outside Miss Flaherty's office as teachers and students had brief sessions with the principal, then left. It was almost three o'clock before the door opened. A tall, very slender woman with neat, graying bobbed hair peered out.

"Mrs. Rosen?"

Hesitantly, Rebecca entered a room that lacked the neatness of its occupant. Files and books were piled haphazardly on her large desk. The bookshelves around the room were filled with a clutter of books, some standing, some leaning, some books piled on books.

The principal stared at her for a moment, appraising her, then shook her head, somewhat dubious. Rebecca took that to be confirmation of her worst fears.

"Miss Flaherty, before you make up your mind, I would like to say something. People judge Elvira before they know her. But they are judging her skin, not the girl herself. There is a very good brain inside that head.

"About that test. Put yourself in her place. She comes to this school, a strange place, where she has never been before. She is the only Negro. Always the only one, the only one. Sometimes . . . sometimes . . ." Rebecca faltered. Despite her efforts at restraint, she felt hot tears starting down her cheeks.

"Sometimes," the principal urged gently.

"Sometimes I wonder if we did her more harm than good by making her part of our family. I tried—believe me, I tried—to find her a place with a nice Negro family. She ran away. She came back to me. I could not find it in my heart to turn away from her. That was five years ago. Now she is so much a part of us, I don't know how we would get along without her. She is a very special, a very unusual child. To watch her grow from day to day, develop, learn, is like watching a miracle unfold before your eyes.

"About the test, I want you to know that she was very sick the day she took it. Maybe I should have refused to let her take it. But she had her heart so set on going to Wadleigh, I couldn't. And I didn't know how sick she really was. Three long days with a temperature so high Dr. Pomerantz was afraid she might be getting meningitis."

"And now?" Miss Flaherty asked.

"Better. Back to normal. In fact, I had her out of bed for a few hours this morning. And if she feels strong enough tonight, she'll have supper with us at the table for the first time."

Miss Flaherty did not attempt to comment.

"So what I am trying to say, Miss Flaherty, is please give her another chance? Just give me the books for her to study. I promise you that next time she will pass. Please? Because she has her heart set on this."

"Mrs. Rosen, I don't know if Elvira mentioned that a part of the examination was to write a composition."

"Yes, yes, she told me."

"Her composition was the reason I sent for you."

"She'll do better next time!" Rebecca interrupted impulsively. "Just give her a chance. Please?"

"Mrs. Rosen, the reason I sent for you was because I wanted to see for myself if you are even half the woman Elvira described in her composition. You are all she described and more—as loving, as concerned, as much a part of her life and she a part of yours as she wrote. And your husband! You might like to read what she wrote about him."

She reached for the test booklet on her desk and handed it to Rebecca.

My Uncle David is a very funny man. He would like to be a grouch, but he does not know how. Even when he complains about the President or the government or *The New York Times,* I can tell he isn't really grouchy or angry. When Aunt Rebecca asks for something, his first answer is always no! But it doesn't take very long before he finds some reason so he can say yes. He is really the kindest man in the world. From what my mama used to say, my father was like him. I hope so.

Tears flowed down Rebecca's cheeks without restraint. "She never said . . . she is so shy and quiet."

"But she *feels,* she *thinks,* she *observes,*" Miss Flaherty said. "And she expresses herself very well on paper. There was only one part of her composition that troubled me. Here, where at the end she writes, 'Someday I must find a way to repay them for everything they have done for me.' That's quite a burden for a child to bear."

"Believe me, we have never asked, or even thought, of being repaid. Her presence in our lives is enough, more than enough."

"I hope one day she, too, will come to realize that. As for Elvira's admission into Wadleigh, we will be very happy to have her." She reached into her middle desk drawer for a long envelope. "Elvira's official certification of acceptance. I think you should be the one to give it to her."

Determined to make a family celebration of Elvira's triumph, Rebecca Rosen stopped to make a special purchase at Olinsky's butcher shop.

When she arrived home, she found Elvira in bed, reading. "Up, darling, up! Into the tub!" Rebecca said. "We'll wash your hair and do it up nicely. Then pick out a dress! Tonight, no supper in bed. You are coming to the table with Uncle David and me."

"You mean we're going to surprise him?" Elvira asked.

"Oh, are we going to surprise him!" Rebecca said, laughing in sole knowledge of her precious secret.

David arrived in more than his usual degree of irritation. Before he had even hung up his hat or slipped out of his topcoat, Rebecca and Elvira could hear him from the hallway.

"If they don't stop him, he will burn up this whole world! Mark my words!"

Elvira came running out of her room to greet him. "Uncle David, who is it this time?"

"Ah, Elvira sweetheart. Out of bed? And so dressed up? What's going on?"

Elvira and Rebecca exchanged the furtive smiles of conspirators, enjoying their little plot.

"So who is it this time?" Rebecca asked.

"Who else? That Hitler! A year ago he passes those laws in Nuremberg! Jews can't be citizens, can't hold government jobs; if a Jew and a gentile happen to . . ."

Sensitive to Elvira's presence, he modified his language. "If something, you know what I mean, goes on between them, they can be executed. Now, you want to know what craziness is, there is in the *Times* today a report that Jews are being put in jail. And for what? For wearing brown pants! Because he says it might be confused with a uniform. He's out to do only one thing, destroy the Jews! And nobody does anything!"

He was on his way to wash up for supper when he called back over his shoulder, "And you, my darling Elvira, are no better off. Much as he hates Jews, he also hates Negroes. White! Blond! Aryan! That's the way this world will be if he has his way."

He came out of the bathroom drying his hands. "And if someone doesn't stop him soon, he *will* have his way." The aromas from the kitchen had reached him. He stopped, sniffed. "Onions! Someone is frying onions! Let me guess. A very very thin steak, with mashed potatoes. The whole thing covered with those soft, wonderful brown onions only my Rebecca can cook!"

Without invitation, he marched to the kitchen table to take his place. He commenced eating heartily.

When he had indulged in more than his share of steak, potatoes, onions, carrots, and peas, he wiped his lips with his napkin, pushed back slightly from the table, and addressed them both.

"All right, ladies. I know when I'm a turkey stuffed for Thanksgiving and ready to be served up on a platter. What is it you two want *this* time?"

The look of total surprise on Elvira's face eliminated her as a suspect. David directed his accusation to Rebecca. "When, in the middle of the week, my wife goes out of her way to prepare a Sunday dinner, something is cooking. And I don't mean in the kitchen. Something is on her mind. Right, Becca?"

"Right," she conceded.

"Well, ask already, so I can say no!"

Instead of responding, Rebecca reached into the pocket of her apron and brought out the envelope. David reached across the table, but Rebecca handed it to Elvira.

"Here, sweetheart, open it. Read it out loud."

Elvira took the envelope, nervously opened it, took out the letter, and began to read:

Elvira Hitchins, care of David Rosen
229 Fort Washington Avenue
New York, New York

Dear Miss Hitchins:

It is my pleasure to inform you that, having passed the entrance examination and fulfilled all the other qualifications for admission to Wadleigh High School for Girls, you are hereby accepted.

Please bring this note with you on Registration Day.

Sincerely,
Marie Flaherty
Principal

While David glanced across at Rebecca, Elvira whispered softly, "She said yes. She said yes. They want me!" She bounded out of her chair to throw her arms around Rebecca, then she raced to David to embrace him.

Her arms around his neck, he said, "I suspected this was a special night. But *so* special I didn't expect. Becca, call your sister, call your brother! Call them! They think *they* got geniuses? Ask them which of their daughters got accepted into Wadleigh!"

"David, please, a little modesty."

"Modesty, shmodesty. When I feel like bragging, I brag!

Elvira my darling, all the time you were so worried about taking those exams, and afterward when we didn't hear, I kept saying to myself, 'She will make it. She will! Because she has not only the brains, but in here'"—he pointed to her stomach—"... in here she has what those Yankee Doodles call guts, courage. So for a prize—whatever you want, just ask!"

The child thought for a moment. A number of childish desires raced through her mind. When she finally spoke, she said, "A new frame."

"A new frame?" David asked, glancing at Rebecca. "What kind of present is a frame?"

"I saw one once in a store up on Broadway. It's a frame that opens up so it becomes two frames. On the one side I want to put this letter. And on the other side I want to put my mama's picture, so she can see this letter always."

"Of course, sweetheart," David said softly. "A double frame. Tomorrow, Rebecca, you two pick one out. Price is no object."

Elvira had gone off to bed with her cherished letter. David sat in the living room, deep in thought. Rebecca was tightening the buttons on one of Elvira's sweaters.

"David?" He looked up, his thoughts interrupted. "What are you thinking?"

"I am thinking about that Hitler. The logical end of all this must be a war. And if there is a war, I have to think of where I get my raw materials. The best grosgrain for hat bands comes from France. The best leather for sweatbands, from England. Last of all I ask myself, how can I be worried about grosgrain and sweatbands while the world is going to hell?"

To lift his spirits, Rebecca told him of her visit to Miss Flaherty and about Elvira's composition.

He asked, "She wrote, 'From what my mama used to say, my father was like him. I hope so.' She said, I hope so?"

"I read the words myself," Rebecca assured.

"Imagine," he said. "Imagine Elvira should say that about me."

His eyes filled with tears. He sniffed a bit. Then, lest he be accused of being sentimental, he said brusquely, "That part about . . . where she said about being a grouch. . . . What did she write there?"

"'He would like to be a grouch, but he doesn't know how.'"

"What does she mean I don't know how? Believe me, if I wanted to be a grouch, I would be a damn good grouch! And don't let her forget it!"

He was silent for a time. "That's still no reason not to celebrate. Tell you what. She has never been to a Broadway show. Tomorrow I'll pick up three tickets for a matinee. After all, a matinee—how much can a ticket cost? A dollar-fifty? Two-fifty in the orchestra? For a special occasion, we can afford it. Maybe we can have dinner out, too. We'll see. How's that for a grouch?"

20

*D*avid Rosen was engaged in his favorite postsupper activity, listening to the radio news while reading those parts of *The New York Times* he had not finished during his subway trip down to business in the morning. Meantime, "the women" as he now called Rebecca and Elvira, were in the girl's room busy with an activity that evoked considerable laughter and excitement.

A major part of David's evening enjoyment was given over to his own comments, at times talking back to the radio, rattling his *Times* in anger, or grumbling about some editorial or article that offended his own view of an issue. At the moment he was reacting to the lead story on the radio news:

Today the Supreme Court of the United States had declared unconstitutional a New York State law providing a minimum wage for women and children.

Recalling his first days in his new country when he rebelled against his Uncle Shiman's exploitation of those women unfortunate enough to work for him, David grumbled, "Unconstitutional . . . some country where it takes nine old men with lifetime jobs to say that to give a decent wage to women and children is against the law. Idiots! Idiots without feeling, without humanity! Some way to run a country!"

Rebecca had come rushing out of Elvira's room to find something at the new walnut sewing machine console, which also served as a piece of foyer furniture. She was searching through one of the drawers for some thread when she heard the tail end of David's protest.

"What did you say, David?"

"What difference does it make what *I* say? *You* don't listen to me. The Supreme *Court* doesn't listen to me. The *Times certainly* doesn't listen to me. What are you two doing in there? What's all the whispering and the laughing?"

"Things. Women's things."

"It's a conspiracy!" David complained. "One man, two women. I will be outnumbered for the rest of my days! If I only had a son—" He interrupted himself abruptly. But unfortunately, a moment too late. The rush of unshed tears to Rebecca's eyes, the look of hurt on her face, made him rise, go to her, embrace her. "I didn't mean anything . . . I mean, what I . . . I was only making a joke. As it turned out, a bad joke. Believe me, I couldn't ask any more out of this life. We've been very lucky, Becca. The business is growing. At the bank I am now considered an important account. A few weeks ago one of the branch vice-presidents said to me, 'Mr. Rosen, if you have any thoughts of enlarging the business, we would look favorably on a loan, a substantial loan.' And at the stores I don't have to wait in line on the buyers' floor. Callahan himself phones me yesterday. 'Davey, I want to see your fall line before I place my orders.' I would be an ingrate to complain about how life has treated us."

He kissed her on the cheek. She returned his kiss and slipped out of his arms, saying softly, "Elvira's waiting for me."

He watched her go down the hall toward Elvira's room. He wondered. Had his apology softened the hurt he had unwittingly inflicted on her?

He went back to his armchair, his *Times*, and the radio, over which the flat but familiar voice of Elmer Davis was reporting that during a parade honoring Adolf Hitler's birthday the Nazis, for the first time, unveiled the true might of their modernized war machine. The sight impressed and startled the diplomats of many nations, especially those of France and Great Britain.

David grumbled, "They want to declare something unconstitutional, declare that bastard Hitler unconstitutional! He is getting ready to blow up the world and nobody does anything! Nobody!"

He rattled his newspaper with more than his usual irritation and resumed reading.

On page seventeen he came across a small boxed headline: NEGRO RAPIST LYNCHED IN GEORGIA.

Again? David thought. *Am I becoming sensitive to these stories*

of lynching because of Elvira? Or are lynchings happening more
often? It seems almost every week I read in the paper, hear on the
radio of another one.

He turned to the financial section. At least there he would
not be confronted by stories of rape and lynching or Hitler.
He glanced down the lists of stocks on the New York Stock
Exchange. Prices were low and getting lower. He considered,
was this the time to buy some stocks? Or should he tend to
the hat business?

On the last page of the business section he came upon a
six-line item, which made David comment with a grunt and a
laugh.

"Last year when I read it I thought it was a mistake. But
here is it again. Japanese making automobiles. A company
. . . what kind of name is that for a company . . . Toyoda Au-
tomatic Loom Works . . . and making automobiles yet. For the
second year. Don't those Japanese ever learn? Loom com-
panies make looms. General Motors and Ford make automobiles. And some name for a car. Toyota. And why would a
company spell its own with a *d* and the car's name with a *t*.
Must be a toy for children."

He could hear them now, coming down the hall. Rebecca
was whispering; Elvira was giggling. Rebecca reached the
archway, but Elvira was not in sight.

"All right, all right," he said, playing the game with them.
"What have you two tyrants schemed up to do to me this
time?"

Rebecca kept a perfectly straight face, but behind her,
Elvira could no longer restrain giggling. Rebecca announced,
"And now it is my extreme pleasure to introduce the valedic-
torian of the graduating class of 1936, Miss Elvira Hitchins.
Da-dah!" With a flourish, she stepped aside to permit Elvira
to enter.

"My, what a magnificent dress!" David exclaimed. "A doll!
An absolute doll! A girl so pretty must take after my side of
the family! Right?"

"Right!" Elvira agreed with a burst of laughter.

"Believe me, sweetheart, after reading and hearing all the
bad news, one look at you makes the whole world brighter.
So you are going to be the class valedictorian!"

He kissed her on the head, and patted her on the cheek. "You make me very proud. Now, take off that dress very carefully, take your bath, and go to bed. Tomorrow is another school day."

Rebecca sensed that David had more in mind than merely sending Elvira off to complete her day's routine. The sound of rushing water from the bathroom was loud enough to assure them that Elvira could not overhear.

"Becca, her being the valedictorian, is that true?"

"The boy or girl with the highest grades automatically becomes the valedictorian," Rebecca said.

"As long as it's the rule. I wouldn't want her to be disappointed."

"They wouldn't dare *not* give her the honor. It's never happened before!" Rebecca protested.

"'Never happened before,'" David mimicked bitterly. "Becca, things are happening now that never happened before. Was there ever such a depression? Did we ever have such a madman as Hitler? Did we ever have so many lynchings? I tell you, what happened before doesn't count. This world is going crazy."

"Well, don't worry about Elvira become valedictorian," Rebecca assured.

By the third week in June, the students in Elvira's graduating class were given their final grades. Elvira's report card carried four A's and one B-plus. With great joy and satisfaction, she ran all the way home. She burst in, calling out, "Look, Aunt Rebecca! Look!"

Rebecca accepted the card, handling it carefully, like a precious artifact.

"And what did Miss Corbin say about your speech? Did she suggest any ideas, any thoughts to express? How long to make it?"

"She didn't say anything about my speech."

"Nothing at all?"

"Not today."

"Not today," Rebecca considered. "There aren't many days left." To avoid arousing Elvira's anxieties, she said no more.

The next morning, Rebecca accompanied Elvira to school.
She sought out Miss Corbin in the teachers' staff room. Since
there were other teachers present having a last cup of coffee
and a last cigarette before starting the class day, Rebecca kept
her voice quite low when she said, "Miss Corbin, I'm Rebecca
Rosen. Elvira Hitchins's aunt."

"Yes, I know."

"I came to discuss Elvira's valedictory. Your suggestions as
to what to say. How long it should be . . ."

"We have had quite a discussion about that."

"We?" Rebecca repeated, aware that despite her best
efforts to keep herself in check, her voice was rising.

"It was decided that Elvira would not be the . . . the
proper graduate to speak for the class."

"Is there any student with better grades?" Rebecca demanded.

"It was a matter of choosing someone representative of the
class and the school."

"You mean someone who is white!" Rebecca accused. "I
won't let you do that to Elvira!" she insisted in a voice so
strong that the other teachers could no longer ignore her.

The only man in the group took it upon himself to intervene. "My dear woman, what seems to be the trouble?"

"She is Elvira Hitchins's aunt," Corbin explained simply.

"Oh," the man said in a manner that revealed that he, too,
had been part of the decision. "Well now . . ."

Rebecca interrupted sharply, "I refuse to hear the explanations of prejudice that usually follow the words *Well now*. If
Elvira earned the honor, she should have it. And she will, if I
have to go to the principal myself!"

"It was Mr. Goodman's idea in the first place," the man
informed, less contentious and more sympathetic. He lowered
his voice. "We can't have all those white parents sitting out
there on graduation night thinking, Some school if the best
they can produce is a Negro valedictorian. There are times
when we do need the support of the community."

"How am I going to explain to Elvira? What do I say?"

"Look at it this way, Mrs. Rosen. This will prepare her for
what she has to face for the rest of her life."

"Yes," Rebecca said bitterly. "Being good doesn't matter.

Even being better doesn't matter. If you are Negro, there is no way you can ever be good enough."

"Mrs. Rosen, if you don't want to break her heart later, you will gradually get her adjusted to her place in life, starting now."

The bell for the start of classes ended the meeting abruptly.

When she reported to David, his first reaction was one of anger. But then he spoke with grave sadness.

"Today it's the valedictorian speech, tomorrow it's something else. Next year another slap in the face. Becca, do you think we are being fair with her, to give her such ambitions?"

"I think of that, too," she agreed sadly. "We look at her, we see the girl we know: sweet, with her bright black eyes, her quick mind, her loving ways. I think of her and I feel her arms around my neck, her soft cheek against mine, her body. But others who don't know her. What do they see? A colored child, a Negro. A nigger."

"Still, how can we say to a child, 'Be less than you can be?'" David said. "'Strive to fail.' If only—" He broke off in futility.

"Life is full of if onlys. If only she had been born white. If only we had had a child of our own . . ." She turned away to hide her tears.

Gently, he placed his hands on her shoulders and turned her back to face him. He used his forefinger to brush aside her tears.

"The best we can do with life is to face it, not try to change what can't be changed. Always remember Disraeli. His father felt the same way about his son as we do about Ellie—if only Disraeli weren't Jewish. So he had his children converted. Eventually, Benjamin Disraeli rose to become prime minister to Queen Victoria. So what does history say of him now? He was the only Jewish prime minister in English history. There is no escaping what *we* are or what *Elvira* is. But to deliberately hold her back, *that* would be unfair."

Sunday morning before Elvira went off to church was the one day of the week when all three of them had breakfast together. It was a treat for David that Elvira scrambled his eggs for him. It was a treat for her to do them. She had learned from Rebecca how to brown the chopped onions first, then drop in pieces of orange-red lox until it turned to a true salmon-pink color. Then she poured in the beaten eggs and carefully tended them, to make sure the mixture did not stick to the aluminum frying pan. When the eggs were done—not runny, not too dry, just as David loved them—she turned the mixture out onto a large plate and set it before him.

He applauded, beaming. "You see, Rebecca. Already your student outshines her teacher!" All three of them laughed. David addressed himself to his Sunday-morning treat. Instead of his usual bagel, he took a piece of the cornbread Elvira had baked early that morning.

They were enjoying their breakfast and making plans for their afternoon outing: a ride atop the open air Number 4 bus to the Metropolitan Museum of Art at Eighty-second Street, a few hours to enjoy the paintings and the statuary in the museum, then to find a nice place to have dinner.

The gaiety and the anticipation of the festive afternoon was interrupted when Elvira asked suddenly, "Will I still be able to wear the dress for graduation?"

"Wear your graduation dress? Of course," Rebecca said quickly. "Why not?"

"You were making it for me to wear for my speech," Elvira said.

David and Rebecca exchanged glances across the kitchen table. His asked, *Haven't you discussed it with her?* Hers admitted she had not found a suitable time to do so.

"I want to apologize for failing to become the valedictorian," Elvira continued.

David put aside his fork. He reached out to her, took her hand and, drawing her close to his side, put his arm around her.

"Darling, for what are you going to apologize? Being the smartest girl in your class? Having the best grades? The honor of being class valedictorian? A trivial honor which you earned but did not get. Because of the prejudice of other people. *They* should apologize, not you."

"You're not disappointed in me?" Elvira asked.

"Disappointed? We are proud! Proud that our girl, in spite of all their prejudice, made the best record in her class!" David said.

"Now go get dressed, darling," Rebecca said, "so you'll be ready for our special Sunday."

Absolved of uncommitted transgressions, Elvira started to her own room. Once she was out of earshot, Rebecca said, "She feels that she's failed. It almost tore my heart out."

"You think it did my heart any good?" David asked.

For the graduation exercises, each student was allotted only four tickets, the expectation being that two would be used by the parents and two would serve for doting grandparents. David suggested that Elvira have the privilege of deciding to whom her extra tickets would be given. She chose Pastor Wilder and his wife.

On the Sunday morning when she informed him, the old man was delighted to accept. He was very meticulous about taking down the information. He made it appear to be one of his most important engagements as he jotted it down on his calendar.

On Tuesday night, June 24, 1936, Reverend Wilder and his wife, Samantha, appeared at P.S. 173, where his brown face was in sharp contrast to those of the other graduation guests. Many assumed Wilder was a member of the janitorial staff dressed up for the special occasion. It was only when the Rosens greeted him and Rebecca kissed him on the cheek that the shock of truth made itself felt. Whispers ran through the auditorium. Only Principal Goodman's signal to the music teacher to give the downbeat to the school orchestra to commence the inevitable "Pomp and Circumstance" caused the shocked whispers to be replaced by the anticipation of seeing the young graduates march in. Each guest strained to identify his or her own special graduate. There were whispered sounds of proud recognition: "Doesn't she look sweet!" "My, she looks so pretty in that white dress!" "Look, Harry, isn't she a beauty?"

Rebecca and David said nothing when Elvira appeared in her place in line but silently they boasted: *She's the prettiest of all. And how she carries herself. Proud. She's proud.* They held hands, each pressing the other's with secret signals.

When Mr. Goodman introduced the clergyman to pronounce the benediction, all heads were bowed in reverence. But many eyes shifted left or right in the direction of the Rosens and the Wilders, wondering at their relationship.

Thereafter, the program followed the time-honored routine. Two songs by the school chorus. Remarks by Principal Goodman to the graduates, complimenting them on their graduation, spurring them on to greater achievements in high school and beyond. Another song by the chorus. Finally came the awarding of prizes, each of which was donated by some local merchant or group. The prize in Latin studies—ten dollars and a certificate—went to Peter Friedman, a plump young lad bursting out of the navy blue suit that had fit him on his bar mitzvah day. To great applause, he accepted the honor. The medal in math—five dollars and a certificate—was awarded to Stella Ostrowitz, who, when she came forward to accept it, tripped and almost lost her silver-framed glasses. Again, loud applause. The medal in civics, donated by the local Democratic Club—ten dollars and a certificate—went to Benjamin Dolan, a tall boy who was already beginning to exhibit signs of the adolescent acne that would plague him for years to come. The applause for him was even stronger. Before announcing the next award, Mr. Goodman paused. Then, unsure of the reception he would evoke, he cleared his throat, smiled beneficently, and spoke.

"And now the award for excellence in history, donated by the Upper West Side Republican Club—ten dollars and a certificate of merit to . . ." He paused before announcing, "Elvira Hitchins." Elvira came forward to accept the rolled-up certificate and the envelope containing her prize money.

David and Rebecca and Pastor and Mrs. Wilder applauded loudly, so loudly that it served to point up the thin, barely polite applause from the others. Rebecca heard a woman behind her whisper, "She's not nearly so dark as I expected."

Elvira accepted her prize. As she started back toward her seat, Mr. Goodman reached out to hold her in place. "And now the prize for the highest grade in English studies, donated by the Neighborhood Merchants Association of Washington Heights—ten dollars and a certificate of achievement—also to Elvira Hitchins."

Again applause, this time only slightly less halfhearted than before. Rebecca was almost out of her seat with enthusiasm until David pulled her back down. "Becca, a little modesty, please?"

"And now," Mr. Goodman announced, "that moment which all of us—faculty, parents, and guests—await with such interest and expectation: the voice of this new generation, our class valedictorian, Edna Schloss!"

To considerable applause, the girl came forward, carrying in her trembling hand the sheaf of papers that contained the speech she had written with the help of faculty members, her parents, and her older brother, who was a student at City College. She was a pretty girl, slightly awkward since she was tall for her young age. She seemed relieved to reach the lectern and be able to put down the papers she was clutching. She looked out at the audience, then glanced in the direction of her parents and her grandparents. She began: "Members of the faculty, parents, guests, and fellow students . . ."

There followed a number of the usual platitudes about education being the cornerstone of their future lives. About obligations to parents, school, and country. Promises to make this world a better place in which to live. She ended with what had become the inevitable and the unavoidable. "And as our president has so eloquently said, we look forward to the future knowing we have nothing to fear but fear itself."

Throughout the entire speech, Rebecca kept pressing David's hand in a manner that protested: *Elvira could have done it better, would have done it better; it's not fair, not fair.*

He pretended to be too involved listening to Edna Schloss to respond, until at the end, while the others applauded, he whispered to Rebecca and Pastor Wilder. "Elvira could have done it better, would have done it better. It's not fair, not fair."

They walked Pastor Wilder and his wife to the Eighth Avenue subway station. Elvira clutched her two certificates and her diploma to her breast as she walked alongside David and Mrs. Wilder, while the pastor hung back to say to Rebecca, "Two prizes, yet she does not seem happy. Why?"

Rebecca explained about being deprived of the honor of delivering the valedictory.

"So?" the old preacher said thoughtfully. "She's still at the age where she has illusions."

At the subway steps, Wilder bent down to be face to face with Elvira. "Child, when you come to school on Sunday, bring your two certificates. I want the whole Sunday school to see them. And I want you to make a speech. I would like to hear the speech you should have made tonight."

"You really want to hear . . ." Elvira started to ask.

"Yes, child. I really want to hear," he said. He kissed her on the cheek.

Together, the pastor and his wife started down the subway stairs.

David, Rebecca, and Elvira walked north along Broadway until they reached the corner of 178th Street, where the German ice-cream parlor was still open, serving the last groups of graduates and their families.

"This is a night for celebration," David said. "So let us celebrate. Elvira, when I first came over to this country and not much older than you the one thing in this world I always dreamed of was a big banana split. Three flavors of ice cream, chocolate, strawberry, vanilla, on half a banana, with whipped cream, wet walnuts, chocolate sauce, and a big red cherry on top. But in those days I never had enough money. After all, when I was young, fifteen cents was like a million dollars. Well, tonight, in your honor, because of your great achievement, *you* are going to realize my dream. You will pick out your own flavors of ice cream—your own sauce, everything exactly the way you want it. What do you say to that?"

"Oh, I'd love that!" Elvira said.

Behind the counter, holding a long glass banana-split boat in her one hand and a ready scooper in her other, the owner's wife trailed along with Elvira as she moved slowly, dawdling over the selection of each ingredient that went into her banana split.

"One scoop of vanilla," Elvira ordered. While the woman dug into the vat of vanilla, Elvira moved on, searching the open containers nestled amid the salted ice that kept their contents frozen. "And . . . and one scoop of chocolate." The woman added a scoop of chocolate. "And one scoop of straw-berry!" That request complied with, Elvira moved back down the long counter, selecting chocolate sauce in which to drown the banana and her three scoops of ice cream. She hesitated before the jars of sprinkles, nuts, and cherries until she de-cided in favor of the wet walnuts. When the woman doled out a generous portion, Elvira insisted, "More!" The woman shrugged, as if complaining, how much can this child eat. But she complied. "And now, now, whipped cream! Lots of whipped cream!" Elvira insisted.

David and Rebecca looked at each other. They had never seen Elvira so self-indulgent.

"She'll make herself sick," David whispered.

"Don't worry," Rebecca assured. "She'll never finish it."

"And on top," Elvira instructed the woman, "a cherry, a big red cherry."

Elvira insisted on carrying the overladen dish to the small, round marble-topped table. Once she set it down safely, she turned and started back to the counter.

"Darling, come back before it melts," David called. He was surprised, then startled, as he watched her. She was ordering another treat. This time the woman reached back for two sugar cones, topping each with a scoop of chocolate ice cream. "Rebecca, what do you suppose—" he started to ask until he saw Elvira reach into the pocket of her graduation dress and take out one of her prize envelopes. She tore it open, took out the ten-dollar bill, and handed it to the woman behind the counter.

"Ellie, no! I pay for them!"

He started toward her, but Rebecca reached out to seize his arm. "No, David. It's something she wants to do." He watched as Elvira carefully placed her change back in her pocket and returned to the table, handing one cone to Re-becca.

"Uncle David, eat your banana split before it melts," Elvira said.

He stared down at the banana split and realized she had selected every ingredient of his version of the most enticing, delicious, colorful indulgence he had ever imagined. And she had insisted on paying for it as well. He shook his head, smil-

ing, picked up the spoon, and began to dig in. Elvira and Rebecca watched, licking at their chocolate ice cream while
stealing amused glances at each other as David ate his way
through his dream.

Once home again, David sank into his favorite armchair
alongside the radio and drew Elvira close. "Sweetheart, I appreciate what you did. It was a wonderful surprise. But you
didn't have to pay for it.

"Yes I did."

"No, darling, no. What I decided when you were up there
getting your prizes, I thought, tomorrow I will take her to the
bank and we will open for her a savings account. You would
put in *your* twenty dollars. Aunt Rebecca and I would add
another twenty dollars, our special present to you, and you
would have money in the bank. That's a wonderful feeling,
money in the bank, now that banks are safe again. And that is
what we are going to do tomorrow. I will pay you back for
tonight so you can start out with an even forty dollars!"

Rebecca noticed it first. David realized only a moment
later, but too late, for Elvira's eyes overflowed.

"Elvira? Sweetheart? What's wrong?"

"*I* have to pay. I *have* to!"

"Who said?" David demanded.

"My mama," Elvira replied.

"Your mama said?" David looked to Rebecca for some explanation, but she was equally puzzled.

"That day . . . that last day . . ." Elvira said.

"Up in Saranac," Rebecca realized.

"My mama said, 'Child, you go through this life, don't
you pile up no burden of debt. Don't you leave this world
owing nothing to nobody.'"

David drew the girl onto his lap. "Elvira my dear, between
us there are no debts. A night like tonight, when we see you
step forward to get not just one but two prizes, we are paid
back a hundred times over for everything we ever did. We get
what my father used to call *naches*. Do you know what—"

Elvira anticipated him. "Yes, Uncle David. *Naches*. The
pleasure, the satisfaction, that parents and grandparents get
from children."

In mock futility, he threw up his hands. "As long as they
were at it, they should have given you a prize for excellence in
Yiddish, too. Just don't use any of those words in your speech
in Sunday school!"

21

"*Rebecca, sweetheart, darling*, the only thing you didn't pack are the Passover dishes!" David complained as he tried to close the second of two large suitcases. "Elvira, come here!" She approached the bed on which the suitcase rested. He picked her up and sat her on the bulging piece of luggage. "Now, make yourself heavy, darling!" He tried once more to bring both sides of the suitcase close enough to engage the lock. His frustration was beginning to show, not only in his eyes but in the film of sweat that broke out on his forehead.

Rebecca tried to explain, "When people go to the country in the early summer and expect to stay till Labor Day, they have to be prepared for all kinds of weather—cold at night, warm during the day, rain, swimming in the pool. They have a pool there at the Concord."

"I know, I know," David said, still straining to close the suitcase.

Elvira timidly suggested, "Uncle David, maybe if *you* sat on the bag and *I* tried to close it, it would work better."

Impatiently, David replied, "Maybe if both my dear wife and I sat on it we would have a chance." With one more desperate attack he managed to bring the top and bottom of the suitcase into sufficient proximity to achieve locking.

"There! Finally!" he said, with a sense of accomplishment. "Now, to get these down the stairs and into a taxi! Come, come, little one. Come, Rebecca! And don't forget the sandwiches."

The journey on which they were about to venture had actually begun on a day in early June, when David had looked up from *The New York Times* and said, "Becca, I must do something about this!"

Expecting David's solution to some problem that neither President Roosevelt nor *The New York Times* had been able to solve, she interrupted mending the clothes that she had promised to repair for Mrs. Feinstein at the Anche Chesed orphanage. Now that Elvira no longer required her full time and attention, Rebecca had volunteered.

Resigned to David's fulminations, criticisms, and solutions, Rebecca had said, "Yes, dear?"

"Rebecca, do not indulge me. This time it is something serious, close to this family, and a problem we can do something about." His tone sounded so immediate that she interrupted her sewing to listen. "Rebecca, it says here in the *Times* that bad as last year's infantile-paralysis epidemic was, this coming season will be worse. You and Elvira have to leave the city for the summer."

"The whole summer? Who'll take care of you?" Rebecca protested.

"Find some place where I can come up every weekend. But never mind me. It's Elvira we have to think of. They call it Infantile Paralysis, but older children, even adults, get it."

"How do we know it's safer in the country than the city?"

"Says here it will be worse in the cities."

"A person can't hide from it," Rebecca argued. "If they could, would a rich man like President Roosevelt have caught it? He could live anywhere he wanted."

"Darling Rebecca, if anything happened to that child and we could have prevented it, I would never forgive myself. Find us a place!"

By the beginning of the second week in June, Rebecca had discovered a place, in the Catskills. It was a new resort, opening for its first season, and its rates were especially reasonable, to draw patrons away from the old, established Grossinger's. This hotel was called The Concord. It was built, out of spite, by a wealthy man who felt Grossinger's had treated him with less than the respect he considered his due as czar of the hair-tonic industry.

Bus and train schedules between New York City and the Catskills would enable David to arrive in time for supper on Friday and leave after lunch on Sunday, without taking time away from his business. That was important during the summer, since all derbies had to be delivered to the stores and be on the shelves by Labor Day. No self-respecting gentleman would wear a straw hat or a Panama a single day after Labor Day, so David's transportation was as crucial to their summer vacation as their accommodations. On all counts the Concord had qualified.

Now, on this last day of June 1936, they were finally on their way.

When they boarded the train at 125th Street, Elvira immediately claimed a seat next to the window. David and Rebecca were content to sit behind her. As the train rattled over the many switches on its way out of Manhattan and into the Bronx, David leaned close to Rebecca to ask, "You're sure there won't be trouble?"

"I wrote to them: one room and all meals for a woman and a child and weekends for her husband. I couldn't be any clearer than that."

"What did you tell them about Elvira?"

"I called her our niece."

"Did you *tell* them?" he insisted, in danger of raising his voice so he might be overheard.

"No."

"Rebecca!" he remonstrated.

"I can't believe they will turn us away. And if they try, I will raise such a *tummel* they'll wish they hadn't," she threatened.

The train had cleared the Bronx and the suburbs and was racing north along the Hudson River. David was engrossed in his *New York Times*, muttering from time to time criticisms that Rebecca did not understand but could well imagine. Meantime, she continued crocheting a collar and cuffs of white silk thread with which to decorate Elvira's dressy dress for special occasions up at the new resort. She had just finished the first half of the collar when she was interrupted by Elvira, who had left her seat to stand alongside David.

David lowered his paper. "We haven't been on the way an hour yet and already you're hungry? I'll get the sandwiches." He rose to get the shoe box in which Rebecca had packed the food.

But Rebecca could read Elvira's eyes. They did not speak of hunger, not the kind that could be satisfied by food. Rebecca beckoned to her. Elvira slipped past David, and Rebecca embraced her. With their cheeks pressed one against the other, Rebecca and Elvira looked out at the scene racing by them, at the Hudson River, at an old oil tanker chugging its way downriver, at small pleasure boats that darted across the water insectlike in profusion now that summer was here.

"There were no little boats the last time, were there, sweetheart?" Rebecca asked.

"Uh-uh," Elvira responded, staring out the window.

"That's because it was almost winter," Rebecca said. "You know, darling, it is very natural to feel sad now."

"It is?"

"Every time you take this ride up the Hudson, you will remember. And you will feel sad. Because that day we were going to see your mama up at Saranac. It was also the last time."

"Then it's all right to feel sad?"

"Oh yes. You are honoring your mama's memory. Even tears are all right at a time like this."

"They are?" Elvira said, relief in her young voice.

Soon tears were slowly tracing down her light brown cheeks. They rode on in silence, except for an occasional gasp from Elvira as she struggled to sniff back her tears.

Almost an hour later, David whispered, "Becca, she must be hungry by now." Rebecca nodded. He rose to take down the shoe box from the luggage rack. He untied it, lifted the lid, and exclaimed, "Does your Aunt Rebecca know how to pack a lunch!"

Elvira turned to him in time to be handed a sandwich of cold sliced chicken between two slices of home-baked white challah wrapped in wax paper. Her eyes still damp, she began to eat.

To lighten the atmosphere, David joked, "Maybe next time we'll take an airplane. I once read in the *Times* that there is an airline called Pan American that is beginning to serve hot meals. In the air. Imagine, flying along a hundred miles an hour, maybe even faster, and eating matzo ball soup! Come to think of it, how do they keep the soup in the bowl while they are going so fast? A matzo ball you can hold in place with your spoon, but soup? I'll take one of my Rebecca's chicken sandwiches any time. Right, Elvira?"

With a mouthful of sandwich, Elvira nodded and smiled. David cast a sly look at Rebecca, indicating, *See, she's feeling better already.*

When the train pulled into the station at Monticello, there were several station wagons waiting to pick up new arrivals. David sought out the one with the name THE CONCORD boldly painted on its wood-paneled side. The driver was eagerly searching for guests for the new hotel.

David called to him, "Hey, driver! Don't just stand there. Lend a hand. These suitcases are not exactly filled with marshmallows."

The driver greeted them with a broad welcoming smile as he started toward them. Then he stopped, drew close, and spoke in a whisper, "Mister, you sure you supposed to come to The Concord?" His eyes, which were directed at Elvira, explained more bluntly.

Rebecca stepped forward. "I made reservations. By mail. Here!" She thrust forward the letter she pulled out of her purse.

The man examined it closely, and shrugged, a reaction that seemed to say, *You're making a big mistake, but if that's what you want* . . . Aloud, he said, "I'm just the driver. I'm not obligated to help with the luggage." Which was an outright lie, but David decided not to argue the point.

The new Concord hotel was somewhat more modest in size than the advertisements had proclaimed. But it seemed clean and suitable. Rebecca and Elvira climbed out. David went to the back of the station wagon to take down the two bags. The driver suggested, "I'd wait if I were you." Despite the warning, David struggled to haul out the two bags. One in each hand to lend balance, he started resolutely toward the entrance, following behind Rebecca and Elvira.

The lobby smelled of new paint, new furniture, and new carpeting. Behind the reception desk a young woman, heavily made up and attired in a bright flowered blouse, assumed her best and broadest smile of greeting.

"Welcome, welcome to the . . ." she started to call out warmly until her eyes fell on Elvira, who, seeing her look, started to draw back. Rebecca seized her hand and made her stand firm.

"We have a reservation," Rebecca said, handing over the letter.

The desk clerk reached for the confirmation as if it were a hand grenade with the pin pulled. She glanced at it. "This letter says woman and child for the week, husband for weekends only."

Rebecca counted off and pointed: "Husband. Wife. Child."

Just a minute," the flustered receptionist said. By now perspiration was beginning to smear her heavy makeup. "I'll be right back."

Moments later she appeared followed by Sol Gordon, a tall, aging man in overalls, flaky white dust coating his thinning hair and his tan face. Gordon had obviously been interrupted in last-minute plastering and painting of some rooms.

"So? What is the trouble?" he demanded with the impatience of a man struggling against a deadline. He interrupted himself once he saw Elvira. "Aha!" he exclaimed. "Seems we got a problem here." Gordon gestured David aside with an imperious forefinger. Not only David but Rebecca, too, complied. When the three were out of Elvira's earshot, the old man accused, "Grossinger's sent you here to sabotage me! Right? I am breaking my—" Rebecca's presence caused him to edit himself. "When I am breaking my *back* to get everything ready for my first summer, my first big weekend, I don't need this kind of trouble."

"There's no trouble," David said. "Just give us our room. Let us get settled. You will find that we are a nice, quiet family."

"But my other guests—" Gordon protested.

"We will not bother the other guests. We're only looking for a place where Elvira can be safe from polio. They say this year is going to be the worst ever."

"I know, I know," the old man commiserated. He shook his head. "I was better off in the hair-tonic business. I made a good product. I had top salesmen. And no trouble. All I made was money. Who needed a hotel?" He scratched his head, dislodging a shower of white flakes from his thinning hair.

"*Bist a Yid?*" David asked.

"What else?" the man replied.

"You ever been turned away from any place *because* you are a Jew?"

"Who hasn't?" the man responded grimly.

"Yet you think it's perfectly all right to turn someone *else* away?" Rebecca asked.

"Look, lady, it's not me. But I am in business to please my guests. This whole hotel—the dining room, the swimming pool, the tennis courts, the theater, the bar—all here for only one reason. To please my guests!" To add to his difficulties, a bespeckled painter came out to harass him.

"Look, Gordon, I got three painters waiting for you to okay the color for the last four rooms. I have to pay them by the hour!"

"Okay, okay, okay already!" the tormented proprietor responded. He turned back to the Rosens. "Look, people, I don't want trouble. And I don't have time. So I'll tell you what. I will find you a nice, quiet room. In the back. And if you just . . . kind of . . ." He groped for the right words. "If you would just—I mean, don't be too obvious. You know what I mean?"

Two minor crises arose during the week. The first occurred when Rebecca brought Elvira to the children's activity counselor. That title was bestowed on the college student whose job for the summer was to keep all children occupied and entertained between meals while their parents played tennis or golf, swam in the pool, enjoyed canasta, bridge, or gin rummy, or just exposed to the strong, hot summer sun as much of themselves as was decent.

The counselor proved to be a stocky young woman, a junior at Savage College, a school for those studying to become physical-training instructors. Her face was strong and well tanned. Hanging around her neck, between her ample breasts, suspended by a leather thong, was a policeman's whistle, which she used to keep her unruly charges in line. She was blowing that whistle when Rebecca approached her with Elvira at her side.

"I'm Rebecca Rosen," she began.

The counselor replied quickly, "Trudy. Trudy Boykin."

"Trudy, this is Elvira."

"Yes, yes, I know. I heard," the counselor said.

"She'd like to join your group."

The counselor glanced at Rebecca, deliberately avoiding

Elvira's eyes. Rebecca replied, "Don't worry. She goes to an all-white school."

"You understand, I have nothing against it. I just don't want her hurt," the counselor explained.

"She does very well with other children," Rebecca replied.

"It's their parents I'm thinking about," Trudy Boykin said. "But we'll face that if it happens. Hello, Elvira. Would you like to join our group? We're climbing the monkey bars this morning. Come. Join in."

Rebecca went off to the pool. There she sat by herself, aware that she was the object of study by the other women, whose husbands, like David, were working in the city.

It was at lunch, after the children had had a chance to report to their mothers about their morning's activities, that the crisis arose. Two mothers, by mutual agreement, descended on Trudy Boykin while she was having her lunch at the staff table.

"Trudy," Beatrice Warshaw began. "What my Rosalie just told me upset me very much!"

Prepared for the onslaught, the counselor decided to pretend ignorance. "I thought Rosalie did very well this morning. Seemed to enjoy herself."

"Miss Boykin, I am not tipping you two dollars a week to take care of my Rosalie so she can play with niggers. If I wanted that, I would move to Harlem!"

"Yes, Harlem!" Hannah Isaacs, the other mother, agreed.

"Now, I know Mr. Gordon doesn't pay you very much. You depend on tips. And every dollar counts. So whatever that Mrs. Rosen is tipping you, I will add that to my two dollars so you don't lose anything. Just get rid of that child so my Rosalie doesn't have to play with—"

"Mrs. Warshaw," the counselor interrupted. "Don't use that word again. Now, if you feel your Rosalie is being hurt by playing with the group, there is a simple way to avoid that. Just keep her out."

"What?" Mrs. Warshaw exploded in outrage. "Why do you think I come here in the first place? All year long, every hour of every day, I devote to my Rosalie. During the summer at least I am entitled to a little freedom."

Hannah Isaacs nodded vigorously in agreement.

"I haven't had any complaints from the children," Trudy said. "Once they realized Elvira was just another child, they all got along fine."

"I don't *like* the idea that they all got along fine," Beatrice Warshaw insisted. "Now, if you don't do something about this, I am going to speak to Mr. Gordon!"

That evening during supper, Mr. Gordon made a conspicuous entrance into the dining room. The grim manner in which he marched down the center aisle to the staff table made all the diners who were aware of the conflict between Mrs. Warshaw and counselor Boykin stop eating and observe his determined journey. He reached the staff table. Though everyone in the dining room strained to eavesdrop, they could not, for Gordon spoke in a whisper.

"Trudy, I guess you know. Mrs. Warshaw came to see me."

"I expected she would."

"Are you going to change your mind?" the old man asked.

"Mr. Gordon, this being your first year, I don't want to create any trouble for you. But I can't do anything to hurt that girl." She glanced in Elvira's direction, at the adjacent table.

"So what do we do?" Gordon asked.

"If you want, I'll quit."

"And waste your whole summer? Where else are you going to get a job now?"

"Call it a matter of principle. But I can't hurt a child. It goes against everything I ever learned in my teaching courses."

"Oy, Trudy, Trudy," old Gordon lamented. Then his face seemed to brighten. "But you know, you gave me an idea. And besides, crazy about that Mrs. Warshaw I'm not. So when I leave this table, don't look happy. Okay?"

"Okay, Mr. Gordon."

"Listen, an actress you're not. But if you could look like you're crying a little, it wouldn't do any harm." With an angry glare at Trudy Boykin, Gordon started trudging back up the aisle toward the table at which Beatrice Warshaw and Hannah Isaacs had interrupted eating to anticipate his arrival.

Gordon leaned between them. "Ladies, the way you two look tonight, I think you belong at the first table near the door. You give the Concord a classy look, real classy. Now, I just had a conference with my children's activity counselor. I laid her out like you never heard. Don't make it obvious, but sneak a look. Is she still crying?"

"Yes, yes, I think she is," Beatrice Warshaw was happy to report.

"Which is what creates the problem. Trudy Boykin has just quit. Here I am with fourteen children and tomorrow no counselor. I have to think of all these mothers, stuck with their own children for a whole summer. You see my problem? And especially my first year in the hotel business. You ladies have to help me out. What I suggest, let your Rosalie and your Seymour make the decision. If they don't like the group, they don't have to be part of it. That's the best I can do. If you ladies want to leave, I will gladly give you back your deposit. More fair a man couldn't be."

"We'll . . . we'll think about it," was as far as Beatrice Warshaw would commit herself.

Hannah Isaacs, however, had another reservation. "And what happens when it comes kiddies' swim time in the pool?"

Gordon's lined face turned pathetic and pleading. "My dear Mrs. Isaacs, how much can one little girl pee in such a big pool?"

The next morning, Rosalie Warshaw and Seymour Isaacs reported to Trudy Boykin. That crisis appeared to have passed.

The second crisis arose in the third week of the Rosens' stay at the Concord.

Having exhausted all the possible games and activities that could command the interest of the children who stayed for longer than two weeks, Trudy Boykin decided to infuse them with fresh enthusiasm by having them perform songs, poetry, and recitations of their own. This was especially helpful on rainy days, when no outdoor sports or hikes were possible.

One boy, Irving Cooperman, who was twelve, had already begun to learn the bar mitzvah speech his Hebrew teacher had written for him for the coming October. He delivered it with studied and appropriate gestures. Rosalie Warshaw performed her imitation of Shirley Temple in *The Littlest Rebel*, since many people (meaning her grandparents) insisted that she looked exactly like that young star. She even attempted the tap dance that Shirley Temple performed with Bill Robinson, except that Rosalie failed to complete it.

To soften Rosalie's embarrassment, Trudy Boykin turned to Elvira. "And now, my dear, what have you chosen to entertain us with? A song? A recitation? A dance?"

"It's sort of all three."

Elvira assumed the stance and attitude of the choir in the Ajalon Baptist Church. In her clear, clean voice she commenced to sing, sway, and clap her hands to accent the words.

> Oh, freedom, oh, freedom,
> Oh, freedom over me.
> And before I'd be a slave
> I'll be buried in my grave
> And go home to my Lord and be free.
> No more moaning, no more moaning,
> No more moaning over me!
> And before I'd be a slave
> I'll be buried in my grave,
> And go home to my Lord and be free!

Her singing, rhythmic clapping, and swaying proved infectious. Other children began to join in. Trudy asked Elvira to repeat the gospel song so they could all sing along with her. By the time lunch was announced the entire group was singing, swaying, and clapping their hands in unison with Elvira, none more enthusiastically than Rosalie Warshaw.

Unfortunately, at that moment Beatrice Warshaw appeared to take her daughter to lunch. She was shocked to find her swaying, clapping her hands, and singing a totally unfamiliar song. What disturbed her most was the realization that her Rosalie was being led by, was imitating, a colored girl in a song obviously meant only for colored people. She stalked into the room, seized Rosalie by the hand, and dragged her out, though the child protested. Beatrice Warshaw went straightaway to seek out Mr. Gordon.

"Something must be done!" Beatrice Warshaw proclaimed, "about that girl! And about that Trudy Boykin!"

After he had calmed her down, old Gordon considered the problem quite gravely. "All right, Mrs. Warshaw, All right! I will put a stop to this at once." He started in the direction of the Rosen table.

"Mrs. Rosen," Gordon began. "Aren't there enough songs, Broadway songs, patriotic songs, school songs? Why did it have to be a Negro song? And on top of that, the other children . . ."

Rebecca turned to Elvira. "What did you sing, dear?"

Elvira said softly, "'Oh, Freedom, Oh, Freedom.'"

"I see," Rebecca said, as the nature of Gordon's complaint became quite clear to her. "And the other children?"

"They were singing right along with her. And if that's not bad enough, they were also clapping their hands and shaking from side to side. So I'm afraid, Mrs. Rosen, when your husband comes up Friday evening, you and the little one will have to leave. I'm sorry. I know how bad things are in the city with polio. Maybe I can find you some small hotel up here that will take you. I'll call around. That's the best I can do."

"I . . . I understand, Mr. Gordon," Rebecca said.

"You'll talk to Mr. Rosen, or do you want me to?"

"I'll do it."

"Becca," David said intensely but softly. "We *can't* leave. Every day you hear on the radio, you see in the newspapers, kids by the thousands paralyzed by polio, dying. We can't go back."

"Mr. Gordon hasn't been able to find us another place. I've been making phone calls. There's nothing. People have fled the city in such droves every hotel and boarding house is full. You'll have to take us back."

"I'm not going to expose Elvira," David said thoughtfully. "I'm not going to risk her life."

He was unusually quiet and thoughtful while he showered, shaved, and dressed for Friday-night supper. Not once did he berate the Supreme Court, the president, or *The New York Times*. To Rebecca, he appeared suspiciously silent for the effusive husband she had lived with for so long.

David had dressed in his slacks and a fresh sport shirt open at the collar. He looked every bit the successful businessman at leisure. The Rosens were ready to go to supper.

As they were about to leave for the dining room, David spoke for the first time, then only to mutter, "Walls . . . walls . . ."

"David?" Rebecca asked, glancing toward Elvira, who shared her puzzlement.

"There has to be some way. But who has seven days?" he asked of no one in particular. "I have only a weekend. Counting leaving after lunch Sunday, a very short weekend."

"David!"

He avoided Rebecca and turned to Elvira. "Darling, there is written in the Torah how when the Israelites reached the city of Jericho and were confronted by those high, thick walls . . ."

Elvira anticipated him. "I know. We sing about it in church." Which she proceeded to do: "Joshua fit the battle of Jericho, Jericho, Jerico, Joshua fit the battle of Jericho, And the walls came tumbling down."

"In church you can do that with a song. In the Torah it took seven days of marching around Jericho to break down those walls. But unfortunately, there are walls that you can march around not for seven days or seven years, or even seven hundred years, and they still won't come tumbling down: the walls of prejudice. Yet it is now necessary for us to find a way in only hours. Hours," he repeated with great concern. "You know what they say about necessity."

"It's the mother of invention," Elvira supplied.

"Right! We have a necessity. We could stand a little invention," he said thoughtfully. "Come! On to supper!"

They arrived at the entrance to the bustling, noisy dining room, full as on every Friday evening, with children and mothers reunited with fathers and husbands. With Elvira between them, David and Rebecca paused at the entrance. David whispered to Rebecca, "No matter what I say, *don't look surprised*. And *you* either, Elvira darling. Now, let's go!"

Thus prepared, Elvira, David, and Rebecca started into the dining room. It was obvious from the sudden silence that greeted them that most of the guests had heard of their expulsion. David pretended not to notice.

Instead, in a voice intended to sound casual and chatty, but loud enough to be heard for many tables around, David Rosen enthused, "Well, soon as I heard that on the radio, right away I sent *your uncle* a cable. I said, 'To hell with Hitler. We are proud you won four gold medals for the United States!'"

A tidal wave of startled whispers followed in their wake.

"Did you hear that?"

"Jesse Owens's niece!"

"Must be. Why else would Rosen send a cable?"

"I never guessed! Jessie Owens's niece."

Throughout supper, the Rosen table was the focus of all eyes. The waiters began to lavish unusual care and attention on them.

After supper, since it was still light enough, David, Rebecca, and Elvira strolled around the pool area. Other guests watched, and many smiled at Elvira. One woman came up to her and said, "Your uncle certainly showed that Hitler with his Aryan superiority."

"Right!" a man seated across the pool chimed in.

When they returned to the hotel Mr. Gordon came out to greet them. He took David by the elbow to walk him a few steps to the side.

"Rosen! Why didn't you tell me we had a celebrity in our midst? I would have given you a rate!" The old man promised, "I can still make an adjustment for the rest of the season."

"No thank you," David insisted. "I, too, am a businessman. I believe a price is a price."

"Meantime, are you satisfied with your accommodations? I could move you to a bigger room. One in front. A suite, maybe."

"Her uncle doesn't like the child to be too conspicuous."

There was never again any mention of the Rosen family leaving the Concord. And every evening when they returned from supper, there was a bowl of fresh fruit in their room.

The summer passed. The polio epidemic had been as drastic and punishing as had been foretold by the experts.

On the Sunday morning of Labor Day weekend, David decided that they would leave early to beat the migration back to the city.

As the driver was loading their suitcases into the station

wagon, Mr. Gordon and Trudy came out to say goodbye. Trudy and Elvira embraced and kissed.

Gordon shook hands with David. He kissed Rebecca on the cheek. "Have a good year, my dear. And you are always welcome here. Also the child. Though through the summer I often thought, if only—"

Rebecca interrupted. "Please don't say it. She *isn't*. She *won't* be. And we love her exactly as she is."

"You're right. She is what she is. A lovely child. And she tells me that next week she is starting at Wadleigh High School."

"Yes," Rebecca said proudly.

"Not only lovely, but smart as well," the old man remarked. "A *Yiddisher kup*," tapping his own temple.

Whereupon he bent as low as his arthritic back would permit, kissed Elvira, and then whispered, "Say hello to your uncle for me. And any time he wishes, he has a free weekend at the Concord."

Gordon was still waving at them as the station wagon pulled out of the grounds of the Concord.

22

*R*ebecca stood at the ironing board carefully pressing the white middy blouse. She used just a touch of starch to give it the gloss and firmness that would make Elvira look her best on this, her first day at Wadleigh High School. It was a big step in a child's life, her first day at a school far from her home. David had bought her a new bookbag, much sturdier, for the bigger, heavier books she would be receiving. He also bought her a fountain pen—a Parker Duofold, bright orange barrel with black tips at either end. Elvira had picked out her own notebooks, with lined pages and stiff covers.

While Rebecca ironed, David was giving Elvira last-minute advice, to which she listened, nodding all the while, though she had heard exactly the same advice from him a number of times before.

"This nickel for the subway downtown. This one for coming home. And this nickel you will keep tied in your handkerchief for just in case. Here is a dime, for milk with your lunch. And make sure it is milk. I hear some kids have sodas with their sandwiches. Milk! You hear?"

"Yes, Uncle David," Elvira said for the sixth time.

"The sandwiches . . . Rebecca, did you make her sandwiches yet?"

"I made them, Uncle David," Elvira said.

"*You* made them? By yourself? What kind?"

"One sliced egg with lettuce. One chicken with mayonnaise. Both on challah."

"No fruit? No cookies?" David asked. "You will be gone a whole day." he lamented, as if malnutrition were an imminent threat.

"David," Rebecca remonstrated. "She had breakfast. She will be back by four o'clock, in time for a snack. She won't starve."

"I remember when I was a little boy, most of the time in cheder all I could think about was food. I was always hungry."

"When you were a boy in Europe, we were *all* always hungry. That's why we're here."

"And yet, did you see those unemployment figures in the *Times* yesterday? With everything Roosevelt is doing, things don't get any better."

"David, it's a little early in the morning for political lectures. Elvira, slip on this middy. Let me see how it looks."

Once Elvira had put on her blouse, Rebecca handed her the navy-blue silk kerchief that, with the pleated navy-blue skirt, completed her outfit. Elvira slipped the kerchief under the wide collar of the blouse, tied it into a neat square sailor's knot, and presented herself for inspection.

David stood back to make his expert appraisal. "Turn around, darling." She turned so quickly her pleated skirt billowed out slightly. "Rebecca, go get the camera!"

"David, there's no time," Rebecca protested.

"Becca! The camera!" he insisted.

She hurried to the hall closet, where they always kept the Brownie. Meantime, David coached, "Elvira darling, close to the window. I will need light. Closer!"

David aimed the camera carefully. "Don't move. Don't breathe. Just smile." He pressed the little lever at the side of the camera. "There! One day, Elvira, one day you will show this picture to your children. You will say, 'This is the way I looked on my first day in high school!'"

Meantime, tense and impatient, Rebecca was slipping into her coat, urging, "David, enough talk. We have to get going! Elvira sweetheart, your bookbag, your notebook, your lunch. Come!"

Elvira did not move. Instead, she wet her lips as if preparing to speak, but she did not utter a word.

"Elvira?" Rebecca called to her.

"Aunt Rebecca, where are you going?"

"Going? Where else? To take you down to school!"

"I . . ." Elvira hesitated, then said bravely, "Aunt Rebecca, I would like to go by myself."

Rebecca looked from Elvira to David.

"Becca, high school. She *should* go by herself. She is not a child any longer."

Painful as it was for her, Rebecca replied, "Yes, of course. I should have suggested it. Go, darling. Go alone. Have a good day. I hope you like all your new teachers."

She helped Elvira with her bag, notebook, and lunch box, followed her to the door, and kissed her. "Good luck, darling!"

David waited in the living room, heard the front door close, and heard Rebecca's slow steps back along the hallway. By the time she reached the archway, she had tears in her eyes. She turned suddenly and started back to the door.

"Becca! Where are you going?" David demanded.

"I will only follow her to make sure she gets to the subway safely."

"Becca, no! Come back!"

She hesitated, her hand on the doorknob. "Becca!" he called once more. As she reached the living room, he said, "Don't you think it was a *shtuch* for me, too? To hear her say, 'I am going alone.' She is making a declaration of independence. And she's right. We have to get used to that."

"But her first day . . ." Rebecca protested.

"What better time to start than on a first day?"

Rebecca nodded and slipped out of her coat. "David, you will be late downtown."

"I told them I would be late this morning. I said, 'Boys, Monday morning I have family business to attend to.' Besides, the way the business is growing, I am entitled to take a little time off. Today I will take the whole day off! I will call and tell the boys that something unforeseen—that's the word they use in the *Times* all the time—something unforeseen has happened and I will not be in today. Then we will take the bus down to Fifth Avenue. We will window-shop. And if we find something you like, we might even buy it. Would you like that?"

"Yes, but—"

"Always a but. What is it this time?"

"Suppose something goes wrong? She has an accident? She loses her carfare? Or her lunch? And she calls here and there's no answer?"

"Rebecca, suppose the Messiah comes and knocks on our door and there's no answer?" he asked. "Put your coat back on! I am not going to let you sit here all day and torment yourself. I think that child is wiser than you are." Then he added grudgingly, "Maybe wiser than me, too. It's not easy, Rebecca, when they decide they are all grown-up."

It had been a bewildering first morning for Elvira. Math class. Biology class. English. Gym. Four different teachers. Four different groups of classmates. No two teachers attacked the first day in the same way. In math, biology, and English, the teacher handed out textbooks. But in math, Miss Stevenson wrote an algebra problem on the blackboard and challenged the class to solve it. Before the bell rang announcing the end of class, she gave her students an assignment to be brought in the next morning.

In biology class, Elvira found the walls hung with giant representations, in full color, of the stages of development of the frog from egg to tadpole to its final form. There were also full-color charts of various forms of plant and animal life. Miss Bogart assigned the girls by pairs to the lab tables that were arranged in rows throughout the room. Elvira was assigned to a table with a very tall red-haired girl who positioned herself at the far end of the table. Miss Bogart either did not notice or else was too eager to get on with her first lecture on the importance of the lower forms of animal life to understanding the human species.

Mrs. Shor, the English teacher, handed out the textbooks first. Then she spent the entire class time speaking of the use of language, the appreciation of literature, and the sound and feel of words.

Elvira listened with total concentration, for Mrs. Shor, a slender, gray-haired woman, spoke as if she were truly in love with language. When she read from a poem by John Milton, even those girls who had been distracted and restless before became still and attentive, so when the reading ended in a whisper, it was heard throughout the classroom.

"That, my dears, is the power of words," Mrs. Shor said. "You come here today fresh from grade school. But by the time you leave my course, by the time you become Mrs.

Shor's girls, a title of which I am very proud, you will be able to express yourselves in a manner that will influence the world around you. We may not all be poets, but we do have thoughts and feelings to convey. Language is the tool by which we do so."

Having secured their rapt attention, Mrs. Shor said, "Each term, with a new class, I have a standard assignment. Since you girls all come from different parts of the city, different homes, different backgrounds, introduce yourselves to me and to the class in a short essay, which is to be entitled, 'Who Am I?' Thus, we will get to know each other. I will expect your essays next Monday morning."

Having been subjected to such a variety of teachers, each an ardent advocate of her subject, Elvira was quite relieved, finally, to come to gym class.

In the locker room with thirty other girls, all struggling to get out of their skirts and into gym bloomers, Elvira was too rushed, too eager to get out onto the gymnasium floor on time to pay heed to the other girls. If she had looked around, she would have caught the glances of the other girls, who were noticeably uncomfortable sharing with a Negro such an intimate experience as undressing and dressing.

Miss Dolan was a robust woman, attired in middy blouse, gym bloomers, and rubber-soled black shoes,

"Line up, girls! Single file. Face me!"

The girls scrambled to form a line, toeing the black line on the floor that marked the border of the basketball court. Each time Elvira sought to take up a place in the line, the two girls between whom she stood moved away to join the line at the other end. After several attempts, Elvira realized the futility of trying to find a place in line and stood off to one side by herself.

This exercise in silent rejection did not escape Miss Dolan. She called out, "You . . . the girl off there . . . what is your name?"

"Elvira Hitchins."

"Well, Elvira, close up ranks. Join the group."

Elvira moved next to the girl at the end of the line. She sensed the girl's impulse to move away, restrained only by the sharp eye of Miss Dolan.

"All right, now, girls! First a little warmup exercise. Watch me and do likewise!"

She jumped to spread her feet apart while at the same time clapping her hands over her head. Then she jumped again while bringing her feet together, again clapping her hands over her head.

"All right now," she called out. "One and two and three and four. Everybody!"

Soon she had the entire class imitating her in unison, except for one girl, who kept raising her hand to explain that she should be excused since she was having her menstrual period.

After gym class and a change back into middy blouse and skirt, Elvira was relieved to find that lunch period came next. Lunch box in hand, she stood in line in the basement lunchroom to buy a small bottle of milk. Other girls who did not bring their own lunch bought sandwiches, plates of baked beans, milk or soft drinks, and cupcakes wrapped in waxed paper. Elvira became aware that though the line was long and slow, the girls crowded together so they created a noticeable gap both ahead of her and behind her.

Undismayed, she stayed in line, picking out her bottle of milk, clutching her metal lunch box. Once she had paid her dime, she was free to find a place at one of the long tables, each long enough to accommodate six girls, three on each side. Elvira scanned the room and recognized the girl who had sat in front of her in English class. There was room at that table. Elvira started for it. She set down her milk and her lunch box. Slowly, one by one, the girls slipped away, taking their lunch with them to find places at other tables.

At a table intended for six, Elvira ended up alone. She opened her lunch box, took out her chicken sandwich, unwrapped the waxed paper, picked up half her sandwich, and began to eat. She felt tears rush to her eyes. But all the girls were watching. She determined she would not cry. But neither could she finish her lunch. She ate only the soft part of the half sandwich and needed sips of milk to get it down. She shoved the uneaten crusts back into the lunch box, closed it, deposited her bottle in the crate at the door, and left.

Alone, sitting on a step in the empty stairwell between the

basement and the first floor, Elvira remained determined not to cry despite how much it hurt. When she heard the excited voices of girls emerging from the lunchroom in response to the clanging bell, she rose, consulted her schedule, and went to her class in American history.

Rebecca had made sure to return early from her venture down to Fifth Avenue with David. She insisted on being there to greet Elvira when she returned. In response to the sound of Elvira's key in the door, Rebecca raced to greet her.

"Elvira darling, how did it go? Tell me, how was it? What is high school like? I always wondered . . ."

Elvira smiled her broadest smile. "It's different—I mean, they treat you so grown-up. I already have homework in algebra, English, and history. They don't waste time, those high school teachers."

Despite Elvira's valiant attempt to appear excited and enthusiastic, Rebecca sensed, *This is not my Elvira. She is smiling too much, trying to cheer me up too much.*

Her suspicions were confirmed when she took Elvira's lunch box from her hand. It was almost as heavy as it had been early that morning.

"Elvira . . . sweetheart?"

"I . . . I wasn't hungry," Elvira tried to evade.

Rebecca took her hand, drew her close, and embraced her. "Tell me, darling."

With her face nestled against Rebecca's cheek, Elvira was able to unburden herself of the hurts inflicted on her in the course of a single day.

"Well, don't you worry, darling. Tomorrow I will go down to that school and talk to Miss Flaherty."

"No, please don't," Elvira protested.

"I won't let them treat you this way," Rebecca insisted.

"Please, Aunt Rebecca, no. If Miss Flaherty does anything, it will only make things worse."

"How can children be so cruel?" Rebecca lamented, shaking her head sadly.

The next morning when Elvira set out for school, Rebecca followed her to the door. "You're sure, darling, you don't want me to say anything?"

"I'm sure, Aunt Rebecca."

By the end of the first week, Elvira's isolation had become a fixed mode of conduct. Only in those classes where girls were made to sit in alphabetical order did she take her place among the H's. In other classes and in gym, where students were free to exercise their preferences, Elvira always ended up alone. In the lunchroom there was one table that all others shunned and had become hers by default.

She covered her hurt by reading her assignments while she ate. But she was determined to have her lunch and, above all, not to give way to tears.

On the second Tuesday of the term, Mrs. Shor arrived early, carrying with her the batch of essays her students had handed in the day before in response to the assignment she had given them on their first day in her class.

She was long accustomed to expecting that among the thirty-odd students assigned to her class some twenty would hand in incomplete essays. Six or seven would have made heroic attempts, at least finishing the assignment. And if she was fortunate, in any given class two or three would have produced essays with a spark of promise.

She knew that many a wooden pen had been almost chewed in half over the weekend by her girls, trying to put down the opening words of this essay in self-revelation. Many an introductory sentence had been crossed out, many a page torn out of the composition book, crumpled in despair, and thrown in the general direction of a wastebasket.

The final results were what Mrs. Shor had expected. Her girls, being a handpicked group, did not lack for writing ability. Inhibition was their enemy. She felt sure that by term's end she would have them all writing well, and grammatically correctly.

What rankled this morning, and had since last night, was the essay of one student.

The hall bell clanged for the end of the first hour. Soon her next class would come straggling in from other classrooms, books clutched to their budding breasts.

Mrs. Shor smiled pleasantly as her charges took their seats. She waited until the last of them arrived before she closed the door. She faced her class. Every girl was very aware of the stack of essays that lay on the corner of Mrs. Shor's desk. Each wondered how her essay had fared under the critical eye of their exacting teacher. They were not encouraged by the sober air of the usually sparkling Mrs. Shor, who made English class such an enjoyable break from biology and math.

"Girls," Mrs. Shor began. "I read and graded all your essays last night. I can't say that I was pleased. But this was only your first effort. Before we are done, you will do better, much better. The main criticism I have is that so many of you did not respond to the assignment. Yes, you did say where you live, who your family consists of, what grade school you attended, how you spent your vacation. Informative? Yes. Revealing? No! Who you really are never came through. Your feelings. Your innermost thoughts. All missing. There was only one essay that really addressed the assignment. I wish to read it to you now.

She picked up a one-page essay that was on top of the pile. She looked about the room, by her stare commanding complete quiet and concentration. She began to read.

Who am I?

I am the girl who sits alone in the lunchroom. I am the girl no one speaks to.

I am the girl who gets a partner in biology lab only when Miss Bogart assigns me to another girl. I am the girl the rest of the girls whisper about. They never call me by name. But there is one name they call me behind my back.

If their aim is to hurt me, they have done that too well.

But no matter how much it hurts, I will not cry. And I will not leave. Like all the other girls, I have earned my place here. And no one is going to drive me out.

I will sit alone. I will eat alone. I will study alone. And, if I have to, I will graduate alone.

But I am here to stay.

As Mrs. Shor read, one by one the girls in the class involuntarily turned their eyes toward Elvira, who sat up straighter, taller, determined, and impervious to their stares.

Mrs. Shor came to the end of her reading. She turned in Elvira's direction.

"My dear, this essay is more what I had in mind than any of the others. So I have graded it an A."

In the lunchroom, Elvira waited in line, purchased her half-pint bottle of milk, and took her place at the table that had come to be accepted as hers. Industriously, she took a sandwich from her lunch box, inserted the straw into her milk, opened her Latin grammar, and commenced to eat her lunch while memorizing her Latin declensions.

Shortly thereafter, Mildred Thomason, a girl now ungainly tall but who would develop into an outstanding beauty by graduation, slipped away from her own table, taking her lunch with her. She approached Elvira's table.

"Do you mind?" Mildred asked.

"No. I don't mind," Elvira said.

For a brief and uneasy time, they ate in silence. Until Mildred said, "I never finished mine."

"Never finished what?" Elvira asked.

"My essay. I got stuck in the middle. After I told all about my family, I didn't know where to go from there," she confessed. "I guess I couldn't write about myself. Talking about yourself isn't so hard. But writing, that's different."

By that time, Gladys Holtzer brought her lunch to the table to join them.

When the gong announced the end of lunch period, Mildred said, "Maybe we can all have lunch together tomorrow. Elvira?"

"I would love it," Elvira said.

1 9 3 7

23

"*So what are* you two scheming behind my back in there?" David Rosen asked as he stood outside the closed door to Elvira's room.

The door opened. Elvira stood there with a sheet of paper in her hand, Rebecca behind her in a show of support.

"Uncle David, I need your permission."

"My permission? You are a young lady. You have been going to school on your own for almost a year now. I didn't think you needed my permission to do anything anymore."

"Uncle David, there is going to be a church picnic and field day next Sunday. Children are not permitted to go unless they have their parents' written consent."

She held out the form to him. He took it and gestured her to follow him. He went into the living room, where his Sunday *Times* was in even greater disarray than usual, indicating to Rebecca that he was not in a very good frame of mind to entertain any new idea. He sat down in his favorite armchair, studied the form for a time.

"Hm!" he grunted. "'Freedom from liability.' This reads like a contract."

"Reverend Wilder said they need it for the protection of the church."

"Maybe I should call a lawyer before I sign it," David joked. He looked up at her. "So tell me, what's it all about?"

"The church has a permit to use one of the ball fields in Van Cortlandt Park for a baseball game and races and a picnic. Everybody will be there—all my friends from Sunday school, my teachers, Reverend Wilder and his wife."

"How long would you be gone?"

"Reverend Wilder said our bus will be back at the church by seven in the evening."

"Seven in the evening," David considered.

"It's still light out at seven o'clock," Elvira pointed out.

"So there'll be ball games and races and a picnic," David pondered.

"And fresh air and sunshine," Elvira added.

"What's the matter, on Washington Heights there is no fresh air and sunshine?" David replied.

"David," Rebecca tried to intervene on Elvira's behalf.

"She doesn't need any help from you," he replied. "She knows all the right arguments. Someday she could make a very fine lawyer. A day in the park with her friends from Sunday school can't be bad. Okay, I give my permission!"

"Oh, thank you, Uncle David." Elvira threw her arms around him.

While they embraced, he continued: "Only one thing, sweetheart. Be careful. And come home while it is still light out. Promise?"

"I promise!"

Early the next Sunday morning, Rebecca and Elvira prepared sandwiches of various kinds: lettuce and tomato, egg salad, sliced chicken. Rebecca filled the sandwiches and Elvira wrapped them neatly in waxed paper, while David hovered in the kitchen doorway supervising.

"You sure you made enough sandwiches, Rebecca? You know kids. Outdoors. Active. They get hungry."

"David, I'm sure we're not the only ones sending sandwiches, so a dozen sandwiches should be enough."

"And drinks, what about drinks? Soda? Celery tonic? Milk?"

"Reverend Wilder said they sell drinks in the park," Elvira replied.

"Then take money," David dug into his pocket and brought out a handful of bills. He peeled off three dollars. "Here, darling."

"Uncle David, that's a lot of money for drinks."

"Elvira my dear, a lesson in life: Never hurts to have a little just-in-case money. Now, enjoy. Enjoy the day. Enjoy your friends. Enjoy being fifteen years old." He urged the money on her. She took it. He leaned over and kissed her on the cheek. "Fifteen," he said. "When I was fifteen, I was already a greenhorn, working seventy hours a week. Have fun, darling, have fun.''

Elvira had been gone less than an hour. Rebecca was cleaning up in the kitchen while David sat in the living room studying his Sunday *Times* and, like Old Faithful, erupting almost on schedule.

"I tell you, the whole world is going to hell!" he exploded. Rebecca came out of the kitchen, drying her hands. He turned from his newspaper. "Rebecca, get ready. Very soon, time for Jews to run again. Hitler reoccupies the Saar. Does any country do anything? No! Italy invades Ethiopia. Does the League of Nations do anything? No. And here. Depression. Unless things get better, this time there will be no place to run. No place!"

"You seem unusually pessimistic this Sunday," Rebecca remarked.

"It isn't me. It's *The New York Times!*" he exclaimed impatiently.

"Frankly, I think it's something else."

"Such as, Mrs. Sigmund Freud?"

"I notice, of late, every time Elvira takes another step on her own, everything seems to irritate you."

"I fail to see the connection between Hitler, Mussolini, and Elvira going to Van Cortlandt Park!" he responded sharply.

"The connection is *you*. Ever since she left this morning, you've been as nervous as a cat."

"A girl of fifteen may feel grown-up, but she is still a child! Anything can happen!"

"David, put down that newspaper. Put on your lumberjacket. Let's go for a walk down by the Hudson—before you drive both of us crazy."

"Talk about driving crazy. Who was it wanted to go with her her first day in high school?"

"David, darling, I'm not saying I'm calm now. But there is such a thing as a proper degree of parental nervousness. You are *too* nervous. Now, get your jacket and let's go."

After the bus had unloaded the congregation of the Ajalon Baptist Church at the athletic field in Van Cortlandt Park, Rev-

erend Wilder assigned the young people to various sports
events—the dashes, the relays, the potato race, the three-legged race, and then, after lunch, the main activity, the baseball
game: Sunday school students versus the deacons.

Wilder selected Elvira for the senior girls' relay team, later
to be joined for the three-legged race with a young man of
fifteen, Willard Johnson.

Running the third leg, Elvira put her team in the lead for
the relay prize, but the girl who ran the anchor leg tripped
and fell, dooming them to last place. Elvira looked forward to
the three-legged race as her only chance to bring home a
prize. She sought out Willard Johnson as he finished the hun-
dred-yard dash in second place. She had noticed him in class
on Sunday mornings and later during services. He was tall
and beginning to be quite muscular. His dark brown face glistened under a coat of sweat as she approached him.

"Hi. I'm Elvira Hitchins."

"I know," Willard replied, mopping his face. "I seen you
in church a lot."

"*Saw*. Or *see*," she corrected at once, "not *seen*." The look
of embarrassment on his face made her apologize. "I'm sorry.
I shouldn't have said that."

"'S all right. You was right."

She was about to correct him once again but stifled the
impulse. "We're supposed to be a three-legged team."

"Yeah," he said, looking down at her. "Don't know how
it's goin' to work, me being so tall and you being so . . ."

"I am not small. Not for a girl," Elvira protested.

"No, not small for a girl, but small."

"We could practice," Elvira suggested.

"Yeah," he said, looking around for a place where they
could practice without being observed. "Whyn't we try over
there, near that big tree?"

He had tied his left leg to Elvira's right leg. The first two
times they tried to stand, they fell.

"This be harder than I figure," Willard said.

"*Is*," Elvira corrected, too quickly.

He did not reply, though it was obvious his feelings had
been hurt once more. He said only, "We try again."

They made several attempts, each of which ended up on
the ground.

"Must be some way to do this," Willard said. "I seen it done before . . ." At once he corrected himself. "I *saw* it done before. Trouble is, either I'm too big or you're too small. So whyn't we try you take a longer step and I take a shorter one? Le's go!"

Half a dozen attempts, with adjustments each time, resulted in a stride smooth and measured enough to please them both. By the time the last event of the morning, the three-legged race, was called they felt ready. Reverend Wilder was at the starting line ready to signal the contestants. Mrs. Wilder stood at the finish line to judge the victors and award the prizes.

"Ready! Set!" Reverend Wilder called out, then, after the briefest of pauses, he shouted, "Go!"

Elvira and Willard started out more slowly than the other teams, at the measured pace they had practiced. The team at their far left had gone only three strides before they fell down, to the laughter of the spectators. Soon the team on their right began to struggle, then fell, to more laughter. Within the first twenty strides, all the other teams had eliminated themselves, so Elvira and Willard were the only team to finish. Mrs. Wilder was at the finish line, laughing as she presented each of them with a small white box tied in purple ribbon, containing a copy of the Gospels bound in white leatherette.

After the three-legged race and before the baseball game, lunch was called. Elvira invited Willard to eat with her.

"I've enough to feed an army," she said.

"Me too," Willard said. "My mama made sure of that. She be believin' . . . she believe . . ."

"Believes," Elvira suggested softly.

"Yeah. She believes no child of hers should ever go hungry like she used to."

"How many are there?" Elvira asked.

"How many what?"

"Children."

"Oh? Seven," Willard said.

"You mean you have six brothers and sisters?" Elvira remarked in envy.

"Two brothers, four sisters. See that girl there under the tree? The one in the pink dress? My sister. And that kid wearin' the green jacket. He my kid brother."

"He's . . ." Elvira started to correct, but stopped herself.

"There ain't hardly no way to say something without you correctin'," he said.

"I'm sorry," Elvira said, trying to conceal her own sensitivity by concentrating on her sandwich.

"That what comes from living with white folks?" he asked. She glanced at him suddenly. "Everybody knows. First time I ever notice you and I ask, someone tell me, that's the little colored girl who lives with white folks. Jews, I hear."

"Yes. The Rosens. And they are Jewish."

"Are they . . . you hear so many things . . . Are they different from other folks?"

"Their holidays are a little different. And they eat things colored people don't, but they also eat lots of things colored people do. Like when I cook for Uncle David—that's Mr. Rosen."

"You cook?" Willard asked in awe.

"Yes. And Uncle David always asks for seconds when I do."

"No foolin'?"

"No fooling!" she replied. Then, after another bite of her sandwich, she asked, "You . . . you noticed me, asked about me?"

"Uh-huh," he mumbled with a mouthful of sandwich.

"Why?" Elvira asked forthrightly.

He chewed slowly and thoughtfully while he debated his response. Once he had swallowed, he licked his lips and seemed determined to attempt an answer.

"I kinda notice how pretty you is . . . are. And your hair looks so soft, I say to myself, I wonder how it'd feel to touch it."

"You said that?" Elvira asked.

"Din' say it, just thought it," Willard said shyly.

"Would you like to?"

"Yeah, kinda."

"I won't mind," Elvira said.

The young man stared at her, trying to determine if she was actually inviting him to do so. When he read the answer in her black eyes, he reached out until the tips of his fingers touched her black hair. He withdrew them quickly.

"Well?" she asked.

"Soft. It is soft like it seems."

"Aunt Rebecca always says that when I'm curious about things, I should ask."

"You love her, don't you?"

"Yes. Very much."

"I can tell, the way you talk about her." He took another bite of his sandwich, chewed slowly, swallowed, then asked, "She the one teach you to go 'round correctin' people all the time?"

"I'm sorry about that," Elvira said. "But as long as you brought the matter up, it's *taught*, not *teach*. As for correcting people, my mama always used to say, 'Elvira, you learn to speak higher than your station and one day you will be.' Sometimes I even correct Uncle David. Especially when he gets excited and talks funny."

Willard shook his head. "I can't imagine how it'd feel living with white folks."

"I don't know about living with white folks, only about the Rosens. I love them. And they love me," Elvira said. "Between us there's no white, no colored. Just us. Of course, it's not that way with many white folks. But I do what Aunt Rebecca always says, 'Proud, Elvira. Be proud.'"

"How's a man to be proud when he can't even get a job to be proud of?" Willard asked. "My papa, he do odd jobs, 'ccpt there was no odd jobs to do. 'N I got one uncle work as Pullman porter and I hear him talkin' 'bout how he got to bow and scrape. 'Yes, sir' and 'No, sir,' just for the tips. Times he has got to go into the club car and get his passengers 'cause they too drunk to make it back to their bedrooms. And they pukin' and vomitin' all the way, which he got to clean up after them. Then next mornin', when they get to Chicago or Cleveland or Detroit or wherever, they get up, get dressed, and come out 'n stare right through the porter like he didn't exist. My Uncle Joab said, 'Funny thing, the ones get the drunkest and vomit the most tips the least. Like they tryin' to make believe we didn't do nothin' for them.' And you tellin' me, be proud?"

"Aunt Rebecca says Negroes and Jews have that together,

the need to be proud—because the world thinks we have no right to be."

"Elvira, you be funny . . . *are* funny."

"I wasn't trying to be funny," she said.

"I didn't mean funny."

"You said funny."

"I mean, I never talk to a girl like you before," he said, then confessed, "I never really talk much to any girl before."

They were both embarrassed by his admission. They stared into each other's eyes. Before either of them could speak again, they heard Reverend Wilder call out, "Time for the ball game!"

Elvira and Willard watched the game together, sitting on one of the few worn, weathered hardwood benches that were behind home plate. The game was a mixture of very skillful play intermingled with some inept play in the field and at bat. On the deacons' team, the pitcher was a man who threw so hard that most young batters had trouble hitting and the catcher had trouble holding on to the ball.

Someone sitting behind Elvira said, "He once be in the Negro Leagues. Some say he throw harder than Waite Hoyt on the Yankees."

By the time Pastor Wilder had to call the game because the bus had been hired by the hour, the score was six to one, with the deacons ahead, thanks to their pitcher.

Elvira and Willard sat side by side on the trip down from Van Cortlandt. The old bus had just crossed the bridge from the Bronx into Manhattan when there was a grinding noise and it came to a halt. The driver got out. Pastor Wilder joined him when he lifted the hood to reveal the steaming motor.

"Got to let the damn thing cool down 'fore we can get goin' again," the driver concluded.

It was just before nine o'clock and quite dark when the wounded bus staggered to a stop before the Ajalon Baptist Church on 138th Street.

In the Rosen apartment up in Washington Heights, David paced back and forth in the living room.

"I never should have given permission. Whatever happened to that girl is my fault!"

"She is in the care of Pastor Wilder. Nothing happened."

"Then why isn't she here? A girl her age traveling on the subway by herself at this hour! Remember what almost happened when she was eight years old and ran away? There are a lot of crazy men in this city, dangerous men. . . . Rebecca, the next time you see me about to give her permission for anything, stop me. You hear?" he shouted.

"Even if I were among the dead I would hear you."

"Don't joke, Rebecca! Not at a time like this. When she gets home, I will give her a lesson she won't forget!" he threatened.

"David, don't you even *think* of laying a hand on that child!"

"Never before. But now, tonight, after this . . . Rebecca, she needs a lesson. Staying out till after dark. Coming home alone on the subway. I don't even like it when she walks home alone from the subway during the day. Tell you what, I'm going down to the station to wait for her!"

"David, no . . ."

He was on his way to the bedroom to get his jacket when the doorbell rang.

"Thank God!" Rebecca said.

"Let's hope it's not a policeman!" David replied as he went to the front door.

Rebecca heard him open the door and start to exclaim, "You call this coming home in day—" Then he grew suddenly silent. She heard Elvira say, "Uncle David, I would like you to meet Willard."

"Willard?" David Rosen was heard to reply.

Rebecca called out, "Elvira, come in and bring your friend." She started for the hallway to greet them. "Come in, come in," Rebecca invited.

Willard hesitated at the door, too timid and embarrassed to cross the threshold until Elvira said, "Come in, Willard. I want you to meet my aunt."

Once they were introduced, Rebecca said, "It's so late I'll bet you're both hungry. Some milk? Some cake? I have some cinnamon-and-raisin cake left from Friday."

"Thanks, ma'am, but I got to go 'fore my mama be worried 'bout me. *Is* worried about me."

"Thanks for bringing me home, Willard," Elvira said.

"I couldn't let you go home alone so late," he said. "Mrs. Rosen, wasn't anybody's fault. The bus broke down. See you in Sunday school, Elvira. Good night, Mrs. Rosen."

He started for the front door. David followed. At the door, he said, "Willard, thanks for bringing Elvira home safely. And so your mother shouldn't worry too long, take a taxi." He tried to press two dollars into the young man's hand.

"Thanks, sir, but I got my fare," he protested.

"I don't want your mother to worry a minute longer than necessary. I know what it feels like. Take a taxi!"

He pressed the money into Willard's hand until the young man said, "Won't do no good, Mr. Rosen. No taxi is going to take no colored boy down to Harlem."

"I'm sorry, my boy. Very sorry. I just hope your mama isn't too worried. Good night, and again, thanks."

While Elvira was taking her bath, Rebecca took the opportunity to point out to David, "So she didn't break her promise. The bus broke down. And thanks to that nice young man, she got home safely. Didn't she?" When David did not respond, she asked, "David? Didn't she?"

"I never realized," he said. "Soon, very soon, too soon, there will be boys . . . young men coming to call on Elvira."

Monday morning when Elvira was rushing to dress for school, Rebecca came to her door to ask, "Sweetheart, what will it be this morning? Eggs? Cereal?"

"Cereal, please," Elvira said as she studied herself in the mirror with a critical yet pleased look that Rebecca recognized as that moment in a girl's life when she wishes to make sure she is pretty and desirable to men. She had felt that way when, for the first time, David had walked her home from night school.

"He seems like a nice young man. Well brought up," Rebecca said.

"His mother is a deaconess in the church. You know, the woman who wears the big hats and the flowered dresses. That's Mrs. Johnson," Elvira explained.

"Oh yes," Rebecca realized. "A handsome woman. It's no mystery where Willard gets his looks."

"Of course his grammar is not perfect. But I think I can do something about that," Elvira said.

Rebecca found herself thinking, *And she will, too. Once that girl makes up her mind to do something, she does it. Just don't let her reach too far, for too much.*

1 9 3 8

24

F or almost a week, Rebecca Rosen had suspected that her husband was harboring some cherished secret. Despite Hitler's annexation of Austria and Prime Minister Chamberlain's assurance of peace for our time, David Rosen had not exploded even once in rage or sarcasm. He had not criticized President Roosevelt as often as usual or mentioned the Supreme Court. His mind seemed to be on other things. Obviously more pleasant things, for several times she had overheard him singing to himself a new jingle he had heard frequently on the radio:

> Pepsi Cola hits the spot,
> Twelve full ounces
> That's a lot.
> Twice as much for a nickel, too.
> Pepsi Cola is the drink for you.

Rebecca wondered, could his secret have to do with the business? Not likely, for he had moved to a larger loft only two years ago and could not be intending another expansion so soon. Perhaps he was planning some special reward for Elvira, since she had come home from Wadleigh with the exciting news that she had been elected to the Artista honor society. She was one of only eight girls in her class to be chosen. Whatever David's surprise might be, Rebecca knew him well enough not to pry. He would not unveil it until he was ready.

She realized the moment had arrived when David returned home from business one afternoon even before Elvira was back from school.

"Isn't she a little late?" he asked, almost peevish.

"This is the afternoon she has Latin club," Rebecca reminded.

"Of course, Latin club. I should have remembered," he said. He went into the living room to turn on the new Zenith radio they had bought only months ago. He settled down with his newspaper, prepared to await Elvira's return. Meantime, the radio news droned on until there was an interruption for what the announcer called a special bulletin. With a civil war in Spain, unrest in Palestine, and Hitler tearing up the map of Europe, a special bulletin was never a harbinger of good news. David lowered his *Times* and turned toward the new radio with grim attention.

"An unconfirmed report from Paris indicates that a distraught young man, thought to be Jewish, burst into the German Embassy and shot a German diplomat there. The first reports state that the diplomat is dead."

"Oh God!" David groaned. "The fool! The crazy fool!"

His outburst was so loud and so unlike his attitude of recent days that Rebecca rushed into the living room. "David, David, what happened?" He told her.

"Oh no!" Rebecca replied. "Reprisals! There will be reprisals!"

"Of course," David said, almost breathless. "What did he expect to accomplish? One young man against Nazi Germany?"

By the time Elvira returned from school, the enjoyment David had anticipated from his surprise had given way to gloomy fears of further news from Europe.

Nevertheless, when supper was over and before Elvira could go to her room, he announced, "Ellie, I want you to know that while you have been making such good grades and being selected for Arista your Uncle David has not exactly been doing nothing."

"You're not moving the business again, are you?" Elvira asked in surprise.

"I am not even thinking about the business. I am thinking to myself, here is a young woman, pretty as a picture, tall, slender, a nice build as any young man can see, and she is also a brain. As Mr. Gordon said, *a Yiddisher kup*. Arista yet. So I ask myself, what does one do to show appreciation for such a fine young lady? Well, I have not been idle. And the result? Just a minute, darling." He went out to the foyer table to bring back a large envelope he had left there. He dug into it, producing three catalogs, which he handed to Elvira one at a time, identifying, "Smith! Mount Holyoke! Vassar!"

The way in which she took each catalog caused Rebecca to suspect that Elvira was surprised but not particularly pleased.

"Take them. Read them. And remember. Whichever one you pick, it's yours. When I wrote them your qualifications, they each said you were accepted subject to an interview. So don't worry about that part."

"It's not that," Elvira said, seeking some way to explain without hurting him deeply.

He anticipated her. "It's the money. Right?" Before she could respond he continued: "Well, my dear, there is right now in the Public National Bank branch on Twenty-third Street a savings account in the name of Elvira Hitchins. In the amount of ten thousand dollars! Enough for four years in any college."

"It's not that," she continued to protest.

"You are going to tell me about building up debts. Believe me, I respect the memory of your dear mother. But I must point out that a debt is only a debt if the other person expects or wants to be repaid. This is a gift."

"Uncle David, Aunt Rebecca . . . I have decided to go to college here in the city."

"Here in the city? Where? Columbia? NYU? Why do that when you can go to one of the best women's colleges in the country?" David pleaded. "Aha! I know. You're afraid that up there in one of those fancy schools you'll be the only one. I asked about that in my letters. There are Negro girls in each of those schools. Not many," he conceded, "but a few." Honesty forced him to admit, "In one school three, in the other two schools only one. So you won't be alone."

"Uncle David, I've been thinking of this for some time now. I decided I would like to go to Hunter College. I want to be a high school teacher. So when a girl like Elvira Hitchins or some Negro boy comes into my school, my class, they will be relieved to see another colored face. Which is more than I have seen in my years of school."

"But, darling, there are colored teachers," Rebecca started to say.

"In Negro schools," Elvira corrected. "I want to teach in a school where there are white students and also some Negro students. I want to be there for the ones who will feel alone and will need me most. So I decided on Hunter College."

Her declaration was so firm that neither David nor Rebecca made any effort to change her mind.

"Of course, darling. You're entitled," David said.

Elvira kissed him and went into her room to study.

"Who knows what goes on in their heads when they grow up?" David said.

"David, she is sixteen, a person in her own right. And who are we to judge? It is one thing to say we understand because Jews, too, are subject to prejudice. But is it really the same, what we suffer and what they suffer?"

"In Germany right now it is even worse for Jews," David replied. "In fact, tomorrow night I will be late for supper. I have to go to a meeting."

"Meeting?"

"Many Jewish businessmen have been called together for a new organization. United Jewish Appeal. To raise money for Jewish relief. Becca, Becca, the old days when charity was a little tin *pushke* on the kitchen wall are gone. Now the need is greater, much greater," he said grimly. "When I think of my Aunt Gitcheh and my cousins who decided to stay over there, I can only thank God they're in Poland, not Germany. And now with that crazy young man killing the Nazi in Paris . . ." He dared not even speculate on what might happen.

The next evening Rebecca and Elvira had supper alone while David attended a meeting in one of the ballrooms of the McAlpin Hotel on 34th Street, across Sixth Avenue from Gimbel's. The meeting was conducted by an attorney David knew only by reputation, having read of him often in *The New York Times*. He was one of the leading corporate attorneys in the nation. Each time David read of his exploits in the law or some huge business transaction, he took vicarious pride in the fact that the man was also a Jew. To think that such a busy and important man could find the time to devote to Jewish affairs was heartening.

The attorney took his place before the lectern, attired as he was in courtroom photos that appeared in the *Times*, in a frock coat and striped trousers, with a wing collar and proper black and gray-striped cravat. He cleared his throat. That alone brought the meeting to order.

"Gentlemen, this morning there came into my hands from secret governmental sources a document which was circulated last year to all German diplomatic offices around the world by Nazi Foreign Minister Von Ribbentrop. I quote from it in part:

> The spread of Jewish influence and corruption of our political, economic and cultural life has perhaps done more to undermine the German people's will to prevail than all the hostility shown us by the Allied powers since the first Great War. This disease in the body of our people has first to be eradicated before the great German Reich can assemble its forces to overcome the will of the world.

"Gentlemen, when a nation talks of overcoming the will of the world, there is only one thing it has in mind: war! Get the Jews out of the way so they can get on with their war against the rest of the world!"

Before the meeting was over, the attorney had donated one hundred thousand dollars to the cause of the Appeal. The other men there also wrote out checks, among them David Rosen, who signed his name to a check for five thousand dollars.

It was past ten o'clock when he arrived home. He was surprised to find both Elvira and Rebecca sitting in the living room staring at the new Zenith, both so intense that when he greeted them, Rebecca impulsively gestured him to silence.

"What happened? What's wrong?" he asked in a terrified whisper. The answer came from the radio.

An excited voice, shouting above noises of shattering glass in the background, was reporting from Berlin. Though static obscured some words, David heard, "Shattering of glass . . . shops and businesses of Jewish merchants. Down the . . . one can see flames . . . have been told . . . several synagogues on fire by Nazi . . . troopers."

"My God, my God," David whispered as he sank down on the couch alongside Elvira, who took his hand.

". . . Jews have been arrested . . . the unconfirmed report . . . set on fire with several hundred Jews locked inside . . ."

Silently, Rebecca began to weep. The voice was drowned out by static so loud and intrusive that the words had become unintelligible. Another voice in the studio took over.

"Wire-service reports confirm that the havoc, called Kristallnacht by the Nazis, is in response to the assassination two days ago of a German diplomat in Paris. Reports, still unconfirmed, say that Jews have been arrested by the thousands and carted off to places unknown."

"Turn it off, turn it off!" David said. Elvira obliged. "It's happening. Happening." He rocked back and forth as he did in synagogue on the holy days. Rebecca wept silently despite Elvira's attempts to console her.

The next morning's *New York Times* not only confirmed in detail the radio reports but added that the more than 20,000 Jews who had been arrested were taken off to places called labor camps.

When David reached his office, he asked Miss Dornan to find the prominent attorney's phone number and place a call to him. Mr. Untermeyer was busy, but his secretary came on the line. David told her he wished to double his contribution. When he hung up, he realized the donation would create a cash shortage for the business. He would borrow from the bank. He was good for the money.

25

*I*t *was early* spring, 1939. Sunday morning. Elvira had had her breakfast of bagels and lox. She went into the living room to bid David goodbye before she went off to church, where she was now teaching seven-year-olds in Sunday School.

"Crazy," he said, "and gets crazier every minute. Not you, darling. The world. Says here in the business section that two months from now Pan American is flying people to Europe in a big plane. Imagine, four engines. Twenty-two people. Separate cabins. Dining salon. Sleeping berths like in a Pullman car. And with a bridal suite. When you get married, sweetheart, would you like to spend your honeymoon in an airplane? I could arrange it. Crazy, no?"

He held up his face to meet her kiss with one of his own.

"Not as crazy as what's going on in Washington," Elvira said more soberly than David.

"Washington?"

"Yes. Didn't you read the front page, Uncle David?"

"First, the business section. After all," he confessed, "I've been picking up a few stocks lately. So what's on the front page?"

"Marian Anderson," Elvira said.

"She didn't die, did she? Such a marvelous voice, it would be a shame."

"The Daughters of the American Revolution won't rent her their hall to give a concert."

"A shame. A terrible shame," David said. "There must be other places in Washington."

"None big enough." Elvira said. "I've got to go."

Rebecca called after her. "Do you have enough for the offering, darling?"

"Yes, Aunt Rebecca," Elvira called back, and she was gone.

David dug in with his business section, rattling the paper more noisily since Elvira had disturbed him with the news about Marian Anderson. Soon his silence was shattered by an outburst. "This is it! The end of the world!"

Rebecca came racing into the living room, expecting some earthshaking development of international consequence. Conditions being what they were, the threat of a war had to be taken seriously.

He pointed his finger at her as he said, "Just listen to this! 'The Warner Brothers Company of Bridgeport, Connecticut, will this season introduce a line of women's brassieres which will be made not only in the usual sizes but by cup sizes as well. A-cups. B-cups. C-cups. D-cups.' Imagine!"

"Women's breasts differ in size and shape, why not brassieres?"

"You mean you wouldn't hesitate to walk into a department store and say, 'I would like a size 36, B-cup?"

"C-cup," Rebecca corrected.

"How do you know you would be a C-cup?" he demanded.

"If there is A, B, C, and D, I think I am a C. What do you think?" she teased, well aware of his fascination with her breasts.

Embarrassed, he retorted, "Don't change the subject. Imagine the inventory problem. To have to stock not only sizes but cups as well. Why can't they leave well enough alone? Of course, could work two ways. Suppose men started to say to a *shadchen*, 'Matchmaker, I would like a wife, size 34-B cup. Or size 36-D cup.' How would women like that?"

"Men do that anyhow," Rebecca replied.

"Not me!" David insisted. "I never even thought of such a thing!"

"David darling," Rebecca asked softly. "What was it that attracted you to me?"

"Not that!" he repeated more firmly, blushing.

"Then what?"

"What?" He began to consider. "Well, remember how it was in night school—everybody sitting by alphabet. Rosen with an *R* comes before Silverstone with an *S*. So I sat in front of you. The first few nights I knew only your voice. Very clear. Very strong. I said to myself, that is a special young woman. Still, how could I turn around and look without attracting attention? I remained in my seat when class was dismissed and I watched. I was sadly disappointed.

"In me?" Rebecca asked, obviously affronted.

"Remember there was a girl, Sarah Teitelbaum, in our class?"

"Yes. The fat one, with the slight mustache on her upper lip.

"I thought *she* was the one who went with the voice," David said.

"You thought she was me?" Rebecca asked, more hurt now than disappointed.

To tease her, David afforded himself the rare privilege of correcting her. "You thought she was *I*, you mean."

"Never mind that! How could you mistake *me* for Sarah Teitelbaum?"

"I told you. I was trying to match a voice with a girl," he said. "Then one night I deliberately came late, so I would have to go to the rear of the room. From there I could see the whole class. When you raised your hand to answer the teacher's question, I finally discovered who you were. What a relief! I said to myself, 'There is the girl I am going to marry!'"

"Without knowing my cup size, how could you tell?" she joked.

He pulled her down to his lap and kissed her. She pressed against him. Soon they were making love.

When they were both satisfied and at rest, David Rosen spoke softly. "Sometimes, Becca, do you realize, with everything that's going on in this world, in other countries, we are very lucky?"

"David, what are you leading up to?"

"The last few years I have been telling you how well the business is doing. Truth is, the business is doing even better than I have let you know. So, last few weeks I have been looking around," he admitted. "You know what would be nice? An apartment on Central Park West!"

"Central Park West? That's for millionaires!"

"Millionaires we're not. But we can afford it. And now with Elvira talking about going to Hunter College, it's right across the park. She could walk to school again if she wanted. It would be nice for us, too. Living right on the park, with a world of trees outside our window. In the morning you can look out and see the sun come up, in the afternoon, the children enjoying the playground. Sundays, we can take a nice walk by the lake."

From his description, she knew that he had not only considered the idea but already selected a possible apartment.

"When do you want me to see it?" she asked.

"After it's painted. A week from tomorrow," he said.

The bus with the banner AJALON BAPTIST CHURCH rippling in the soft Washington breeze had slowed down as it approached the tall, white granite spire that was the Washington Monument, thrust upward into the blue sky of this mild Easter Sunday.

Elvira Hitchins pressed her face against the window of the bus to stare at the monument and the flags that bordered the area from which it rose. In the distance, beyond cherry trees in full bloom, she recognized the tall white columns of the Lincoln Memorial.

Hindered by streams of traffic that converged in the vicinity of the Memorial, the Ajalon bus had come to a halt. On signal from one of the hundreds of policemen who had command of the streets, the driver started to edge his cumbersome vehicle to the side and into an area designated for parking. As the bus came to a stop, Pastor Wilder stood up from his front seat.

"We will leave the bus, assemble, and march to the Memorial in a group. Stay together, so when it comes time to leave we are still a group."

They piled out of the bus—young people, their parents, some grandparents, even aging Mrs. Powell, who had been prohibited by her doctor from making such a long journey from New York.

But she had responded, "Doctor, it cost me my life, I ain't gonna miss this day!"

With the pastor leading the way, the contingent of sixty-eight members of the Ajalon Baptist Church started forward to join the crowd, which now numbered more than seventy-five thousand—Negroes and whites, Catholics, Jews, and every denomination of Protestants. They had reached the pool that led to the Monument itself. The still waters of the pool mirrored the blue sky above and the few white clouds that drifted by slowly.

Despite her height, Elvira had to stand on tiptoe to look over the heads of the crowd toward the Memorial itself. Before the tall white pillars several rows of chairs had been set up to accommodate special guests. Between the columns she could make out the huge form of Abraham Lincoln, a figure in white stone. She had seen the imposing statue before, but only in photographs. She had to see it for herself, and as close as she could manage. She pressed forward despite arousing some resentment from more than one spectator. But the words of the old gospel song compelled her:

> Oh, freedom, Oh, freedom.
> Oh, freedom over me.
> And before I'd be a slave
> I'd be buried in my grave
> And go home to my Lord and be free.

She was close enough to the white granite steps and the tall white pillars to be able to see the statue in all its majesty: the thoughtful, somber face of Lincoln; his huge hands resting on the arms of his stone chair; The folds of his coat, so real that white stone seemed soft fabric. He stared out at the more than seventy-five thousand human beings who crowded before him waiting to hear the golden voice that all America waited to hear, if one could judge from the battery of microphones that were clustered before the platform.

Elvira peered between the columns at Lincoln until she thought, *Any moment he will start to breathe.* Her concentration on Lincoln was broken when, in single file, a group of men and women came from inside the memorial to take their places in the chairs that were lined up to the left of the columns. At once Elvira recognized the tallest woman. She had seen many pictures of her in the newspapers and in newsreels. She was the driving force behind this great day, and the wife of the president of the United States. At her appearance, the entire crowd erupted in a burst of cheers and applause. Elvira found herself crying out, along with the others. Her voice was strong and clear and continued longer than most of the others, until she became self-conscious and looked around sheepishly to see if she had been observed. Alongside her was a young man with a smile on his dark-brown face. Evidently, he had been aware of her for some time. She looked away quickly.

Taller than she by at least half a head, and with the sturdy, well-formed body of an athlete, the young man said, "I felt the same. But I didn't have the courage or the voice. You have an excellent voice."

She half turned back to see if he was teasing. He smiled. She could not resist and said, "Thank you."

"Do you know who those people are up on the platform?" he asked.

"Some of them look familiar, but I don't know their names," Elvira said, though she did. But she had learned from Aunt Rebecca's actions that there were times when a woman must appear in need of help to make a man feel needed.

"That tall man with the glasses, he's the secretary of the treasury."

"Henry Morgenthau," Elvira said.

"And that other man, just a little shorter, he's the secretary of the interior."

"With the funny name. Ickes."

"Oh, you know," he said, somewhat surprised.

"Isn't he the one who invited Miss Anderson to give her concert here today?"

"Yes, yes, he is," the young man confirmed. "And that other tall man, the tallest one, that's Hugo Black."

"The Supreme Court justice," Elvira admitted, then felt obliged to apologize for her knowledge. "I saw his picture in the *Times* only last week, with some opinion he wrote in an important case."

"You read the *Times*?" the young man asked, impressed.

"When I can pry it away from Uncle David. No, that isn't fair. Ever since I became a senior, he's been saying, 'You can't be educated without reading the *Times*.'"

"You're a senior? Where?"

"Wadleigh."

"Wadleigh High School in New York?"

"Yes," she admitted, thinking, *He seems old enough to be a senior too.* "You a senior, too?"

"Junior," he admitted.

Elvira thought, *He looks too old to be a junior. Too bad.* "Where do you go to school?"

"Here."

"Washington?"

"Yes. Howard."

"The university?"

"Yes."

"And you're a junior?" she asked, impressed.

"Yes."

She felt considerably more encouraged.

"You going to college?" he asked.

"Hunter."

"Oh, that's a great school. One of the best," he was saying as the entire crowd became silent, for Secretary Ickes approached the bank of microphones and newsreel cameras.

"Welcome," Ickes greeted. "Welcome to this day of renewal, which is not only Easter Sunday but a day of renewal of our faith in the ideals of democracy."

Elvira and the young man, along with seventy-five thousand other voices, joined in agreement.

"Genius, like justice, is blind. For genius has touched with the tip of her wing this woman, who, if it had not been for the great heart of Lincoln, would not be able to stand among us today, a free individual in a free land. And so it is fitting that Marian Anderson should raise her voice in tribute to the noble Lincoln, whom mankind will ever honor."

He turned back to hold out his hand in a gesture of invitation. From the protected area of the monument emerged the tall, regal, graceful woman with a deep brown face. She was dressed in a long gown of black velvet, a mink coat thrown over her shoulders. As she appeared between two of the white columns, a cheer of greeting exploded from seventy-five thousand throats, sending its echoing sound across the city.

The moment was so thrilling to Elvira that she felt herself

tremble with excitement. The young man at her side realized this and extended his hand to her. She was relieved to grasp it and cling to it.

The crowd's welcome had died down. Elvira whispered, "If she only stands there, this is an important occasion."

The accompanist at the piano played the introductory bars of Miss Anderson's first number. The crowd recognized the melody at once. When she sang, "Oh, say you can you see . . ." the entire crowd began to sing the national anthem with her. From the steps of the Memorial, along all four sides of the pool and as far back as one could see, thousands upon thousands of people of all colors joined in song along with the world-famous concert artist. When they had finished singing, their cheers were even louder.

The assemblage had grown silent. Marian Anderson looked to her accompanist and gave an almost imperceptible nod. He played the introductory bars. She began to sing a gospel song that Elvira had sung on many Sunday mornings in church. She found herself humming along until she became embarrassed. She fell silent, then glanced at the young man to see if he had overheard her. He smiled at her, then turned his attention back to Miss Anderson.

Each spiritual Marian Anderson sang evoked applause that seemed endless. Each time Elvira expected that the applause could not possibly go on, but it continued, longer and louder. This was more than a concert now; it had the fervor of a religious service.

It was late afternoon. The sun was far to the west. The air was cooler, the breeze a bit stiffer. Still the crowd would not permit Miss Anderson to stop. She sang on until, with an air of finality—and a song, the spiritual feeling of which would signal the end of her concert—she began to sing, "Ave Maria . . ."

Her deep voice, the religious feeling with which she invested the song, had turned the huge open area into a church, the crowd of thousands, a congregation. When she had finished, the applause itself admitted that the historic event was over. Mrs. Roosevelt rose from her chair and went forward to embrace Miss Anderson.

At the sight of the two women embracing, Elvira said, "It makes you feel we really are part of this country, finally."

"Not enough a part, but more than we were," the young man said.

"I was just thinking," Elvira said. "If the Daughters of the American Revolution had let her sing, the crowd would have only been two thousand, maybe twenty-five hundred."

"Are you leaving now?" the young man asked.

"First I would like to see Lincoln. Close up," she said. "But I suppose you've done that many times."

Unwilling to let her go, he protested. "No. In fact, I've never done that."

She knew he was lying. But since she had no desire to end their brief moment, she said, "Then why don't we do it together?"

Making their way against the crowd that was breaking up and departing, they held hands so not to be separated. They finally reached the steps and started up to join the throng that crowded around the statue. They passed so close to Mrs. Roosevelt that Elvira could not resist reaching out to touch her. At the contact, Mrs. Roosevelt glanced at her. Embarrassed, Elvira stammered her apology, "I'm sorry. I didn't mean . . ."

Mrs. Roosevelt smiled. "It's quite all right, child. Quite all right." She fixed her stare on Elvira. "My, but you're pretty." She turned to the young man. "I hope you realize what a lucky young man you are."

Both Elvira and the young man blushed.

They reached the foot of the statue and stared up.

"He seems so alive, he looks like he could breathe," she said.

"He worries a lot, too," the young man said.

"Is one permitted to touch?" Elvira asked.

"I always do," he said.

In recognition of his admission that he had lied before, they both smiled. She reached up in an effort to touch the cold stone of Lincoln's boot.

"There's a story they tell," the young man said. "When he was president, he used to polish his own boots. One day a cabinet officer who needed him in a hurry found him in the White House kitchen polishing them. In stunned surprise, he asked, 'Mr. President, do you polish your own boots?' And Lincoln replied . . ."

"'Whose boots *should* I polish?'" Elvira supplied quickly. A moment later, she realized and apologized, "Sorry. It was your story."

"That's all right," he said. "It's nice to meet a girl as bright as you."

His eyes spoke more than his words. Much as she would have liked to stay on, she felt compelled to say, "I have to go. The congregation . . . the bus . . . they're waiting for me."

"They haven't waited for you as long as I have," he said.

Her heart as well as her young body responded to him. She had never felt this way before.

"I really have to go," she said. "My bus."

"We'll find it together," he said, holding out his hand.

They started away from the monument and along the pool. Most of the crowd had disappeared.

"I don't even know your name," he said.

"Elvira. Elvira Hitchins."

"That's a nice name. Elvira. I like it. In case you care about . . ." he started to say, hoping to be encouraged.

"I care," she admitted softly.

"My name is Drew. Drew Armstrong."

"Drew. That's a nice name, too," she said.

"If I wanted to write you, where would I write?" he asked.

"Two twenty-nine Fort Washington Avenue, New York City," she informed. As he took a small pad out of his pocket to make a note of the address, she added, "Care of Rosen."

"Rosen? Isn't that a Jewish name?"

"Yes. My aunt and uncle, Rebecca and David, are Jewish.

"You live with them?"

"Ever since I was eight years old," Elvira said.

"They're white and Jewish and you've lived with them since you were eight?" he asked, unable to conceal his astonishment.

"It isn't really so strange, it only sounds that way."

"Yes it does," he admitted.

"If you ever met them, you'd know what wonderful people they are."

"When?" he asked directly.

"When what?"

"When will I meet them?" Drew asked.

Too fast, she thought. *This is going too fast. I've never gotten to*

feel so close to any young man in so short a time. She was relieved
to avoid answering by pointing out, "That's it! The Ajalon
bus! See, they *are* waiting for me." She waved to Pastor
Wilder, who stood next to the bus seeking some sign of her.
Relieved, the old man waved back, urging her to hurry.

As they reached the bus, Drew Armstrong said, "I will
write you. But you must promise to answer."

"Hurry, child, hurry," Pastor Wilder insisted. "We're late
enough as it is."

"Will you?" Drew asked.

"Yes, yes, I will," she said softly, withdrawing her hand
from his tight grasp.

It was long past ten o'clock at night when the bus arrived
at the church. All the way uptown in the cab to Washington
Heights, Elvira kept thinking, *Will he write, will he really write?
A junior in college, and Howard, one of the best Negro schools in the
country. I wonder where he comes from. I should have asked. I will
ask when he writes. What if he doesn't write? He must! He will! A
young man so handsome, he must have lots of girls. With his looks he
can have any girl he wants. I wonder if he really would come all the
way to New York?*

By the time her cab pulled up in front of the building on
Fort Washington Avenue, Elvira had explored all her hopes as
well as all her fears. David was waiting out front, looking at
his wristwatch. Before she stepped out, he was paying her
fare. As the cab pulled away, he felt obligated to make some
excuse for being caught waiting for her.

"Gets kind of stuffy in the house. A Sunday evening, with
what's on the radio, Eddie Cantor, Ed Wynn, all the other
comedians, and Dinah Shore, a man feels like a prisoner. So I
said, I'll go out, get some fresh air, stretch my legs a little. You
all right?"

"Fine, Uncle David."

"You had a good time?"

"A wonderful time!" Elvira said.

"Then come up. Aunt Rebecca is waiting."

Rebecca Rosen had witnessed Elvira's homecoming from
the window three stories up. She was waiting at the door
when they reached the landing. Before Elvira was inside the

apartment, Rebecca said, "Go, darling, wash up. We were waiting for you to have a snack with us."

"I'm really not hungry," Elvira said as she started for the bathroom to freshen up.

The airy way in which she walked by made Rebecca remark, "Something has happened to our little Elvira."

"Of course. She was telling me, it was the most exciting day of her whole life. That Marian Anderson, a God-given talent."

"David, if I'm any judge of young women, something has happened. And it hasn't to do with singing."

Over a snack of freshly fried blintzes and milk, Elvira described the events of the day, the crowd, the dignitaries, her moment of contact with the First Lady. "'My, but you're pretty.' Mrs. Roosevelt said that to me."

"And why not?" David asked. "She is a woman of excellent taste." He turned to his wife. "Becca, are you going to tell her or should I?"

"Tell me? What?" Elvira asked.

"Tomorrow, darling, you and I are going to go down to Central Park West. I'll pick you up at school," Rebecca said.

"Central Park West? What for?"

"Your Uncle David thinks we have outgrown Washington Heights and this apartment."

"We're moving?" Elvira asked, startled. "Leaving here?"

"And about time," David affirmed. "You'll be closer to Hunter. I'll be closer to the business. And my darling wife will be a *balabustah* in a nice, big, bright apartment with six, count them, six big windows on the park. So tomorrow, go and take a look."

After she had taken her bath and was dressed for bed, Elvira came into the living room, where David was catching up on the last news broadcast of the night. In the Holy Land violence between Arabs and Jews had flared up once more. The news from Spain was also grim. Franco was setting up a system that mirrored the ones in Nazi Germany and fascist Italy.

"Uncle David," Elvira interrupted. "If we were to move, what would happen if a letter was sent to me here?"

"The post office would forward it."

"It wouldn't get lost or anything, would it?" she asked.

"No, I don't think so, sweetheart. So don't worry about it. Tomorrow you'll go, you'll see, and tomorrow night we'll talk. But don't lose any sleep. You had a long day. You need your rest."

She kissed him, then kissed Rebecca and started for her own room.

David was troubled. "Why should she suddenly be worried about a letter? What kind of letter?"

Rebecca continued to write out envelopes that solicited contributions to the Jewish National Fund. In the morning, she would slip one under the door of each apartment in the building. As she wrote, she continued to think. *Something has happened to our little girl. Something good, I hope.*

26

*R*ebecca Rosen *and* Elvira Hitchins climbed the subway stairs to the street. They looked across at Central Park, where the trees were just beginning to bud, sweetening the air and creating a vista of fresh light-green as far as they could see.

"Uncle David was right. It is beautiful down here."

"Beautiful, yes, but it smells expensive," Rebecca said in her practical way.

They started south, passing apartment houses that, unlike the five- and six-story ones up in Washington Heights, were ten and twelve stories high, a few even taller. Some of the buildings were old, some very new. Among the new ones Rebecca noticed that many had unwashed and undraped windows, indicating they were vacant. These were buildings obviously planned and under construction in more prosperous times. The Depression continued to take its toll.

They passed one very old building, so dour and apparently impenetrable that Elvira remarked, "Seems more like a fortress than a place to live." Then she noticed, "And it has a name. A very strange name for a house in New York. The Dakota."

They were approaching a new building that boasted a bright blue canopy on the side of which in fresh white numerals was the address David had given them. A strapping doorman stood guard, attired in a crisp blue whipcord uniform with epaulets and a military cap with a shiny black patent-leather visor.

The doorman was crisp and obligingly affable in response to Rebecca's request to see the building superintendent. Soon, a short, stout man came bustling through the ornate art deco lobby of silver and black. He greeted them effusively.

"Ah, Mrs. Rosen! I was expecting you. I must say it was a

pleasure meeting your husband. A very fine man. Very fine." He glanced at Elvira but made no comment. "Come, Mrs. Rosen, the elevator is on the left. Actually, we have two banks of elevators, to serve each side of the building. Of course we also have two service elevators—for deliveries, tradesmen, maids. We run a very high-class building. The best on Central Park West."

The apartment David had chosen was on the twelfth floor. Mr. Hanley inserted his master key in the lock and, with great pride, threw open the door, as if unveiling a monument. They were greeted with a flood of sunshine from the unshielded windows. This was indeed the brightest apartment Rebecca Rosen had ever seen. The foyer alone was larger than their present living room. Beyond it stretched an even longer, wider living room. Large by any standard, the rooms seemed gigantic in their present empty state.

Elvira started quickly across the foyer and down two steps into the living room. She approached the wide windows and looked out.

"So high above the park you can see almost to Queens!"

Hanley did not appear to appreciate her enthusiasm. He urged, "Mrs. Rosen, don't you want to see the bedrooms?"

He led the way, explaining, "The master has windows facing east and south, so you get the park view—from two sides. Naturally, it has its own bathroom."

Hanley led the way to the second bedroom, pointing out, "Notice that this also has its own bathroom. Makes a perfect room for a young woman. Your husband said you will have a niece living with you."

"Yes, yes, we will," Rebecca said. It was apparent that Hanley had not yet identified Elvira as the niece.

"And now," Hanley was saying, "something you will find in only the best apartment houses in New York! A dining room big enough to entertain twenty, thirty people at one time! Naturally, we have kitchens to service such a dining room."

He swung open the door, pointing out, "Not only a large kitchen with the latest and best in gas ranges and ovens, but double sinks—one in the kitchen and one in the butler's pantry. Your cook will find it a pleasure to work in this kitchen!"

Hanley started for the door that led beyond the kitchen.

"And this,"—he glanced at Elvira, "is the maid's room. Also with its own bath." He opened the door wide, gesturing Elvira to enter.

"We hadn't planned on having a live-in maid," Rebecca said.

Hanley appeared startled. "What do you mean? This girl . . . isn't she . . ." he stammered. "Mr. Rosen didn't say anything about . . . all he said was you, himself, and a niece. A family of three."

"We *are* a family of three," Rebecca said.

"You don't seem to understand, Mrs. Rosen. We run a very high-class building. Domestics, deliverymen, and Negroes ride the service car. House rules!"

"Who makes the house rules?" Rebecca asked.

"The owner, Mr. Proctor. He's a very stubborn man. When he makes a rule, it's carved in stone."

"Get him on the phone!" Rebecca ordered.

"It won't do any good, but if you insist. . . ." To emphasize his point, Hanley chose to bring them down to his office in the service car. While he was trying to raise Proctor on the phone, Elvira edged Rebecca to the side.

"Aunt Rebecca, it's futile, so don't demean yourself by pleading."

Rebecca remained firm. Hanley held out the phone to her.

"Mr. Proctor, this is Mrs. Rosen. We came here prepared to see apartment . . ."—she looked to Hanley, who supplied the number. ". . . apartment 12C. It seems adequate for our needs. And my husband is prepared to sign a three-year lease. However—"

Proctor interrupted to volunteer, "Mrs. Rosen, if there is something not to your liking, say a door you want put in or taken out, or additional cabinets in the kitchen, we are prepared to be reasonable and cooperative."

"Good. I appreciate that," Rebecca said, thinking, *The man is anxious to make a deal. Now, let's see how anxious.* "The problem isn't in the apartment. It has to do with the elevators."

"The elevators?" Proctor replied, surprised and greatly puzzled. "We've never had a complaint about our elevators. And even if we did, there isn't much we can do about them now."

"Ah well, too bad," Rebecca said, as if concluding the conversation.

Unwilling to allow a new tenant to slip through his fingers, Proctor asked quickly, "Mrs. Rosen, if you told me . . . if perhaps it has to do with access . . ."

"It has to do with my niece."

"Your niece? Does she have some difficulty walking? Is she on crutches or in a wheelchair? We could build a movable ramp. No problem. We like happy tenants in this building. So anything we can do . . ."

"Mr. Hanley says it's impossible," Rebecca said.

"Mr. Hanley does not run this building! I do!" Proctor insisted. "Put him on!"

Rebecca handed the phone to Hanley, who accepted it very cautiously. She discovered why when she could hear, even at her distance from the phone, Proctor's onslaught.

"Pat, what the hell is the matter with you? Here we have a hot prospect, a potential three-year lease for an apartment that's been standing empty for two years, and you're willing to let her walk out! What's the problem?"

"Mrs. Rosen's niece is a Negro."

All three of them could hear the explosion that greeted that announcement.

"A *what?* Did I hear you correctly? Did you say she is a Negro?" Proctor bellowed.

"Yes, sir," Hanley said softly.

There was a long silence before Proctor was heard to say, "Put Mrs. Rosen on."

"Yes, Mr. Proctor?" Rebecca said.

"Mrs. Rosen, you realize it isn't just me. There is not a single apartment house on Central Park West that will allow a Negro to ride in a passenger elevator. Besides, I have to consider the feelings of my other tenants."

"Mr. Proctor, I hate to point this out, but you don't have that many other tenants to object. In fact, you have a building here that is more than half empty. Now if you want a family of quiet, responsible people who will pay their rent promptly on the first of the month—for an apartment that has been standing empty for two years—you will change your rules to permit a young, attractive soon-to-be college student to ride your front elevator."

"Mrs. Rosen, you don't understand the position of a land-lord in these times. When it comes to the matter of color—"

"Mr. Proctor, in these times the only color that counts is not white or black but green. You will find that Mr. Rosen's money is as good as that of any tenant you have. So I want your answer. And I want it now!" Rebecca insisted. "Or do you want that apartment to be vacant for another two years?"

"You're a very tough woman, Mrs. Rosen," Proctor protested.

"Actually, I'm a very sweet woman, Mr. Proctor. I just seem tough when I confront prejudice. Now, I want your answer!"

"Against my better judgment . . ." Proctor started to say.

"Does that mean yes?" Rebecca asked at once.

"Well, I . . . guess so. Yes! Have your husband call me about the lease."

It was the second Sunday in May. Elvira was in her room cramming for her senior finals and her Regents examinations. She had her heart set on winning one of the Regents Scholarships. Not for the money, which was comparatively very small, but for the honor involved.

David sat in his usual place, Sunday *Times* in hand, cup of neglected cold coffee on the end table beside him, as he exploded: "Unbelievable!" He was so vehement that Rebecca came racing out of the kitchen. "When I heard it on the radio last night I didn't believe it. Either they said it wrong or I heard it wrong. But it couldn't be!" By now, Elvira had abandoned her studies to rush in to discover the cause of Uncle David's outburst, unusual even for him.

"Uncle David?"

"Nine hundred Jews lucky enough to get out of the hands of the Nazis. They come on a leaky boat, seeking safety here. And my government? President Roosevelt says no!"

"Roosevelt said that?" Elvira asked, unbelieving.

"Where will they go now? Back to Germany? To concentration camps?" David demanded. "They are killing Jews, and people still don't believe!" Aware that he had diverted Elvira from her studies, he regained a sufficient measure of composure to urge, "Go, darling, back to your books. While the world is wrestling with great events, each of us has his own day-to-day things to do. Hats. Studies. The little things that make up life. By the way, any news? About that young man?"

"He *was* coming up for my graduation," Elvira said.

"*Was* and *is* are not the same. What happened?" David asked.

"He got a summer job, teaching backward children. It starts too early for him to get up here for my graduation."

"Ah, too bad. But on the other hand, it's nice he got a job. Especially in these times. Sounds like a serious young man."

Once Elvira had gone back to her room, David spoke softly, "Becca, you think she is depending too much on that young man? After all, they saw each other only once, for a few hours."

"He writes very often," Rebecca said.

"Yes, but what does he say in those letters?"

"She showed me one. He writes well. Like a young man in love," Rebecca said. "And every few weeks he calls. Long-distance," she pointed out.

"I just don't want her heart broken," David said. "She is strong in many things, but very sensitive, too. I would hate to see her suffer."

Though Drew Armstrong could not attend Elvira's graduation, there were sufficient honors to brighten the day for her. She was one of six seniors at Wadleigh who were awarded Regents Scholarships. She won first prize in creative English and second prize in history. When the issue arose as to which girl should be class valedictorian, Miss Flaherty made the decision. As her last official act before resigning to become a dean at Hunter College, she insisted that the honor go to Elvira Hitchins.

As Elvira approached the lectern to deliver her speech, Rebecca grasped David's hand and clung to it. When Elvira concluded and the applause swept through the auditorium, Rebecca said, "Just to see her up there, so proud, all these years were worth it."

When they claimed their graduate, who was kissing some

of her classmates farewell, David and Rebecca had the opportunity to greet Miss Flaherty.

"You can be very proud of the job you've done, Mrs. Rosen," the principal said. Turning to David, Miss Flaherty remarked, "And this, I assume, is the grouch?"

"Miss Flaherty, I would rather be called a grouch by that young woman than a king by anyone else."

Miss Flaherty turned to Elvira, whose black eyes were sparkling more brightly than ever, in pride at David Rosen's compliment. Miss Flaherty hugged her, saying, "I'm happy that you chose Hunter. I'll have four more years of watching you grow. Now, go off and celebrate. God knows, you've earned it!"

For the rest of that summer, Rebecca and Elvira devoted their time to selecting bedroom, living room, and dining room furniture, fabrics, draperies, carpeting, and other decorations for the new apartment on Central Park West. They spent days going from one furniture house to another, from one fabric house to another, from one carpeting house to another.

Each time Rebecca suggested they might move some of their furniture from Washington Heights down to Central Park West, David Rosen said, "A move like this we make once in a lifetime. A new life demands everything new!"

Rebecca and Elvira continued searching. Many days they returned to the empty apartment on Central Park West to lay out on the floors of the various rooms samples of all kinds of upholstery fabrics, carpeting, drapery fabrics to see how they harmonized in the bright sunlight, how they contrasted. They debated various combinations, arrived at their selections, then after they came upon another new color suggestion, they threw out all their previous decisions and started all over again.

When, after almost a whole summer of debating, choosing, eliminating, and combining, they presented their selections to David, he said, "Perfect!"

They felt gratified until he commented, "If you had showed me this on the first day, it would have saved you ladies a lot of trouble. What took you so long?"

Rebecca and Elvira were too exhausted to explain.

It was mid-August before the new apartment was in good enough shape to allow them to move from Washington Heights.

Mrs. Dwyer had tears in her blue eyes as Rebecca and Elvira said goodbye.

"You won't forget us, will you?" she asked. They embraced. "My, child, when I think of how you've grown up. So pretty. So bright. I feel proud to think I may have had a little to do with it. You take care, child. Take care." She kissed Elvira and was reluctant to let her go.

Dwyer took the cigar out of his mouth. "And nothing for an old man?" Elvira kissed him on the cheek. "Good people," he said. "Good people. Sorry to see you go."

The first few days in the new building were tense. The reaction of their new neighbors was, at first, one of surprise and some resentment. But after they observed Elvira conduct herself in her usual friendly but reserved fashion, their initial feelings turned to quiet acceptance.

The transition from Washington Heights to Central Park West was accomplished without undue incident.

It now afforded David Rosen a great sense of fulfillment each morning when he came out of the building and the doorman greeted him respectfully, "Shall I get you a cab this morning, Mr. Rosen?"

"No thank you, Tom. This morning I think I'll walk a bit."

After a full day at work, he returned home to relax in the new large living room, in his comfortable new armchair upholstered in maroon velvet, to read his *New York Times*. However, his new surroundings did not moderate his views about the reportage or the editorials he found in the *Times*. If anything, this new, larger living room seemed to invite louder, more explosive opinions.

Once Rebecca had their new household running efficiently, it was her duty and pleasure to take Elvira shopping. A young woman entering college should start off with a wardrobe that befit her new situation.

At the dinner table every evening, David would inquire, "And what did we find today, ladies?"

"Today," Elvira reported, "skirts and tops."

"Skirts and tops is no description, darling. What kind? What colors?"

"Gray plaid skirt with a red sweater."

"Gray plaid skirt, red sweater? What a combination!" David said. "Just so happens I was making my usual call on Lord and Taylor this morning. To get up to the buyer's office, the elevator goes by the ladies sportswear floor, so I stop off there. Just to browse. I happen to find there a sweater. A beautiful shade of red. And soft as cream. One hundred percent cashmere. I say to myself, this is for Elvira."

"Uncle David," Elvira protested. "Cashmere is too expensive."

"What makes you think I'm spending my money? Your college fund is still in the bank. It's drawing interest, so I'm spending your interest," he joked. "Well, now that financial matters are out of the way, anything interesting in the mail today?" It was his way of keeping abreast of the situation between Elvira and Drew.

Elvira's face flushed slightly. "As soon as his teaching job is over, he promised to visit," she said.

"A serious young man. Works. Teaches. Nice."

But David's moment of calm enjoyment was suddenly disrupted by the sound of the radio from the kitchen. He held up his hand in a signal for absolute quiet. He bolted from his chair, muttering, "I can't believe my ears!" He raced into the kitchen. Elvira and Rebecca stared at each other. With his ear ever tuned to the grim news coming out of Europe, what had David heard that they had not?

Moments later he returned, a man stunned, in shock.

"I heard it. But I don't believe it."

"David? What?"

He did not reply but hurried out to the living room, where a new Stromberg-Carlson radio had been installed in the walnut secretary.

The unemotional, flat voice of Elmer Davis was delivering his commentary: ". . . despite Hitler's extreme and intemperate outbursts against Communism, it is clear now, with this official announcement in Moscow and Berlin, that both powers have today signed a nonaggression pact. The inevitable consequence is that with his eastern flank secure, Hitler is now free to pursue further adventures in the west."

"Further adventures!?" David shouted back at the radio. "He is free to go to war against England and France! Rebecca, Elvira . . . we are looking at the end of the world, the end of the world."

"Uncle David, do you think we'll get into it, too?"

"We did the last time," he reminded. "One thing I know. This will be bad for the Jews. It always is."

One week later, On September first, German troops and planes attacked the defenseless country of Poland. England and France, in accord with their treaty obligations to Poland, declared war on Germany.

27

*F*_{our days after} Hitler invaded Poland, Elvira received a letter bearing a Washington, D.C., postmark, with precise hand lettering on the upper left-hand corner: DREW ARMSTRONG. She tore open the envelope, read the note hastily, then called out, "Aunt Rebecca! He's coming! If it's all right with you and Uncle David, he would like to come up to New York next Saturday!"

It was just past two o'clock on Saturday afternoon. Elvira had changed her dress three different times, each time coming out of her room to present herself for their approval.

"Do you think he'll like this one or was the blue one better?" she asked.

"If he has eyes in his head he'll love you in any dress, darling," David assured, while for the hundredth time he glanced furtively at his wristwatch, an unusual action of which Rebecca was aware but that Elvira was too excited to notice. "Sweetheart, what time did you say his train from Washington was due?"

"Two twenty-five, Uncle David. Why?"

"Just asking." He folded his rumpled *New York Times*. "Becca, I think I will go for a little stroll. After all, when is the park so nice as on an early fall day like this?"

He slipped into his navy-blue cardigan. Rebecca pursued him and caught him at the door just before he left.

"David, the young man will be here any minute. How can you leave now?"

"Just a short walk. A *shpatzier*," he replied.

"David . . ." Rebecca hesitated. "She has her heart set on this meeting. What if he isn't everything she thought? Worse, what if he doesn't like her as much as she likes him?"

"I thought years ago we decided to ignore the what ifs.

You're more nervous than she is. Relax. The way I figure, if it was meant to be, it'll be. If not, better she finds out now. Now, if you don't mind, I got to get in a little walk."

David Rosen stepped out of the elevator car into the clean, spacious, well-furnished lobby with its accents of silver and black. He was greeted by the uniformed doorman and he returned the greeting with equal politeness. He crossed Central Park West, but instead of taking his usual route, he sat down on the wooden bench opposite the building. From time to time he consulted his wristwatch. He found himself growing so nervous that he determined not to look at his watch again. Two minutes later he did. As he looked up, he noticed at the corner a tall, dark-skinned young man, who consulted a note he held, checking it against the number on the canopy.

Must be him, David decided. *And if it isn't, so I'll look like an idiot. Won't be the first time.* He started back across Central Park West. Before the young man reached the building, David approached him.

"Tell me, young man, would you by any chance be named Armstrong?"

"Yes, sir. Why?" the startled young man asked.

"Drew? Drew Armstrong?" David asked, while thinking, *Our Elvira has very good taste.* Then, as was his cautious nature, he warned, *So far.*

"Yes, Drew Armstrong," the young man said, apprehensive. Why?"

"My name is Rosen. David Rosen. I figured if it it was you, since I am going back up anyhow, we could go up together. Do you mind?"

"No, no, of course not."

David walked Drew Armstrong past the doorman, who greeted them with a more guarded, "Hi, Mr. Rosen," while he appraised Drew with noticeable suspicion.

Once they had stepped out of the elevator and approached the Rosens' front door, Drew stopped.

"Mr. Rosen, were you purposely waiting down there for me?"

"And if I was? If they made you go around back to the service elevator, what would you prove? That there is prejudice? Do you need any more proof?"

"The old Jewish attitude: Don't make trouble, eh?"

"My boy, to make trouble, all a Jew or a Negro has to do is be born. Now, let's go in. She is waiting."

He unlocked the door, calling, "Rebecca! Elvira! We're here!"

Rebecca came racing out of the bedroom area in response to this strange announcement. "What do you mean we're . . . oh!"

"Rebecca, I would like you to meet Drew Armstrong. I think the name is familiar to you."

"Yes, yes, of course," she said. As they shook hands, she glanced toward David, her eyes approving. *Elvira was right, he is nice-looking.*

David explained, "We happened to be coming into the building at the same time. So where is Elvira?"

"She'll be right out."

It was David's turn to respond with his eyes. *Don't tell me. Yet another dress?* Aloud, he said, "Come, young man, into the living room. We might as well wait in comfort."

He gestured Drew to precede him. "So, my boy, I know you are starting your senior year in college. What do you intend to do?"

"Maybe education. Maybe sociology. I will have to decide pretty soon."

"Teaching. Sociology," David evaluated. "That's nice. But a young man should also be open-minded. Sometimes life makes decisions for us that are wiser than we make ourselves. Take me. When I was a child, my whole career was to be devoted to religious studies. But life said no! So what am I? I am in the hat business.

"Which reminds me, you college men, what is this fad lately about going around without hats? To be well dressed, a gentleman should always wear a hat. Especially when a young man goes in to apply for a job. Listen, tell you what. Give me your size. I will have a few hats sent down to you. What are your favorite colors?"

"Please, Mr. Rosen, I really don't need—"

At that moment Elvira, followed by Rebecca, entered the living room.

"Drew," she said.

He rose at once to greet her. "Elvira . . ." Their eyes spoke
of their mutual great relief, for their memories of each other
had just been confirmed.

In the manner of all new suitors, Drew was awkward as he
said, "I . . . I don't know New York well, but I thought if you
don't mind, we might go down to Times Square. I was told
there's a place there—Gray, or something like that—where
one can get theater tickets at discount prices. Would you like
to do that?"

Elvira realized at once that he had made considerable sacrifice to afford this trip to New York and that he had inquired
about all possible forms of entertainment in keeping with his
stringent budget.

"Drew," she started to say, then confessed, "Funny thing.
I've thought your name a thousand times, but when it comes
to speaking it aloud, it feels strange."

"Get used to it. Because you're going to be saying it a lot
from now on."

She looked up at him. He was smiling. She smiled back
shyly.

"All I was going to say is that if I'm to practice saying your
name, I can't very well do that during a play. So why don't
we go for a walk in the park? It's lovely this time of year."

"Okay, if you'd rather," he said, betraying slight relief.

They started across into the park. They walked along a
paved path, passing elderly people seated on park benches
who held their faces up to the sun in the pursuit of health and
longevity. They passed baby carriages tended by nannies.
They passed children as young as two or three or four playing
in the grass or digging in the moist earth of early fall. Two
children began fighting over a metal toy. Their nannies intervened, trying to make peace between them, but it ended in
tears.

All this Elvira and Drew observed without comment. Until
they were deeper into the park.

"Negro," Elvira said. "All the nannies are Negro. All the
children white."

"When I was just a little one, my grandma used to say,

'Seems colored women was born to take care of other women's children.'"

"That what she did?" Elvira asked.

"After she died, my father said she spent so much time taking care of others that she had little time for him. And most of that was spent taking him to church on Sundays. She was a very religious woman."

"She had to be, to endure the *new* slavery," Elvira said.

"New slavery?"

"Free is a hollow word, without equality."

He stopped walking to stare down at her. "That's a powerful thought for someone just starting in college. I think, Elvira, that we are going to get along very well. So, start practicing."

"Practicing?"

"Drew!" he said.

She laughed. "Drew." Changing her reading, she repeated the name. "Drew? Drew. Drew!" She spoke it loudly, then not so loudly, then firmly, then sternly. Until she stopped to comment, "Mr. Armstrong, I don't know if I like your name."

"Why not?" he demanded indignantly.

"Past tense," she said. "I think a name that is future tense would fit you better."

"I could change it," he volunteered in jest.

"How did you come to have a name like Drew in the first place?"

"My grandma. Seems in the early days of movies there was a popular actor named John Drew. Somehow, Grandma took a fancy to it. So here I am. Drew Armstrong. What are you going to do about it?"

"I don't know," Elvira pretended great dismay. "It sure is a problem."

"I could change it."

"What would your grandma say?"

"Don't think she isn't up there watching right now. She wasn't the type to give up easily."

"She's watching you now?" Elvira asked. "Walking in Central Park in New York with a strange girl?"

"Bet on it. I can picture her up there—her hands clasped in her lap, rotating her thumbs in a fury. When she was thinking hard or observing hard, her thumbs were going like sixty. And she rocked. Her favorite chair on the porch of her old house . . . house? It was a shack. With tar paper to hold the walls together. But there she was up on the porch, rocking away and twiddling. I see her doing the same now as she looks down on us."

"What's she thinking?" Elvira asked. "About a Negro girl who was brought up by Jewish people and is going to do something outrageous like go to college?"

"She's thinking, 'My, Drew, what makes you think you deserves such a pretty lady?'"

Elvira felt herself blush.

"'Not only pretty. But that girl has a mind, and ain't afraid to use it, too. Son, she going to make some lucky man a very good wife. And some man's sons a mighty good mother.'"

Elvira felt herself scarcely able to breathe. Matters had gone far beyond what she had anticipated. She was tense, unable to respond. She looked off into the park seeking something to engage her eyes, for she could not look up at him. She thought, *If he is toying with me, I can't bear to know it. If he is serious, why am I frightened?*

He sensed her feelings, for he said, "And right about now my grandma is saying, 'Son, don't you hurry that girl. Maybe you say too much already. You ain't talkin' about nothin', son!'" He paused before asking, "You know what that means, or have you been away too long?"

"I know, I know," she protested. "It means, Son, stop talking."

"Right. Sorry."

Elvira found the courage to say, "That's only what your *grandma* said."

"You don't mind, then?" he asked. Her silence was encouragement enough. "On my own I wouldn't have had the nerve to say it. And I still haven't said it all. I keep remembering the first moment I saw you there at the Memorial—the look on your beautiful face, your eyes. All the feelings of all the colored people were in your eyes—sensitive to their suffering, but strong as you looked to the future. I watched as your bus pulled out. Watched your face as you looked out the window at me. When you were gone, I kept watching till your

bus was out of sight. After, I went back to the Memorial. I
stood there, between the columns, looking up at Mr. Lincoln.
And I thought, 'Mr. Lincoln, you may go down in history for
freeing the Negroes. But to me you'll always be the way I met
Elvira.'"

They had arrived at the boathouse deep in the park and at
the shore of the large lake.

"Would you like to?" he asked.

Elvira debated the cost. He sensed that. "I've been saving
up for this for four long months." He laughed. She relented
and laughed along with him.

They were drifting out in the center of the lake. On all
sides were boats with other young couples, several with couples accompanied by a young child or two.

They had been silent for a time until Drew said, "You
haven't said."

"Said? What?" Elvira asked.

"That day, that first day. After the bus pulled out. What
you did, what you thought."

"I wish I had a grandmother to help me out now," Elvira
said.

"Pretend to have one, if it'll make it easier," he urged.

"Okay. She'd be up there saying, 'Elvira, don't go setting
your mind on him. After all, compared to him, by age and
learnin' you be just a chile. That young man, he be a junior.
In a big college like Howard. And you not even started in
college yet. Why, he forget you the first minute you is out of
sight. Though was nice 'n thoughtful of him walkin' you back
to that bus to make sure you all right. Same as if he takin' care
of his lil' sister. So don' you go gettin' any fancy ideas 'bout
him. Likely you never see that young man again.' But I said,
'He took my name, my address, surely he'll write!' She said,
'Chile, you is mistakin' courtesy for somethin' else. You be
wise to forget about him.' But I said, 'No, no, he will write.
He must write.'"

"Which only goes to show that grandmothers, wise as
they are, don't know everything," Drew Armstrong said.

Having confessed her feelings, Elvira glanced shyly at
Drew for his reaction. He was staring at her with such concentration that his oars no longer guided the rowboat, which

drifted aimlessly. Their eyes were in close communion when they were suddenly jolted by another boat.

An angry, hoarse voice called, "Stupid nigger! Why the hell don't you watch where you're going?"

They were both startled back into reality. Anger swelled the veins in Drew's neck. He was about to shout back when Elvira said, "No, Drew! What good would it do?" He restrained his fury, plunged his oars into the water, and started to row swiftly away.

They were seated on a park bench trying to enjoy their ice cream cones. But it was impossible to recapture the easy, delightful aura of earlier in the day.

"Will it ever get any better?" Elvira asked suddenly.

"It must," Drew resolved.

"I don't know," she remarked sadly. "The last time I saw my mama alive, she told me how my father died, how she tried to warn him to keep his mouth shut. Yet I warned you to do the same. Are we ever going to be free enough to speak our feelings? To answer back when an answer is called for?"

"We will!" Drew said with great conviction. "Someday. If the generations before didn't do it for us, we will have to do it for our sons and daughters."

"And we can," she agreed. "Those thousands who stood with us at the Lincoln Memorial that day won't be denied forever."

He reached for her hand to press it as if sealing a compact.

28

*O*nce *Elvira and* Drew had left the apartment, David Rosen stood at the living room window, staring down to see them emerge from under the canopy. He watched them start toward the corner, stop, exchange brief conversation, then start across the street into the park.

"Good!" he announced to Rebecca. "Instead of wasting a lot of money trying to make an impression, they went into the park," David had said, still watching the young people. "I like a young man who knows the value of a dollar." Once he had lost sight of them amid the green trees, he turned back to ask, "So? What did you think?"

"He's nice-looking. Well-behaved."

"Of course. But to be a good match for Elvira, a man should be special."

"Good match?" Rebecca responded. "They are having their first real date. She is just entering college. And you're thinking about marriage?"

"Becca, when they come back, ask him to stay for supper."

"They may want to be by themselves. They have so much to learn about each other. Why would they want to waste time with two old folks like us?"

"Old? Forty-four is old?" he demanded resentfully, Then he admitted, "Of course, nineteen I'm not. Remember, Becca, when I was nineteen and you were sixteen?"

"And the Lower East Side was the whole world to us," Rebecca recalled. "We courted walking along Delancey Street. Among pushcarts and peddlers. When you felt rich enough, we had a potato knish for three cents and plain seltzer for a penny a glass."

"You're forgetting, sometimes we had a frankfurter on a roll for *five* cents," David reminded proudly. "The way things change. Today you can't get a decent frankfurter for less than a dime. A kosher one, that is. Thank God the subway is still a nickel. If they ever raise the subway fare in this city, there will be a revolution! So what are you going to serve?"

"I didn't plan anything. I never expected—"

"Becca, a young man comes all the way from Washington, D.C., to call on our Elvira. How would it look we don't show him a little hospitality? Not nice. Not nice!" he reprimanded.

"I could try out something that I happened to get yesterday. It's the newest thing, but Mr. Birnbaum recommends it very highly."

"So what is it, this new wonder?" David asked.

Recalling only too well the trauma precipitated by introducing him to Martha Custis's recipes, Rebecca announced with some trepidation, "Tuna fish."

"Tuna fish?" he evaluated. "Is it anything like gefilte fish?"

"No. It comes in cans."

"A fish that comes in cans and it isn't salmon?" He sounded highly skeptical.

"Tuna fish."

"There is no such thing as a fish in cans that is not salmon or tomato herring!" he declared flatly.

"There is now. Tuna fish," she insisted.

"This I got to see."

He was on his way so quickly that Rebecca barely managed to precede him into the kitchen. There she produced two cans of the new fish. He examined them closely, with great suspicion.

"Open one," he said. As if she were about to disarm a bomb, he warned, "Be careful!"

She sank the blade of the opener into the metal top of the can. She worked it around, stroke by stroke, until she had removed the lid. She held it out for David's inspection. He stared at the round section of white flaky fish swimming in oil.

"Any fish this pale must have been sick," he diagnosed.

"Ridiculous."

"To be good, a canned fish has to be red. Like salmon," he pontificated. To appear reasonable, he conceded, "Or at least pink. But this? A healthy fish should have a healthy color."

"Mr. Birnbaum said they are just beginning to can tuna fish. Maybe they have to learn how."

"So what am I, a guinea pig?" His curiosity overcame his skepticism. "Did he say what you're supposed to do with this stuff?"

"He said it can be used in different ways. Cold, in a salad. Hot, with noodles. Mixed up in sandwiches. Maybe that's what I'll do for tonight. Tuna-fish sandwiches."

"Oh no!" David protested. "I'm not taking any chances that we poison that young man. Elvira likes him too much."

When it was eight o'clock and Elvira and Drew had not returned, Rebecca decided to prepare their own supper. She mixed the tuna fish, as Birnbaum had suggested, with some mayonnaise and a touch of onion. She made up sandwiches on slices of challah left over from Friday evening's Sabbath supper. She set the platter down on the dining room table.

David leaned back to examine the platter from a greater distance. If he could have walked around it, he would have. He lifted half of one sandwich and inhaled the aroma. "Could be worth a try," he said. With the courage that emboldened history's explorers and pioneers, he bit into it. Rebecca stood by, awaiting his verdict.

"Well?" she was forced to ask to end the suspense.

"I think you can now serve my coffee."

Supper ended on a note of triumph for Rebecca when he said, "Tuna fish, eh? And it comes in a can? What will they think of next? Becca, we could stand this again sometime. Soon."

It was almost ten o'clock when Drew Armstrong brought Elvira home. Anxious to interview the young man at length, David invited him to stay for coffee and cake. But the last train back to Washington would leave Penn Station at eleven, so he had to leave. Elvira saw him to the street. She was gone for what seemed to David a long time. When she returned, he asked, "So? What happened?"

"David, please!" Rebecca remonstrated.

"Young people are gone for hours, ever since this afternoon. I have a right to ask."

Elvira appeared oblivious of David's comment. With a sigh

and sense of reliving cherished secrets, she said softly, "We talked."

"Eight hours, naturally you talked. But about what? What did he say? About his family? His plans for the future? He must have said something."

"He talked about his grandmother," Elvira said, smiling.

"Tell me, Becca, when you and me first started to go together . . ."

"Even in those days I had to correct you," Rebecca said. "It's when you and *I* first started to go together."

"So! I stand corrected! But tell me, when you and I started to go together, did we spend eight whole hours talking about my grandmother? He must have said more."

Elvira continued to smile. "That was the part I'll always remember best." She started off to her own room.

"The young man must have said something," David protested to Rebecca.

"David, can't you see? She is a girl in love. So in love that the rest of the world, including you, doesn't even exist."

"Becca, any girl with such a look on her face is so in love that she has no judgment."

"I was in love like that once," Rebecca pointed out.

"Meaning?"

"I had the good judgment to pick you," Rebecca said.

It was difficult for him to rebut that.

"Now, you listen to the eleven o'clock news," Rebecca advised, "and I will go in and talk to her."

Elvira had just slipped out of her dress. She stood in her bra and panties, staring at herself in the full-length mirror inside the door of her clothes closet. Rebecca knocked and entered to find her that way.

Her immediate thought was, *God, what a lovely young woman. Beautiful, with such a long graceful body. And with her hips and those young full breasts, she is born to become a mother. I only hope . . .* She deliberately resisted pursuing that thought, which could lead only to reliving her own disappointments.

"Elvira darling, I can tell from the look in your eyes how it went. Is there anything else you want to tell me?"

"We did talk about his grandmother. And the war. And

what would happen if somehow this country got involved in it."

"He sounds like a very serious young man," Rebecca said.

"He . . . he wants me to go steady with him."

"After only one date?"

"Yes."

"And?" Rebecca asked.

"I told him I'd think about it," Elvira said in such a way that Rebecca knew she would consent. "Meantime, we promised to write every day."

"Every day?"

"And call once a week. We'll alternate calls. He can't afford to call more often," Elvira said. "Do you think Uncle David will mind?"

"You know your Uncle David. He still needs lessons in being a grouch."

They both laughed. Rebecca embraced Elvira and kissed her on the cheek.

"See," Rebecca said. "When you were young, I had to bend down to kiss you. Now you're so tall I have to stand on tiptoe."

Three weeks later, on September 28, Hitler and Stalin officially announced the division of Poland.

David came home late that evening. Rebecca had already promised to attend a meeting of a women's committee formed to press for the admission of more refugee Jews into Palestine. She asked Elvira to serve David his supper.

When Elvira heard David unlock the door to the apartment, she put aside her *Basics of Pedagogy* to greet him.

"Uncle David, Aunt Rebecca had to go to—" She did not complete the thought. "Uncle David? You look so pale. Uncle David, don't you feel well? Uncle David?"

As if he had not heard, he removed his hat and coat and tossed them to the foyer bench. The hat fell to the floor and rolled away. He made no effort to retrieve it. He trudged slowly into the living room. Elvira followed him.

"Uncle David, what happened?" Never in the nine years she had known him had she seen him so distraught and defeated.

"It happened. That bastard Stalin, he has delivered all Polish Jews into Hitler's hands. I have family there—a greatuncle, three cousins. They have children. I have just come from a meeting, to raise funds to get more Jews out of Europe. A man spoke, a man who was able to escape from Warsaw. The stories he told us tonight! Half a million Jews in Warsaw alone! The same thing will happen to them as is happening to Jews in Germany! I wrote out a check immediately. But is it enough? Will it help? Who knows?"

"Uncle David, there is more money."

"What do you mean, more? You have a *knippel* too? Money you saved from your allowance?"

"My tuition money, *Ten thousand dollars.* It's still intact, in the bank."

"Darling, I am touched, deeply touched. But this is not your fight. It's ours."

"Uncle David, it's all one fight. Drew says that if we get into it, he'll volunteer."

"After the way this country has treated him?"

"He says it isn't just for this country. It's for freedom for the entire world. Because without this country, there can't be any freedom anywhere."

"I like that young man more and more."

"About the money, Uncle David. I'd like to give at least some of it," Elvira insisted.

"If I thought money would do it, believe me, I wouldn't hesitate. But those madmen in Germany. They have only one thing in mind, one plan: exterminate all Jews."

"God wouldn't let that happen," Elvira said.

"God?" David considered. "I think God has looked down on this earth and said, 'This creature man which I have let loose on the earth, he is a mistake. I have given him an earth that is rich and plentiful. I have given him a brain that makes possible undreamed-of inventions. He can fly through the air like a bird. He can send voices, music, laughter through the air, like magic. With all that to enjoy, what does man do? He fights wars. He is ready to kill anyone who is not the same religion or the same color. I have come to the sad conclusion that man is indeed my worst mistake. So I will give him the means to destroy himself. Thus I will be rid of that problem and perhaps invent some other form of life that will reflect glory on me.' That, Elvira, is what I imagine God is thinking now. If that makes me an apostate Jew, God Himself has driven me to it."

Elvira noticed that unlike in other times of distress, when he would take down his battered copy of the Torah to seek refuge in his beloved learning, on this night he sought neither consolation nor courage in religious study.

He only sat there shaking his head in disbelief.

29

*E*lvira *waited outside* the office of Dean Flaherty until she was admitted by the dean's secretary. Flaherty rose to embrace her.

"I've seen your first-year grades. Very good, Elvira. Not surprising. But extremely good. So I am most curious. What is this summer project you mentioned in your note?"

"I would like permission to attend summer courses."

"Now I *am* surprised. With grades of A, A, A, and B-plus, what is there to make up? You want to raise that B-plus to an A?"

"Time, Miss Flaherty, time. I would like to finish in three years and get my degree."

"Is there any special reason?"

"Yes. To catch up with Drew, before the war catches up with both of us," Elvira said.

"Of course, my dear, of course. I will see that permission is granted."

"Thank you," Elvira said.

Flaherty watched her leave, thinking, *That young woman— strong, determined, with purpose. And the way she carries herself. Whoever that young man is, I hope he's worthy of her.*

Elvira left Hunter College, started across Park Avenue toward Madison, then Fifth and into the park to walk home along paths overhung with cherry trees in full pink bloom.

She clutched her purse, in which reposed her official record of grades for her first year. When she called Drew tonight, she would tease that her first-year grades were better than his had been. Not by much. But enough to let her boast a bit.

She arrived at the house and was greeted by the doorman. "Beautiful day, Miss Hitchins, lovely."

"Yes, Pat, just made for walking through the park."

She unlocked their door, called, "Anybody home?"

Greeted by silence, still she sensed there was someone there. She started toward the living room. Aware that the shades were drawn, she slowed to a cautious walk and peered in. In the darkened room, she found Uncle David seated on a low box, his shirt open at the collar, with no tie. On his feet were not shoes but bedroom slippers.

Elvira realized he was sitting shivah, mourning for some close relative. She approached him and spoke softly: "Uncle David? What happened? Who?"

He waved his hand in a gesture of futility, his grief too heavy to explain. He fingered his shirt where the prescribed rent in his garment had been made.

Elvira heard the front door being unlocked. She started toward the foyer. Rebecca came in hurriedly, calling, "David," When she caught sight of Elvira, she dropped her voice to explain. "The news came this morning, just after you left for school."

"News?"

"You know how he's been worried. The Nazis taking over Poland, Holland, Romania. First thing they round up the Jews, send them off to camps, and they're never heard of again. Well, early this morning . . ." Rebecca found herself unable to continue.

"Aunt Rebecca?" Elvira urged.

Rebecca began to weep. She patted Elvira on the arm and went by her to the living room. Elvira followed, then waited at the archway as she saw Rebecca approach David. "I went to the synagogue. The rabbi wasn't there. I spoke to the sexton. He promised he would be here this evening, with a minyan."

"Thank you, Becca," he whispered.

She kissed him, went to join Elvira, and led her toward her bedroom.

"What happened, Aunt Rebecca?"

"For weeks now he has been writing and calling, pleading for some word from home. No word. Nothing. Until this morning. A Jewish welfare agency had word. Our village wiped out. Every Jew there was taken away. What else can he do but sit shivah? It is the least the dead are entitled to—to be remembered, their souls commended to God."

"If there were anything I could do . . ." Elvira volunteered.

Rebecca wiped her eyes dry and tried to summon up a smile as she asked, "So? Last day? Grades?"

Elvira handed her the slip on which her end-of-year grades were listed.

"Ah," Rebecca said. "Wonderful!" Impulsively, she kissed her.

"Right now my good news seems so unimportant."

"Wrong," Rebecca said. "In times like this, more than ever we should savor what good news there is. Tomorrow you will tell him. It will help to cheer him up." She shook her head in great regret. "Last night he and I were discussing where to go this summer. This morning he is sitting shivah. Life! Who knows?"

She was on her way back to the living room when she was reminded. "Oh, darling! With everything that is going on, I completely forgot. He called!"

"Drew?"

"Who else? He wants to invite you down to his graduation. But first he wanted Uncle David's permission. And"— Rebecca smiled, saving the best for last, "he wants you to meet his parents."

"His parents," Elvira considered, with full appreciation of what that meant.

"I know exactly what you should wear," Rebecca said. "That light blue linen we found at Best's. And with it you should wear a hat. A big wide straw in white, to frame your face. I can just see you now. A picture!"

They embraced. As they were parting, Elvira said, "Aunt Rebecca, about the summer . . ."

"Yes, darling?"

"Because of my grades, I have permission to attend summer school."

"Sweetheart, you have just spent nine months studying, with classes during the day, and the library until late at night, staying up to write term papers, exams. You deserve some time off. What's the rush? To catch up with him? For a girl like you any man would wait."

"He'll wait. But the world won't," Elvira said. "When the British had to start evacuating Dunkirk, I said to myself, 'The

Nazis will never be satisfied. Our turn will come. Sooner than we think.' So I figured it out. If I go to summer school this year and next, I will graduate in three years instead of four. We can be married sooner. Before . . . before he has to go."

Rebecca agreed grimly. "Of course. You are right. Summer school. Now, call Drew, tell him you are coming to his graduation!"

The train from New York pulled into Union Station in the nation's capital. It ground its way slowly, bell clanging. The acrid smell of smoke reminded Elvira of another train trip of years ago. Trains would always remind her of that day. That pungent odor seemed lodged in her nose. That day she had had the comfort of Aunt Rebecca. Today she was alone. And doubly tense. Despite Drew's assurances that his parents would love her, she felt insecure, her stomach tense and crampy, as if she were getting her period.

Though the uniformed Negro porters approached most white passengers with obsequious deference, no porter approached her. She carried her own bag, following the signs that said TO STREET AND TAXIS.

Elvira was brought to an abrupt halt by the sign on the door to the ladies' room: WHITES ONLY. Despite all the barriers she had encountered, for the first time she had come up against the prejudice that prevailed in the nation's capital. Her first reaction of anger gave way to a feeling of hopelessness. *If this is the attitude of the nation's capital toward Negroes, what hope is there for the rest of the South, the rest of the country?*

She continued toward the exit, her nervous anticipation now overshadowed by a feeling of depressed futility. She wondered, *Have I been shielded too much? So much that when I come up against the hard reality of true second-class citizenship I am unprepared? What would they have done to me if I ignored the sign and entered the WHITES ONLY room? Would they arrest me? How do they treat Negroes who either don't know their place or refuse to accept it?*

She deliberately started back, determined to find out. She reached the forbidden door and was about to push it open when a uniformed guard called, "Hey, you! Can't you read?" When he was only a few feet from her, Elvira thrust the door open and entered, defying him to follow. The two women inside, touching up their makeup, caught her reflection in the mirror. They both turned, shocked but silent. Elvira put down her bag, took her place before the mirror to powder her nose, and added a touch of color to her lips. She ignored their resentful glares, determined to be neither self-conscious nor hurried.

When she was done, she picked up her bag and started out. Just before the door closed, she heard one woman say, "Must be the daughter of some diplomat." The other responded, "Still, it was a shock. Pretty, though."

The frustrated guard was waiting for her. "You know, I could arrest you for that!"

She was about to challenge him to do so when she heard Drew's voice call out: "Elvira!" He raced to her side, colliding with two other men in his haste. He embraced her with such force that he lifted her off her feet.

Once he set her down, the guard rebuked, "Do you know what she just did?"

"No," Drew replied. "But whatever she did, she must have done it well. She does everything beautifully."

He seized Elvira's bag and led her out of the station. Once in a taxi, he seemed less exuberant than when he had first greeted her. Was he as nervous as she about her first meeting with her parents?"

"Honey," he began. "You won't like this, but I've reserved . . . had to reserve a room for you in a . . . a Negro boardinghouse. That's the way things are down here."

"Will your folks be staying there, too?"

"Yes."

"Then it's all right."

"You won't mind? After all, you're not used to—"

"No," she interrupted." And I *won't* get used to it! Nor will any child of mine ever get 'used to' it!"

They were silent the rest of the way.

The Armstrongs were waiting in the modest sitting room of the boardinghouse on a side street in a Negro neighborhood in Washington. Elvira had no difficulty recognizing them. Not only did they rise at the sight of their son, but she realized that Drew got his height from his father and his dark color from his mother. Susannah Armstrong embraced Elvira, then held her off so she could study her face.

"My!" Mrs. Armstrong exclaimed. "Drew been tellin' us what a pretty girl you be. But you exceeds pretty. Don't she, Joshua?"

"She do, she do indeed!" Armstrong agreed. He reached for Elvira's hand and held it between his two large hands, which, Elvira realized, were accustomed to hard physical labor. They were strong, and callused; still, their touch was gentle.

They had supper in the small dining room of the boardinghouse. At a table in the corner, they had the opportunity to talk privately, to discover each other. Throughout the conversation, Elvira sensed that Drew was uncomfortable at the way his parents spoke, because they used language that both he and Elvira had learned to abandon years ago. The line between the two generations was clear every time the Armstrongs spoke. Aware of Drew's discomfort, Elvira was tempted to say, *Don't, Drew, don't feel that way. I understand. My mother spoke the same way. Don't suffer so.*

She was forced to abandon such thoughts when Susannah Armstrong remarked, "Drew tellin' us you lives with Jewish folks."

"Yes. Since I was eight years old."

"Are they . . ." Mrs. Armstrong started to ask, but she glanced across at her son and decided not to.

Elvira smiled. "Are Jews different from other folks? They have different holidays and different food. But they're like us in many ways. They can't go everywhere they want to go, either."

Drew felt obliged to explain. "Elvira made the mistake of going into the whites-only toilet at the station."

"It wasn't a mistake, Drew," she pointed out.

"You do that on purpose?" Joshua Armstrong asked, startled.

"Yes, Mr. Armstrong, I did that on purpose."

There was a marked lull in the conversation. The Armstrongs exchanged concerned glances across the table. Elvira could read their thoughts: *What kind of woman is our son mixed up with, going into whites-only places? Don't we have enough trouble?*

The silence became too oppressive. Drew said lightly, "Elvira makes the most delicious fried chicken and gravy. And her cornbread!"

Susannah Armstrong asked, "Real fried chicken? Real gravy?"

"Yes, Mrs. Armstrong," Elvira said. "Mrs. Rosen taught me all about Negro cooking."

"I didn't know Jews ate colored."

"The Rosens do," Drew volunteered. "And Elvira cooks it. I've had it. Real fried chicken, real gravy, and real cornbread."

That seemed to take the chill off the disturbing news of Elvira's rebellion.

The next afternoon Elvira and Susannah and Joshua Armstrong sat in the hot sun of a Washington summer day fanning themselves with their graduation programs. Along with more than a hundred other young men of various shades of brown, Drew Armstrong received his diploma certifying that he was now a fully accredited Bachelor of Arts in Sociology.

The main commencement speaker—a white man, and a lesser official of the war department—made an effort to hold out some signs of progress to this graduating class. He laid great stress on the efforts of the navy to open its enlistment to Negroes. So that "white and Negro can serve side by side in the cause of freedom." He did not mention that the activities of the Negroes would be limited to serving the officers' mess aboard ship.

Later that evening, Drew and Elvira bid his parents farewell at the bus station and watched them board the bus for the small town in Virginia where they had lived all their lives.

Hand in hand, Elvira and Drew walked back toward the boardinghouse through the summer evening. The heat of the day had slackened, but the air was still. From open windows they could hear the sound of radios pouring out the war news. From the snatches they picked up, the most important news concerned the war in the air over England. The loss of life and property in London and other cities was mounting. But so too was the cost to the Luftwaffe of planes shot down by the RAF.

"It's a question of who quits first," Drew said in a dispirited tone that indicated he feared the British would be bombed into surrender.

"We had a guest lecturer at Hunter, an expert on military air war. He said it's a matter of acceptable losses. If the British can inflict unacceptable losses on the Luftwaffe, that should stop them."

"When young men are being shot out of the sky, what's an acceptable loss?" Drew asked.

"He said anything up to ten percent."

"Does that mean if you send out a hundred planes and five hundred men and ten planes and fifty men don't come back that's acceptable? Not to the men who don't come back, I'll bet."

Elvira realized, as did Drew, that they were both thinking about the same thing. When it came Drew's turn to go, as appeared certain now, would he become one of the acceptable losses? They spoke no more about war, air raids, or losses.

It was past ten when they arrived at the boardinghouse. They were admitted by an elderly watchman who had to be roused from his nap on the sitting-room couch. They climbed the stairs to the second landing, where they had rooms at opposite ends of the hallway. He saw her to her door. There they kissed. A long kiss. He held her close, so close that she became aware of his passion as well as her own.

"Uh-uh," she resisted in a whisper. "And please, don't ask. Because if you do, I'll say yes. And that's not the way I want our life together to start."

Reluctantly, he released her. She unlocked her door and went into her room. He waited a moment, then started down the hall toward his room. She waited at the door until she no longer heard his footsteps.

The next morning, Drew took her to Union Station. Before she boarded her train, Elvira said, "You understand about last night, don't you? It wasn't from want of wanting you, but wanting you too much."

"You were right," he conceded. "We'll be married soon enough."

They kissed.

"You never said anything about my folks."

"I think they'll make very doting grandparents."

"How could you tell?"

"By the pride in their eyes when they look at you."

"'Board!" the conductor inside the gate called. "All aboard!"

Drew picked up her suitcase. They raced through the gate, found her car. She started up the steps of the Pullman, then turned on the top step. He leapt up to meet her. They kissed. He jumped off as the train began to pull out. Elvira started into the car, passing the white-coated Negro porter.

30

It was ten o'clock on a hot July night when Elvira returned from the library, where she had been doing research on a paper for her summer course in psychology.

Drew had called and left a message for her to call back the moment she got in. He refused to tell Rebecca his good news. That was for Elvira's ears only.

Once she went to her room to make her call, David divided his concentration between the war news on the radio and the outcome of Elvira's call. While Quentin Reynolds was reporting the toll that the RAF was taking of Nazi bombers over England, David asked impatiently, "Becca, what's taking her so long?"

"Young people in love have lots of things to say to each other, though you don't seem to remember," Rebecca rebuked.

He held out his hand to her, lifted her from her chair, and looked down into her face. "So I don't remember, eh? I remember the first night I ever saw you. The first night I walked you home from school. The look in your eyes the night we were married. I used to say to myself, What does a girl with such a lovely heart-shaped face, with that dimple in her chin, with those bright, eager eyes, what does she want with a greenhorn hat worker who earns eighteen dollars a week? She must be crazy. Beautiful, but crazy!"

Rebecca laughed. "Silly! I saw you and I said to myself, 'He's a nice-looking young man. Tall, not too bright. But I will take him and make a success out of him.' And I have."

They both laughed. He embraced her, and while close, he said softly, "Becca, those two young people are only going to be young once. What would be so bad if I just offered—"

Before he could complete the thought, Elvira came bounding back into the room.

"He got it. The appointment! He got it!"

"That appointment with Professor Worley?" Rebecca asked.

"What appointment?" David asked.

"Drew is going to be Worley's research assistant for a year!" Elvira said.

"Marvelous!" David enthused. "Does it pay well?"

"Not much," she admitted. "But to be assistant to a man like Professor Worley is a great start for a man who wants to teach sociology."

"Does it pay *enough*?" Rebecca asked.

"Not at the start," Elvira admitted. "But by the time I graduate, between the two of us . . ."

David glanced at Rebecca, ignored her forbidding look, and asked, "Tell me, darling, if it was possible . . . I mean, if it could be worked out some way, could you transfer from Hunter to some college down there?"

Suspecting what David had in mind, Elvira said, "No, Uncle David. It couldn't be worked out!"

"How can you say no without hearing what I have to say?" he asked.

"We are not going to accept any money from you."

"Aha! You see? Right away you jump to the wrong conclusion," he accused. "Becca, did you hear me offer her any money?" With the injured air of the wrongfully accused, David continued, "Women just don't understand business. What I was about to suggest is this: You go to a bank. You take out a loan—three, four, five thousand dollars. Whatever it takes for you to marry, settle down, and finish college down there." He looked at Rebecca as if to say, *See, I didn't offer her any money.*

"I, a Negro woman, walk into a bank, say I would like to borrow five thousand dollars, and they just hand it over? I would have a better chance with a gun."

"Try it," David urged. "See what they say!"

"They'll want security or someone to cosign the note."

"So? What are uncles for?" David asked.

"That would just be a way for you to give us money. Drew *wouldn't* do it. And I *couldn't* do it."

"Still your obsession with being in debt," David complained. "Darling, what do you think business runs on? Debt! Everybody borrows from the bank—manufacturers, suppliers, stores. We all need cash to tide us over while we are waiting to get paid by others who need cash to tide them over."

"Not I!" Elvira insisted.

Exasperated, David shook his head. "There is *will*power. And then there is *won't* power. When you decide to go to summer school to make up time, to catch up to Drew, that is *will*power. But when you refuse a little innocent help from me that is *won't* power."

"I'm sorry, Uncle David, but . . ."

"I know, I know, you promised your mother. I understand. I also admire you. I only want to help out, because none of us knows how much time there is going to be."

Before he was to begin his assignment with Professor Worley, Drew was able to make a trip up to New York. They had twenty-seven hours. Twenty-seven hours to kiss, talk, make plans, dream dreams, avoid talking about the war, resist making love, and hardly have time or even the desire for food, wanting only to be with each other and near each other.

When Elvira left him at the gate in Pennsylvania Station, he assured her, "It won't be forever. The time'll pass more swiftly than you think."

On September 15, having completed her summer school courses, Elvira embarked on her regular fall semester.

On September 16, the United States Congress, by a margin of only one vote, passed the Selective Service Act.

That night Drew called.

"What will it mean, darling?" Elvira asked.

"I'll have to register, of course."

"And then?"

"I don't know. I guess nobody knows," he said grimly.

On October 16, Drew Armstrong, along with millions of other Americans between the ages of twenty-one and thirty-five, lined up to register for the draft. From that moment on his fate would be determined by the national draft lottery.

More than ever, Elvira felt the urgency of time.

1941

31

W*hen David heard* the door being unlocked, he put aside his Sunday *Times* and started toward the foyer calling, "So, darling? How was your weekend?" He tried to relieve Elvira of her heavy suitcase. She insisted on carrying it herself. He protested. "What's the matter? You think I'm too old, maybe?" He wrestled it away from her. "So? Talk already."

"It was fine. Wonderful," she said, starting down the hall to her room. He trailed along, realizing her suitcase was indeed heavy.

"Any word?" he asked, which meant only one thing: *Where does he stand in the draft?*

"Professor Worley wants to ask for a deferment for him."

"And?"

"Drew won't let him. He says it's his duty to serve, and he will."

"Look on the bright side, darling. There's a chance we won't get into the war after all, so maybe he never has to serve. Besides, after this summer you will be a senior. Then only one more year to go." Trying to sweeten her situation, he pointed out, "Not even a year. Ten months. Not exactly a lifetime, though it can seem that way. I know. Don't forget I was young once myself. And in love, like you. Before you know it, it'll pass."

Elvira kissed him on the cheek. "Thanks, Uncle David. For trying."

"But I didn't exactly succeed, did I?"

"All the way up on the train it hurt. Not a real pain. A fear, actually, that something will happen, we won't be able to get married."

"Don't think that way, darling. Please."

She seemed to shake off her forebodings. "Aunt Rebecca?"

"Another meeting," he said. "These days that woman belongs to more committees to help refugees than I even knew existed. Trouble is, there are always more refugees than they can provide for. Come, into the kitchen. She left fresh bagels for you. Also a nice salad. You must be hungry."

"No, I'm fine. I'm okay," she insisted.

Aware of her resentment at being treated like a second-class citizen in dining cars, he pointed out, "You didn't eat on the train."

"I wasn't hungry," she avoided.

"So you must be hungry now. Take your shower. Relax. Then eat."

While she showered, David continued to read the *Times*, devouring every dispatch. He studied maps of the progress of the Japanese thrust into southern Asia, where they were making fierce inroads into Indochina, taking Hanoi and leaving a trail of blood and deaths numbering into the millions. In Europe, the prongs of the Nazi penetration reached into a dozen nations. In each nation they occupied, the first thing they did was round up the Jews.

There was one hint of a promise of better times. Jewish men from Palestine were fighting alongside British troops by the thousands in Beirut against Arab forces from Syria and other Middle Eastern countries.

Maybe, David thought. *Maybe when this is all over the British will remember and reward the Jews of Palestine.*

But less optimistic, he rattled his *Times* and continued to read.

Sometime later, Elvira came racing out of the kitchen.

"Uncle David! Uncle David, did you hear?"

"What?" he asked. "What happened?"

"Turn on your radio!"

He reached to snap on the set.

". . . from first reports, the movement is on a broad front, stretching from the Arctic in the north to the Black Sea in the south."

"What? Who?" David asked. Elvira gestured him to silence.

The reporter continued: "Neither the Führer, nor Foreign Minister Von Ribbentrop, has issued any formal explanation of the attack on the Soviet Union . . ."

The radio blared on: ". . . the suddenness and the size of the attack has caught the Russians by surprise. Some Nazi tanks and motorized cavalry have penetrated more than twenty miles into Soviet territory."

They listened in silence through the report, which ended with a promise of bulletins and confirmations as soon as available.

"So! The animals are now at each other's throats," David said. "Let them devour each other and leave us out of it. Your Drew may not be drafted after all."

"And what about the Jews in Russia if the Nazis have their way?" Elvira asked.

David nodded his head sadly. "We seem always to be in the way of history. In ancient days, the Greeks and the Romans. Yet they are gone and we are still here. If only the price of surviving wasn't so high."

By midsummer the Russians had mounted a defense against the surprise offensive. But the Nazis had almost reached Leningrad and were threatening important anchors of the communist defense line such as Kharkov and Smolensk.

The Western powers watched, with the knowledge that Hitler's strategy called for defeating the communists so that he could turn the full force of his military might on England.

Meantime, with the approval of the Vichy French, the Japanese tide flooded into Cambodia and Thailand.

The world was aflame.

In the Rosen household, every activity took on increased pace and gravity. David had to convert his business from the manufacture of civilian headgear to producing caps, hats, and helmet liners for an increasing number of army and navy troops.

Rebecca found herself devoting more time to committees, charity functions, and old-clothes collections. Elvira, in her haste to finish, spent more hours at Hunter, coming home later and later, and eating her meals alone while poring over books she brought to the kitchen table.

All three had become transients in their own home, passing each other only early in the morning or late at night.

It was a cold cloudy day in early winter. On a more normal Sunday morning, the Rosen family would have been having breakfast together. But by now David's plant was working overtime, Sundays included. Rebecca was off at a breakfast for the women's auxiliary of an organization for relief of refugees fortunate enough to escape the Nazis and land in Palestine, albeit homeless and destitute. In her haste to win her degree, Elvira was at the library researching her paper on advanced theories of education, her senior thesis.

David returned home just after noon. He unlocked the door to the apartment, sensing it was empty. He called out nevertheless. "Becca! Ellie!" No response. He hung his coat and hat in the hall closet and carried the heavy Sunday *Times* into the kitchen to scan it while he ate lunch. He never could figure out when Rebecca found the time, but she always made sure that there was lunch for Elvira and him in the icebox. He kept calling it an icebox, from their early days. Actually, it was an electric refrigerator, with a clump of round coils on top, and it was called a Frigidaire.

He looked in. Neatly arranged on a platter was some cold chicken—Elvira's contribution, he knew. There was also a bowl of cole slaw: Rebecca. And if he wished something hot, there was a large pot of chicken soup with matzo balls, which he had only to reheat. Solitary eating had never appealed to him. He missed the conversation, the arguments, the chance to voice his opinions. This day he settled for cold food and the kitchen radio.

He began to eat, scanning the *Times*. The radio droned on with inconsequential chatter. Some program or other which, to David, merely filled in the time between news broadcasts. The front page of the *Times* seemed repetitious from day to day. In Europe, the Nazis were holding on the Western front but advancing in the East. In North Africa, the general they called the Desert Fox was chasing the British across the desert once again. Until he outran his lines of supply. Then it was the turn of the British to drive him back. So it seemed to go. However, in Southeast Asia the Japanese kept moving, moving, moving, gobbling up territory, countries, and people.

There was one optimistic article. Since Japanese diplomats had turned down his proposals for a Pacific settlement, President Roosevelt had made a personal appeal to Emperor Hirohito to use his influence to avoid a war. Today FDR was awaiting the emperor's response, the *Times* reported.

David was turning from page one to page fourteen to read the rest of the article when the radio went dead. Silence accomplished what the program had failed to do. It demanded David's attention. He looked up. He was about to switch the dial, thinking that his station had gone off the air, when suddenly it came alive once more.

"We interrupt this program to bring you a special bulletin. According to news reports which have reached this station, at seven o'clock this morning Hawaiian time, Japanese planes bombed Pearl Harbor."

David's first reaction was, *No, it can't be. It's a mistake.* He rose from his chair to stare at the radio.

". . . At this time there is no estimate of damage, though it is known that the bulk of the Pacific fleet was in Pearl Harbor at the time. There has as yet been no comment from the White House or the state department."

David went into the living room and turned on the big radio, as if hoping it might offer different, and less shocking, news. He tuned in another station and heard: "We will report further details as soon as they are available. But for the moment, we repeat: Japanese planes have bombed American naval installations at Pearl Harbor in Hawaii."

He had never felt so alone. His mind reached out. *Becca! Elvira! Where are you? Did you hear? Do you know? War! It means war. We kept thinking, hoping we would escape it. But it is here! It has happened!*

David felt a compulsion to do something. Anything. But what? He realized there was nothing he could do. The phone started ringing. He seemed unable to pick it up. Finally, he did.

"Hello?"

"David?" He heard Rebecca's voice. She was as startled and frightened as he.

"Yes, Becca."

"In the middle of the meeting someone came in. . . . It seems . . . we couldn't believe it . . ." She was not her usual coherent and precise self.

"Becca, I know. I heard it on the radio. Pearl Harbor!"

"My God, what will happen now?"

"I don't know. . . . Just . . . just come home. At a time like this, it's not good to be alone. So come home."

"Elvira? Where is she? Does she know?"

"She's not home, either. Just come home, Becca."

After the longest half hour of David's life, Rebecca finally arrived. Without a word, they embraced. While he held her, he said, "Before you came back, I was thinking. This is the first time since I came from Europe that I have been in a country that is in a war. Before, it was always somebody else's war—Germans, French, English, Japanese, Chinese. Always somebody else, always just a story in *The New York Times*. Not anymore. Now it's ours. Ours."

He turned on the radio once more. They sat and listened.

It was late afternoon when Elvira arrived, burdened with several books and two pads full of notes. At the sound of her key in the door, Rebecca called out, "Elvira!"

The manner in which Rebecca's voice reached out to her made Elvira race to the living room.

"Aunt Rebecca?"

"You didn't know? You don't know?"

"I've been in the libr—" She interrupted herself. "What happened?"

"War!" Rebecca said.

"The Japanese attacked Pearl Harbor," David explained.

"War, war . . ." Elvira repeated, breathless now. She went to the phone at once. She dialed the operator.

"I want to place a person-to-person call to Washington. To Mr. Drew Armstrong." She gave the woman the number.

All three of them waited, silent, expectant. Elvira eventually hung up the phone.

"He's not there," she said softly. "I wonder if he knows." She sank down onto the sofa, stunned, fearful. "He'll go now. He'll surely go now."

Two hours later, after Elvira had failed to reach Drew four times, he called. She was so relieved to hear his voice, she started to cry.

"Honey, no, please don't cry," Drew implored. "It will be a long time, months, before most men will be called up. In months you'll graduate. I'll finish my assignment. We can be married as we planned."

She sniffled her way back to control of herself. "I'm sorry, darling. I'm not a very good example of a Negro woman, am I? We're supposed to be the strong ones, and here I am crying."

"My mama says there's a way Negro women got that reputation—they save their tears for when they're alone. You can cry if you want."

"I'm all right," Elvira said. "I'm . . ." She searched for a word and had to settle for "fine . . . I'm fine."

"I figured it all out," Drew said. "We will stick to our original plan—unless I get called up sooner. Then we'll get married right away."

"Yes," Elvira said. "Yes, we will, we will."

The following day, Franklin Roosevelt made his historic speech in the Congress of the United States. Standing in the well of the House of Representatives, on legs supported by heavy steel braces, Roosevelt began, "Yesterday, December seventh, a day which will live in infamy . . ."

The next day the Congress voted to declare that a state of war existed between the United States and the empire of Japan.

On December 9, Roosevelt spoke to the nation at large, to prepare them for a long, hard war. But he assured them, "We are going to win!"

There was talk of ration coupons for food, for gasoline. David volunteered for service as an air-raid warden. He spent two evenings a week in the local police station learning his duties through the new television set that had been installed there for that purpose.

Rebecca spent more time in her charitable activities. Those few bits of information that managed to filter through pointed to quite terrible things happening to Jews in Poland, in Russia, and in Romania. The reports were so frightening that most people wrote them off as wartime propaganda, like the stories in the First World War, when the Germans, Huns then, were accused of cutting the breasts off Belgian nurses.

Elvira redoubled her efforts at Hunter. Each paper or report assigned to her was finished before its deadline, as if she could hasten her graduation by being ahead of schedule.

Twice Drew managed to spend a day in New York by taking an early-morning train from Washington and returning on
the midnight milk train. The second time, Elvira took him
down to Pennsylvania Station, kissed him, and watched as he
went down the long, drafty corridor toward the coach that
would take him back to Washington. At the door, he turned
and waved back to Elvira. She watched until the train pulled
out. When she turned away from the gate, she discovered
David waiting a short distance away.

"Uncle David!" she rebuked. "I'm not a child! You don't
have to keep watch over me."

"I have air-raid duty at two o'clock in the morning. Who
can sleep? So I thought I would come down, pick you up, and
we could go have a coffee. Then I would take you home in
time for me to go on duty."

There was an all-night cafeteria on Seventh Avenue across
from Penn Station. Once they were seated at a table away
from the main aisle, David pretended to cut up his coffee cake
into bite-size pieces. But it was a diversion from what he was
leading up to.

"You know, darling, while I was waiting for you I figured
out, maybe it could be a mistake."

"Mistake? What?" Elvira asked.

"Waiting until June to get married," David suggested gingerly.

"But it's what we planned. I'll be done. Drew's grant will
be over."

"That's my point, darling," David pointed out. "You and
Drew and a million other young couples are all planning to
get married in June. There'll be a rush for wedding gowns,
hotels, caterers, ministers. This way, if you were to get married, say, in March, or even April, you beat the rush. Yet there
is still time to plan. You know your Aunt Rebecca when it
comes to planning. Makes sense, no?"

Elvira's black eyes filled with tears. Her chin began to
quiver.

"Ellie darling, did I say something wrong?"

"You think he'll be drafted before June. That he'll go. That
something will happen to him."

David was forced to admit, "It pains me to see two young people so in love be kept apart, maybe for a long time. Maybe . . . maybe forever. So I ask myself, What's wrong if they get married now? What's involved? A little money? What does money mean in a time like this?"

"Drew and I talked about that too, Uncle David."

"What?"

"We decided when we start out, we will be on our own," Elvira declared. "No gifts, no loans."

David smiled sheepishly at the recollection of his previous attempt.

"We have a good example—you and Aunt Rebecca. I remember when I was eight years old and you took me in. That little apartment. That simple furniture. But there was love there. Respect. Admiration. We want the chance to start off that way. We even know where we want to live. Up on Morningside Drive."

"But that's—" David started to protest until he caught himself.

"Yes, it's a Negro neighborhood. But we could afford a small place there."

32

*R*ebecca watched with delight, yet some small regret, as Elvira modeled her graduation gown and cap. Tall and slender, she wore the gown with dignity and grace, her mortarboard cap at a defiant tilt. On her face was a smile of achievement and victory.

Rebecca thought, *She is getting a college diploma tomorrow. How I would have liked to do that. But that is what this country is for—to give children opportunities their parents never had.*

From the misty look in Rebecca's eyes, Elvira sensed the depth of her thoughts.

"Aunt Rebecca," she said softly, as if tiptoeing into her reverie. "Do you think he'll get here in time?"

"These days, with the army moving so many trainees and troops and equipment, *nothing* runs on time," Rebecca replied.

The invitations read, "Ceremonies commence promptly at 7:00." Graduates had been given instructions to be present by 6:30. At 6:15, David said, "Here, sweetheart, here. Take a cab. You get there on time. We will bring Drew."

At 6:45, he said to Rebecca, "Darling, you go! You can still make it on time. I will bring Drew."

At 7:05, David said to the doorman, "Ben, you know that young man comes to call on our Elvira? When he shows up, give him this ticket. Give him this five-dollar bill. Tell him to take a cab across the park to the college."

It was a warm June evening. The auditorium was filled to capacity. Standees overflowed into the corridor. Women fanned themselves with their programs. Men dabbed at their warm faces with once crisp pocket handkerchiefs.

The opening orchestral number, under the baton of a young woman majoring in music, was almost completed when a perspiring David Rosen edged his way through the standees, ignoring their glares. He recognized Rebecca's blond hair, tidy, braided into a halo. Alongside her was the empty seat she had managed to save for him.

Whispering his excuses, he made his way, brushing by resentful parents and friends until he reached Rebecca's side.

Behind her program, she whispered, "Did he?"

"Not when I left," David whispered back.

"She'll be so disappointed."

The ceremonies included the baccalaureate address by an undersecretary of the army, who pointed out that now that President Roosevelt had established the Women's Army Corps, the WACs needed officers as well as privates. Who better to fill that need than young women college graduates?

Next on the program was the awarding of prizes and honors. There were prizes in language studies, French, Latin, Spanish. The prize for German was eliminated this year. The English prize was awarded to Elvira Hitchins.

When she went up to receive it, she noticed the look of pride concealed behind the smile on Dean Flaherty's face. She accepted the prize, stared out at the audience, was able to spot Rebecca and David, but found no sign of Drew. She accepted her prize with far less joy than she had anticipated. Three years of accelerated work to secure her diploma, yet now it seemed an empty achievement because he wasn't here.

The ceremonies over, graduates and families found each other. There was much laughter, hugging, and kissing.

By the time David and Rebecca managed to fight their way down the aisle to claim Elvira, they found Dean Flaherty embracing her.

"Elvira, dear, now that you've finished, don't lose touch," the dean said. "I want to know everything about you. Everything!" Reluctantly, she surrendered Elvira to her uncle and aunt.

They embraced. Rebecca and Elvira. Elvira and David. Then all three together. Elvira said not a word about Drew's absence. But David knew the signs, so he felt compelled to urge, "Come, darling, give back the gown, that flat hat. Let's go. We have a reservation and we don't want to be late."

Rebecca's eyes flashed a signal to David. With a gentle finger under Elvira's chin, he lifted her face. "You don't feel like it, do you, sweetheart?" She had no need to respond. "We'll go home. Maybe he'll call."

The phone was ringing while David fumbled with his keys at the front door.

"Hurry, Uncle David. Hurry!" Elvira urged.

As the door yielded, Elvira pushed past him toward the hall phone. "Drew?"

"I've been calling all evening."

"We just got home."

"I couldn't be there. But it's not all bad news. There's good news, too. I'm coming up there. To stay."

"Here? To stay?"

"I'll explain when I get there tomorrow," he said. "Meantime, I'm sorry I couldn't see you with that mortarboard on your beautiful head. Were you cute? Or stately?"

"A little of both," she teased now that her fears and disappointments had been tempered by the good news.

"Tomorrow," he promised. "Tomorrow."

While the women were out in the kitchen preparing lunch, David had the opportunity to discuss Drew's new situation.

"You get sworn in as a second lieutenant and you're assigned to Columbia?" David considered. "That's nice. Very nice, my boy."

"When the army consulted him, Professor Woley recommended me. I'll be able to start on my master's and carry out my army assignment at the same time."

"And this assignment?" David asked.

"That part's not so nice," Drew replied. "They are forming Negro battalions in the army, with white officers. Men like me will indoctrinate the white officers in how to deal with Negro troops. It seems Negroes can fight, but they can't command."

"I know the feeling. Right now, Jews are fighting in Palestine, in Lebanon, in Syria, in the underground in France and Poland and Russia, yet we are considered cowards." Before he became mired in regrets, David forced himself to brighten and ask, "So? What happens now?"

"That's why I wanted to talk to you, sir," Drew said.

"Sir? Since when did I become a sir?" David asked.

"The way I was brought up," Drew began. "The way it was with my mother and father, when it came time for a man to consider marriage, he first spoke to the girl's father. Elvira has no father, so I feel I have to ask you."

"It is very considerate of you," David replied. "Because she is as much our daughter as if Rebecca had given birth to her. In fact, I can see traces of Rebecca in Elvira. Warmth. Graciousness. Now, about marriage and permission. You are an intelligent, responsible young man and you love her. That would seem to be enough. But there is more. Marriage is a lifelong undertaking. It has its joys, also its disappointments. The essence of marriage is for love to grow stronger out of the disappointments. If you are prepared to love her that way, then yes, you have my permission."

Plans for the wedding had to be fitted in with Drew's move to Columbia and Elvira's taking her written exams and her orals for teaching certification. Rebecca and Elvira shopped for the wedding gown and arranged the church, the floral decorations, and the reception. All was done in haste, for once Drew accepted his commission, despite Army promises, he might be assigned anywhere. It was also understood that if he was shipped out, Elvira would not be able to accompany him. The women found a small but suitable apartment in a part of Harlem close to Columbia, in an old building more usually referred to as a tenement.

When Elvira and Rebecca were first shown into the small flat by the elderly Negro superintendent, they both were aware of the paint that made the doors stick, testament to the many paintings the place had endured through long years.

There was a cramped entryway, a short hall that passed a tiny kitchen, with a chipped, discolored white porcelain sink and an old stove and oven. Beyond the kitchen, a small living room adjoined a single bedroom.

Elvira walked through, in her mind arranging furniture, allotting space, changing her plans, walking the rooms again and then again.

Rebecca fought to control her own thoughts. *This place is not suitable, not after what she has been used to.* She beckoned

Elvira into the bedroom, out of the superintendent's presence. "Darling, before you decide, let's talk to Uncle David."

"So he can offer to pay half our rent and we can afford a better place, a bigger place?" Elvira asked with a smile, but shook her head.

"I guess he'll have to content himself with your wedding present."

"He has plans for that, does he?" Elvira asked.

"He told me he would like to furnish the place."

Elvira shook her head again, slowly.

"Not even that?" Rebecca asked. "He'll be very disappointed."

"This has to be our own. All of it. As soon as Drew gets out of class this afternoon, I'll drag him up here. If he likes it as much as I do, we'll take it."

While Rebecca and Elvira attended fittings of the wedding gown, David took Drew downtown to a men's rental establishment that David supplied with silk top hats.

The owner himself brought out a selection of tuxedos for their approval. David rejected them.

"Sol," he said. "At an afternoon wedding, *Gentleman's Quarterly* says, swallowtail coats, striped gray trousers, and ascot ties. So let's see the best in swallowtails!"

Attired in swallowtail coats that fit, trousers that needed shortening, and silk top hats delivered from David Rosen, Hatters, David and Drew admired themselves in the full-length mirror.

"Well, Drew, do I look ready to give the bride away?"

"Do I look ready to receive her?"

"Soon as Sol shortens those pants."

They both laughed. While Drew was in the dressing booth getting out of his semiformal attire, Sol took David aside to ask with great concern, "Dave, your niece is marrying a Negro?"

With a wicked twinkle in his eye, David said, "I wouldn't have it any other way."

The shocked tailor did not respond.

In the bridal department on the third floor of Saks Fifth Avenue, Elvira Hitchins was enduring her last fitting of her wedding dress, which was of ivory satin, with a stand-up collar, an empire waistline, and a train that stretched for nine feet behind her. She stared at herself in the mirror, first from one angle, then from another.

My, Rebecca thought. *What beauty. And how her light brown skin enhances the luster of ivory satin. If magazines ran photographs of Negro brides, she would be the one. Look, just look at what has happened to the frightened little girl I first found.*

The wedding ceremony of Elvira Hitchins and Drew Armstrong took place at the Ajalon Baptist Church. Now in his mid-seventies, leaner, his face more deeply ingrained with wrinkles, Pastor Wilder had delayed his retirement in order to perform the ceremony. Over the last dozen years, Elvira had endeared herself to the members of the congregation not only for her kindness and devotion but for the distinction she had added to the church by virtue of her degree and honors at Hunter. So the church was crowded, more so than on any other Sunday except Easter.

Mothers and fathers of children in the Sunday school held Elvira up to their own young as an example of what could be accomplished despite the barriers that hindered them.

Pastor Wilder was in his place before the altar. Behind the altar, the choir stood in their white-and-crimson robes, singing in rhythm, swaying, clapping. Members of the congregation hummed along, some singing aloud, many clapping in rhythm with the choir.

As had been rehearsed, Drew's parents walked down the aisle to take their place in the front right pew. One of the older deacons, dressed in white and wearing spotless white gloves, escorted Rebecca Rosen down the aisle to the pew on the left. She was attired in a gown of light blue, which contrasted with her blond hair, no longer as bright as it had been a dozen years ago.

Once she was seated, she smiled up at Pastor Wilder, sharing with him the satisfaction of the occasion. Two of Elvira's schoolmates from Hunter—one white, one Negro—and two girls who had gone to Sunday school with her served as bridesmaids.

Along with four of his classmates from Howard, who had

come up from Washington to serve as his best man and
ushers, Drew Armstrong waited to the right of the altar.

When everyone was in place, Pastor Wilder signaled the
organist. The organ began to peal out the wedding march.

David Rosen, tall, feeling impressive in his diplomatically
correct swallowtail coat and striped trousers, held out his arm.
Radiant in her ivory satin gown, Elvira gripped it.

They started down the aisle. Slowly. In measured pace to
the music. Elvira's eyes were fixed straight ahead, on Drew.
David's eyes subtly flicked from side to side, at the faces on
both sides of the aisle. Old, middle-aged, young—they stared
at Elvira with admiration and love.

It was the first time that David Rosen had been inside this
church, or any church. He had been relieved to yield that
duty to Rebecca. Now, as he led Elvira down the aisle, he felt
far less uncomfortable than he had anticipated.

At the altar, he presented Elvira to Pastor Wilder. David
kissed her and retreated to take his place alongside Rebecca.

During the wedding ceremony, when Rebecca cried, David
passed his breast pocket handkerchief to her, only to discover
a moment later that he needed it himself. They passed it back
and forth between them for the rest of the ceremony.

If David had had his way, the reception would have been
held at one of the hotels—the St. Regis, or even the Waldorf.
But after a few inquiries, Rebecca had discovered that at the
better hotels there was no enthusiasm for a function at which
most of the guests would be Negro. The banquet manager at
the Waldorf phrased it more directly than the others.

"Mrs. Rosen, if you don't mind your guests being asked to
take the freight elevators, it might be arranged."

Pastor Wilder suggested the reception take place in the
church basement. The ladies of the congregation would provide the supper.

Long tables had been set up laden with platters of the kind
of food that David had grown used to over the years: fried
chicken, chops, collard greens, mustard greens, peas, beans,
mashed potatoes, bowls of gravy, cornbread stacked in neat
squares, chitlins, and beef in gravy.

A large woman who seemed to be in charge of the arrangements approached David, took him by the arm, and pulled him close enough to whisper, "You can eat everything here but the chitlins. The chicken and the chops came from a kosher butcher."

The three-piece band, composed of musicians from Small's Paradise, played during the reception. After the bridegroom and bride danced the first dance, Rebecca urged David out on the floor to dance with Elvira.

"I'm no dancer," he protested.

"David! Go out and dance!" Rebecca urged in a whisper.

He ventured out onto the floor. Someone began to applaud. Soon they all applauded, surrounding the small dance floor. David took Elvira in his arms. They started to dance. When he faltered, she was secure. When he misstepped, she kept their rhythm. By the time they had circled the floor once, he felt at ease and was even beginning to enjoy it. He relaxed enough to abandon his stiff, fixed smile. He looked into her dark eyes. She was beaming, happy. In that moment, all the years seemed worth it. Yet he was sad as well.

Throughout David's dance, Rebecca and Pastor Wilder stood at the side of the dance floor.

"Seems only yesterday you were bringing that timid little child here for the first time," Wilder said. "She was pretty even then. But so shy. Now she is no longer pretty, she is beautiful. And full of confidence. You can be proud, Mrs. Rosen, very proud."

"Happy? Yes. But proud? She did it all by herself. I think her *mother* would have been proud," Rebecca said.

Once the bride and groom had departed, David and Rebecca danced one dance together. They bid the pastor and the other guests farewell and left.

David had reserved a limousine to take them home. Seated in the backseat, David unbuttoned his frock coat, relaxed, and sighed with relief. He had eaten more than he intended.

"Nice people," he said.

"Very nice."

"I should have gone there before. I could have taken her down to Sunday school too."

"You had no time. You were busy expanding the business."

"Not on Sundays," he said. "Yes, I should have done it. When I think of it now, there were other things I could have done to make it easier for you, Becca."

He suspected that she was in pain.

"Becca, are you all right?"

"I think I ate too much," she said.

"I know I ate too much," David replied. "But it was good. You sure you're all right, Becca?"

"I'm fine, fine. Why?"

"When we were dancing I said to myself, she feels thinner somehow. You're working too hard. Tell you what. Tomorrow, call the doctor. Tell him you want a checkup."

"I don't need a checkup. Besides, I don't have time."

Impatiently, he asked, "Becca, can't there be just one committee meeting of Hadassah, or the ladies' auxiliary of fifty other organizations, that can go on without you?"

The taxi bearing Mr. and Mrs. Drew Armstrong arrived at the old, weathered apartment house on Morningside Drive. Several neighbors were gathered on the front stoop to enjoy the late-afternoon sun. They were amused and delighted to watch the elaborate ceremony involved in Drew assisting Elvira out of the cab in her wedding dress. Once free, as she passed between them she heard whispers.

"My, she be lovely!" a child exclaimed.

"And he not bad either," one of the women remarked.

At their front door Drew swept her up in his arms, pushed the door open, and carried her in. In the small living room he set her down. They embraced, kissed. Then held each other for a long time. Since most of their modest furniture had not yet been delivered, they had room to dance. She hummed a waltz. They circled the small room several times.

He spoke into her ear: "I would have wanted it to be so different—a honeymoon, a bigger place. So many things."

"The war isn't your fault. Class tomorrow morning at Columbia isn't your fault. We're luckier than most," Elvira said, pressing her face against his shoulder. "We have each other. That's enough for me."

They kissed again. He lifted her and started toward the bedroom.

*   *   *

David fumbled with his keys before he found the right one. Once inside, he said, "Strangest thing. Suddenly it feels empty in here, like there could be an echo."

Rebecca said nothing, just started toward their bedroom. David went into the living room, slipped out of the frock coat, unbuttoned the gray double-breasted vest, and took off the cravat. Suddenly, he realized, and called out: "Boy, some hat man I am! Becca, you know what . . ." He started toward their bedroom. But as he passed Elvira's room, he caught sight of Rebecca lying on the bed. "Becca? You all right?"

"I'm fine," she said. But her eyes were damp.

"You know, maybe this place is too large for us now. Maybe we should go back to what we had. I don't mean uptown. I mean down here, some nice neighborhood. But a living room, a bedroom, and a kitchen. That's all we need now."

"No. We'll stay," Rebecca insisted. "She will be coming to visit, to have dinner. If Drew is busy or away, she might stay over from time to time."

"You think she will?"

"I think so," Rebecca assured.

"She is moving into a different world. Out of ours and into her own."

"This will always be her room. Always," Rebecca said. "What did you want to say before?"

"Say? Me? About what?"

"Hat man, you said."

"Oh yes. What an idiot! I went to all the trouble to get silk hats for Drew and for me and we forgot all about them. Never wore them."

"You looked handsome anyhow, darling."

"I did?"

"When you danced with Elvira, you were a picture of elegance," Rebecca said. "Beautiful bride, handsome man, a picture!"

"Becca, remember our wedding? You were a little doll. So pretty. That dimple in your chin shone. Your hair was so bright and golden. Everybody said, 'Where does she get such beautiful blond hair? Not from her mother. Not from her father's side. Where?' And I said, 'She is a gift from God.'"

"You never said that," Rebecca replied. "You just invented that. To cheer me up."

"Yes," he admitted. "I just invented it. To cheer *me* up. But you *were* a beautiful bride." He patted her on the thigh. "I suppose it's normal to feel a little lonesome at a time like this."

He went out to the living room, where his Sunday *Times* still lay untouched. He glanced at the front page. There was one note of good news. For the first time there was a victory to announce. An American fleet had engaged in a naval battle with the Japanese at a place called Midway. The size of the victory was not known as yet, but it was clearly a defeat for the Japanese.

Maybe, David thought, *just maybe the tide is beginning to turn.* He had little time to savor that crumb of encouragement before he noticed a small boxed item farther down on the page: NAZIS WIPE OUT TOWN. He read on. A week ago, a Czechoslovakian patriot had assassinated a Nazi officer named Heydrich. In reprisal, the Nazis had executed 1300 men, women, and children and razed every home in a town called Lidice.

How can you look into a child's eyes and then shoot him? Very hard to believe in God in times like this.

He went into the kitchen to perk some fresh coffee. As he entered, he heard the phone ring. Before he could answer, Rebecca had picked up the extension.

"Hello?" he heard her say from the bedroom. Then, "Oh, Elvira darling! Is everything all right? Or did you forget something?"

He picked up the kitchen phone to hear. "I just wanted to tell you I'm lonesome. For you. And for the grouch." She was laughing. From the way she laughed, he knew that she was delighted with her husband. The marriage had been consummated. So he took the liberty of intervening.

"My dear Mrs. Armstrong, this is the grouch in person. If you are lonesome for me, I would like to hear it myself. Not secondhand."

Elvira's voice was lower and a bit sadder as she said, "Yes, Uncle David, I'm lonesome for both of you. I wanted you to know that."

"We are a little lonesome too," he said. "But don't you worry about us. We'll get along fine, just fine. Listen, we'll talk. And we'll have supper from time to time. Say, like every Wednesday evening?"

Rebecca intruded, "David, they're just married. They're entitled to some time alone."

"Right," David agreed, then added, "Elvira darling, tell you what. Drew is taking classes at night, no?"

"Yes."

"So what would be wrong every night he's at school you come down for supper? H'mm?"

"Uncle David, let's just say every Wednesday evening," Elvira replied.

"Whatever you say, darling. And if some Wednesday night Becca has a meeting, you'll cook me up a little fried chicken, a little cornbread, maybe a little kasha and drippin's."

"Of course, Uncle David," she agreed readily.

He hung up the phone. "Now, that is a very sweet, thoughtful human being. A real *mensch*. She knew how we felt."

33

In the archaic Hall of Philosophy at Columbia University, Second Lieutenant Drew Armstrong waited outside the office temporarily assigned to the major in command of his section. Though Drew had qualified for his rank in all respects, physical and educational, he felt ill at ease in uniform. He had not yet become accustomed to the salute with which the corporal had greeted him when he entered Major Hassey's waiting room. For the first time in his young life he had been addressed as sir. He recovered in time to return the salute and announce, "I have an appointment with Major Hassey."

"Yes, sir," the corporal responded. "Lieutenant Armstrong. One moment, sir."

The corporal started for the inner door, stopped, and looked back. That particular look was not unfamiliar to Drew Armstrong. It meant: *He really is Negro, and above his station. What's this world coming to?*

Major Hassey was standing at the window. His back to the door, he was staring out at the yard around which the most ancient of Columbia's buildings were clustered.

"Armstrong?" he called, without turning.

"Yes, sir!" Drew responded crisply.

"You come well recommended. Professor Worley wrote very highly of you."

"Thank you, sir."

"You understand the nature of the assignment, I assume."

"Yes, sir," Drew replied. "To indoctrinate white officers who will be leading Negro troops."

"Right," Hassey said, turning to confront Drew for the first time. He was a clean-shaven man with a ruddy complexion that spoke of much active outdoor service. With a brief gesture of his large hand, he invited Drew to be seated. "I assume you have had a chance to acquaint yourself with the manual?"

"Yes, sir," Drew responded.

"Follow that and you should have no trouble," Hassey assured. "Of course there will, from time to time, be an officer who doesn't cotton to the idea of leading black troops, because other white officers tend to look down on men who have to command Negroes."

"Yes, sir, the manual explained that. And when I read that I thought, sir, if there is this reluctance, maybe it would be better to have Negro troops commanded by Negro officers."

"You thought that, did you?" Hassey asked. "And just where would you get enough Negro officers to do that?"

"I realize, Major, that on Pearl Harbor day there were only five Negro officers in the entire regular army."

"And three of those were chaplains," Hassey was quick to point out.

"But there are over three hundred college-trained Negro officers in the reserve corps who would be available for the regular army."

"So?" Hassey challenged.

"It would seem more logical to bring them into the regular army to command Negro troops rather than try to train white officers for the job."

"Would you like to know what seems logical to *me*, Armstrong?" Hassey asked. "That you do what you were sent here to do. And thank your lucky stars that your ass is safe as long as you are in the confines of these hallowed halls. Do we understand each other?"

Drew Armstrong hesitated to respond.

"I asked you a question!"

"Yes . . . yes, sir . . . we understand each other."

Later that evening, when Elvira asked how it had gone on his first day, rather than share his humiliation, he said, "Okay. Of course, it's the army. I'll have to get used to that."

After supper, while Elvira was doing the dishes, Drew was in the living room going over the manual for the course he would start in the morning. She called to him: "I was glancing through that while you were out."

"Oh!"

He reacted so defensively she thought she had committed

some breach of army regulations. "It's not considered classified, is it?"

He attempted to avoid any discussion. "If there was any reason to keep it secret, it would be the lousy way it's written."

"It seemed quite clear to me," Elvira said as she came out of the kitchen, drying her hands. "They start out saying, 'The first thing white officers must be taught is not to use the word *nigger* when addressing Negro troops.' Is that the type of officers you'll be working with?"

"That's why they need indoctrination," he said, trying to avoid further discussion.

"And what it says in there, that Negro troops need fifty percent more officers than white troops?" Elvira challenged.

There was no avoiding it now. He put aside the manual.

"The army's theory is that Negro troops need more officers because they are less educated and of lower class."

"First they deny them a decent education, then they fault them for being uneducated. They won't give them decent jobs, then they condemn them for being lower-class. It's difficult to fight that kind of logic," she said.

He reached out to take her hand and pull her down into his arms. "Elvira honey, it is not my job to correct all the evils of the system. As it is, I'm lucky to be here wearing a lieutenant's bars instead of being somewhere in Georgia or Texas or Oklahoma taking basic training."

"That's right," she pretended to agree. "Walk in the gutter instead of on the sidewalk. Take off your hat before you dare to talk to a white man. Isn't it ever going to change?"

He kissed her eyes, which had filled with tears.

"My son," she said, "my son is not going to live that way."

"One war at a time, darling, one war at a time," he said sadly.

"At least this isn't a benefit," David Rosen said as he was tying his tie. "This is an evening I can look forward to! Our first dinner at Elvira's!"

He turned from the bedroom mirror to find his wife at her vanity table completing her makeup.

"Only today I asked my secretary to figure out how many benefit dinners and theater parties you have dragged me to in the last ten months. Would you like to guess? British War Relief. French War Relief. Russian War Relief. Orphans of the War. Jewish Refugees. Aid to Jews in Palestine. But do I have to go? Why can't I once just send the check? Otherwise, I am a delivery boy in a tuxedo."

"You set a good example by being there," Rebecca said.

"From setting good examples I have worn out two tuxedos in the last few years. Tonight at least I will be seeing Elvira. And remind me to take the bottle of champagne."

He kissed Rebecca on the neck and inhaled her fragrance. "You smell so good, if we hadn't promised to be at Elvira's by seven, oh boy, what would be happening now!"

He had engaged a limousine to take them up to Elvira's and wait for them until it was time to return home. On the way up, Rebecca remarked, "Was it necessary to rent a limousine for the whole evening? It's expensive."

"Nothing is expensive if you can afford it," David said, making light of her comment. "Besides . . ." But he thought better of it and did not continue.

"What you mean is, it could be dangerous late at night on those streets up there and who knows if we can get a taxi," Rebecca corrected.

"That did enter my mind," he confessed.

To change the subject, he asked, "So what do you think she'll serve? Fried chicken? You know, Becca, I can confess to you now that girl has a way with fried chicken even better than yours."

"That girl . . . that girl . . ." Rebecca said. "She is a woman. A married woman who has been certified to teach. High school! We have to stop thinking of her as eight years old."

"Okay, okay," he agreed. "Let's get back to the menu. Fried chicken. Mashed potatoes. Cornbread. Greens." He was suddenly reminded, "You sure she said we will be the first guests in their home since they moved in?"

"Yes."

David Rosen did not respond, but the smile on his face

was more expressive than any words. He reached out to draw the bottle of champagne closer to him.

They were rounding the third floor and starting their climb to the fourth when David noticed and remarked, "Am I going too fast for you, Becca?"

"No, No, I'm fine, fine," she protested. But he noticed that she seemed winded. "I guess by now I'm too used to elevators."

David rang the doorbell. They could hear the rush of Elvira's footsteps. The door was flung open.

Simultaneously, Elvira called out, "Aunt Rebecca!" as Rebecca cried out, "Elvira darling!" They embraced and kissed until David said, "For old uncles not even a hello?" Elvira embraced him and kissed him on the cheek.

David sniffed the air. "Ah! There is a real cook in this house!" He handed her the bottle of champagne. "Here! For special occasions. If you got a towel, I'll open it."

"Save it for later," Elvira said. "Because first, *your* drink."

"Mine?"

"In the early days, every evening when you came home you would have a drink of *bronfen* before supper. Well, I would like tonight to be like those early days. So first, your drink."

They entered the little living room. David looked around. *Small, but nice, neat and clean, the kind of home Elvira would run. Of course if she had permitted it I would have been willing to provide a larger place, in a better neighborhood.* He abandoned such thoughts when she handed him his drink. With the gesture of a toast to the ladies, he downed his drink of straight whiskey.

"So where is the man of the house?" David asked.

"He's working a little late this evening. The way the war is going, they need more and more men. They're even talking about drafting down to the age of eighteen. That'll mean many more Negro troops—and more white officers to lead them. So there's more work for Drew."

Drew returned, so impressive in his second lieutenant's uniform that David regarded him as an expert in all matters military. While the women bustled about in the little kitchen, he plied Drew with questions.

"So how is it going? The war? You military men must know a lot more than they tell us on the radio. I mean, at Stalingrad, are the Russians really pushing the Nazis back? Or is that only propaganda? And on Guadalcanal, did we win or lose? Those communiqués sometimes conceal more than they say. What is your opinion?"

Drew smiled, the muscles in his lean jaw evident under his brown skin.

"Uncle David, this may come as a surprise to you, but I don't even have time to keep up with the radio news."

"Look, Drew, we are both grown men, so if you don't call me uncle I won't call you nephew. From now on, Drew and David. Okay?"

"And Elvira?" Drew asked.

"Ah, to her I hope I will always be Uncle David."

They were called to table in the kitchen. David entered and one look told him all he had to know. Instead of the fried chicken David had expected, there was pot roast swimming in rich gravy, ringed by mounds of brown kasha. Collard greens David had grown to love. Fried okra, mashed potatoes with gravy. And at each place a colorful salad. The crowning touch, a bread and butter plate with a square of Elvira's golden cornbread plus a slice of dark brown cornbread with a crust like shoe leather.

Deeply touched, David tried to pass off the moment by pretending to disapprove. "Beef? In times like this you spent ration points on beef? However, I will do my best."

Throughout dinner he was as good as his word, talking, eating, reaching from one platter to another.

Once the main part of the meal was over and the table cleared for coffee and dessert, Elvira said, "Now, Uncle David! Time to open the champagne."

She brought the champagne out of the refrigerator and handed him a fresh white linen towel. Despite his pretensions to being a man of the world, David failed to uncork the bottle. Drew had to take over. He grasped the bottle by its bottom, then, holding the cork firmly, he twisted the bottle slowly, gradually raising the cork until it popped and champagne gushed over the side.

Impressed by Drew's skill, David said, "You're going to have to teach me how to do that. Where did you ever learn?"

"My first two years in Howard I worked summers at the Homestead in the West Virginia mountains, as a waiter."

"They must drink a lot of champagne there."

"They do," Drew said.

"Well," said David, raising his glass. "A little toast. May this be the first of many many dinners we enjoy together. Here. And also in our home, which, far as we're concerned, will always be Elvira's home."

They drank. Elvira rose to her feet, lifted her glass, and said, "Now a toast of my own. To me. And my baby."

Rebecca felt a rush of tears to her eyes. "Elvira darling, sweetheart, you mean it? You're pregnant?"

Elvira nodded. The two women embraced. David seized Drew's hand and shook it vigorously, saying, *"Mazel tov, mazel tov!"* Then, realizing, he began to translate. "That means . . ."

"I know," Drew anticipated. "Elvira warned me. 'When Uncle David says that, and tonight he will, it means good luck.'"

"That girl . . . that woman . . . she has made me into a project. She knows everything I say before I say it." He chattered on because the excitement of the moment was too great for him. "Listen, Drew. Did I ever tell you about what she wrote about me in a composition at Wadleigh?"

Though he had been told more than once, Drew chose not to deny David his enjoyment, so he said, "No, she never told me."

"She wrote, 'He would like to be a grouch, but he doesn't know how.'" David laughed and Drew joined in. "This is a great moment, Elvira darling. So, tell you what. Tomorrow, first thing—"

Elvira interrupted to complete his announcement: "Elvira and Rebecca will go shopping for a layette, a bassinet, and a crib!"

"How did you know?" David demanded, deprived of his great announcement.

Elvira and Drew laughed. It was obvious that they had anticipated David's reaction even before he arrived.

Pretending indignation, David said, "Well, one thing you two didn't know. *Where* to buy a layette! Only one place—

Macy's. They got twin insurance. If you have twins, they supply the second layette free!"

"We hadn't planned on having twins," Elvira said.

"'Planned!' In such matters things don't always go as they are planned. I know!" Though he had not intended it, a pall fell on the little celebration. The unfortunate history of Rebecca's numerous miscarriages came to her mind, and to David's, and Elvira's as well.

34

With the coming of the September term, Elvira was placed on the list of approved but unappointed teachers. She was free to seek substitute day-to-day employment at any school that would have her. She had listed herself at four schools—two in her own neighborhood, both Negro schools, and two farther downtown on West End Avenue, where the student body was almost exclusively white. She had received an occasional day of work, sometimes as many as three days a week at the Negro schools, but none at all at the other two. Which made her determined to break down that barrier. So much so that even on days when she might have received employment at the Negro schools, she persisted in appearing at one or the other of the schools downtown.

Along with a few white women, she waited patiently outside the principal's office until he received the report that told him how many temporaries he would need to complete his teaching staff for the day. He chose his substitutes in the order in which they sat. Those who had arrived earliest were appointed first. The rest were sent away with a, "Sorry, young ladies. That's all for today."

Determined to be first in line, Elvira arrived earlier each day. When her presence became more obvious and her place in line too obvious, the principal altered his method of selection. He no longer chose the first in line but only from among those with experience in his school.

After a number of such days, once the principal had dismissed the rest with a polite, "Sorry, ladies, that's all for today," Elvira did not depart with the others. He started back into his office with a self-conscious half glance at her. Elvira came to his door, knocked, then knocked again. When he pretended not to be aware, she entered.

"Mr. Green."

With considerable annoyance, he replied, "Yes?"

"Mr. Green, I have come here day after day. I am as qualified as any teacher I've seen here. In fact, more qualified, since I am certified to teach at the high school level—English and history. Yet you've passed over me every day."

"Miss—" He was asking for her name.

"Mrs. Elvira Armstrong."

"Mrs. Armstrong, I was hoping it wouldn't come to this. But you seem intent on making an issue of it. You understand that I, personally, have nothing against Negroes. I am a very tolerant man. Ask anybody who knows me. But I must think of my students first."

"What harm could possibly come to your students if I were to teach them?" Elvira asked.

"You would be a distraction. Since they are not accustomed to being taught by Negro teachers, they would be thinking about your color instead of the subject you are teaching."

"If you've never had a Negro teacher here, how do you know I'd be a distraction?"

"My dear young woman, believe me, after twenty-seven years in the educational system of this city, nine of them as a principal, I *know* they would be distracted. I'm sorry. I wish I could be more encouraging because you seem like a very nice person. But that's the way things are."

"Why not put your theory to the test?" Elvira challenged.

"Mrs. Armstrong, I'm a busy man. I have more important things to do than carry out experiments in pedagogy. So if you don't mind . . ."

Aware that she could not convince him, Elvira left. Two more such direct confrontations convinced her to confine herself to substitute work at the Negro schools within her own neighborhood. On those mornings when she waited outside the offices of principals of Negro schools she often wondered, *How different am I now from those Negro women I used to see years ago on my way to P.S. 173, the ones who waited at the subway station for a day's work as cleaning women? At least these days, with war work, those lines at the subway have disappeared.*

Still, her hurt and resentment continued to rankle. Not wishing to burden Drew, who had problems enough of his own with his heavy schedule at Columbia as both instructor and candidate for a master's degree, Elvira chose an outlet most natural to her from her earliest schooldays. She wrote out her feelings.

Virtually all my life I have been told about the plight of colored people in the South. Mainly, I have been told it by decent, well-educated Northerners who point long accusing fingers at Southerners who pronounce the word Negro so that one can barely distinguish it from that other, hated word.

Northerners, particularly educated Northerners, would never be guilty of such slurs and insults. They are far too enlightened, far too tolerant, a word on which they pride themselves.

That word could bear closer examination. Webster defines it as "inclined to tolerate others' beliefs, practices . . ." Mind you, not eager to tolerate, not even willing to, only inclined.

And if one reads on, one discovers some of Webster's secondary definitions. To tolerate means "to put up with."

It turns out that I am one of those Negroes whom nice, polite, educated Northerners refuse to put up with.

I am an educator, trained, tested, and certified to be capable of teaching English and history to students of high school level.

Nowhere in my studies was I warned that I would be qualified to teach those subjects only to Negro children.

Nor, when tested on my written and oral examinations, did anyone ask me to speak Negro, think Negro, or give Negro answers.

Does a historical fact change if taught by a Negro teacher?

Does a sentence parse differently in the hands of a Negro teacher?

Are there different rules of grammar for Negro people?

I believe I am qualified to teach children, all children, regardless of their color—or mine.

Until that is recognized by all educators we cannot honestly call ourselves enlightened or progressive or, yes, even tolerant. The educational community may be willing to tolerate me only so long as I am willing to be tolerated.

But I demand more. I will not be "put up with."

I will keep knocking on the doors, hammering at the walls, until one day they give way. Educated prejudice, prejudice softly spoken, prejudice disguised as polite refusals will no longer satisfy me.

I want what I have earned: the right to teach children in this city's high schools—all children, white and Negro.

After she had read over what she wrote, she decided, *Why not? Why not send it to* Teachers' Quarterly? *The worst that could happen would be that they reject it.*

"The key to commanding Negro troops, like any troops, is to realize that they react in accordance with their treatment," Second Lieutenant Drew Armstrong declared as he stood before his class of first and second lieutenants in the small lecture hall at Columbia. "Men treated with respect, with regard for their ability and courage, will *act* like men with ability and courage. Therefore, it is the duty of the officer in command to treat them that way. The use of such demeaning terms as *nigger* or *boy* or *blackie* is strictly forbidden, either directly to or in the presence of Negro troops."

From the back of the room, in a whisper that could be heard by everyone, one officer remarked, "What are we supposed to do, call 'em sonny? And tuck the bastards in at night?"

Most of the men pretended to ignore the remark. But since it had been heard by all, Drew could not. He could feel himself flush. Part of him cautioned control, moderation. A deeper part of him urged: *Face it down at the outset.*

"The man who made that remark, stand up!" he ordered.

There was a tense silence in the room. Drew glared toward

the back of the hall. The men down front turned to look. Finally, a tall, beefy officer in the last row untangled his crossed legs and rose to his full height.

"Lieutenant, do you know why you're here?"

"I sure do," the man responded. "I am here because it is well known that Negroes do not have leadership qualities. So it is up to us white officers to lead them in battle."

"Well known by whom?"

"By everybody. That's what well-known means," the man replied quickly. "Anybody but a dumb nig—" He cut short his reply.

Drew completed it for him. "Anybody but a dumb nigger knows that. Right, mister?"

"You said that, not me," the man replied with a smirk.

"Well, mister, are you familiar with the word *assumption*?"

"I've heard of it," the man replied.

"Do you know what it means?" Drew asked.

"It means . . . to assume." The man began to lose his smirk and become more openly hostile.

"For your information, mister, the dictionary says an assumption is the act of taking for granted or supposing a thing without proof. 'Everybody knows' is an assumption, a supposition without proof. Now, I am going to give you five minutes to tell us all the proof you have that Negro troops are dumb and that they lack leadership qualities. Commencing right now!"

Drew pulled back his sleeve to stare at his wristwatch. The man's face was red with anger. With the others staring at him, he felt compelled to respond to the Negro officer's command.

"Well, it is well known . . ."

"By whom?" Drew demanded.

"It's always been true—"

"Who proved it?" Drew interrupted once more.

"Back where I come from . . ." the man began once more.

"Mister, we are here now. Proof! I want proof!" Drew insisted.

"Damnit, I didn't come here prepared to prove what everybody already knows!" the man shouted.

"Back to 'everybody knows,' are we?" Drew shot back. "Well, let me tell you something else 'everybody knows.' You, mister, are a second-rate officer. Else you wouldn't be here. How do I know? Because 'everybody knows' that white officers who are selected to command Negro troops are not as good as other white officers. Now, is that true? Has it ever been proven? No. Yet 'everybody knows.' That, mister, is another false assumption. Like your assumption that Negro troops are dumb. Or that Negro officers lack leadership qualities. That's the last I want to hear about this in this course. From anybody!"

There was a moment of respectful silence before Drew resumed his lecture.

The next afternoon, when Drew finished his lecture, he was handed a slip with a note requesting his presence in Major Hassey's office.

"Well, Lieutenant, I hear you had a bit of a set-to in class yesterday."

"I wouldn't exactly call it a set-to, sir."

"Oh? What would you call it, exactly?"

"A lesson in semantics, sir."

"See-man-tics, eh?"

"The meaning and definition of words, sir."

"The way I heard it, mister, it would seem semantics means insulting and degrading a fellow officer before other officers of similar rank. Well, you are certainly not here to be a smart-ass . . . Negro. And to show off your college education. That was a mistake, mister. So you may get the chance to show off *your* leadership qualities somewhere else. Dismissed!"

Drew started for the door. But Hassey was not quite finished. As Drew reached for the doorknob, he heard, "You didn't know when you had a cushy situation, did you? Couldn't leave well enough alone."

Sporadic teaching assignments afforded Elvira days off, when she and Rebecca went shopping for all the things that a modern infant would require. Elvira had decided the living room would become the baby's room. She would shift the living room furniture to one side and balance it with the baby's needs on the other. Drew would have to do his work on his master's thesis in the kitchen instead of the small desk in the

living room. But one day, soon after the baby was born and
when their lease expired, they must find a bigger apartment.

Elvira stood naked before the long mirror in their bedroom. She was proud of her tall, slender body, her full
breasts. She turned to view herself in profile, to see if she
could detect that bulge that would reveal to the world that she
was pregnant, that she would one day be giving birth to a
child. Drew hoped for a boy. She wanted a girl, to name her
in memory of her own mother. But boy or girl, it must be born
healthy, she insisted.

She could now detect that first slight bulge. She took great
pride in it. In four months she would be giving birth, in four
months Drew would receive his master's in sociology and be
ready at war's end to receive an appointment at some good
college. Her plans and her ambitions for herself, for Drew,
and for the little one were within her grasp. She wished her
mama were alive to see how much she had progressed from
the condition into which she had been born almost twenty-
one years ago.

She proceeded to dress so she could meet Rebecca for another round of shopping. Rebecca would be free after one of
her charity luncheons in a midtown hotel. Rebecca attended
more luncheons and dinners than any woman could possibly
find time for, yet she never gained weight. If anything, she
seemed to grow thinner with each passing week. It seemed
the woman who arranged the luncheons, the menus, and the
program, who made the speeches appealing for funds, for old
clothes, and for donations of food had no time to eat.

Early in the evening, Elvira returned to the little flat on
Morningside Drive. She followed her routine of opening first
the lock built into the door, then the auxiliary double lock that
Drew had insisted on installing. That lock was not secured,
yet she could clearly recall locking it when she left. Timidly,
and with caution, she pushed the door open.

She heard movement. Hasty movement. Someone was
there. She was undecided—to enter and confront the intruder
or run and seek help? She decided to confront whoever it
might be. She started in, slowly. She passed the kitchen and
realized the intruder was in the bedroom. Frightening

thoughts shot through her mind. This was one of the days Drew also had night classes for his master's, so he was not due home until late. If anything were to happen to her now, there would be no one to help.

She was fearful more for her unborn child than for herself. She could not run that risk. She started toward the front door. Out of the bedroom came the intruder, with an armful of clothes.

"Elvira!" she heard him call.

In pained relief, she cried out, "Drew? Darling? Is it you?" She broke down.

He took her in his arms, holding her close, kissing her wet face to reassure her.

"Sorry I frightened you."

"What are you doing home at this hour? And on a Tuesday?" she managed to ask through her sobbing.

"Come," he said, guiding her into the living room. "Let's sit down and discuss this calmly."

"What do we have to discuss? And why do I have to be calm about it?"

"Darling, once a man is in the army, he does what he's told."

"Such as?"

"I'm being transferred."

"But they promised," Elvira protested. "For the duration, they said."

"There was a . . ." he started to explain, then decided on the plain truth. "I had a confrontation with another officer."

"A white officer?"

"Yes," Drew said.

"So you're being transferred out of Columbia," she realized, feeling a sudden vague pain in her belly.

"I've been assigned to a combat unit."

"Without warning, without time to prepare?"

"In the army when you get written orders to report, you report."

"Oh, darling," she responded, instinctively embracing him.

To calm her he tried to reassure, "At that, I'm lucky."

"Lucky?" she disputed.

"They've formed an Air Force unit entirely composed of Negro fliers. They need noncombat personnel as well. So I've been transferred out of the Army into the Air Force."

"When do you go?" she asked.

"My orders read: Report to McGuire Air Base tomorrow morning. That's why I had to rush home to pack."

She held fast to him. Moments later she said, "You won't be here when the baby comes. God knows where you'll be."

"There's always Rebecca and David," he pointed out. Then confessed, "You know, darling, there have been times when I felt David was trying to take over our lives. Now it feels good to know they're here when you need them."

"Maybe I should call them," she said.

"No. Tonight is for us. Alone. Once I'm gone, call them."

It was a night of hopes, fears, promises, making love, a night of tears, more plans for the infant yet to be born, plans for themselves, their careers, and more love.

By dawn they fell asleep. Drew woke two hours later. He set out breakfast for her, took his shower, shaved, picked up his bags, and was gone. He left a note: "Soon as I know where I'm assigned I'll write or call. Take care of my son. All my love."

Several hours later, Elvira woke. She found his note and wept over it. He was still sure he would have a son.

Later in the morning, she called Rebecca to tell her. Within minutes Elvira's phone rang. As soon as she picked it up, she heard that familiar brisk voice: "Elvira darling, Becca just called me. Now look, don't panic. I will be right up there with a limousine. Meantime, pack whatever you want, especially the things for the little one. We're moving you down to our place."

"Uncle David—" she tried to interrupt.

But he continued, "A time like this, no woman should be alone. Especially if she's carrying. And in her fifth month."

"Uncle David!" she insisted. "I have decided to remain here."

"But it doesn't make sense," David tried to point out. "Down here you'll have Aunt Rebecca. You'll have me. You won't be alone."

"Uncle David, I have to face this alone. That's what my mother would have done."

After a moment of silence, she heard him say, "Darling, I . . . I understand. . . . Well, really, I don't understand. But whatever you say is the way it will be."

"I'll teach as long as I can, wherever they'll have me. Then I'll have my baby to take care of. This war can't go on forever."

Three months after Drew had been called away on duty, Elvira received a telephone call. The voice was tantalizingly familiar, the attitude crisp and reproachful.

"Elvira, bad enough you haven't kept in touch. But not to advise me about your article was not very considerate. Not at all."

Elvira recognized the voice. "Miss Flaherty?"

"Yes, Miss Flaherty," the woman replied. "Quite an article. And quite a reproach to the entire educational fraternity."

"Article?" Elvira asked.

"Your article. The *Teachers' Quarterly*. Didn't you know?"

"They actually dared to print it?" Elvira said.

"Dared or not, they printed it. Elvira, this is not a request. This is an order. Come see me before the week is out. Understood?" Miss Flaherty spoke in an attitude Elvira remembered very well from her days at Wadleigh.

"Yes, ma'am," Elvira agreed. "Tomorrow?"

"Tomorrow will not be too soon," Miss Flaherty responded crisply.

"If only you'd told me," Miss Flaherty said, once Elvira had apprised her of Drew's unfortunate experience and her own failed efforts to obtain teaching assignments at any but Negro schools.

"I didn't want to ask favors," Elvira explained.

"I do not consider it a favor to appoint a teacher to a post she deserves and that deserves her," Miss Flaherty replied. "Nor do I intend to do you any favors now or show you any favoritism. You know my policy well."

"Yes, ma'am. A student must earn her way," Elvira recalled.

"What I propose now is that you work hard to earn your

master's degree. And if you do and you achieve the grades I
know you're capable of, then I promise to consider you for a
teaching position here in the English Department at Hunter.
You'll be in competition with other very capable young
women. But I promise you a fair shot at it. The rest is up to
you."

"A master's degree. . . . Soon I'll have my baby to take
care of, and Drew's second lieutenant's pay means I have to
work."

"Elvira, you never used to give me excuses in the past. I
won't hear any now. You know the requirements; you know
the possibilities. What you make of them is your own doing."

Elvira knew the interview was over. She rose. Flaherty
held out her hand. As they shook hands, the dean said, "One
thing I want you to promise me now: if you are not the one
who is selected, you won't blame it on prejudice."

"I know you too well for that," Elvira said.

35

It was late on the night of June 2, in the war year 1943.

The Rosens were returning from an emergency meeting held at the home of one of Rebecca's committee members. As they stepped out of the cab, the night doorman greeted them with a friendly, "'Evening, Mr. Rosen, Mrs. Rosen." He was surprised that the usually pleasant Mr. Rosen did not respond. He did not even greet the elevator man, but was silent and morose until they were inside their apartment.

When Rebecca offered him a cup of tea, he waved her invitation aside with a weary gesture and went into the living room to turn on the radio. He was rewarded by the usual wartime bulletins and correspondents' reports. The Nazis, having been turned back at Stalingrad and Rommel having been defeated in North Africa, the situation seemed favorable for the first time. In the Pacific, the Americans had begun to win back, island by island, that part of the world made bloody by the Japanese invaders.

Still, David was not encouraged. Rebecca brought him a cup of tea and then, to encourage him, said, "Things are getting better. Another year, two maybe, and it will be over."

"Becca, from the orders I get for hats and caps from army procurement, it won't be over soon." Then he added, "That man who spoke to us at the meeting, he should be on the radio so the whole country could hear him!"

He sipped his tea in silence for a while, then continued: "I must have had two cousins there in the ghetto in Warsaw. My father had a brother, Feivele. When I was about four years old he came to the house with his two young sons. Came to say goodbye. They were moving to Warsaw in the hope things would be better there. He was a giant of a man, so his two sons must have been big and strong. They must have fought those Nazi bastards with their bare hands. Against tanks, mortars, machine guns, flamethrowers. If I was there, believe me, I would have fought!"

He pushed aside his cup.

"Just think. For years, half a million Jews in Warsaw. When the uprising started, only sixty thousand left. By the sixteenth of May, not a single Jew alive. But they fought back. They fought back!"

"David, what you said, about a long war. What about Drew? And Elvira? And, soon, the baby?"

Avoiding Rebecca's question, David said, "At least now Drew has more to fight for. An order came down from the War Department this week. No manufacturer can get a defense contract if it practices race discrimination."

"About time," Rebecca said.

"If they knew what I know, such an order wouldn't even be necessary."

"What do you know that's such a secret?" Rebecca asked.

"Months ago, with orders piling up, even with night work, I asked myself, if our Elvira can be so bright once she had the opportunity, how many other Negroes are there like her? So I called Pastor Wilder. He recommended several men from his community who are too old for the draft. You know what I discovered? They are not only quick to pick up the work, but they are anxious to do well."

"They're grateful to finally have a decent job," Rebecca said.

"With the way the Army is taking my younger men, this week I will call Wilder again."

"David, what you said about a long war . . ." Rebecca asked.

"Becca, based on the orders we get, they either expect a very long war or else a very bloody one, with lots of casualties."

"Poor Drew, poor Elvira . . ." Rebecca said.

Still under the pall of the sad report he had heard earlier in the evening, he said, "I'm going to bed. Until morning they will have to run the country and the world without the advice and opinions of David Rosen."

* * *

David had fallen asleep. Rebecca was in the bathroom taking another dose of bicarbonate of soda to relieve the heartburn that of late she suffered more frequently. Too much coffee during her meetings, too many meals of cold sandwiches at hurried and irregular hours. Despite David's pleading, she had not been able to change her ways.

The phone rang. *A phone call at two-thirty in the morning? Can't be good news*, Rebecca thought. In her haste to reach the phone before it could wake David, she turned from the sink too quickly and dropped the glass, which shattered on the tile floor. She was torn between answering the phone and dealing with the shattered glass. When the ringing was interrupted, she knew that David had answered.

On bare feet, she went cautiously to the door of the bathroom to hear:

"Never mind about waking us. What happened? It broke? We'll be there in fifteen minutes! Meantime, call your doctor!"

He hung up, leaped out of bed, and started to dress, calling, "Becca! Her water just broke. Get dressed! Quick!"

Twenty-one minutes later, David and Rebecca Rosen assisted Elvira into the waiting cab.

"Doctor's Hospital!" David ordered.

Elvira's obstetrician, Dr. Wilmot, was waiting for her. Before he led her away, David took him by the arm and whispered into his ear.

"Doctor, whatever it costs, the best. You hear? The best!"

"Mr. Rosen," the doctor answered. "She is an intelligent young woman, physically strong. She followed my instructions. We shouldn't have any difficulty."

"With these things you never know. I tell you this from experience. So remember, everything she needs. And the best!"

At 6:34 on the morning of June 3, 1943, Elvira Armstrong was delivered of a baby boy, six pounds thirteen ounces and in obvious good health. Ten minutes later, Dr. Wilmot came down to the main floor waiting room to inform the Rosens.

"Thank God!" Rebecca whispered.

"When can we see her?" David asked.

"Give the nurses a chance to get her back to her room and freshened up," Wilmot advised.

Almost two hours later, David and Rebecca Rosen tiptoed into Elvira's room. She was awake and propped up in bed.

Smiling, Rebecca observed. *Her eyes have never looked brighter*. She went to the bedside, embraced Elvira and kissed her. She held her tight as she said, "My little girl is a woman now, a mother! Where have the years gone?"

The nurse brought in what appeared to be a bundle of white blanket. David stopped her to peer in. A tiny light brown face was nestled in the folds of white, wrinkled, eyes closed, lips making a sucking motion. The nurse brought the infant to the bed and placed him in Elvira's arms. She took him gently and looked up at the nurse seeking permission.

"Yes, yes, my dear, now. That's what he's here for."

Elvira reached into her nightgown, lifted out her breast, and guided the nipple into the infant's mouth. At first he did not suck. Then, once accustomed to the process, he sucked with great hunger.

Rebecca and David watched in pride and admiration, as if their little girl had invented this natural phenomenon.

When the infant had fed sufficiently and was asleep again. Rebecca asked, "Can I . . . may I hold him?"

Elvira surrendered him to her. Rebecca parted the folds of the blanket to stare down into his wrinkled face; even in sleep he continued making a sucking motion.

"Who does he look like? David? What do you think?"

David Rosen studied the little face, the tiny nose, the light brown skin.

"In my expert opinion, this child is lucky enough to look like his mother, with also a little of his father thrown in. Which is not bad, considering he is a handsome young man. May he be handsome, bright, and smart like his mother! And most of all, by the time he grows up, may this be a better world!"

"Drew!" Elvira said. "I must get word to Drew!"

David handed her the phone. She had no need to refer to the number. She knew it as if it were engraved on her heart as well as her mind. She gave the information to the hospital operator. After what seemed too long a time, the phone rang. As Elvira reached for it, David called, "Tell him hello for us, too."

Elvira lifted the phone. "Drew! It's a boy . . ." But she never completed the word *boy*. "Was shipped out? When . . . where? Of course they couldn't say. I understand." Tears filled her eyes and ran freely down her cheeks. "I promised him he'd know soon as it happened."

Rebecca handed the infant back to her. "Here, darling, and don't let him know you're crying. Drew will be fine. You will write him and somehow the army will get the letter to him."

"Better yet," David said, "I will call the Red Cross. There must be some way they can get the word to him."

Early in the evening, when the Rosens returned to the hospital, flowers had already started to arrive. There was a modest selection of early-summer flowers from the Armstrongs. Pastor Wilder and his wife sent a dozen pink roses. There was a bouquet from the deacons and deaconesses of the Ajalon Baptist Church and a dozen red roses from David's office staff.

The room was fragrant with the mingling perfumes of many flowers.

"Ah," David said, inhaling. "Smells like the country. Or is it the mother who smells so sweet? Darling, I called the Red Cross. They said not to worry. Wherever Second Lieutenant Drew Armstrong is, they will find him and get the word to him."

"Thanks, Uncle David."

"So where is that hungry little boychick?" he asked.

"They'll be bringing him in soon for his seven-o'clock," Elvira said. "The way he eats, he's going to be a big boy, a very big boy."

Rebecca smiled. "They say you can tell from the minute they're born what they're going to be like. They have a personality of their own right from the start."

"If that's true, he's going to be great," Elvira enthused.

Seven days later, Rebecca and David took Elvira and little Samuel Drew Armstrong home.

Rebecca cut down on some of her other activities to go up and spend time with them. She took great pleasure in watching Elvira nurse the child, bathe him, and change him. At times when Elvira was taking her afternoon nap, Rebecca delighted in taking care of the baby.

This, she reminded herself from time to time, *this is what it would have been like if I had had a daughter. I would have been a grandmother by now.*

After days of such devoted care, Elvira said, "Aunt Rebecca, it isn't necessary to come every day. I'm not afraid to handle him anymore. I'm not going to drop him or break something."

"Of course, darling," Rebecca agreed. Almost too readily, it seemed to Elvira. Until Rebecca added, "So I'll come only on those days when you have to go to class."

"That would help," Elvira conceded. "I just didn't want to take so much of your time away from your charity work."

"Take time, darling, take time," Rebecca insisted. "How is it going at the college?"

"Tougher than I expected. But I'll be damned if any other woman is going to get that appointment," Elvira promised.

"I'll see you get all the time for study that you need," Rebecca said. "Oh, there is one thing you can do for me."

"Anything, Aunt Rebecca," Elvira was quick to offer.

"Wednesday nights, for David's sake, come to supper again. He looks forward to it so."

"Of course. Every Wednesday night, as usual."

They kissed, held each other for a long moment, and then Rebecca departed.

Elvira went to tend her son and found him asleep. She stood over him watching him, so peaceful and innocent. *I wonder what this world will do to him because his skin is brown?* Then she settled down with the books she had borrowed from the college library to help her write her first paper in pursuit of her master's degree.

David Rosen folded his *Times* and picked up his predinner scotch and soda. After a sip, he said, "Rebecca darling, I was thinking . . ."

She looked up from the seating plan she was working on

for the dais of the charity dinner she was running for United Jewish Appeal.

"I was thinking, sweetheart, it's already the twenty-first of June. Before you know it, it will be July. What if we were to take a summer house out on Long Island? On one of the beaches. Far Rockaway, Arverne, Long Beach?"

"It's a little late in the season to start looking for a house," Rebecca pointed out.

"How could we make plans when Elvira didn't even have her baby yet?" David responded. "What do you think?"

"To spend the summer out there where I don't know anyone?" Rebecca questioned. "I would feel isolated."

"Isolated? With Elvira and the baby there, you'll have your hands full. I'm going to tell her Wednesday night."

"That's what you really had in mind. To find a summer place for Elvira and the baby."

Pretending ingenuousness, David replied, "I figured as long as we're renting a house and you're going to be out there all summer, what would be wrong for Elvira and the little one to enjoy the ocean too?"

"David, darling David, Elvira and the little one are their own family. We can no longer make plans and expect she will be part of them."

"But summer in New York, hot, muggy," he protested. "Out on the Island it's cooler. At night there's a breeze. Remember two summers ago we were invited out to the Callahans' for a weekend? Wasn't that a pleasure? At night, Dennis and me, sitting out on the back porch looking at the ocean, enjoying that cool breeze while we were having a cocktail. Wasn't the Callahans' daughter Marie there with her two little ones? It's the way families are. The way—"

By which time David had realized the point Rebecca had been trying to make.

"You're right, Becca. Elvira is a grown woman, a wife, a mother. She has her own family now. I just thought, as long as we're renting a house . . ." Rebecca's look vetoed the idea. "So we're not renting a house," he conceded. He started toward the radio, but before he turned it on he grumbled, "Suddenly it's a crime to make a suggestion in this house."

Rebecca resumed work on her seating chart. David concen-

trated on the radio news, which was concerned mainly with
the war in Europe. Pressure was building for a second front,
an invasion of the Continent. There was a limit to how long
the Soviets could maintain their defense against the Nazis.

"Second front, second front," David muttered. "Why
don't they talk numbers? How many men will be killed? How
many wounded?"

His plaint was interrupted by a second voice from the radio: "We interrupt our regularly scheduled newscast for further word about the riots in Detroit."

"Riots? Detroit?" David asked, startled. "Becca, did you
hear?"

They both turned to the radio.

"While the authorities have not yet been able to determine
what caused race riots to erupt in the motor city, based on
reports from hospitals in the Detroit area, there are more than
twenty-six confirmed dead. Some reports say the injured ex-
ceed five hundred. The mayor of Detroit has made a radio
plea to all citizens to return to their homes and for whites and
Negroes to remain in their own separate neighborhoods . . ."

As the report droned on, Rebecca said softly, "Riots between whites and Negroes. More than twenty-five killed. In
America? Can't be, can't be."

"Can't be?" David asked sadly. "But it is. Who started it?
Why?"

"Does it matter who? Or why? People are being killed,"
Rebecca lamented.

The radio continued with fragments of news from Detroit
until suddenly the voice of the announcer took on a more immediately urgent tone: "Word has just reached the studio
that, possibly in response to the news out of Detroit, rioting
has just broken out up in Harlem."

"Rebecca!"

They both leaned closer to the radio. The announcer spoke
in more impromptu fashion, as if being handed fresh news
dispatches.

"First reports indicate that rioting, which broke out along
One Hundred Twenty-fifth Street, is spreading. Store windows have been shattered. Looting is taking place. And there
are physical confrontations between police and Negroes. The

sound of gunshots is being heard in other Harlem neighborhoods as well . . ."

"Becca, come!"

"Where?"

"Up to Harlem. To get Elvira, her baby!" David said.

"David, we don't even know if her neighborhood is involved."

"Should we wait until it is? Come!" David said. He interrupted his own sudden start from the room. "Hold on! If we bring her down here where she'll be safe and the baby will be safe, we will have to take all those things with her, bassinet, diapers, powder, and God knows what else. We will need a little truck."

"David, please, first call."

"You know how independent she is. She'll say everything is fine. A truck, we need a truck. I know! Muscarella!" He consulted the Manhattan phone book, then dialed the number.

"Muscarella's? I want to talk to Ray! Who am I? Rosen. David Rosen. You make the deliveries of all my hats to the department stores. I need a favor. And I need it right now! Put Ray on." After a moment of silence, David continued: "Ray, Dave. I need a small truck. I need it now. How long would it take to get it up to my place on Central Park West? Only big enough to move a woman and her baby with all the things that babies need. Where? Up in Harlem, that's where! No, I am not crazy. I know about the riots. That's why we have to go up there! Ray! Just send the truck! I'll be responsible for everything! Good! Good! We'll be waiting downstairs!"

Even from a distance they could see beams of powerful searchlights flashing across the sky. As the truck drew closer, they could hear the sound of sporadic gunfire. Sirens cut through the night. Police cars sped by them, escorting ambulances commandeered from hospitals outside the riot zone.

"The war has come to New York City," Rebecca lamented.

David urged the driver to go faster, but the man remained cautious, as if feeling his way along a dark and dangerous alley. As they passed a side street, Rebecca and David caught sight of the glow of fire and battle several blocks away.

"Who could believe it?" David said. "Such a thing happening in New York City!"

"It happened, and worse, a long time ago, during the Civil War," Rebecca reminded. "They burned down a Negro orphanage with the little children still inside."

"That was history. This is now."

"One day this will be history, too. Unless people forget."

The street Elvira lived on was dark and quiet. Usually, on a summer evening, people would have been sitting out on the stoop, the women to gossip, the men to talk about baseball—the Yankees, the Giants, the Dodgers. On this night not a person was to be seen on the entire block. Every stoop was clear. Every door was closed. Every window seemed dark. The whole neighborhood was dug in against the danger.

The truck pulled to a stop.

"Wait here," David said to the driver.

"Don't be too long. No telling what can happen with these savages," the driver replied.

"Just wait!" David ordered.

The front door was locked. David banged so hard that Rebecca warned, "You'll break the glass." He continued to pound. Finally, a door inside the dimly lit hallway opened. An old man, his white hair contrasting with his black face, peered out cautiously to stare at them through the glass. At first he judged them to be a danger and turned back toward his flat. Then he appeared to recognize them. Still unconvinced, he came toward them slowly, studying their faces in the night. Now, at last, he unlocked the door, opened it slightly, using his foot as a doorstop.

"You the white folks be comin' to see that Mrs. Armstrong on the fourth floor," he said, more a question than a statement.

"Yes. We're the Rosens. We have to see Mrs. Armstrong," David insisted.

"Why? You got some word about her husband?"

"No, no word. Just we have to make sure she's all right!"

"Okay, then, come on in."

As they climbed the stairs, they could hear through every locked door voices on radios, excited, backed by distant sirens, as they described riots that were going on only blocks away. No one was asleep in this building, or in this part of Manhattan, on this night.

They reached Elvira's door. They could hear the same voice describing the same tragic events. David rang. Evidently, Elvira did not hear. David knocked, then again, louder. Soon they heard her footsteps approach. She called, "Who is it?"

"Uncle David, Aunt Rebecca," he called back.

They heard the door being unlocked. Rebecca rushed past David to embrace Elvira.

"Darling, are you all right? And little Sam?"

"We're fine, fine," Elvira reassured.

"Look, darling," David said. "Gather up the baby's things. I'll fold up his bassinet, his other stuff. We'll take you home, where you'll be safe."

"Uncle David, this is my home."

"You know what I mean. Downtown. Where everything is peaceful and quiet."

"Suppose Drew calls and I'm not here? He'll be worried."

"Better he should worry than you and the baby should be in danger. If he was here, even he would say that. So, come!"

In the living room, despite the radio's excited voices, little Samuel Drew Armstrong slept peacefully.

David noticed that on a chair alongside the bassinet were stacked a number of tiny shirts, a pile of fresh-smelling diapers, baby powder, oil, and other necessities. He turned to Elvira with an inquisitive look.

"Yes," she admitted. "My first impulse was to gather up his things and run. Until I thought, This is my home, these are my people. This is where I belong."

Reluctantly, David was forced to concede, "Of course." He took Elvira by the arms and kissed her on the cheek. "Forgive me, darling, for trying to run your life. It's a habit, I guess. After all, how many years has it been—twelve?"

"Thirteen," Elvira corrected.

"Look, darling. Wednesday, come early so you and the baby can enjoy the park during the afternoon."

Elvira smiled, shook her head, and glanced at Rebecca.

"What's so funny?" David asked, offended.

"Uncle David, Wednesday afternoon I have a class in Medieval Ecclesiastical Literature," Elvira explained.

"Perfect!" David exclaimed, to the astonishment of both women, until he explained, "You'll come down early, leave little Sammy with Becca. You go across the park to the college. And then when you come back, you meet Rebecca in the park and spend a few hours in the fresh air. Then we all have supper. Like I said, perfect!"

Elvira could only laugh and agree.

Back in their own apartment, David was locking their front door when he grumbled, "What was so funny about what I said? At this time of year, the park is delightful."

"David, David." Rebecca smiled and shook her head.

"There!" he accused. "You're doing it, too!"

"David, she is a grown woman."

"Grown women sit in the park with their babies. I see them every day!" he argued.

"I'm happy to have her come for dinner every Wednesday. And to baby-sit little Sammy when she needs me."

David went into the living room to turn on the radio.

The announcers sounded less agitated. There were fewer sounds of sirens than there had been. The worst of the rioting was over. The confirmed number of dead in Harlem was only six; the number of wounded and injured was still being counted at various hospitals.

David commented grimly, "Becca, did you hear what he said? Isn't that reassuring? Confirmed dead were 'only' six. Only! Six men are dead. Six wives are widows. And maybe twenty-five kids are orphans. You'll excuse me, I don't think *only* is the proper word."

36

Darling,

Still can't tell you where I'm stationed, but the weather is hot, very hot. And the native spaghetti is very good.

Being a morale officer in a squadron like this is possibly the best job in this whole air force.

I get more morale from them than they get from me.

What an outfit! In just twenty-four hours they shot down 17 Nazi F-W 190's.

Remember, I used to speak of a guy named Raymond, who was ahead of me by two years at Howard? He got three kills by himself.

By the time this war is over the Black Eagles will have made history. Someday little Sam will be bragging about his old man being part of them. Of course, being a brilliant kid, he'll have the good sense not to mention that I was only a morale officer, not a fighter pilot.

Send more pictures. He seems to grow with every one. And say my name to him every day. I don't want to be a stranger to him when I get home.

Got to run now. They're bombing our airfield again.

All my love,
Drew, present tense.

The letter, dated July 5, 1944, reached Elvira Armstrong eleven days later, along with a letter of condolence and praise from Colonel Benjamin Davis, Jr., commander of the Black Eagles Fighter Squadron.

Due to a snafu somewhere along the line, there had not been the usual "the War Department regrets" telegram. Elvira had been able to delude herself into excusing the lapse in Drew's letters by blaming the exigencies of combat. This last letter and his colonel's postmortem praise struck her with shocking surprise.

She sat stunned, dry-eyed, disbelieving, even unaware of the sounds of her one-year-old son, who sought her attention. When he crawled to her feet, she picked him up and held him to her breast. She began to rock back and forth.

"Mama . . ."

She held him tighter.

"Mama . . ."

"Shh, Sammy . . . shhh," she whispered through her tears. "You poor baby. Like your mama, you are never going to see your papa. He is just going to be a name to you, like my papa was to me. Poor baby, poor baby . . ."

Only then did she begin to weep.

Hours later, cried out and numb except for the vague pain in her belly, she realized, *I must call them. Aunt Rebecca and Uncle David should know.*

"Hello," Rebecca Rosen said briskly, expecting a report from one of her committee ladies.

"Aunt Rebecca . . ." Elvira began, then broke down and sobbed.

"Elvira sweetheart, what is it? Something about the baby?"

"Aunt Rebecca . . . no, not Sam . . . Drew . . . Drew!"

"Oh my God! I'll be right there! Right there! Is there anything you need—anything?"

"Just you, Aunt Rebecca, just you!"

"Of course, darling. I'm on my way."

Rebecca paused only long enough to call David at the office.

By evening, Pastor Wilder, his wife, and many friends from the Ajalon Church had come to call. Rebecca took care of Sammy, changing him, feeding him, bathing him, and putting him to bed after David had moved his crib into the bedroom. Tired as the child was, disturbed by the hectic and unaccustomed activity of the day, he was restless and unable to fall asleep. Elvira had to go in and breast-feed him, though he had been weaned weeks ago. Finally, he fell asleep. She placed him in his crib, her tears falling gently on his small face. But he was unaware.

By the time Elvira returned to the living room, the other visitors had departed. Only Rebecca and David remained.

"Elvira darling . . ." David began, glancing at Rebecca as if to gain her support. "At a time like this . . . a woman in your situation . . . with a year-old baby, with this terrible news about Drew . . . You have to take a realistic view of things. At least for the time being, to get adjusted, give yourself a chance to figure things out, make plans . . . We think it would be a good idea to move in with us."

"Uncle David, you and Aunt Rebecca have already done too much."

"'Too much,' 'not enough,' 'too little' . . ." David disparaged. "Right now you are too overcome to decide. So, here—"

He held out his keys to her.

"Keys to the apartment. Think over what I said. Anytime you feel like, you are welcome."

He placed the keys in her hand and closed it tightly.

Alone, sitting alongside her son's crib in the early hours of the morning, Elvira Armstrong was forced to put aside grief and mourning long enough to consider her situation.

Twenty-two, well-educated, certified to teach, she must make plans for the future of her little son who lay asleep, unaware of the tragedy that had robbed him of his father. She might be forced to take a teaching appointment in an all-Negro school. But not for long, she vowed. She would manage somehow to combine working with taking courses at the college and caring for her son. It was a comfort to know that Aunt Rebecca and Uncle David were there to help. But for her own salvation and her son's future, she must secure that appointment at the college.

She placed the keys David had given her in the same drawer in which she kept Drew's letters and the little mementos he had sent her from overseas.

Within the week she registered with the local high school. Because so many male teachers were being drafted into the army, by early fall she was notified that she had been granted a temporary appointment to teach first-year English and composition. So as not to burden Rebecca too greatly, she arranged for Sammy to be cared for during the day and some evenings by a deaconess of the Ajalon Baptist Church. She transferred all her courses at Hunter to evening sessions.

If it meant working fifteen or sixteen hours a day and spending less time with Sammy than she would have liked, Elvira was determined to extend herself to the utmost for the next year in order to achieve her goal.

Though at least once every day she spoke to either Rebecca or David and still had supper with them most Wednesday nights, she had never used the keys David had given her. Until late afternoon Monday, the seventeenth day of October. Since that day was a school holiday, she packed sufficient changes for Sam and headed downtown to Central Park West.

She arrived just before sundown. The doorman was delighted to see her.

"Ah, Miss Elvira! And little Sammy. My, he gets cuter every time. Unfortunately, the Rosens are not back yet."

"Yes, I know. Synagogue. Yom Kippur. Don't tell them I'm here."

She let herself into the apartment. Once she set Sammy free to explore, Elvira went to the kitchen. She opened the refrigerator, where she found all the foods she had expected. Aunt Rebecca always prepared well to break the twenty-four-hour Yom Kippur fast.

Elvira set the table in the dining room—four places, for David and Rebecca and for herself, and for Sam the high chair that David had insisted on having ready for their visits.

She set the large pot of chicken soup and *matzo* balls over a low flame to heat up slowly. As it heated, the fragrance of parsley and parsnips in rich broth made a delectable perfume.

On a large platter she laid out portions of cold gefilte fish with decorations of golden jelly and brightly colored carrots. She filled a small bowl with red horseradish. She sliced the challah twist and covered it in a white linen napkin to prevent it from becoming crusty and stale. And she set out a plate of what had become David's favorite coffee companion, crumbly cornbread with Rebecca's own strawberry jam.

When the table looked in all respects as Rebecca herself would have set it, Elvira went into her room to find that Sam had fallen asleep on the floor. She cradled him in her arms and lay down on her old bed.

Only at evening time, when she heard David's key in the front door, did she stir. She listened closely, anticipating their reaction.

First she heard Rebecca, half surprised, half suspicious. "David?"

Then she heard David. He sniffed the pleasant aroma but seemed suspicious as well. "Rebecca, you didn't leave the soup on this morning when we left for synagogue, did you?"

"Would I even touch food on Yom Kippur?" Rebecca asked. "I'm going to find out." She started for the kitchen. "David! Look! Everything is ready!" Then it struck her. "Elvira! Darling! It's you!"

Elvira came out of the bedroom to greet them.

"Happy New Year!" they wished each other.

"Darling, what a surprise! No wonder the doorman looked at us so funny," Rebecca said. "And the little one?"

"Asleep, in my room."

"Then don't disturb him, let him sleep," David ordered, but he went in to take a peek.

In the kitchen, Rebecca and Elvira embraced once more.

"I was lonesome," Elvira said, "for the old times up in Washington Heights. When you and Uncle David went off to shul on Yom Kippur and were gone all day, I'd wait for you to come home, because it was so festive, so warm. Today I missed it."

"And I can't tell you what a wonderful surprise. To open the door, to know there was someone here to greet us."

David returned to the kitchen for his usual drink to break the fast.

"You know, every time I see that little one, I say to myself, no question about it. He takes after his Uncle David."

They all laughed. He raised his glass.

"*L'chayim*. To life. Long, long life!"

He downed his drink. Then in a softer, more troubled tone he said, "And let's hope this war is over soon. There has been enough killing, too much killing."

Elvira's eyes brimmed over and tears streamed down her cheeks.

In the late spring of the school year, when marks were posted on the bulletin board outside the office of the English department, Elvira Armstrong was listed as having achieved two A's, one B-plus, and one B. There was another name on the list, Naomi Rothenberg, who also had two A's, one B-plus, and one B, though her grades were achieved in different courses.

Attached to the bulletin board was a sealed note addressed to Elvira Armstrong. When she opened it, she found a note from Dean Flaherty. It said simply: "Elvira, see me!"

Late that afternoon, Elvira waited outside Flaherty's office while she presided over a conference of a small, select group of English Department faculty. When the meeting broke up and they were leaving, they seemed surprised, and some almost embarrassed, to come face to face with Elvira. She took that to be a discouraging omen. She was prepared for the worst when Dean Flaherty finally called her in.

"Elvira . . ." Flaherty began. "I suppose you know that in year-end grades there was a tie between you and the Rothenberg woman."

Assuming that to be a precursor to a rejection, Elvira said, "Yes, I know. I think I might have done better than that B in Comparative Lit, but I just couldn't manage the time."

"It hasn't been easy, has it?" Flaherty asked.

"But we survived, Sammy and I," Elvira said proudly. "We survived. And if I have to, I can go on teaching at the high school level until I secure a permanent appointment."

"That would be the dead end of what could have been a promising career," Flaherty pointed out.

Elvira felt a sudden flush of hope, which she dared not express.

"From the time I read your first essay about the Rosens, I have looked upon you as one of my special students, the group that I like to follow through their careers. Since I feel that way, I did not think I could be impartial. So rather than rely on my own judgment, I convened a small group of the English faculty to let them vote on the matter."

"So I thought," Elvira said. "I noticed their faces when they saw me."

"There was rather sharp dissension. In fact, I was quite surprised at the bigotry that exists among our intellectual elite—which explains why we have never had a Negro on the faculty at Hunter."

"I understand," Elvira said, prepared to concede defeat.

"Because the vote was so close, it was up to me to find some way to resolve the question."

"I told you I did not want or expect any favoritism," Elvira said.

"Yes, I know. And I respect your feelings. That's why I refrained from voting."

"You mean the issue is not yet decided?" Elvira asked.

"Oh, it's been decided, but without my vote," Flaherty said. "To avoid casting the deciding vote, I decided on a different strategy. I let you vote."

"Me? Vote? How?"

"I produced your article from the *Teachers' Quarterly*. And I read it to them. When I took the second vote, you were the clear winner. So you see, no favoritism. No undue influence. You won it on your own."

"I . . . I don't know what to say."

"Don't say a word," Flaherty advised. "Just feel wonderful. Enjoy it!"

Elvira started to nod, but her eyes filled up. Then she confessed, "My first thought, my first impulse was, I must tell Drew, he'll be so proud. But there's no Drew to tell. No Drew."

On September 10, Elvira Armstrong attended her first meeting as a member of the faculty of the English Department of Hunter College. Three days later, she greeted her first class.

1949

37

September 1949. *David* and Rebecca Rosen were making last-minute preparations for their pilgrimage.

"Becca, the passports? What did you do with the passports?"

"What I did," she called from their bedroom, "was put them in the pocket of your travel coat, as you said."

"Oh yeah, yeah, right, right," David recalled. "And the tickets too?"

"Yes, David, the tickets too," she called back.

He checked his coat and found the passports and tickets. He called down to the front door to make sure the limousine was waiting. For the third time, the doorman assured him the car was waiting.

David went into the bedroom to find Rebecca giving her face one last pat of powder. He stood behind her, staring into the mirror.

Tired, he thought. *She is tired from so many years of giving herself to her causes. But still that heart-shaped face, that dimple in her chin. Hair a little less blond, well, actually, more gray than blond. But on her it looks good. It will be nice to take her away. She could stand a vacation. And what a vacation! Israel! The Promised Land!*

She turned from the mirror to catch him staring.

"David?"

"I was just thinking, years ago when we first were married, did you ever in your wildest dreams imagine that one day we would be spending Rosh Hashanah and Yom Kippur in Jerusalem?"

"Never," she admitted. "In childhood when we used to say at Passover, 'Next year in Jerusalem,' it was like a fairy tale."

"Well, not *next* year in Jerusalem but *this* year!" David ex-

ulted. "You, at least, earned it. During the war I always wondered if they knew that without you the war couldn't be won.
You deserve a good long vacation, my darling."

"And you didn't earn it?" Rebecca asked.

"For what? Writing a few checks?" he disparaged.

"It wasn't your fault," Rebecca pointed out. "When the
army says you are essential to war production, that's what
you do."

"And when the Arabs attacked Israel last year and I went
to volunteer, what did they say to me? 'Sorry, Mr. Rosen, but
fifty is too old.' Too old! Me? Why, I am better today than I
was twenty years ago!"

Rebecca smiled. "David, you told them you were only
fifty? Last year you were fifty-two."

"So what? In a crisis, who has time for details?" he
evaded. Then he added, "I would have felt better if they took
me. Once in my life I would like to do more than grumble
about the state of the world, more than just shake my fist at
The New York Times. Always, since childhood, I had this fan-
tasy that one day I would do something heroic. But first I was
too busy. Then I was 'essential.' And finally I was too old.
That's the way a lifetime passes."

The doorbell rang.

"Aha! That's her now," Rebecca brightened.

David started for the door. He greeted Elvira with a kiss
and looked down at Sammy, who clutched his mother's hand.

"Well, well, well, growing every day. One day soon you
are going to be taller than your mother. Come in, Sam, come
in!" David tried to sweep him up in his arms, but the boy
resisted, preferring to walk into the apartment on his own.
"Independent, just like you," David said to Elvira.

The two women embraced. "It was nice of you to come to
say goodbye. It would feel like unfinished business if you
hadn't."

"I'd go to the airport with you, Aunt Rebecca, but today is
a big day for us too. Samuel Armstrong starts school today."

"Marvelous!" Rebecca said. She beamed at little Sam, who
looked up at her, his face creased in a shy, self-conscious
smile.

"He'll be smart," David said. "Just like his mama. And his

papa. I can see it in his eyes. When they're smart, you can tell
from the eyes."

"Just to make sure, Uncle David, I want you to do for him
what you did for me on that first day."

"What I did . . ." he started to protest, then remembered.
"Of course! Becca, the honey! I will get a book! Quickly, Becca, quickly!"

When he opened the honey jar, he dipped in his little finger and deposited a single drop of honey on the page of the
open book, urging, "Taste, Samuel, taste. The sweetness of
honey. So you will always remember that learning, too, is
sweet. It is one of the sweetest pursuits of a man's life."

Samuel Armstrong licked the honey drop off the page.
Elvira nodded and smiled at Rebecca, whose eyes were glazed
over with tears at the memory of that earlier day and a timid
little eight-year-old girl.

The first sign of trouble came two hours after the plane
started east over the Atlantic. After staring out the porthole
for a time and finding endless stretches of ocean boring,
David settled back in his seat prepared to snooze a bit. Rebecca was busy with what seemed an armful of travel folders,
marking off places in the Holy Land that she had learned
about in childhood and looked forward to seeing for the first
time. One of the stewardesses came by to offer coffee or other
drinks. David refused because he wanted to nap, Rebecca because she had a slight burning sensation in her chest. She dismissed it as the tension involved in taking her first long flight
overseas.

By the time lunch was served, the burning sensation became more pronounced, so she declined lunch and settled for
a fizzing antacid. When David inquired, she assured him,
"Nerves, darling, just nerves."

As the flight continued, David became aware of her discomfort. Before they landed in Paris, he asked the stewardess
to get word to have a doctor meet the plane. Rebecca protested. "David, don't embarrass me. I'm fine. I just have a
little indigestion."

After an examination, the physician at Le Bourget advised
against continuing the trip. He recommended the excellent

American hospital in the city. But Rebecca insisted, "David, if I'm going to be sick, I want to be sick at home. Take me back to New York."

On a hastily arranged flight, David and Rebecca Rosen arrived back at Idlewild Airport in New York only twenty-three hours after they had departed. When David called Dr. Bannerman from Idlewild, he advised, "Get her right to Sinai. I'll meet you there!"

The doctor had preceded them to the hospital, arranged for a room, and set up tests with the various departments he felt might be involved. He detailed a wheelchair to meet her at the door. When Rebecca refused, David insisted. "If the doctor said a wheelchair, then you'll ride in a wheelchair."

"I'll feel like an invalid," she protested before surrendering to David's persistence.

Dr. Bannerman pored over the lab report and the tapes of Rebecca's electrocardiograms. David could not understand or interpret the results, but he insisted on looking over Bannerman's shoulder.

"She didn't have any pain?" Bannerman asked in surprise.

"Just a little heartburn," David said.

"With such an EKG I would expect she'd have considerable pain."

"Doctor, what are you saying?"

"Cardiac infarct. Extensive, from the look of it."

"Which means?" David persisted.

"A serious heart attack, Rosen. Very serious."

"Listen, doctor, whatever it takes, I don't care what it costs. Call in specialists! The best—you hear me, the best! If not in New York, fly them in. From the Mayos in Minnesota. Or from Johns Hopkins. Fly them in!"

"Rosen, Rosen, get hold of yourself!" the doctor cautioned.

"My Rebecca has a serious heart attack and you say get hold of myself? Do something! Do something!" he shouted.

"First thing, lower your voice. If there is one thing your wife doesn't need now it is excitement, added to the fears she must now be experiencing."

"Afraid, she's afraid? How do you know?"

"Patients have a sense of these things," the doctor said. "They know when it is serious and when the outcome is in doubt."

"The outcome, the outcome . . ." David repeated the phrase, aware that it was a euphemism for a word the doctor chose not to use. In a tense whisper, he asked, "Doctor, what can we do?"

"What we're already doing: keep her on oxygen, ease her pain, and let her rest."

"Isn't there anything else . . . anything?"

"Maybe someday there will be. But right now that's all we can do. All any specialist can do."

David nodded. "Doctor, can I . . . is it all right if I go in and sit with her?"

"Yes, but don't encourage her to talk. And don't say anything that might excite her. Rest. That's the key. Rest."

He entered her room. He was startled by the sight of his Rebecca, the strong one, the active one, always on the run, now lying there helpless, oxygen tubes in her nose, an intravenous drip taped to her arm. Her eyes were closed. Her graying blond hair was in slight disarray.

It's a good thing she can't see herself, he thought. *She wouldn't be pleased at looking so untidy.* He tiptoed to the armchair and sank into it.

The sigh of air escaping from the cushion caused Rebecca to ask weakly, "David . . . darling?"

"Yes, Becca. Just be quiet, please. Get some sleep."

"All right," she said softly. "I'll try."

She was silent for a time. He strained to watch her from his chair but dared not move for fear of waking her again. She seemed to breathe evenly, her coverlet rising and falling with shallow regularity. That reassured David somewhat.

"David," she whispered suddenly, to make sure he was still there.

"Yes, darling, something you want? I'll call the nurse."

"No. I was just thinking . . ."

"Becca darling, please, the doctor said just rest. Don't even think."

She persisted. "I was thinking how funny life is. We started out to see Israel, Jerusalem, the holy places. Mount Sinai. I didn't get to see Israel or Jerusalem. But here I am at Mount Sinai."

"Yes, darling . . . life is very funny. Now, rest. Please."

Rebecca grew silent. David sat there frozen by fear and indecision. He could not decide—to call Elvira or not? She would surely resent not being called. On the other hand, why disturb her if it became unnecessary? After Rebecca rested through the night and had improved, he could call Elvira with good news.

At eight o'clock in the evening, when all other visitors were told to leave, David insisted on remaining. When they ordered him out of Rebecca's room, he retreated to the visitors' lounge, insisting he be called if there was any change in Rebecca's condition.

During the night, he went out into the corridor frequently to listen for any sounds of unusual activity that would signal an emergency. By three o'clock, he fell asleep on the couch in the lounge.

At 4:17, an hour in the early morning when human resistance is at its lowest ebb, peacefully and without pain, Rebecca Rosen died.

he synagogue was more crowded than David had anticipated. There were faces he recognized as women and men he met at the many fund-raising functions he had attended at Rebecca's insistence. There were even more faces that were unfamiliar to him. He had had no idea of the breadth of her acquaintanceships and her charitable activities. People, some he knew, some he didn't, came up to him, pressed his hand, whispered condolences, praised Rebecca. Some even called her a saint. He nodded in appreciation of the words he barely heard.

In the first few pews were relatives—cousins, nephews, nieces, and Rebecca's sister and her brother's widow.

Among the other mourners sat elderly Pastor Wilder attended by his wife.

When the rabbi took his place at the pulpit, David sat down in the first pew alongside Elvira. They held hands throughout the service and the eulogy, which, to do justice to Rebecca's varied charitable activities, was longer than usual.

On the ride out to the cemetery, David insisted that only he and Elvira occupy the first limousine. He had not the patience to endure any other mourners.

Ahead, he could see the hearse bearing the plain pine coffin that was mandatory for Orthodox Jews.

"So many people," he said. "She had friends I never heard of. They talked to me as if I should know them, but I didn't."

Elvira patted his hand to comfort him.

"The little boychick, Sam . . . where is he?"

"At the house," Elvira said. "Mrs. Prescott from the church is taking care of him."

"Did she order food? Enough food? There'll be a lot of people tonight and the next few nights," David said.

"I ordered the food. From Fine and Schapiro, the kosher delicatessen on Seventy-second Street."

"Good, darling, thanks," he said. "I never realized how helpless I would be at a time like this. I'm so used to giving orders, getting things done. Now, without her, I feel . . . it's not the same. It will never be the same again."

"I know how that is," Elvira said.

"Forgive me for thinking only of myself at a time like this. But in recent months I've been thinking about you, too. Elvira, you should consider remarrying. Five years is a long time. And Sammy needs a father."

"Sammy *has* a father," Elvira replied. "As for myself, should I ever meet someone who is the man Drew was, I might consider it. But not until then."

"I know what you mean. There'll never be another Rebecca, either," David said sadly.

They were quiet for a time. The cortege had started up the ramp to the Triborough Bridge toward Queens, where the cemetery was.

"You know, Elvira darling, it worked out all wrong. I should have gone first. She would have known what to do. With her activities, her charities, her desire to travel, she would have had a full life ahead of her. But me . . . what am I?"

Elvira did not attempt to respond, for it was obvious that Uncle David had a great need to talk about Rebecca.

"You know the big difference?" he continued. "With Rebecca, if you said someone is in trouble, someone needs help, a little girl of eight needs a place to live, right away she would *do* things. Find an apartment. Find a school. A church. But if you say to me, Someone is in trouble, I say, I'll write out a check.

"That was the difference. I gave money. She gave herself. The sad part is, she gave so much of herself, to so many causes, that when she needed strength, there was not enough left for her."

He sniffled back his tears. When he chose not to wipe his eyes, Elvira reached out with her handkerchief, which was damp from her own tears.

"To the very end, no matter what I said to her, I always had the feeling she felt guilty, blamed herself for not having given me a child. Did she ever say anything to you?"

"No, never."

"I would hate to think she died feeling guilty about that," he said.

The limousine sped along the highway behind the hearse, followed by eight more limousines and twenty-four other cars.

"Like Moses," he said suddenly, then fell quiet. After a while he explained: "In the Torah it is written that after all Moses went through, freeing the Jews from Egypt, guiding them forty years through the desert, when it seemed he was about to realize his dream, God took him up to the mountaintop and permitted him only a glimpse of the Promised Land.

"So it was with my Rebecca. All her activities. For the war. For Israel. For refugees. The war is over. Israel is finally a country. The refugees are mostly settled. But God said, 'Rebecca Rosen, you cannot enjoy the final triumph.' He must have thought a great deal of her to accord her the same treatment as Moses."

The cortege had reached the gates of the cemetery.

They returned from the cemetery. The rabbi and some of the mourners accompanied David and Elvira back to the apartment.

In accordance with custom, and at Elvira's instructions, Mrs. Prescott had covered all the mirrors. She held Sam's hand so that he would not interfere with the mandatory ceremonies that now took place.

David slipped off his shoes and changed into slippers. He held out his vest for the rabbi to make the time-honored rent in the garment. He went to the low box near the window, sat down, clasped his hands between his thighs, and stared down, seeing nothing, aware of nothing.

Elvira, meantime, had gone into her old room. She took off her own shoes and put on a pair of slippers she had brought. She slipped into an old dress and came out to the living room to present herself to the rabbi.

"Go ahead," she said. The rabbi was puzzled. "Make a slit. A deep one."

"My dear young woman, it is only required of close relatives," he explained.

"Make the slit!" Elvira said.

The rabbi realized, nodded and proceeded to abide by her request. Once he had done that, Elvira went to David's side, sat down on the box alongside him, and took his hand in hers.

The mourners who had returned from the cemetery lingered only long enough to partake of a cup of coffee and a bit of cake and speak the usual condolences. Not long after they departed, the rabbi returned with the minyan he had gathered for the afternoon and evening prayers so that David Rosen could say the Kaddish in the traditional way. Elvira stood beside him and repeated the words.

Later in the evening came those mourners and bearers of condolences who had not been able to attend the funeral. The apartment was filled with them: men and women from the synagogue, from Rebecca's many organizations, and a delegation of men and women from the Ajalon, including aging Pastor Wilder and his wife. They crowded into the living room, where David and Elvira sat on their crate. Men shook his hand in sympathy. Women kissed him on the cheek. Those who knew Elvira kissed her and pressed her hand as consolingly as if her own mother had died.

People spoke to David of charitable acts Rebecca had done with which they assumed he was familiar. He was not. Smiling, they recalled her usual reply whenever money was suddenly required for some good cause and she supplied it.

"Just say I am an old-fashioned Jewish housewife. I still have my *knippel*."

Their remembrances, which were intended to console and cheer David, had the opposite effect. More and more, he complained within himself. *She was such a fine woman, such a warm human being, why did He take her so soon? Why?*

He was relieved when the last of the callers were at the door, where Elvira waited until the elevator arrived to take them down. She came back into the living room.

"Uncle David, what can I get for you?"

"Nothing, darling, thanks anyhow."

"You haven't eaten all day."

"So? Starve I won't," he said. "Let's go clean up. Must be lots of cups, saucers, and plates in the kitchen."

"Everything's been cleaned up."

"The ladies from the church?"

"Yes."

"Nice of them to come. Becca would have been pleased."

"They loved her," Elvira said.

"Everybody loved her," David said, sighing. "The little one, he's asleep?"

"The last time I looked."

"Look, darling, it would be foolish to wake him just to take him home. Do me a big favor. Stay the night. Stay the whole week so this place won't seem so empty all of a sudden. Please?"

"Of course, Uncle David."

He reached for her hand, turned the palm up, and held it against his bristly cheek.

"When I think . . ." he started to say, but did not continue. "When I . . ." he began once more. "Eighteen years ago, or was it nineteen? No matter. She said to me, 'David, there is this little eight-year-old girl. She's alone. Her mother is sick. She needs love, needs a home.' And I said to her, 'Becca, are you crazy? A Negro child? A Christian child? Impossible!'

"But she knew. Not only *what* to do, but *how* to do it. Imagine if she had been foolish enough to listen to me. I would like to tell her now. 'Becca, every time this old grouch said no to you, he was wrong.' Oh, the things I would like to say, should say now . . ."

"I know the feeling," Elvira said. "I'm in her debt for all these years. I was always intending to repay. Always promising, someday, one day. But that day never came. That debt will always be the great regret of my life. And now it's too late, too late . . ."

"Mama . . ." She heard the timid voice of her son. She glanced toward the door where he stood, forlorn and uneasy, after waking up in a bed not his own.

Elvira went to him and took him in her arms.

"Sammy sweetheart, did you wake up and miss your mama? Well, we'll get you some juice and back to bed you go." She turned in David's direction. "Say good night to Uncle David."

"'Night, Uncle David."

"Good night, Sammy. Sleep well, son, sleep well."

She was tucking him in, and he was already half asleep when he asked, "Mama?"

"Yes, dear?"

"Mama, a . . . a debt. Is that the same as dead?"

"Oh no, dear. A debt, spelled *d e b t*, is something that one person owes to another person. And which that person must repay. My mama used to say to me, 'Elvira, don't you leave this world owin' nothing to nobody.'"

"Even if it's too late, Mama?"

Elvira stared down into her son's black eyes. "Sam, were you standing there at the door listening?"

"Only a little, Mama."

"I'm afraid there are some debts that never get repaid. Never," she said sadly.

She lay down beside her son Samuel and sang softly to him until he had fallen asleep. She began to weep for all the years, all the memories. And, like all loving mourners, she spoke to herself all the words she had meant to say but never had.

After the formal week of shivah, once the deep mourning was completed, Elvira and her young son left for their own home. Before she departed, David had said, "Darling, remember, every Wednesday for supper like always."

"Of course, Uncle David."

They kissed and held each other close. Elvira took her son by the hand and entered the same elevator from which she had almost been barred years before.

For the first week after she returned home, she felt the continuing pangs of mourning. On Wednesday evening she and Sammy went to have supper with David. She came away feeling her pain even more deeply. By the third week, after supper with Uncle David, she began to recognize the feeling not only as mourning for a deep loss but one of guilt as well.

By the end of the fourth week she felt so burdened that after church service on Sunday morning, she went to call on Pastor Wilder, who was now so frail that he could no longer attend church regularly. With Sammy at her side, she sat in the pastor's modest parlor and confessed her feelings freely, and, at the end, tearfully.

The old man listened patiently, recalling the early days of Elvira's attendance at Sunday school and at services. And he thought, *What a fine woman she has turned out to be.* She had finished describing her desperate need to repay the love and care and devotion that Rebecca had lavished on her for all those years.

"No matter what I think or what I say to myself, I cannot say it to her now. I feel I shall carry this burden like an unpaid debt for the rest of my life. What can I do to repay it?"

"Child, have you forgotten what you learned at our church? God grants salvation even to the undeserving. For He feels that all His children are worthy. Rebecca's love was given to you freely because you were worthy of it. Why should you feel it imposed a debt on you?"

"If only I'd been there before she died. I might have said something. If only I'd kissed her for the last time," Elvira said, weeping. "Why do I have this feeling that things are so . . . so unfinished?"

"Because they are. Life is an unfinished process. As is love. Love is an endless gift passed on from person to person. The love Rebecca gave to you, you will pass on to others. You have a long life to live, much love to give—to Sammy, to friends, to students, even to strangers. No more is required of you."

"But still . . ." Elvira started to say.

"Always you will have that regret," Wilder observed sadly. "Child, be content to remember her love. Do not confuse the pain of mourning with a debt no one has laid upon you. If in God's eyes more is required of you, in His time He will provide a way."

1963

39

*W*eighed *down* *by* a heavy bookbag, Sarah Marshall, a young Negro student, reached the door of the English Department of Hunter College with a sense of trepidation. She had succeeded in being granted a conference with Professor Elvira Armstrong, her departmental adviser, but now the girl felt intimidated by second thoughts.

Professor Armstrong had become an institution at Hunter, being the only Negro on the faculty. She had also established a reputation for being quite exacting with students when the situation called for it, so many legends had grown up about her.

However young Sarah pushed her silver-framed glasses up on the bridge of her nose and, determined, she knocked. She was greeted by a pleasant voice calling, "Come in, Sarah." To be addressed by her first name encouraged her.

Sarah entered. To her surprise she found Professor Armstrong to be a much younger woman than she had expected, in her early forties. She was also a handsome woman, her lean, light-brown face crowned by soft black hair that only recently had begun to exhibit strands of gray. When the professor smiled, her face lit up with a warm and inviting glow.

"Sit down, my dear. Do get comfortable," Elvira invited.

Once Sarah was seated, freed of her burden of bookbag and purse, Elvira looked into her troubled young face.

"Now then, Sarah, according to your note you are having trouble with your instructor, Mr. Haines. What sort of trouble?"

"I think . . . I think he's picking on me."

Though Elvira Armstrong had been hearing such complaints for half a dozen years now, she did her best to appear surprised. "Oh? And in what way does he seem to be picking on you?"

"He has nothing but criticism to make of my work, even my best papers."

"What sort of criticism?" Elvira asked.

"Nothing I write seems to please him. When I recite in class, he finds fault with me. He's always correcting me. Personally . . ." Sarah paused and leaned forward to speak more confidentially, as if she might be in danger of being overheard. "The reason I asked to talk to you is because I knew you would understand. Being one of us, you must have had to face this kind of thing very often."

"What kind of thing?" Elvira asked, anticipating the response.

"Bigotry. Prejudice."

"Oh yes, I've had my share," Elvira admitted.

"It's not much fun being one of the only two Negroes in my class."

"My first year here, child, I was the only Negro in the entire college," Elvira pointed out.

"I can imagine how that must have felt," the student said. "So I knew you'd understand. Mr. Haines deliberately picks on us because we're Negroes. He likes to ridicule us before the white students."

"Does he ridicule the white students, too?"

"Yes, but not as much. I almost get the feeling that few of us as there are, he'd like to be rid of us."

"Strange," Elvira said.

"Ma'am?" the puzzled student questioned.

"Most student complaints in the English Department come to my desk. But I have never before received one from a Negro student about Mr. Haines."

"Of course not," Sarah defended quickly. "Because we're afraid. Afraid he'll flunk us. Or we'll get expelled if we complain."

"Sarah my dear, we have never expelled anyone from Hunter for complaining. Else, considering some of the protests and petitions we've had, this place would be empty by now. In fact, we are constantly being accused of running a college solely to educate revolutionaries and communists. Now, suppose you become more specific about Mr. Haines and his criticisms. What sort of thing does he say?"

"Well, he writes nasty comments on my papers. For instance, I did this short story about visiting my grandma down in Baltimore for Easter Sunday. I thought it was a good story. A very good story. My best. But he wrote across the top of it, 'I can abide a twice-told tale better than a half-told tale.' And he gave me a C-minus."

"And you took that to be?" Elvira asked.

"Very sarcastic," Sara replied. "Humiliating."

"Since the comment was written on your paper, meant for your eyes alone, it was evidently not intended to humiliate you before the class, was it?"

"No," Sarah conceded.

"So perhaps Mr. Haines had something else in mind," Elvira pointed out. "I've known Mr. Haines ever since he's been in the English Department. I've always found him to be a fair man. Demanding, but fair. Very devoted to his students. If he has any fault, it's that he wants every student to achieve to the utmost of her ability. He does not like lazy students or students too easily satisfied with their own work. It's not good enough for a student to think that she's written a 'good' story or her 'best' story."

Sarah pulled back slightly in her chair at this unexpected rebuke from Professor Armstrong.

"Sarah, when he wrote 'a half-told tale' on your paper, I think he was trying to say that this story has more to offer than the author found in it. And this writer has more to offer than she herself knows. She must learn to extend her talents."

"You don't think he's being . . . biased?"

"Oh, he's being biased all right," Elvira admitted freely. "I've heard him say many times, 'Give me the Negro students, because I want every one of them to excel. I want to prove to the bigots that Negroes not only belong in a college like Hunter but can be outstanding.' He evidently sees you as one of the potentially outstanding ones. Believe me, if he didn't think you have the ability, he wouldn't drive you as hard as he does."

Sarah Marshall absorbed Elvira's words in silence.

"My dear, if I were you, I'd go back, rethink that story and rewrite it, several times if need be. And I would submit it again. If Mr. Haines thinks you can do better, I know you can."

"You really think—" the girl started to say.

"Yes, my dear, I really think," Elvira said.

The phone on her desk rang. Elvira lifted it to say only, "Hold for a moment, please!" She turned back to Sarah. "And one thing more, I think. Don't go suspecting prejudice where it doesn't exist. God knows there's still enough of the real thing around."

Sarah Marshall nodded as she pondered Elvira's advice. "I want to thank you."

"Don't thank me. Get to work on that story!" Elvira advised sharply.

As Sarah Marshall gathered up her things and left, Elvira gave her attention to the phone.

"Yes? Hello?"

"Mama," she heard the anxious voice of her son.

"Sammy? What are you doing out of class at this hour? Is today some kind of holiday down there at Howard?"

"Haven't you heard the news?"

"News? What news?" Elvira asked with a pang of fear reminiscent of the day more than twenty years ago when that same inquiry meant that World War Two had started.

"Birmingham!" young Sam Armstrong said.

"What happened this time?"

"Today the police used fire hoses and guard dogs on black college students who dared to protest," Sam said, seething at the injustice. "Governor Wallace meant it when he said, 'Segregation now, segregation tomorrow, segregation forever.' Well, we decided he won't get away with it."

"We can't let him get away with it!" Elvira insisted. "Your daddy didn't die to make the world safe for Governor Wallace!"

"Why I'm calling, Mama, is the guys here at Howard and guys at Georgetown and a few other colleges are organizing a group to go down to Birmingham and protest. I want your permission—though I've got to tell you, even if you say no, I'll go."

"You're your father's son, all right," Elvira said. "Any women going along or just men?"

"Why?"

"If there's room for one woman, I'm going with you—though I've got to tell you, even if you say no, I'll go."

Sam laughed. "Okay, Mama. You come down here to Washington, join up with us. We'll all go together. How's that?"

"Son, I'll be there!"

She was about to inform her secretary of her change of plans when she remembered, *Today is Tuesday, tomorrow's Wednesday, Wednesday is supper at Uncle David's. I'd better call him.*

Where would David Rosen be at this hour? At his office, of course. Despite her urging and his doctors' advice, he persisted in going to work every day. No amount of Elvira's pleading could convince him to sell out and retire to some more hospitable climate.

"And what would I do there?" he would always respond. "Spend my time fighting off widows. Elvira darling, you and I are alike. For you there is only one Drew, for me, only one Rebecca. So I do not wish to be pounced on by a hundred widows, each of whom would like to take my nice, quiet life and reorganize it into bedlam. Besides, what would David Rosen, Hatters, be without David Rosen? That son of yours, that Sammy, he gives me heartburn. When he works here during the summers, I can see he has a head for business. If, instead of studying sociology like his father, he would come into the business full-time, when I'm gone it'll be his. But go make sense to these young squirts these days. They know everything, everything!"

Occasionally, though, David Rosen would pause in his plaint to admit softly to Elvira, "You know, I envy that young man. He is doing what I always wanted to do. He's a student. Of philosophy. Of life. With him it's sociology. With me it was Torah. Even now, nights when I can't sleep, I read Torah, Talmud, Rashi. And I think of what might have been. On the other hand, if I had done that, today I would be dead. Burned to death in some oven in some concentration camp. He's a wise young man, your Sammy."

He had always held Sammy in great affection. At the beginning, after Sammy's father had died in the war, David was his foster grandfather. Later, if Elvira had not prevented it, he would have spoiled the boy shamelessly.

Such thoughts went through Elvira's mind as she dialed David Rosen's private line at his office.

"Hello?" she heard his singsong greeting. It seemed to her that the older David became, the more a Yiddish intonation crept into his speech. Or was it that his beloved Rebecca was no longer here to correct him?

"Uncle David."

"Ah, Elvira, thank God it's you and not my stockbroker with another of his hot tips. From following his tips I could go bankrupt. Well, darling, nice to hear your voice for many reasons. One of which is that tomorrow night I gave orders to my cook to prepare a very special dish."

"Uncle David, that's exactly why I'm calling you."

"How could you know? Who told you?"

"I mean, I can't be there tomorrow night."

"You can't—you mean some meeting . . . or some trouble at the college?" the distressed man asked.

"I have to go down to Washington."

"Washington! About time President Kennedy recognized your ability! What kind of appointment! What did they say?" David asked eagerly.

"No, Uncle David, no appointment. No call from the White House. I have to meet Sammy and a group of students from Howard and some white colleges to go down to Birmingham."

"Birmingham?" David Rosen exploded "Elvira, it's dangerous down there! Don't you read the newspapers? Listen to the radio? Watch television?"

"That's exactly why we have to go," Elvira said.

His sense of alarm diminished to a soft, resigned, "Aha. I see. To protest."

"Exactly."

"I . . . I can understand that. Only, darling, be careful. You are dealing with storm troopers down there, storm troopers," he warned.

"Somebody has to do it, Uncle David."

"And my little Elvira has to be that somebody. But if Rebecca were still here, she'd be down there with you. Look, darling, what time are you leaving? Are you flying or going by train? Whichever, I'll have my car pick you up."

"No need, honestly," Elvira tried to resist.

"Elvira, this is your Uncle David the grouch speaking. When I say my car will pick you up, it will come to pick you up. If nothing else, it will give my driver something to do for a change."

"I'll be going by train from Penn Station. The same train I take when I go to visit Sammy. I'll leave the house at ten."

"My man will be waiting downstairs for you!" David announced, before adding a soft but deeply concerned, "Good luck, darling. Take care."

Promptly at 9:45 on Wednesday morning, David Rosen's black limousine was waiting at the modest apartment building on East Seventy-first Street and Lexington Avenue where Elvira Armstrong had lived for the past eight years. Promptly at ten o'clock, attended by the doorman who carried her one piece of luggage, Elvira came out. The driver was at her side quickly to stow the luggage in the trunk. He opened the door, and as Elvira stepped in, she found the backseat already occupied.

"Uncle David!" She was surprised. "There's no need to see me to the train."

"Who is seeing you to the train?" He pretended to be annoyed. "*I* happen to be going to Washington. And *you* happen to be going to Washington. So we'll go together."

"Uncle David, you can't be thinking—"

"You're such a mind reader, tell me what I'm thinking!"

"Uncle David, are you planning to go to Birmingham with us?"

"No, I am not planning to go to Birmingham," he declared, then, "I am *going* to Birmingham!"

"You can't. You mustn't!" Elvira protested. "Have you talked to your doctor?"

"I did better than that!" David informed.

"Such as?"

"I talked to my rabbi!" David replied.

"And what did he say?"

"He didn't have time to say much. He was busy packing a few things. Seems he, too, is going to Birmingham. With a group of clergymen from New York. Priests, ministers, rabbis—a whole delegation. So all he could say to me was, 'David, Leviticus nineteen.' Since I have been one of his most faithful students in his Sunday afternoon Torah discussion group, he assumed that I knew. Frankly, I had to look it up. I discovered what he meant: 'The stranger who sojourns with you shall be to you as your own and you shall love him as yourself, for you were strangers in the land of Egypt.' Meaning, a people who have been persecuted, who have been slaves themselves, cannot sit by and watch others suffer the same fate. Jews and Negroes belong together at a time like this."

"Yes, Uncle David, but for a man of your age . . ."

"Age, age," David disparaged. "I am a healthy man of a mere sixty-five."

"Sixty-seven," Elvira corrected.

"You are even worse than your Aunt Rebecca when it comes to correcting. Okay, sixty-seven. So what? I have to go! Rebecca would understand."

"Right now Rebecca would be insisting, 'David, take care of yourself!'"

"No, Elvira darling, I don't think so. She would understand. When I said to her, 'Becca, when the war against Hitler came I was "essential." When Israel had to fight for her survival, I was already fifty and I was "too old."' Now, Elvira, for once in my life, I have to be part of the fight. After all, how much time do I have left?"

"I wish you had talked to your doctor," Elvira insisted.

"Darling, when you have lived as long as I have, you learn one thing. Doctors and lawyers grow rich by telling you what you *can't* do. Now, let's go else we'll miss the train. Charles, Penn Station. And step on it!"

He settled back and took Elvira's hand. From time to time he patted it, though he seemed lost in a reverie at which she could only venture a guess.

Rebecca. He is thinking of Rebecca, justifying this journey to her.

When the train pulled into Union Station in Washington, Samuel Drew Armstrong was waiting. Tall and muscular like his father, though somewhat lighter skinned, he was a handsome nineteen-year-old with all the fervor of a young man on fire against injustice. At his first sight of David Rosen, young Sam's face reflected his reluctance. David was prepared to overcome his resistance.

"Sammy, I can't get over you. Every day more and more like your father. Did I ever tell you the first time I saw him? The first time he came to New York to call on your mother? There I was sitting across Central Park West and I see this handsome young man coming along, checking the address on a slip of paper against the address on our canopy, and I said to myself, 'That must be him!' So I cross the street—"

From the look on Sam's face, David was forced to admit, "I guess I told you this before."

"Many times," Sam Armstrong said. "Uncle David, what are you doing here?"

"The same thing your mother is doing here, the same thing you are doing here!" David said.

"Do you realize it's going to be a long march and we are going to meet a lot of opposition? Violence, possibly. Brutality."

"Yes, Sam, I realize. And still I am going," David insisted. "If you have any regard for me, for the years I have treated you almost as a son, you won't try to stop me," David said.

Sam looked at his mother.

"Sammy, he's determined. You'd better let him come."

"Okay. The bus is waiting," Sam said, picking up their luggage and leading the way.

The way toward the bus passed the ladies' room. The sign WHITES ONLY was no longer on the door.

Elvira thought back to that day so long ago when it was considered daring, even criminal, for her to have disregarded the sign and entered there.

Such a long time to make such a little bit of progress, she thought, *almost twenty-five years. Tomorrow we make another step.*

40

*T**he caravan of* buses had traveled through the night. Just before dawn, the spring rains began. By the time the buses had ventured as far as the drivers dared to go without incurring reprisals from the local and state police, the downpour had eased off to a light but steady rain.

Out of the lead bus climbed a succession of men, all clothed in black, some with clerical collars visible, but all representing the many faiths who had joined in the protest. They were men of all ages, from their twenties up to the white-haired, tall minister who seemed to be in his seventies but was actually older.

Black and white, young and middle-aged and elderly, the priests, ministers, and rabbis joined hands to present a phalanx behind which all the others proceeded to form ranks.

Elvira and Sammy Armstrong took places on either side of David Rosen and each took his one of his hands. They fell in behind the men and women who had formed long lines. They started forward along the glistening-wet highway. Trucks and cars coming against them honked their horns in anger. The marchers persevered. Some of the drivers surrendered and drove off the highway, their horns blaring their resentment. Other vehicles remained on the highway. The protesters flooded around them, surrounded them, and swept on by.

Someone far back in the line of march began to sing. Others picked up the melody and the words. Soon the air was filled with thousands of voices.

> We shall overcome someday
> Oh deep in my heart I do believe
> We shall overcome someday.

At the words "We'll walk hand in hand/ We'll walk hand

in hand/ We'll walk hand in hand someday," marchers gripped more tightly the hands of their companions and marched on, singing, despite the rain, which was beating down harder now. They continued to sing:

> Oh, deep in my heart I do believe
> We shall overcome some day.

Elvira Armstrong marched, sang, rain flowing down her lean face. She kept a tight grip on David Rosen's left hand, glancing at him from time to time, fearing that she had been wrong not to persuade him to remain on the bus. The rain, the chill in the air, the exertion could only endanger him. But he had been so determined, it would have been unfair to prevent him from joining.

The singing was interrupted by sounds of a confrontation at the head of the line. The singing died out sporadically until only the sound of a voice on a bullhorn could be heard.

"You people are all in violation of the law!" a harsh voice bellowed, reinforced and magnified by the electrical power of the horn.

The voice of one of the clergymen responded, "We are American citizens availing ourselves of our right to protest peaceably under the Constitution of the United States!"

The voice bellowed back, "According to section nineteen, paragraph twelve of the city code, no one can hold a parade without securing a license. You have no license. So you will either disband or we will be forced to take steps to see that you do!"

At the threat of physical force, Sam Armstrong released his hold on David's hand and started forward through the crowd.

"Sammy!" his mother called out instinctively, though knowing it would not dissuade him.

Other young men, black and white, started forward, an impromptu, unofficial pickup protection squad to become a cordon of defenders around the clergymen, who were in the lead and most vulnerable to official assault.

The voice on the bullhorn continued: "You've been given fair warning as the law requires. Now, this is an order. Disperse! Failure to do so and we will have to resort to force. You young bucks, stand aside! All right! You're asking for it! Okay, men! Let 'em have the water hoses!"

The sounds of rushing water, voices raised in anger and fear, and the barking of police dogs became a confusion of noises that filled the air with terror and panic.

"They can't—people don't do such things!" David Rosen protested.

"Sammy, Sammy," was all that Elvira Armstrong said as she started forward through the crowd, some of whose members had now begun to disperse and turn back out of fear. Elvira fought her way through them, David trailing behind, calling, "Elvira, wait! Wait for me!" He was pushed aside by some of those who were trying to flee. He slipped and fell to the wet road, picked himself up, and pressed on, calling, "Elvira! Elvira!"

Elvira Armstrong fought her way toward the head of the line. She could already see the physical confrontation. She saw the old minister go down and disappear from view, but not before a red smear of blood stained his white hair. She witnessed young black men, one of whom closely resembled Sammy, being struck across the head and face with clubs and dragged off to the waiting police vans.

"Sammy!" she continued to cry out. "Sammy!"

Only the sounds of the clash, the cries of pain, the voice on the bullhorn answered her.

She pressed forward, barely evading a club swung not at her but at the priest alongside her. She had reached the thick of the melee but saw no sign of her son. She strained to see if he was one of those who had fallen or were being dragged off, but before she could discover that, a blow from a club struck her across the back of the head and she fell unconscious.

David Rosen kept trying to press forward, breathless, his legs weak and beginning to tremble. He continued to call, in a voice of diminishing strength, "Elvira . . . be careful. Elvira!" Finally, he could not go on. Around him on all sides were those who pressed forward to confront the troopers or those who had given up the fight and were retreating. Finally, he stood there, lost, alone. Until a young black woman approached him.

"You all right, sir?"

"I'm . . . I'm fine . . . No, frankly, I am not fine. I'm tired, very tired," David said.

The young woman put her arm around him and led him off to the shoulder of the road, where she helped him down to the rain soaked steel-cabled railing.

"Elvira," he said. "She . . . God knows what she . . . I have to find her."

"Wait here till the fighting's over. Then we can go look for her."

"Yes. We'll look for her, we'll go look," David said, not fully aware of what he was saying, or what it might mean.

The rain had stopped. The highway had been cleared. The marchers were either all under arrest or had reboarded their buses and were no longer considered a threat.

David's new companion felt it was safe to move now. "Rabbi, it might be safe now to go looking for her."

David summoned a weak smile. "Rabbi? You call me rabbi?"

"I assumed you were," the young woman said.

"Once, a long time ago, possibly . . . then I was a *yeshiva bucher*—you know what that means?"

"Not exactly," the young woman said.

"I was a student of Torah in my young days. You know what Torah is?"

"Yes," she replied. "I know that from my course in comparative religions."

"Comparative religions, that's nice. Very nice," David said. "But a rabbi I'm not. Now, I have to find Elvira. And Sammy."

"There are only two places to go now. The hospital or the jail," she said.

"I'll find them," David said with renewed determination.

"I'll help you," she offered, turning up his collar, for he was beginning to feel a chill.

They set out on the shoulder of the road, as trucks and cars raced by them.

As they slogged through the wet earth and the mud, he asked, "You're from up north?"

"New York."

"Obviously a college girl, no?"

"A college girl, yes!" she responded proudly.

"Possibly from Hunter?"

"Yes."

"You know maybe a Professor Armstrong there?"

"Everybody knows Professor Armstrong," the girl said. "She is one tough lady. Very determined! And there isn't a black student there who doesn't aspire to be like her."

"That's my Elvira," David informed.

"And she was out there in the midst of it? Then we've got to find her!" the young woman said. They began to walk even faster. "Tell me, how does she happen to be your Elvira?"

"She's my niece," David said. "And you want to know something? She was very determined from the time she was a little girl."

At the local community hospital, David Rosen, accompanied by the young woman, whose name, he discovered, was Leora Coops, made his way through the corridor leading to the emergency room. It was difficult to proceed in a straight or orderly path since both sides of the corridor were blocked by stretchers or patients lying on the floor awaiting treatment for head wounds, fractures, and other injuries.

Nurses, mostly white, made their way along the corridor trying to determine which patients were in most dire need of emergency treatment by a staff that had been overwhelmed by this sudden influx of wounded.

David edged along slowly, tiptoeing here, squeezing by there, looking for some sign of Elvira or Sammy. When he could find no sign of them, he asked of one of the nurses, "Is there some other hospital where they would take the wounded?"

"The ones that ain't here are in the jail, sir," the nurse said, making no secret of her distress at the entire situation. "This city is like a war zone. Broken heads, fractures, dog bites. There must be another way."

At the city jail, David Rosen refused to be pushed aside by one of the officers who had orders to keep out anyone who even appeared to be a lawyer. He made his way to the desk to demand, "I wish to know if you have here a person named Professor Elvira Armstrong from New York City."

"And who the hell are you?" the desk sergeant demanded.

"I am David Rosen!" he declared. "The name may not mean anything to you, but back in New York I am a very important man."

"Well, down here, mister, you are shit!" the officer said.

"I still demand to know if you are holding a person named Elvira Armstrong!" David insisted.

"And if we are?"

"I wish to post bail for her. I want her out. Free!"

"You have the money to post bail? Five thousand dollars maybe?" the desk sergeant asked.

"Give me the phone!" David demanded.

With a condescending smirk, the desk sergeant shoved the phone forward.

"Operator, I wish to make a collect call from David Rosen to Mr. George Twining at the Public National Bank on Twenty-third Street in New York City. The number is Gramercy two-six one six one. Yes, I will hold on."

The sergeant continued to smile at a man he considered slightly daft. In the meantime, Leora Coops stood slightly to the side of David, hoping he was not making a fool of himself, for he seemed a bit peculiar even to her.

In a few minutes, David heard a response that caused him to reply, "Mildred, I want to talk to your boss. Is he in? Put him on!" He glared at the desk sergeant. "George? Hello, George! This is Dave. Listen, George, I've got a problem . . . Where am I calling from? From Birmingham, where else? Never mind what I'm doing in Birmingham! I need you to vouch for my credit. No, no, not fifty thousand, not twenty-five thousand, only five thousand dollars. For bail money! George, I am not in jail! My niece is in jail! Never mind how! Just let me put you on the phone with this officer here and tell him my check is good for five thousand dollars."

He urged the phone on the sergeant. "George Twining, vice-president of the bank."

The sergeant took the phone gingerly. "Yes, sir?"

"Officer? What in the world is going on down there that got Mr. Rosen's niece into trouble?"

"Never mind that. Is he good for the money?" the sergeant asked.

"Mr. Rosen's credit is good for anything up to half a million dollars at this bank!" Twining said.

"Is that so?"

"Yes! That is so!"

The sergeant hung up the phone and, with respect for David's credit rating, if not for his views, said, "Your check will be acceptable, sir."

"Now, so where is my niece?" David demanded.

The sergeant signaled one of his officers, who had witnessed the entire procedure. The officer led the way down a short corridor that opened onto a longer one, this one flanked on both sides by iron-barred cells that were so full that most of the occupants had no room to sit down and were pressed up against the bars.

Accompanied by his newfound companion, David Rosen started slowly down the corridor, searching through the bars for a glimpse of Elvira's face. He could not find her.

In frustration, he cried out, "Elvira! Where are you? Elvira!"

Her response came not from one of the cells but from a room at the far end of the corridor.

"Uncle David!"

In moments she emerged from the room, angrily pulling on her dress. She glared back into the room, then started forward to meet David. Behind her, a smiling policeman came to stand in the doorway.

Elvira reached David. They embraced. As they held each other, he whispered, "What is going on here?"

"He was starting to strip-search me," Elvira said.

"Animal!" David replied, casting the epithet in the officer's direction. The man only seemed amused. "Come, darling, come. I'm posting bail for you."

"No, Uncle David, I will stay here. Until all of us go free."

"But . . ." he tried to argue.

"Uncle David! It's all of us or none of us."

"Ah, I should have known," David lamented.

"Sammy. Just find Sammy. Make sure he's safe," Elvira pleaded.

David Rosen managed to locate the prisoner named Samuel Drew Armstrong in a makeshift holding pen, one of many set up in advance to accommodate the more than one thousand persons, black and white, taken prisoner on that day. David was shocked. The young man's head was wrapped in a rough bandage through which blood had seeped and caked. His face was bruised, blue around his right eye, and he had a nasty lump on the left side of his jaw.

Almost in disbelief, David asked, "Sammy?"

"Yes, Uncle David."

"Oh my boy, my boy, what happened? No, don't even try to tell me. I can see. Gangsters. Gangsters in uniform." David sighed. "I could bail you out. You need medical treatment. But I know you—you're your mother's son. So I just want you to know you have not been abandoned. I am here. Ready to help. Just ask."

"I'll wait my time like the rest," Sammy said.

Four days later, under pressure from President Kennedy, all prisoners were released and permitted to return North.

David Rosen, Elvira Armstrong, her son, Samuel, and Leora Coops were on the same bus headed north from Birmingham. Sammy's head had been rebandaged with fresh, clean gauze. The lumps on his jaw and around his eyes had subsided and changed color. Only his mood had not softened or subsided.

He announced his feelings with a blunt, "I am through with sociology!"

"Sammy?" his mother asked in surprise.

"I am no longer interested in the general study of human social behavior. There is only one species and one area of human behavior I want to study—law and those who enforce it. If what we've lived through in the last week can be done to human beings in the name of the law, then either the law has to be changed or the people who carry it out have to be changed. I want to be one of the new people!"

In the face of such a strong statement of his feelings, and knowing her son as well as she did, Elvira Armstrong said nothing, but she exchanged glances with David Rosen. Hers said, *He's his father's son, all right*. David's said, *I like that boy more and more*. Sharing their mutual pride in Sam Armstrong, they were silent the rest of the way to Washington.

41

*O*n *Wednesday evening*, when Elvira arrived for dinner with Uncle David, she found him attired in pajamas and robe, unusual for him at such an early hour. He tried to belittle her concern.

"I got up this morning and I suddenly said to myself 'David Rosen, take the day off. You're entitled. For one day become a bum. Sit around. Read the *Times*. Yell a little. Watch maybe some television.' You know, they got these soap operas on all day. You wouldn't believe what goes on there. Such trouble. Real life seems wonderful by comparison."

But Elvira was not deceived.

"Uncle David, have you spoken to your doctor today?"

"Why should I talk to him? So he can ask my advice on the stock market? While he is taking my blood pressure or my cardiogram, he talks not about me but about what I think about the market. I tell you, these doctors are more greedy than all the businessmen I know."

"Uncle David! Did you talk to him?" Elvira persisted.

"We . . . we had a little conversation. On the telephone."

"What did he say?"

"Well, actually, he was up here. Dropped in on his way to the office. He gave me a quick once-over. He said I had a little . . . I forget the word."

"Congestion?" Elvira supplied.

"What are you suddenly, a doctor?" David bristled, before admitting in desultory fashion, "Yes, congestion. In the lungs."

"From being out in the rain all that day and the next," Elvira concluded.

David was forced to admit, "I . . . I didn't exactly tell him where I had been."

"Well, you will have your dinner in bed tonight," Elvira ordered.

"In all the years we've been having dinner together, never have I had dinner in bed!" David protested.

"You will tonight!" Elvira said, calling toward the kitchen, "Hilda! Get a tray ready for Mr. Rosen, please."

"My fate in life," David pretended to grumble, though he was secretly touched by Elvira's concern. "The first half of my life I was run by Rebecca. The second half by a tyrant named Elvira." As he made his way toward the bedroom, he called back over his shoulder, "I am not one of your students at Hunter. I am a grown man!"

When he was comfortably settled in bed, Elvira sat alongside it, overseeing his dinner and making sure he ate all of it.

As he ate, he continued to complain. "You know, darling, that Hilda is a very nice woman. Very eager to please. There is no dish she won't try. But between you and me, she will never make pot roast like Rebecca or fried chicken and gravy like you. And as for cornbread? A lost art in this house."

"Next Wednesday I'll come early and bake some of my own," Elvira promised.

"As long as you're coming early, a few fried veal chops and mashed potatoes wouldn't be bad either," David suggested.

He continued to eat but with little appetite. As she watched him, she said, "You shouldn't have gone. It was too much for you. And marching in the rain for hours—that wasn't the best thing, either."

"You know," David replied sadly, "I thought about that. And I said to myself, 'David Rosen, you did it again. Came time to act, and what did you do? Again you wrote out a check.' You know, Elvira, in the ten days between Rosh Hashanah and Yom Kippur, each man's fate is being decided. Then on Yom Kippur his destiny is written in the great Book of Life. For me it must be written every year, this David Rosen is never allowed to be a hero, never allowed to do something of importance. He will for the rest of his life make hats and write checks."

"Checks are important, too, Uncle David," Elvira observed.

"You don't understand," he protested. "Rebecca didn't understand. A man needs to take a risk, to fight the fight, to make a stand for decency, freedom. You have no idea how I admired, and yes, how I envied your son when at the first sign of the struggle he raced forward to be part of it. To help protect those ministers, those rabbis, those priests. How I wished I could have done that. But no. Always it is my fate to be denied even a single moment of heroism." Sadly, he said, "In the book of life I am inscribed as David, the check writer."

Elvira noticed tears in his eyes, but whether they were a reflection of a fever or of his emotions, she did not know. But she said, "Rebecca knew. I always knew. To us you were a hero."

"Ah," he tried to disparage. "You know," he confessed, "I wasn't even a very good grouch. I just made a show, that's all."

"You're still the best grouch I know," Elvira comforted.

She insisted that he take several aspirin, and promise not to listen to the late news on television lest he become too wrought up and unable to sleep. Then she made sure he was comfortable, put out the bedroom lights, and left.

When she called the next morning, she did not like the way he sounded. She insisted he stay home from work. She also called Dr. Steinfeld. By late afternoon, David Rosen was admitted to Mount Sinai Hospital with a bad case of pneumonia in both lungs.

At the end of the week, Elvira sent for Sam to come to New York. David had asked to see him. By the time Sam arrived, David Rosen was in an oxygen tent. It was obvious from the attitude of Dr. Steinfeld and the nurses who attended him that the end was close at hand.

When he spied Sam, David tried to smile. He raised his hand to beckon him. The young man leaned close. David whispered, "Sam . . ." But what he had intended to say would remain a secret, for with a sudden sigh, David Rosen slipped into unconsciousness, from which he did not recover.

The synagogue was crowded to the doors for the funeral of David Rosen. The beneficiaries of his charity and his good works were there. People who worked for him and had worked for him in the past attended in large numbers. People from the Ajalon Baptist Church came to express their sympa-

thy to Elvira and to Sam, to whom David had been more father and grandfather than uncle.

At the graveside, the rabbi handed the shovel to Elvira so
she could drop the first clump of earth on the plain pine casket of David Rosen. Sam Armstrong spread the second shov-
elful.

As the other mourners dispersed, Elvira and Sam remained. She tended the grave of Rebecca Rosen, the greenery
of which needed trimming. She found a small stone and
placed it on top of the white granite gravestone, as is the Jewish custom.

She stood a slight way off and stared at the stone on which
was carved:

ROSEN

Rebecca
1899–1949

The other half of the stone was yet to be engraved:

David
1896–1963

Elvira stared at the gravestone through eyes filled with
tears. Until Sam said, "Mama, we have to go. They're waiting
at Uncle David's house."

She nodded, wiped her eyes, and said softly, "Remember,
Sammy, when you were very little and Aunt Rebecca died,
that night?"

"Yes, Mama."

"And you overheard me talking about debts unpaid,"
Elvira said. "I still can't help feeling that way."

"You told me Pastor Wilder said that if more was required,
God would find a way," Sam reminded her.

"He never did," Elvira said sadly. "Well, we had better go.
I must sit shivah for Uncle David. And say Kaddish. He will
not go unremembered."

1 9 8 9

Epilogue

On the dais of a hotel ballroom that was filled to over-flowing, Elvira Hitchins Armstrong, sixty-seven, gray hair contrasting with her aging but smooth face, was enduring yet another testimonial speech from colleagues who had served under her in the English Department at Hunter College.

She made her best effort to smile modestly, even to appear embarrassed at tributes to her character, her devotion to teaching, her service to the community, and to her students of all races, in high school early in her career and at Hunter College later in her career.

Beside her, attired for the occasion in his bemedaled navy-blue uniform as New York City police commissioner, sat her son, Samuel Drew Armstrong.

Aware of her impatience with such flowery praise, Sam shared his mother's impatience—especially when confronted by praise from colleagues, white and black, who had always considered her too tough, too exacting, and not sufficiently receptive to revolutionary techniques of teaching.

These same colleagues had often accused her of being "of the old school," the worst epithet that could be leveled at an educator in times of great change and even greater confusion.

Her conviction was, "Making things easier for minority students may be good politics, but it is bad pedagogy. Teaching a student to confront and overcome difficulty makes for better character and education." That statement had been quoted back to her many times, not in commendation but in accusation.

Now these same accusers spoke so flatteringly of her that her son leaned close to her to whisper, "Mama, how does it sound after all these years?"

"Sam, they're only heaping all this praise on me so I'll be too embarrassed to *un*retire. But if this keeps up, maybe I will!"

The moment came for Elvira Armstrong to accept the inscribed silver vase and to acknowledge the tributes that had been lavished on her.

"I thank all of you for the many flattering things that have been said about me today. And I shall do my best to believe them. But it would not be fair to accept so much praise without sharing it with two other people, Rebecca and David Rosen, who, if they had been here today, would have enjoyed great *naches*—great pride and satisfaction. If my career has accomplished only half of what you kind people have said, I offer it in part payment of a debt I failed to pay."

The final applause was reaching its peak when Sam Armstrong hastily kissed his mother and said, "Have to leave. An important meeting."

In his office at Police Plaza, Sam Armstrong was concluding another of those frustrating meetings that every police commissioner in recent history had been forced to endure: one minority group was demanding police protection from another minority group.

If it wasn't the blacks, it was the Jews. And if not the Jews, it was the Koreans, or the Chinese, or the Vietnamese or, among Hispanics, it was the Puerto Ricans against the Colombians.

The meeting over, the latest delegation of outraged citizens having filed out, Armstrong remarked wearily to his secretary, "Clara, you know the trouble with this city? We have no real population. Just minorities."

Accustomed to his complaints about a job that was impossible to accomplish, she nodded sympathetically. That Sam Armstrong was black made him a special target of criticism from all groups. White groups accused him of favoring blacks, while blacks accused him of bending over backward to favor other groups in order to curry political favor. Among some blacks he was taunted as Uncle Sam, a parody of the old Uncle Tom.

In the main, he was inured to most criticism. One could not long survive in his job otherwise. However, in some infrequent situations, Sam Armstrong was intensely sensitive. That arson case months ago, the synagogue in Brooklyn in which two Torahs had been burned, was an act of ruthless destruction and rankled more than most, because the perpetrator turned out to be a teenage black.

No matter how long Sam Armstrong held the job of police commissioner, he would never overcome the special personal sense of shame he felt when the criminal was a black.

Among minority groups, the crime of one comes to be considered the crime of all. In that, Sam Armstrong's thinking was no different.

The only fact that served to ameliorate that sense of guilt about the torched synagogue in Brooklyn was that most people in the neighborhood, black as well as white, had contributed sufficient funds to restore the modest building.

What brought the subject of that synagogue to Sam Armstrong's attention so vividly today, months after the crime, was the letter that lay on his desk. Addressed to both the mayor and himself, it invited them to the reconsecration service of the rebuilt synagogue later this afternoon.

Across the invitation, the mayor had written, "Sam, this one we've got to attend."

"Don't let anything interfere," Armstrong ordered his secretary.

"Yes, sir," Clara replied crisply while handing him a long list of phone calls that had accumulated during his meeting.

Just scanning the names on the list, the commissioner could anticipate the complaints.

He was reaching for his phone to instruct Clara to return the first call when his attention was drawn back to the invitation from the synagogue. He picked it up and stared at it.

The memory of that early dawn in Brooklyn came back to him very strongly. The odor of smoke, of burning wood, seemed lodged in his nostrils. The blackened water running deep in the gutter was still a vivid memory, as were the revolving red, white, and blue lights on the police and fire vehicles. Most graphic of all was the sight of that fireman, with a smudged face and glistening-wet raincoat, coming toward him clutching two burned scrolls of the Torah.

Those memories were as real now as they had been early that morning. It was another unfortunate act of vandalism in a

city in which vandalism was becoming routine. Yet this particular crime continued to trouble him.

Was it his memory of the old rabbi as he clutched to his
breast the remains of two burned Torahs, shedding tears of
mourning?

Surely something could be done to make up for the destruction of those two holy scrolls. He had heard that some
group had started to gather a fund to purchase two new ones.
But that took a great deal of money, since it took more than a
year for a scribe to write out the first five books of the Old
Testament in Hebrew script on sheets of sheepskin joined together to become a single long, continuous scroll.

Recalling that old rabbi brought back other memories as
well. Memories of his boyhood, when Uncle David would lecture him on the joys of learning, especially before his first day
of school, when Mama had taken him to the Rosens' so David
could give him a taste of honey from the page of a book.

And other times when Uncle David would intone: "Learning is the highest activity of a civilized man, and the study of
Torah is greater than all others."

Sam Armstrong could still recall the regret in Uncle
David's eyes when he spoke those words, regret for a dearly
held ambition that he had never fulfilled to his own satisfaction.

He recalled other times his mother had taken him to visit
the Rosens. David was always ready with a new toy, and in-
evitably with some advice as well. Ah, but Aunt Rebecca, she
had always baked and cooked in anticipation of his visit. Always, when they were leaving, she had secretly pressed into
his hand a bag of cookies, whispering, "Don't let your mama
know until you get home." As if it were possible to conceal
such a large bag. Every Christmas there were gifts from the
Rosens. Every Chanukah, Mama took him down to Central
Park West to deliver gifts to the Rosens.

There was the day that phone call came. Aunt Rebecca had
suffered a heart attack. She had died during the night. And
Mama had never had a chance to see her again.

When they had returned from the cemetery, Mama had
shed her shoes and put on slippers. She had the rabbi make a
slit in her garment. She sat alongside Uncle David on the low

box, as custom required. When Uncle David spoke the Kaddish, she spoke the words along with him.

Sam Armstrong had to subordinate those warm memories to the long list of phone calls that Clara forced on him. Resigned to enduring complaints, accusations of prejudice, even vilification, Sam Armstrong instructed her to put through the first call. He was not surprised—not by the first call or the second or the third. Though he tried to listen conscientiously, his memories of Rebecca Rosen, of David and his reverence for Torah, persisted until they overshadowed the abuse to which he was being subjected.

Finally, he ordered, "Clara! Cancel all calls for the time being!"

He pushed back from his desk to concentrate on one memory that persisted most vividly—the image of the old rabbi weeping: "With all your new inventions, there is no proper way to produce a Torah except by the careful, precise hand of a holy scribe. Word by word, letter by letter. How will we replace these? How?"

How will we replace these? How?

To Sam Armstrong, those words had now become a personal challenge. The longer he pondered them, the more another long-ago memory insinuated itself into his mind. That other crime, too, had involved two Torahs. He had been in his rookie year. What made that crime so memorable was that the monetary value of the Torahs and their ornaments made it the first felony that he and Mike Conlin had been sent out to investigate. Mike was a rookie at that time, too.

Later, Mike was reassigned to the 46th Precinct. Sam had been sent to the 31st. They had never worked together again. But when he was appointed commissioner, he had received a warm letter of congratulation from Mike. And he had sent an equally warm note of thanks. On the one occasion when their paths crossed and they talked of the old times, Sam had not asked, nor had Mike, about their first felony case.

It had troubled Sam Armstrong from time to time why he had never been called to testify in that case. He assumed that the district attorney in charge of the case had, for reasons of his own, decided to go with a white witness, since the defendants in that case were also white. Racist though such a decision appeared to be, in practical, courtroom terms a district attorney going for a conviction used race for only one purpose: What would play best before the jury?

Curiosity provoked Sam Armstrong sufficiently to buzz his secretary. "Clara, find out where Detective First-Grade Mike Conlin is assigned. And if he's on duty, get him."

Some minutes later, his phone rang. He lifted it. "Armstrong here."

"Commissioner, you called for me?" Conlin asked.

"Mike, what the hell is this commissioner stuff? How ya been?"

"Pretty good, Sam, pretty good. Putting in for retirement in seven months. Doesn't seem like it, but we've been around a long time—too long, maybe. What can I do for you, Sam?"

"Mike, remember our first felony? That synagogue burglary?"

"Yeah. What about it, Sam?"

"What was the outcome of that case?"

"You're asking me?" Mike Conlin protested. "You're the one who testified."

"I didn't testify," Sam denied.

"Well, I sure never testified," Mike said.

"But the D.A. couldn't make the case without your testimony," Sam said.

"Oh, a couple of different young D.A.s talked to me from time to time, but I never got called to testify. I always figured they thought that with all your college degrees, you'd make a better witness."

"If *you* didn't testify and *I* didn't testify . . ." Sam began to speculate.

"Probably was plea-bargained," Mike concluded.

"Plea-bargained or not, one thing is sure. That case never came to trial," Sam Armstrong decided. "Mike, you said a couple of D.A.s talked to you—"

"You know how it goes. Cases get kicked around down there. New young D.A.s come and go. Must have been at least five or six who talked to me," Mike recalled.

"So that case never came to trial . . ." Sam Armstrong considered.

"What did you say, Sam?" Mike asked.

"Just considering the possibilities, Mike," Sam replied. "Mike, one day soon, before you retire, let's have lunch together. We'll sneak off and talk about old times."

"Sam, with your job, your visibility, you are going to sneak off? I'm afraid lunch will have to wait until we both retire." Conlin hung up laughing.

Sam Armstrong was laughing too. But only for a moment. For his mind returned to pondering the problem of the Torahs for that rebuilt synagogue in Brooklyn.

If it were true, as now appeared, that there never had been a trial in that old case, it could very well have been plea-bargained. And if it had been, then all the evidence would have been returned long ago.

On the other hand, it could have been one of a great number of criminal cases in which, through delays invented by a skillful criminal lawyer and indulged by a harried, overworked prosecutor, the case becomes dormant by the sheer erosion of time and is eventually ignored completely.

If that case had not been plea-bargained or come to trial but continued to be listed as pending, the evidence would still be held, as is all material evidence, in the property clerk's office of the police department.

Too often, after years of discouraging postponements and frustrations, complainants and witnesses in criminal cases either die or become so disillusioned that they decide to abandon the prosecution and go on with their lives. In his years in the department, Sam Armstrong had seen many discouraged witnesses drop out and too many prosecutions abandoned, the evidence abandoned as well.

Determined to pursue every possibility, Sam reached for his phone.

"Clara! Get me the property clerk's office!" Immediately, he countermanded his order. "Never mind! I'll find out for myself!"

The policeman behind the protective grille of the property clerk's office was startled, disbelieving, that the police commissioner himself would visit his drab department.

The shelves and cabinets behind him contained handguns, rifles, sawed-off shotguns, machine guns, Uzis, AK-47s, machetes, knives of all sizes—weapons of all kinds that had been used to threaten, and many to take, human life. The shelves contained marijuana wrapped in burlap; cocaine in plastic bundles; clothing of women who had been raped or murdered; jewelry that had been stolen; gold chains that had been snatched from the necks of women and men who displayed more wealth than caution; hi-fis; stereos; VCRs, all stolen from broken-into homes and cars. All variety of evidence of almost any crime committed in New York City was to be found here.

Startled, the clerk stumbled over his words as he said, "Yes, sir . . . uh, Mr. Commissioner. Anything . . . I mean, what can I do for you, sir? Something wrong, sir?"

"At ease," Armstrong said. "I'm only here to get some information."

"Yes, sir!" the uniformed clerk replied. "Anything I can tell you, sir?"

"Years ago," Armstrong began, then a smile broke out on his face. "Before you were born, son—I was just a rookie at the time—we had a case involving a break-in in a synagogue on the East Side. I don't recall the name of the case or even the synagogue. But I remember that the evidence included two Torahs."

"Toras?" the puzzled clerk asked. "Oh. Japanese. Like in the movie Tora, Tora, Tora."

"Holy scrolls," Armstrong explained. "Two Torahs. And the silver and gilt ornaments that were on them. What happened to all that?"

Fearing that his performance of duty was being impugned, the clerk defended, "If it was during my time, sir, then anything that was taken out was signed for. You can inspect the register."

"No, no, no, nothing like that, son," Armstrong said. "I don't know if that case was plea-bargained or abandoned, if the evidence was ever released. But if those Torahs are still here, I'd like to get a look at them."

"If it was that long ago, they may not be here any longer. But I'll make a search, sir."

The clerk started away until he was lost from Armstrong's view among shelves, cabinets, and crates from which untidy evidence could be seen protruding. Armstrong grew impatient, thinking of all those calls still waiting to be returned, new calls that had come in, possible emergencies that might have arisen since he left his office. But if there had been any emergencies, his beeper would have found him.

It seemed a long time before the clerk returned.

"Commissioner, I found a load of stuff back there. Looks like it hasn't been touched in years. Might be what you're looking for."

Armstrong gestured for him to open up. The clerk opened the grille gate. Armstrong followed him down one long aisle, then another, and around the far end of a set of shelves. There, behind all the other shelves, was a collection of cartons, each with a tag that bore the number of the case and the year involved. The clerk dropped to one knee and pulled out some bulky articles covered in dusty felt cloth. He proceeded to unwrap the covering until he produced a platter-sized engraved shield of tarnished silver and gilt. Armstrong recognized it as one of the decorations that usually adorned a Torah once its velvet cover is in place. The clerk unwrapped another cloth, bringing into view a pair of silver decorations that fit over the top rollers of the holy scrolls. Old as they were and discolored, the tiny gold bells on them had not lost their timbre.

Armstrong was encouraged. With the shield and the decorations at hand, the Torahs must be here as well.

"Keep going, son."

The clerk dug deeper and unwrapped another roll of cloth. Armstrong leaned in and stared down. There they were—two ancient scrolls. He carefully lifted the Torahs from their resting place. Their purple velvet coverings, with faded gold embroidery, were crushed and untidy. Armstrong tried to smooth them but could not eliminate the wrinkles that so many years had pressed into them. But he was relieved that the scrolls themselves appeared undamaged. He handed one to the clerk.

"Hold this!"

When the clerk grabbed the Torah by its middle, Armstrong said, "Not that way, son. Hold it by the bottom rollers." The clerk complied. Armstrong hung the shield over the purple velvet cover. He placed the ornaments on the top roller of the Torah. He stood back to see if it was as he remembered from the times his mother had taken him to a synagogue. Satisfied, he dressed the second Torah in the identical manner. Then, holding one in each arm, he started out.

When he entered his office, still carrying the two Torahs, his startled secretary was waiting with a fistful of messages. The most important one was from the mayor.

"The mayor's picking you up in half an hour."

"Call his secretary. Tell her I will be going out to Brooklyn on my own. And get my mother on the phone!" He continued into his private office, leaving his secretary shaking her head in dismay, not only at his refusal of the mayor's order but in puzzlement at the sight of the black police commissioner carrying two holy scrolls.

Moments later, she reported, "Commissioner, your mother is on the line."

"Mama?"

"Sam, something wrong?" Elvira Armstrong asked.

"No, Mama. Why?"

"Your secretary sounded so strange," she started to say.

"Never mind her, just tell me one thing: How do you get the wrinkles out of the velvet covering that fits over a Torah?"

"You mean the velvet mantle that protects the Torah?"

"Exactly! What do you do about the wrinkles?"

"Steam them out."

"Could you do it?"

"I didn't raise an active, energetic, mischievous boy without learning how to take care of a few wrinkles—and worse," Elvira said with a laugh. "Any steam iron'll do it."

"Then, Mama, get ready for a surprise."

"Surprise? Sam, what kind of surprise?"

"I'm only sorry that old Pastor Wilder isn't alive to see this."

"Sam Armstrong, what in the world are you talking about?"

"Just get your steam iron ready, Mama. I'm coming up!"

When the commissioner's car turned the corner into the Brooklyn street where the newly restored synagogue stood, so many people had come to celebrate the rededication that they not only filled the sanctuary but overflowed onto the steps outside and down into the street, filling it from sidewalk to sidewalk. Slowly, the driver edged the commissioner's car through the crowd, which gave way when they recognized the official shield and license plates.

At the foot of the steps, the car came to a halt. Sam Armstrong climbed out. From inside someone handed him a Torah, dressed now in a smooth purple velvet embroidered mantle, with newly polished ornaments and shield in place. He was handed a second Torah. Then there emerged from the car his tall, distinguished, gray-haired mother.

"All right, Sam, let's go!" Elvira Hitchins Armstrong said.

To the surprise and consternation of the onlookers, many of whom were Chasidic Jews in long black coats, Elvira Armstrong and her son, who carried two Torahs in his arms, mounted the steps to the synagogue.

They made their way through the crowd outside the sanctuary and finally entered it as the old rabbi was concluding a prayer of hope and promise before the open ark. The old man turned to tearfully address the congregation and the visiting dignitaries: "I am shamed before you and God that our holy ark still remains empty. For after all, without Torah, what is Jewishness? We tried to secure two Torahs to replace those that were desecrated in the fire. But Torahs are very costly. And thus far we have not yet been able to secure even one. So we are destined . . ."

But his tear-filled eyes fixed suddenly in such a stare of surprise that the entire congregation turned to look back. They saw a tall black man in the police commissioner's uniform stride down the aisle toward the altar. In each of his arms was a Torah, its horns triumphantly crowned by silver decorations whose tiny gold bells tinkled as he walked.

Alongside him strode his mother.

At the altar, Sam Armstrong surrendered one Torah to his mother. She gently passed it to the old rabbi, who stared at her, speechless. She took the second Torah from her son's arm and handed it to the old man.

"From where . . . how? . . ." The old rabbi was too startled to phrase this question properly.

"A gift, rabbi," Elvira said. "In memory of Rebecca Rosen and David Rosen, a man who revered *Torah*."

"A gift? No, my dear, a miracle," the rabbi said.

"A wise man once said to me, 'If in God's eyes more is required, in His own time, He will provide a way.'"

"It seems He has, He has," the rabbi said, tears of joy forming in his eyes as he embraced both Torahs.

As Elvira Armstrong had seen Uncle David and Aunt Rebecca do earlier in her life, she reverently touched each Torah with the tips of her fingers, then brought them to her lips and kissed them.

She turned, and with her son at her side, she started up the aisle of the synagogue, tall, erect, and proud—as Aunt Rebecca had always taught her to be.